Praise for the Masterful *from the Mind of Allan Topol*

China Gambit

"*The China Gambit* is a choice pick for those who love high end military plots, very much recommended."

Midwest Book Review

Spy Dance

"It's a smooth and exciting ride. You'll want to see these characters take on another problem or two. Yep, I was sorry the story stopped."

Carnegie Mellon Magazine

"The story takes off at warp speed."

Washington Magazine

"*Spy Dance* is a must-read for fans of espionage thrillers, and deserves a place on the bookshelf alongside the works of Tom Clancy, Robert Ludlum, and even John LeCarre."

Hadassah Magazine

"This is a superb first novel . . ."

Newt Gingrich

Enemy of My Enemy

"Topol's turf is the old-fashioned novel of international intrigue. His scene shifts constantly from trendy clubs in Moscow to three-star restaurants in Paris to strip joints in Montreal to Cabinet-level confrontations in the Oval Office."

The Washington Post

Dark Ambition

"Topol might be the most riveting spy-adventure writer in America today . . . I found myself solidly immersed in Topol's multi-faceted conspiracy and am eagerly anticipating his next work."

Newt Gingrich

"Unlike most other members of the lawyer-novelist fraternity, Topol turns out good old-fashioned spy stories that leave the corridors of big law firm business far behind in favor of the broader stage of foreign affairs, political intrigue, and the murky recesses of human desire."

"In this tightly written novel, Topol captures well the quiet neighborhoods of Washington, D.C., and the occasional ruthlessness of its people."

Legal Times

"John Grisham and Richard North Patterson may have a new successor in Topol . . ."

Publishers Weekly

Conspiracy

"Seethes with political intrigue, a cast of shady characters, and enough deception, smart dialogue, and behind-closed-doors deals to keep readers hooked until the final."

Publishers Weekly

"An entertaining and suspenseful thriller with a well-crafted plot . . ."

Stephen Frey, *New York Times* best-selling author of *Silent Partner*

"*Conspiracy* is a perfectly executed combination of the best elements of legal and political thrillers. With a lightning-fast pace, a compelling story, and an insider look at Washington, Topol takes his readers on a memorable thrill ride. Find a comfortable chair and plan to stay up late. Highly recommended."

Sheldon Siegel, *New York Times* best-selling author of *Final Verdict*

"[Topol has] managed to weave a convincing conspiracy theory into near worldwide conflict. And it's done with the extreme finesse that keeps us guessing all the way, also hankering for more of Topol's penetrating portrayal of inside-the-Beltway deceptions."

The Sanford Herald

"A paranoia-inducing thriller . . . The action scenes and telling details linger long after you have finished the book."

Legal Times

"This Washington, D.C.-set thriller from Topol (*Dark Ambition*) seethes with political intrigue, a cast of shady characters and enough deception, smart dialogue and behind-closed-doors deals to keep readers hooked until the final scene."

Publishers Weekly

A Woman of Valor

"Few novels have kept me as involved as this one."

South Bend Tribune

"Topol has written an evenly paced story, introducing his characters slowly so that each has a chance to come alive before the plot takes off on a convoluting and deftly interwoven path leading to the climax."

The Free Lance-Star

The Fourth of July War

"The book is remarkably reflective of contemporary affairs."

Chicago Tribune

"Topol creates believable characters with real problems and emotions; he constructs a tight, suspenseful plot that has us flipping pages as fast as we can find out what happens while we root 100% for a hero we don't altogether like."

The Los Angeles Times

"Topol's scenario for this fast-paced, gripping novel has the ring of inevitability . . . Should be a best seller."

Houston Chronicle

"It's a screamer of a novel . . . So real it makes you believe it could happen."

Natchez Democrat

THE RUSSIAN ENDGAME

THE RUSSIAN ENDGAME

ALLAN TOPOL

To TOM
An Avid reader of
mysteries with
my hope that you
enjoy this Book
Best Wishs
Allan Topol

SelectBooks, Inc.
New York

Copyright © 2013 by Allan Topol

All rights reserved. Published in the United States of America. No part of this book may be reproduced or transmitted in any form or by any means, graphic, electronic, or mechanical, including photocopying, recording, taping or by any information storage or retrieval system, without the permission in writing from the publisher.

This edition is published by SelectBooks, Inc.
For information address SelectBooks, Inc., New York, New York.

First Edition

ISBN 978-1-59079-999-4

Library of Congress Cataloging-in-Publication Data

Topol, Allan.
  The Russian endgame / Allan Topol. – First edition.
    pages cm
  ISBN 978-1-59079-999-4 (paperback : alk. paper)
  I. Title.
  PS3570.O64R87 2013
  813'.54–dc23
                            2013006688

Manufactured in the United States of America

10 9 8 7 6 5 4 3 2 1

Dedicated to my wife, Barbara, my partner for all nine novels.

Acknowledgments

I wish to thank my agent, Pam Ahearn, who helped me develop all three books in this trilogy, *The China Gambit, The Spanish Revenge,* and now, *The Russian Endgame,* with great wisdom and tremendous insight. It has been a pleasure working the people at SelectBooks. I very much appreciate Kenzi Sugihara's enthusiasm for the project from our first discussion. Nancy Sugihara and Molly Stern did an outstanding job of editing, and I'd like to thank Kenichi Sugihara for his work as the marketing director.

Thanks to my wife, Barbara, for her enormous assistance. She read each draft and offered valuable suggestions. She helped me shape the characters, and shared the fun of visiting the places in this book.

PROLOGUE

November, Six Months Ago

Moscow

Enraged, Dimitri Orlov stood in Red Square at noon watching Russian President Fyodor Kuznov's motorcade leave the Kremlin through Savior Gate and race past. Heavy snow was falling. Orlov paid no attention to the flakes caking in his blonde hair, the water running down his face past the scar on his right cheek, the result of a knife wound in a battle with a Chechnya terrorist. At six foot two, and powerfully built, standing tall in his military coat, which he had found in the back of his closet, and staring at the Kremlin, Orlov was a forbidding presence. People crossed the street to avoid him. Orlov ignored them.

Orlove vowed never to take "no" for an answer. He had always been this way. That was part of the reason for his meteoric rise to Major in the Soviet Army and then to section head in the KGB in the good old days of the Soviet Union. "Yes I can" was his creed. "Yes I can" was his answer to any question. For example, "Orlov, can you break though the defense lines of the Chechnya rebels?" Or, "Orlov, can you force the American spy to tell us whom he's working with?"

After the breakup of the Soviet Union, which would never have happened but for that self-aggrandizing coward Gorbachev and that worthless drunk Yeltsin, Orlov moved on. He took his can-do approach to Vasily "The Venal" Sukalov, an oligarch in the new Russia who became incredibly wealthy, five billion dollars' worth, as a result of stealing the telecom monopoly from the State. After ten years of being

Vasily's enforcer while skimming twenty million euros he socked away in a Swiss bank, Orlov severed his relationship with Vasily. He was now ready to serve Mother Russia. And he knew exactly how.

Orlov had only one problem: he needed a meeting with President Kuznov, and he hadn't been able to get through Kuznov's layers of bureaucrats to schedule it. Orlov even knew Kuznov from his KGB days when Orlov played a minor role in a Kuznov operation to spread disinformation to the Americans in Germany. He was confident Kuznov would remember him.

Though Orlov explained this to the secretary to Kuznov's secretary, he received the stock answer given to any lunatic who tried to approach the president's suite in the Kremlin. "Submit your request in writing. You will receive an answer in six to eight weeks." Unfortunately, using Vasily to gain access to Kuznov wasn't an option. Those two hated each other. Vasily was even worried Kuznov might issue an order for his arrest for theft of State property.

Submitting a request in writing wasn't an option. What Orlov had to say to the Russian president couldn't be put in a letter. Besides, he guessed all those letters were routinely dumped, unread, into a trash can. So he had only one choice: to force his way past Kuznov's layers of protection. That would be next to impossible to do if Kuznov was in the Kremlin. But today was Friday and two days ago when Orlov sat cooling his heels for the fifth time in the office of the secretary to the secretary, he overheard the fat, redheaded swine say in a phone conversation, "President Kuznov will be leaving for his country home Friday afternoon."

Orlov decided that must be where the presidential motorcade was now headed. He zipped up his black leather jacket, climbed on his Harley, and sped off, following the motorcade but hanging back just far enough to avoid attracting suspicion.

As he rode, Orlov thought about Kuznov. The Russian president, like Orlov, had been a distinguished army officer who was recruited by the KGB. But unlike Orlov, who fought against the changes convulsing the Soviet Union with the rise of the so-called Democratic Movement, Kuznov, with loyalty to no one, manipulated the new system for his own advancement. He became the Director of the FSB, the KGB's domestic successor, then Mayor of Moscow, and finally president of Russia. In his early contact with Kuznov, Orlov found the man impressive. Yes, but president of Russia? Orlov would never have imagined it.

Orlov had to admire Kuznov. Somehow, he was now in a presidential motorcade while Orlov, binoculars pressed against his eyes, stopped to stretch out on the snowy ground on the crest of a hill, literally freezing his dick, while watching the motorcade pass the guardhouse at a break in the twelve foot high stonewall that surrounded Kuznov's country estate on three sides. On the fourth, it bordered a circular lake roughly two kilometers in diameter.

Orlov focused on the guardhouse. Four men were inside, all armed with machine guns. He considered his options. Forcing his way through the guardhouse would be tough. It meant killing or incapacitating the four guards. They would no doubt sound an alarm and bring every other security man on the property. And no doubt there were plenty of them. Scaling the wall under the cover of darkness was more likely to succeed, but if he was spotted at or near the top, he'd be a sitting duck.

He didn't like either option. Then it hit him. He had a third way.

Orlov rode back into the center of Moscow to gather what he needed.

*   *   *

Orlov had always been a student of history. It was his favorite subject in school. Even while in the KGB he was a voracious reader of history books about each area in which he operated. He was convinced that people shaped world events. Not just leaders. But others. Those with courage and daring. The assassin of the Austrian Archduke in Sarajevo was responsible for the outbreak of the First World War. Then there was Philbrick and his colleagues who spied on England for Russia and the American scientists who beat Germany in the race to develop the atomic bomb.

Orlov had always dreamt that one day he would be someone who influenced world events. In that way, he would achieve immortality. That was why he had joined the KGB.

So far, he hadn't affected the course of the world. He had merely been a low-level agent. Now, finally, his time had come. He was determined to take advantage of it. And something else was motivating Orlov as he prepared for this evening's encounter with Kuznov. He had money, but he sought power. He wanted to be the head of a new, revitalized, and even more dreaded KGB, making him the second most powerful person in Russia. If he accomplished this mission for Kuznov and delivered what he was promising, a grateful Kuznov would readily accede to Orlov's request.

At eleven thirty that evening, with the sliver of a moon concealed by thick clouds, he rode his motorcycle back to a park across the lake from Kuznov's estate. The snow had stopped. Orlov parked the bike in a thick clump of trees and pulled out the materials he'd packed in the side bags. First the black wetsuit, mask, and flippers. Then the Glock, knife, and rope in a watertight container, which he tied around his waist. Orlov donned the wetsuit over his slacks and shirt and dove in. He swam on a straight line toward Kuznov's house with smooth strokes. No splashes to alert anyone to his presence in the water.

As he approached the other side, Orlov saw two guards, sitting on lawn chairs facing the house, their backs to him. They were each holding a bottle and talking loudly. They had to be drunk, he decided, from the sounds of their voices.

He pulled the Glock from the pouch at his waist. All I want to do is knock them out, Orlov decided. No need to kill the fools. But I can't give them a chance to call for help.

On the toes of his feet, gripping the gun by the barrel, he advanced stealthily across the wet grass. He was right behind them. Neither man had turned in his direction. The man on the right looked larger and tougher. Orlov decided to attack him first. In a single swift motion, he swung the gun and smashed it against the side of the man's head. Before he passed out, the cry of "Ah . . . ah . . ." came out of his mouth. Enough to alert his colleague, who shot to his feet and wheeled around to face Orlov.

"Who the hell . . ."

Before the startled man could finish the sentence, Orlov slammed a fist into his stomach, doubling him up. He followed that with a viscous kick to the balls. The guard dropped to the ground. Orlov fell on top of him, raising his pistol to smash against the man's head and finish the job. Before he had a chance, the man lunged for Orlov's face, scratching and punching, going for his eyes. The gun fell from his hand. Momentarily stunned, Orlov recovered quickly and fought back. They rolled on the muddy ground. Orlov ended up on top. The guard was trying to force him off, but Orlov had his hands around the man's thick neck. He was squeezing tightly. Squeezing and squeezing until the man stopped moving. Still squeezing until the man stopped breathing.

Orlov stood up and peeled off his wetsuit. He tossed it on the dead man's body, recovered his gun, rope, and knife, and looked at the house. No one was at any of the rear windows. Chances were no one had seen or heard what happened. Orlov breathed a sigh of relief. He studied the house some more. Undoubtedly, Kuznov's bedroom suite faced the back. That way he'd have a view of the lake. Lights were on in only one room facing that direction. It had to be Kuznov's. The Russian president was well known to be an insomniac.

With the knife in one hand, gun in the other, and rope over his shoulder, Orlov snuck to the back door. He could pick most locks with a knife, but maybe he wouldn't have to. Maybe he'd get lucky.

He turned the doorknob slowly and the door opened, without creaking, leading into the kitchen. The house was quiet. He saw a young woman in her twenties dressed in a pink flannel robe leaning into the refrigerator, her back to the door. She must have heard him because she suddenly turned around. Orlov saw she was preparing to scream. He lifted his right hand with the gun and pointed it at her. At the same time, he raised the forefinger of his other hand to his lips, signaling her to be quiet. She stood mute, frozen to the spot.

"Who are you?" he asked.

"One of the maids."

"If you tell me what room President Kuznov is in, I won't harm you."

She pointed to the ceiling confirming what he suspected. The room faced the back.

"How do I get there?"

She gestured toward a closed door in a corner of the kitchen, "A staircase behind the door," she stammered in a frightened whisper. "Will you kill him?"

"That's none of your business. I'm going to tie you up."

She nodded. He used the rope to tie her torso to a chair, legs and arms as well. He grabbed a kitchen towel and tied it around her mouth.

Then he opened the door, concealing the wooden staircase. Climbing the stairs, Orlov heard the sound of a television. A movie was playing in English. He had read that Kuznov liked Americana movies.

When Orlov reached the second floor landing he saw five closed doors in a dimly lit corridor. On the tips of his toes, he walked softly toward the room in which the television was playing.

Gun raised, Orlov twisted the doorknob, kicked open the door, and looked inside. He saw Kuznov leaning back on a sofa. With him was a gorgeous, busty, blonde woman, half Kuznov's age at best. Definitely not the frumpy Mrs. Kuznov. The Russian president's pants were unzipped and she had his dick in her mouth. *The Manchurian Candidate* was playing. The Russian president pushed aside the blonde, grabbed a cell phone from the table, and shot to his feet.

Kuznov was not a dominating physical presence, Orlov recalled from their prior meetings. He was thin with a receding hair line. No more than five foot eight. A contrast to the strapping Orlov. But Kuznov did have those hard, cold, black eyes. And they were boring in on Orlov while the blonde raced behind the sofa to hide.

"All I have to do is press one button on the phone," Kuznov said, in a steely cold voice, devoid of emotion and fear, "and four armed guards will come. You'll be a dead man."

"I'm not here to harm you."

"Who the hell are you? And what do you want?"

Orlov realized Kuznov was staring at him, the president's face showing partial recognition.

"Dimitri Orlov. We were . . ."

Kuznov completed the sentence. "In the KGB together. You worked for me on a disinformation project in Berlin involving the Americans."

"You have a good memory."

"You did an outstanding job. And now you've become insane, breaking in like this."

"I didn't have a choice. I was desperate to talk to you about something extremely important and confidential. Those morons who guard access to you refused to schedule me. I had to take matters into my own hands."

"Why should I believe you?"

Orlov handed the gun to Kuznov. The former KGB operative kept the knife in his hand. If he thought Kuznov intended to shoot him, Orlov planned to open the knife blade and hurl it at the Russian president.

Orlov held his breath for a long minute while Kuznov stared at his surprise visitor and moved the gun around his hand.

Finally, Kuznov looked behind the sofa and called to the blonde, "Wait for me in the bedroom and don't tell anyone about this."

She practically flew out of the room.

Kuznov pointed to a chair. When Orlov sat down, Kuznov settled into the sofa facing him. He rested the gun on the end table where it could be easily reached. Now confident of the outcome, Orlov put the knife in his pocket.

"Are you still working with Vasily Sukalov?" Kuznov asked.

"I quit two months ago."

"Good for you. Sukalov's a gangster. A criminal. Since then?"

"I'm freelancing."

"Who sent you to talk to me?"

"Nobody. This was my idea."

"It better be good."

"It is."

"Start talking."

Orlov took a deep breath and began. "Most Russians believe that the events of 1991, culminating in the collapse of the Soviet Union, were a tragedy. Even that spineless Gorbachev, who is referred to in the media as Jell-O, has conceded that the Soviet Union could have and should have been preserved. Yeltsin, after him, was a disaster for Russia."

"You're here to give me a history lesson."

Orlov ignored the sarcasm and continued. "Under Putin, Medvedev, and now you, our economy has prospered. We are once again an economic force in the world, thanks in part to our energy resources, but also because of the drive of our top businessmen. The State has created stability in the country, which is key. Every recent survey shows that the Russian people don't want democracy or human rights. They want order and stability. The FSB, while not as effective as the KGB in our day, has solidified domestic control."

"So you're telling me that Putin, Medvedev, and I have been successful. We've given the people the order that they want as well as economic growth."

"That's true, but . . ."

Orlov paused for a minute and looked at the Russian president. He was confident Kuznov wanted to hear what was coming next.

"But," Orlov continued, now treading carefully because his views could be considered criticism and Kuznov was thin-skinned, "we are still viewed as a joke militarily. The sick man of Europe."

"Are you aware that I have been quietly rebuilding our army, navy, and air force?" Kuznov sounded defensive.

"Of course. But no one in Washington regards Russia as a resurging superpower prepared to compete with the United States and China."

"American arrogance is unbelievable. They view themselves as the dominant superpower. The world's judge and police. All this from a country whose own government is dysfunctional."

"I couldn't agree more. That's why I'm here. I have a plan to restore Russia to its prior greatness before Afghanistan, Gorbachev, and the fall of the Berlin Wall while, at the same time, inflicting a mighty blow to the U.S. The Russian people will revere you for doing this. Most look back longingly and yearn for the good old days when we were a world force."

Kuznov walked over to the credenza, poured two glasses of vodka, and handed one to Orlov. They each took a gulp. Kuznov said, "That's an extremely ambition objective. How do you propose to do this?"

It was a lob up to the net. Orlov was ready with his response. "We form an alliance with China. Then in a joint operation, we strike at the United States and Europe."

Kuznov was shaking his head. "I'll be very frank with you, Dimitri. I've met Chinese President Li twice. I've never been able to develop a relationship with the man. He's gutless and two-faced. An alliance with China is out of the question."

"Change is in the wind in Beijing. A beneficial change for us. Li will not be the president of China much longer. He will be succeeded by General Zhou."

"You're wrong. Zhou was exiled."

"Respectfully, I hate to disagree with you. Zhou will be back in Beijing sometime next year. And he will become the next Chinese president."

Kuznov looked skeptical. He finished his vodka. "How do you know all this?"

"My sister Androshka is General Zhou's mistress living with him in Paris. Though I'm ten years older, we always had a close relationship, in part because our father died when Androshka was only a year old."

"I've heard of your father. He was well respected as a high-ranking Communist Party official."

"Thank you. Well, anyhow, I had a secret meeting with Androshka last March in the south of France. She told me precisely what I told you about General Zhou's plans to become the next Chinese president. She also told me that General Zhou hates the United States."

While Kuznov paced with one hand on his chin, undoubtedly assessing what he had just heard, Orlov recalled that meeting with Androshka.

He hadn't seen or heard from her in two years and he hadn't been able to locate her. It was as if she had vanished from the face of the earth. The last he heard, she was in a relationship with Mikail Ivanoff, another Russian oligarch. Word had reached Orlov that Androshka had stolen money from Ivanoff and fled the country and that Ivanoff wanted to find and kill her. None of that made sense to Orlov, who had plenty of money to give to Androshka. All she had to do was ask.

Then out of the blue, she called and asked him to meet her in the south of France. "I'm staying at the house of Chinese General Zhou. He's away for a few days. Come now. Please."

So Orlov took the first plane to Paris where he connected to Nice. It was a huge estate with a swimming pool and a red clay tennis court in the hills above the town of Cap d'Antibes. Androshka, with tears running down her cheeks, told him how, back in Moscow, Mikail had beaten her when he was drunk. One night it was too much for her. While he slept, she gathered up the money he had in the house and fled to Paris. There she had no choice. She had to earn money the way good-looking women have since the beginning of time.

"You were a prostitute?" Orlov said horrified.

"I had no choice. But I had good luck. I met General Zhou. He's been good to me."

"You should have called me," Orlov said angrily.

"I didn't want to make trouble for you. I know that Vasily and Mikail were friends."

"They were. Now they hate each other. But why did you call me now?"

"Thanks to General Zhou, Mikail is dead."

Orlov stopped thinking about his meeting with Androshka and looked at Kuznov, who was staring at him.

"Alright," the Russian president said. "I'm willing to accept everything you've told me about General Zhou and his hatred for the Americans. If and when he becomes president of China, I would like to meet with him. Here in Moscow. But I can't arrange that meeting myself. And it can't be a public meeting. That would raise suspicions around the world. Feed paranoia. Particularly in Washington. They'll see it as Stalin and Hitler joining forces and take strong action. We have to form our alliance secretly. Do you understand?"

These words were music to Orlov's ears. "Absolutely. That's where I can help you," Orlov added.

"How?"

"Androshka promised to get me access to General Zhou—as your representative of course. As soon as he becomes China's president I'll call her and arrange to visit Beijing to meet with Zhou and invite him to Moscow. If that's what you want."

Orlov was trying to sound deferential.

Now Kuznov was smiling. And he almost never smiles, Orlov thought.

"I like that plan. Good you came to see me. I promise you won't have trouble getting in the next time. By the way, how many of my guards did you kill to get his meeting with me tonight?"

"One dead. One unconscious. Both on the back lawn."

They were just the beginning as far as Orlov was concerned. He was prepared to kill more—as many as necessary to fulfill his mission and make himself the second most powerful man in Russia.

PART ONE

April, the Present

Paris

Craig Page, Director of the EU Counterterrorism Agency, leaned back in the chair in his Paris office and closed his eyes. It had only been ten days since his successful defense of the Vatican and the battle for Southern Spain, and he was still emotionally strung out.

He realized that he had plenty to be pleased about. He had thwarted the daring plan of Musa Ben Abdil to launch a rocket attack on the Pope and the Vatican on Easter morning, while at the same time creating a Muslim enclave in Southern Spain. Many had perished in that lunatic's march across Southern Spain to the Alhambra, but Musa Ben Abdil and his lieutenant Omar had died rather than surrender, which the remains of his ragtag army were all too happy to do to save their lives. The Alhambra had been spared damage. And Craig had managed to rescue Elizabeth from her captivity unharmed.

Despite all of that, for Craig, it was a bittersweet victory. The ruthless General Zhou, whom Craig was convinced was the brains behind Mohammad Ben Abdil's plans, had managed to escape, along with his mistress, Androshka. A year and a half before these attacks, General Zhou had planned the murder of Craig's daughter, Francesca, his only child. All Craig could think about was gaining revenge over Zhou. After these separate encounters, Craig's animosity toward General Zhou had reached gargantuan proportions. No matter what he did, he kept thinking about it.

Last night, in bed in their apartment in Montmarte, Elizabeth had held him and said, "General Zhou is becoming an obsession with you. Believe me, I want to get him as much as you do. I was his prisoner, but we don't even know where he is. He's probably back in China where we can't reach him. We can't let him destroy us."

"I know that, but . . ."

She had pulled away and sat up, wrapping a sheet around her naked body. "I feel so bad. It's all my fault that Zhou got away. If I hadn't been so stupid and let myself get caught . . ."

"That's not fair. You can't blame yourself."

But he knew she did. And he did as well. She should have been suspicious that they were trying to trap her in Paris.

He wouldn't tell her that. He didn't want to hurt her. So instead he said, "I'll try to move on."

But he knew it was futile. As time passed, it would be more difficult to get at General Zhou. He needed something damn soon.

Finally, this morning, he caught a break. When Craig had ridden in the back of the car with Androshka, taking her to the exchange for Elizabeth in Gibraltar, he had secretly slipped a tiny, but powerful tracking device into her bag. He had enlisted the aid of his friend Betty Richards at the CIA in Langley to use American satellites to pinpoint Androshka's location. No doubt she was with General Zhou. But that had taken time because Norris, the CIA Director, despised Craig. So Betty had to work surreptitiously. For several days, General Zhou and Androshka had been on the move, undoubtedly to give the slip to anyone trying to pursue. This morning Betty called on an encrypted phone with precise coordinates. General Zhou was in Bali. Craig now had his exact location.

That left Craig with a dilemma: how to get at General Zhou in Bali? While Craig's title was impressive: Director of the EU Counterterrorism Agency, the reality was he had no legal authority to seek extradition. Nor did he have any military or security personnel at his disposal. Quite the opposite, the EU resolution creating his office specifically provided that he was dependent upon member nations for legal and military support. That wasn't surprising. The EU member nations, particularly Germany and France, had a strong prejudice against relinquishing any of their sovereignty.

Now that he had General Zhou's location, if Craig built an ironclad case against the Chinese General, he could take his evidence to Spanish President Zahara. Craig was confident that Zahara would authorize the Spanish Justice Minister to seek General Zhou's extradition from the Indonesian government. Then the Spanish government could try him for the murder of the Spanish people who died on the Easter morning attack in Southern Spain. The prosecutor's theory would be simple: General Zhou wasn't there with a gun. But he was the mastermind. In legal terms, a co-conspirator.

The idea was a good one, Craig was convinced. But how to build the case?

The Spanish government had directed and was holding in prison the remnants of Musa Ben Abdil's army, which had surrendered at the Alhambra. Craig could interrogate them to determine whether any of them had seen or heard General Zhou involved in planning the attack. Craig was convinced that would be futile. At the time of the Alhambra surrender, Craig had spoken informally to a number of Musa's troops. He was convinced that other than Omar, who was dead, none of them had knowledge of the planning of the operation.

A better possibility, Craig decided, was Elizabeth. When she had been captured and taken to Musa Ben Abdil's house in Marbella, she had heard conversations between General Zhou and Musa. Her testimony might be enough to persuade the Spanish Justice Minister to seek extradition. Even to obtain a conviction of General Zhou.

Buzzing on the intercom brought Craig back to reality. His secretary said, "Time for you to leave for lunch with Elizabeth."

"Oh, yeah," he said. He had totally forgotten that she had called an hour ago and said, "I have good news. I'm buying lunch."

Craig stood up and headed toward the door. It was a gorgeous spring day in Paris. He would have preferred to walk, but he'd never make it in time from his office in La Defense to the excellent little restaurant, Arome, off the Rue St. Honore, close to Avenue Franklin Roosevelt. They both liked it and the restaurant was equidistant between his office and hers at the *International Herald*, where she worked as a reporter. So he took a couple of gulps of outdoor air and climbed into the back of his waiting car. When he entered the restaurant, he saw Elizabeth seated at a corner table, looking radiant, dressed in a simple Chloe sheath. Though they never drank at lunch, she was sipping champagne. After he kissed her, she signaled the waiter who brought a glass for him.

"Guess what happened?"

"I'll bet it has to do with your book."

"Correct."

"The publisher has no more revisions to the first part?"

"We're not there yet. However," she was dropping the words like pearls, "I received an email from Harold, my agent in New York. He sold French rights for 200,000 euros and they love my title: 'Heads in the Sand: Europe Ignores Islamic Threat.'"

He whistled. "Wow. What great news. Congratulations."

"Thanks."

"You're definitely paying for lunch. Even though you know where I think their heads are."

"Very funny."

They had a wonderful lunch with Elizabeth talking about some of the things she'd do with the money. She wanted to finance a long overdue vacation for them. Renovate the apartment. Send money to her father in New York. As she talked, sounding excited, Craig tried to be fully engaged with her. But he was only half there. Despite his best efforts, he could never block General Zhou from his mind.

He didn't want to spoil her celebration, but he had to tell her about what he had learned from Betty this morning.

He waited until they were sipping espresso. Then he decided to wade in, "I was thinking," he said.

"Here you go again about General Zhou."

"Yeah. How'd you know?"

"Your face gets a certain expression and your voice has an edge."

She was frowning. She reached across the table and put her hand on his. "I'm so sorry. It's all my fault. If only . . ."

Craig interrupted. "You can forget about all that. We now have a way of catching Zhou and making him pay for what he did in Spain. And to Francesca." Craig sounded excited.

"What happened?"

"Betty came through. I have a precise location in Bali for Zhou and Androshka. All we have to do is build the case against him, take it to the Spanish Prime Minister, and have him seek extradition from the Indonesia government. In Spain, General Zhou will stand trial for conspiracy and murder for the death of all the Spaniards who died in Musa Ben Abdil's war in Southern Spain."

Elizabeth wrinkled up her nose. He recognized that as a good sign. It meant she was willing to help him, rather than telling him to forget Zhou. She, too, must believe they now had a chance.

"How do you intend to build your case?" she asked.

"By using you as a witness to implicate Zhou in planning the attack on Southern Spain."

"But what can I testify?"

"You overheard conversations between Zhou and Musa Ben Abdil. Didn't you?"

She shook her head. "It won't fly. Nothing I heard directly involves Zhou in the attack."

"You were with me in Morocco when we saw Chinese instructors training Musa Ben Abdil's troops."

"Correct. But we don't have evidence General Zhou sent them."

Craig's spirits sagged. "You know how to deflate a boy's balloon."

"Look, I'm happy to give it a try. Just the fact that Zhou was in the house with Musa Ben Abdil and that he held me as a captive until you worked out the exchange for Androshka may be enough to build a case that he was co-conspirator."

"Good. Let's do it."

She held up her hand. "Whoa boy, there might be another way."

"Yeah."

"What's the status of General Alvarez, the former Spanish Defense Minister?"

"Carlos called yesterday from Madrid. Carlos was formally appointed Defense Minister. He's no longer Acting Minister. I asked him about Alvarez. He said the Argentine government approved Spain's extradition request. Spanish agents were in Buenos Aires to fly him back to Madrid. He should be arriving later today."

"What are they charging him with?"

"That he gave the order to move Spanish troops from the south to the north right before the attack. And he received a large amount of money for doing it. That makes him a co-conspirator. He could be charged with the murder of all the people who died." Craig was warming to her suggestion. "We don't know how directly Alvarez was involved with General Zhou. If he was, then Alvarez's testimony could give us what we need to build the case against General Zhou."

"Alvarez hates you. Persuading him to tell you about General Zhou's involvement won't be easy."

Craig finished his espresso while thinking about what she had said. "I'm sure Carlos will give me the freedom I need to interrogate Alvarez. With that I'll make him cough up enough of the story."

"I'm glad I'm not Alvarez."

Craig barely heard what she had said. He was planning logistics in his mind. "I'll call Carlos and set it up. You want to fly to Madrid with me this afternoon?"

"You're damn right. I have my own score to settle with those bastards who locked me up in the dungeon in Marbella, planning to rape and kill me."

Madrid

Notwithstanding General Alvarez's arrest in Argentina and his extradition to Spain, Craig didn't expect Alvarez to look beaten down and despondent. And Craig was right. When four Spanish soldiers led Alvarez into the interrogation room, the former powerful Defense Minister was dressed in prison blues and his wrists were cuffed behind his back. But he had the same arrogant, haughty expression Craig had seen on his face each time they had met, beginning with their initial encounter prior to the Spanish train bombing. Today, it was accompanied with a look of defiance.

This won't be easy, Craig thought.

Craig, Carlos, and Elizabeth were seated along one side of the battered wooden table. According to the prearranged plan, the soldiers forced Alvarez into a chair on the other side.

"Take off the handcuffs," Alvarez barked to one of the soldiers.

He didn't respond. Instead the four soldiers left the room. "What is the purpose of this gathering?" Alvarez asked.

Carlos said, "We want to question you about your role in the events leading to the attack in Southern Spain."

Alvarez was sneering. "I understand you managed to get my job, you despicable little worm."

Carlos showed no emotion. Craig, who wanted to smack Alvarez, admired Carlos' self-control. Carlos reached into his briefcase, removed a recorder, and placed it on the table. He didn't press the start button. "Craig will begin the questioning," Carlos said.

"I don't care who begins it. I have nothing to say."

"Are you certain of that?" Carlos asked.

"Yes. Very certain."

"That's unfortunate," Carlos replied. He nodded to Elizabeth. She and Carlos stood and exited the room.

"Where are you going?" Alvarez called after them.

Neither responded.

For the next two minutes, neither Craig nor Alvarez said a word. The former Defense Minister was shooting poison darts at Craig with his eyes.

Then the door opened. A man wearing a suit and tie and carrying a black leather doctor's bag entered. He was Philippe, the Director of the Science and Medical Section of Craig's counterterrorism agency.

Philippe put the bag down on the table. Calmly, with quiet efficiency, he removed a syringe with a long needle at the end, then a liter bottle with a clear liquid. In an instant, Alvarez's expression changed. The swagger was gone. He now looked worried. "What is this?" he demanded.

Craig replied, "We can do this interrogation the easy way or the hard. Either you answer my questions voluntarily or . . ."

Craig paused for a minute, letting his words sink in, while watching Alvarez squirm in his chair. "Or my associate will inject you with increasingly larger doses of a substance which will work on the nerve junctions in your body. Do you know what nerve junctions are?"

Alvarez shook his head.

"That's where bundles of nerves come together. You'll feel excruciating pain. More pain than you've ever experienced. And I will tell my colleague to increase the dose until you answer my questions. Traces of the chemical will disappear rapidly from your body. If you die, and you may hope for that, even a skilled medical examiner will conclude it was due to a spontaneous heart attack."

Alvarez pulled back in his chair, a terrified expression on his face. He let out a blood curdling scream. "Help . . . help . . . help!"

"No point dong that," Craig said. "No one can hear you. I asked Carlos to select a soundproof room."

Alvarez sprang out of his chair, to a standing position. Craig immediately pushed him back down.

"You won't get away with this," Alvarez shouted.

Craig laughed. "Do you really believe that? You are now hated by the entire Spanish nation. Your powerful friends will have nothing to do with you." Craig turned to Philippe. "Full body restraints."

Philippe reached into his bag and pulled out two rubber straps. He hooked one around Alvarez's chest, tying him to the chair, and the other around his legs. Alvarez was now locked in place.

"Skip the lowest dosage," Craig said to Philippe. "Begin at the mid level."

"The pain may be too much for him to bear."

"I don't care. He's scum. If his heart gives out, it means nothing to me."

"No," Alvarez pleaded. "No. Don't do this."

Philippe rolled up the sleeve on the right arm of Alvarez's blue shirt. He poured liquid into the syringe, picked up the needle, and approached Alvarez.

"No," Alvarez cried out.

Perspiration was dotting his forehead, running down the sides of his face, wetting his mustache. Craig saw that his shirt was wet under the arms.

"No. I'll tell you what you want to know."

"Hold up." Craig said to Philippe. "We'll give him a chance. Personally, I doubt if he'll answer my questions so be ready to shoot him up."

Philippe moved away and sat down. Craig pressed the record button on Carlos's machine. Then Craig gave today's date and the place, Madrid, Spain. He continued. "This is an interrogation of former Defense Minister General Alvarez being conducted by Craig Page. General Alvarez has voluntarily agreed to answer my questions. Is that correct, General Alvarez?"

Craig was staring at Alvarez.

"Yes," Alvarez said softly.

"Please speak louder. I want to make sure the recorder picks up your words."

"Yes," Alvarez replied in a louder voice.

"When did you first meet General Zhou?"

"Saturday, March 21. This year."

"And the occasion?"

"General Zhou invited me to his house in Cap d'Antibes in the south of France."

"What did you discuss?"

"He offered to make a payment to me of ten million euros if I agreed to provide China with an opportunity to compete for a Spanish Air Force order of planes."

"And did you accept his offer?"

Alvarez hesitated. Didn't respond.

Craig pressed the off button on the recorder and pointed to Philippe who picked up the needle.

"Give him an injection," Craig said, sounding exasperated.

Alvarez looked ready to cry. Craig noticed his pants were wet in front, liquid dripping from his chair onto the floor.

"No. I'll answer," Alvarez stammered.

Craig pressed the play button and repeated the question.

"Yes," Alvarez answered in a soft voice.

"Louder," Craig said. "The recorder has to get it."

"Yes," Alvarez repeated in a louder voice.

"Did you receive the payment?"

"It was deposited into a Singapore bank account in my name."

"What else happened at that meeting?"

"General Zhou's girlfriend, Androshka, had a friend named Masha in the house. Masha and I spent time together."

"So General Zhou provided a woman for you for sex in addition to paying you money?"

"Correct," he mumbled.

"Speak up," Craig said.

"Yes. That's right."

"When was the next time you saw or spoke with General Zhou?"

"The following day, Sunday. I was in Paris for a meeting of EU Defense Ministers. Afterwards, I went to his apartment. I had dinner with him and Androshka. And Masha."

Craig was confident he knew what meeting Alvarez was talking about. But he had to nail it down. "That was the meeting at which I urged the EU Defense Ministers to take action against Musa Ben Abdil in Morocco. And you argued successfully against it. Am I correct?"

"Others were against it as well." Alvarez's tone was hostile.

"Did you report to General Zhou what happened at that meeting?"

"Yes."

"Did you tell him that I named a young French woman, Lila, as a witness who identified the voice of the perpetrator of the Spanish train bombing?"

"Yes," he muttered.

"Are you aware that Lila was savagely murdered shortly after that meeting?"

"I read something about it."

"Then you realize that you are responsible for her murder?"

Craig had never expected to establish responsibility for Lila's murder today, but it was now perfectly clear.

"I deny that," Alvarez said.

"But you told General Zhou. And he told Musa Ben Abdil."

"I don't know who General Zhou told."

Craig didn't take issue with that. He moved on. "When was your next meeting with General Zhou?"

"Saturday, March 27th. He summoned me to a meeting at Parque de Retiro in Madrid at seven in the morning."

"What happened there?"

"He threatened to disclose that I took a bribe in connection with the airplane purchase order unless I—bastard had made a secret tape at Cap d'Antibes . . ." Alvarez was growing red in the face.

"Unless you what?"

"Unless I agreed to move troops from Southern Spain to the north."

"Why did he want you to do that?"

"He told me to say I had learned of a Basque threat in the north."

"Had you?"

Alvarez looked away. "No."

"What did you understand to be his real motive?"

"I didn't know."

"But you ran away from Spain to Argentina. So you must have known he was involved in a plan to launch an attack on Southern Spain."

"I went on vacation."

"The Defense Ministry travel office has told us you didn't make your plans until that morning. My advice is that you don't use the vacation lie in front of a judge. He'll never believe you."

"Fuck you."

"Let me ask you this. In hindsight, do you believe that General Zhou wanted you to move the troops to the north to facilitate Musa Ben Abdil's attack in the south?"

Alvarez didn't respond.

"What's the point of covering for General Zhou? When it all turned to shit, he let you swing. Made no effort to protect you. Hung you out there alone in Argentina while he escaped."

Craig sensed that Alvarez was close to turning on General Zhou, but he wasn't quite there.

Time for the carrot, Craig decided. He turned off the machine.

"If you give me what I want, what I need to nail General Zhou, I will tell the prosecutor that you cooperated. I'm certain he'll take that into account in deciding how aggressive to be in proposing your punishment."

Alvarez blinked his eyes. "Okay. Repeat the question."

Craig did. And then he turned back on the recorder.

Alvarez took a deep breath and said, "I believe that scheming bastard General Zhou concocted the bribery for the airplane purchase to get me hooked so he could later use that to blackmail me and secure the troop movement. He had this whole thing orchestrated from the get go. I fell right into his trap." Alvarez paused for a moment, then added, "Truth is, General Zhou is as guilty in all of this as Musa Ben Abdil. By getting me to move our troops from the south to the north, he was facilitating the attack."

Craig had gotten exactly what he hoped for. He wanted to shout, "Yes!" but he remained still. Amazing what can be accomplished with water in a syringe.

*   *   *

Craig followed Elizabeth and Carlos into the office of Spanish Prime Minister Zahara. Standing next to the Prime Minister's desk was a tall, thin, baldheaded man with wire frame glasses who Craig recognized as Justice Minister Garcia.

Zahara immediately took charge. He walked over to his desk and picked up one of three burgundy boxes. With a dramatic gesture, he opened it and removed a gold medal suspended by a purple ribbon. Zahara held it in front of Craig so he could read the inscription: "With gratitude from the Spanish people." Zahara hung it around Craig's neck then kissed him on each cheek.

Craig was deeply touched. He recalled a similar ceremony in the Oval Office when President Brewster presented him with the Medal of Freedom for stopping a terrorist attack in Madison Square Garden when it was filled to capacity for a Knicks game. At that ceremony, Craig was accompanied by his beautiful and talented daughter Francesca. Then a second time when Brewster presented the Medal to him as well as Elizabeth and Francesca, posthumously, she wasn't there because General Zhou was responsible for her murder. Thinking about her intensified Craig's hatred for Zhou.

Zahara returned to his desk, picked up a second box, and repeated the presentation to Elizabeth, who had worked with Craig in exposing and defeating the plot by Musa Ben Abdil and the general against the Spanish nation. Craig saw tears in her eyes. Zahara's presentation was sincere and unexpected. He was confident Elizabeth was as startled as he was.

Zahara then presented the third metal to Carlos.

Afterwards, the Spanish Prime Minister said, "If it weren't for the three of you, I believe that we would have lost control of the southern portion of our country to the man calling himself Musa Ben Abdil and his co-conspirators."

Craig said, "I'm rarely speechless, Mr. Prime Minister, but I cannot think of adequate words to express my appreciation."

After Elizabeth and Carlos added their own thanks, Zahara pointed to the conference table in the corner of the large office. While the others settled in, Zahara returned to his desk and picked up what Craig recognized as the transcript of Craig's interrogation of Alvarez.

Clutching it tightly, Zahara took a seat at the head of the table. Craig recalled the first time he had been seated at this table. Hard to believe it was only seven months ago when he and Elizabeth had been summoned from Paris by Zahara to provide advice to the Spanish Prime Minister about how to deal with the threat of a train bombing planned by Musa Ben Abdil. That had been the opening salvo in Musa's effort to reestablish Muslim control over a portion of Southern Spain.

While Justice Minister Garcia pulled the transcript out of his briefcase, Zahara slammed his copy down on the table. He looked squarely at Garcia. "I'm so furious at Alvarez. I want him to get the maximum punishment. The death penalty."

"Under our law, he can't get that."

"Well then, life in prison and no chance of parole."

"I agree. I'll make sure it happens."

"I still can't believe he did it. I thought I knew the man. Well anyhow, Carlos, you said we have some unfinished business."

"Yes, Mr. Prime Minister. General Zhou has to be brought to justice for his role in this conspiracy."

"I agree. I'm not a lawyer, but when I read Alvarez's testimony, it seems absolutely clear to me that General Zhou has criminal responsibility for the Spanish people who died in the invasion of Southern Spain and the march to the Alhambra. Am I correct?" Zahara was looking at the Justice Minister.

"Yes, sir. You are," Garcia replied in a subservient tone.

"Good. Then we have to make Zhou pay for his crimes."

"First, we have to find General Zhou and seek his extradition," Garcia said. "I doubt very much that he's still in Spain."

Craig spoke up. "I know precisely where General Zhou is. Even the location of the house he's occupying."

"Where?" Zahara asked eagerly.

"He's on the island of Bali in Indonesia."

"How do you know that?" Zahara said in a voice suggesting both admiration and disbelief.

"Before I made the prisoner exchange between Elizabeth and Androshka in Gibraltar, I slipped a powerful tracking device into Androshka's bag. Thanks to a friend in the CIA, I now have precise coordinates for where they've been the last three days."

Zahara smacked his right fist into his left palm. He turned back to the Justice Minster. "How long will it take you to draw up a petition for extradition?"

Garcia was squirming in his chair, a frown on his face.

Uh-oh, we have a problem, Craig thought.

"Unfortunately," Garcia said in a halting voice. "We do not have an extradition treaty with Indonesia."

Zahara reddened with anger. "You damn lawyers. Always telling me what I can't do."

"I'm sorry, Sir."

"So we're stymied. Stuck." Zahara sounded outraged. "I can't believe that."

"Unfortunately, that's the situation."

"Suppose we negotiate an extradition treaty with Indonesia right now. Let's do that."

Garcia was shaking his head. "Won't work."

"Why not?"

"Even if Indonesia would be amenable, which I doubt, it'll take too long. Also, it couldn't be applied retroactively."

Zahara turned away from Garcia, toward Craig and Elizabeth. "Have you ever noticed that lawyers always tell you what you can't do?"

Craig was in agony. His great plan for bringing Zhou back to Spain to stand trial never got off the ground. It was D.O.A. His successful interrogation of Alvarez was all for naught. He was right back where he started. Nowhere. But he couldn't accept that. Zahara was willing to try Zhou. A Spanish court would convict him. Craig couldn't let this opportunity disintegrate. He had to find a way to get Zhou back to Spain to stand trial.

Then it hit him. There was a way. Risky to be sure, but Craig was willing to gamble everything, even his own life, to get revenge over Zhou. Life had no value for Craig unless Francesca's murderer was made to pay for his crime.

"Here's what we should do," Craig said. He coughed and cleared his throat. Through the corner of his eye, he saw trepidation on Elizabeth's face. He could guess what she was thinking: you should discuss this with me first. But there was no time for that.

All eyes were on Craig.

"Mr. Prime Minister, I'd like to request you to authorize Carlos to assemble a strike force of four special ops troops. Carlos will remain here in Madrid. I'll head up the unit. Our mission will be to go into Bali, under the cover of darkness, abduct General Zhou, and bring him back to Madrid to stand trial."

As Craig's words sunk in, an eerie silence settled over the room.

"You really think you can do that?" Zahara asked, the doubt evident.

"I executed similar missions when I was with the CIA."

"But you had a great deal more technical support for those. Didn't you?" Elizabeth interjected, disapproval in her voice.

"Technology only goes so far," Craig said.

"But you'd be exposing yourself to great danger," Carlos added.

"I won't deny that. In selecting your special ops men to join me," Craig said, "you should seek volunteers. No one should be compelled to do this."

Carlos nodded.

Craig turned back to Zahara. "It's up to you, Mr. Prime Minister. Whether you wish to authorize it. I'm afraid the operation may provoke a major diplomatic incident for Spain with the government of Indonesia, the largest Muslim country in the world."

"I'm prepared to accept that," Zahara said. "They've granted sanctuary to this criminal responsible for killing so many of our people."

"Are you certain?" the Justice Minister asked. "The fallout could be serious. Perhaps you should analyze our commercial dealings with Indonesia before you give this risky operation a green light."

"There comes a time," Zahara said boldly, "for any leader when principles trump business. For me, this is one of them."

Craig's high opinion of Zahara was raised a notch.

Zahara turned back to Craig. "If your abduction gets into trouble, don't hesitate to kill General Zhou."

"Thank you, Sir. I appreciate having that authority. Now I'll go with Carlos to plan the operation."

Carlos, Elizabeth, and Craig left the Prime Minister's office. None of them said a word until they hit the street. Then Elizabeth, eyes blazing, said, "Are you crazy? Out of your fucking mind."

Carlos backpedaled. "You two should talk about this by yourselves. I'll be at the Defense Ministry."

"You don't care what I think, do you?" Elizabeth cried out. "That's the most insulting part."

People passing by were staring at them.

"Can we at least go somewhere private to talk," he said.

"Whatever you want."

He led the way to a nearby park. They sat down next to each other on a bench.

"Loving you is about the stupidest thing I ever did." She was crying. She pounded her fist against his chest. "We're not even married, and I feel like a widow already. That's quite a trick."

"You don't have to worry. I'll come back alive," he said displaying a bravado he didn't feel. "This operation won't be riskier than many I undertook with the CIA."

Of course, she was right in what she had said in the meeting. In his CIA operations, he'd always had lots of high tech support which made a difference. Also he knew that Carlos's special ops troops wouldn't have had much, if any, experience in the field. The odds of him coming back alive were long. The odds of abducting General Zhou even longer. But he couldn't admit that to her.

"What really upsets me," she said, "is that I know I'll be responsible for your death. If I hadn't been taken prisoner in Paris, you would never have let General Zhou get away."

"Totally irrelevant. All that matters now is he's eluded me twice. He was responsible for my daughter, Francesca's, death. It's time for my revenge."

"That's absurd. It's time for you to forget the past. Time for you to move on."

"I wish I could."

He reached for her hand. She pulled it away, then stood up and left the park.

Watching her walk away, he had no second thoughts about what he planned to do. Yes, he loved Elizabeth, but he rejected her opinion on this issue. She never had a child. She couldn't understand the pain of losing one. Perhaps he was a fanatic. And obsessive. Call it what you want, but all that mattered to him right now was getting Zhou for Francesca's murder. This was the best chance he'd ever had. Perhaps he'd never have another once Zhou was safely back in China. Either he'd bring Zhou back from Bali to stand trial or he'd kill him. Not with a gun. But with his bare hands, so he could watch Zhou die. Painfully and slowly.

Bali

In the balmy evening air, General Zhou sat on the verandah, rocked while smoking a Cuban cigar, and stared out at the sea. He viewed his stay in Bali as a pleasant interlude. The calm before the storm.

His brother Zhou Yun in Beijing still didn't know when President Li planned to have surgery for colon cancer. Once that occurred, General Zhou was confident he would be returning to China to assume the presidency. Though he didn't have a precise date, he knew it was a matter of days or weeks. No longer.

Meantime, thanks to his brother having promised a major investment in the Indonesian oil industry, General Zhou and Androshka were being treated as honored guests.

They occupied a compound, encircled by a six-foot-high stone wall, located on a promontory at the top of a steep hill that ran down to the sea. He had a car and driver at his disposal. His aide, Captain Cheng, was living in the compound. Two servants maintained the house. Two others cooked incredible meals from local products. Androshka was insatiable in bed. It was an ideal existence.

Still, after only a couple of days in Bali, his mind was racing ahead, formulating plans for changes he would make in China, its military and foreign policy, once he became president. He would challenge the U.S. directly on every issue. The days of Beijing being subservient to Washington would be over. China would take the premier place in the international order, consistent with its economic might.

His thoughts were interrupted by Androshka, who came through the screen door shouting, "What the fuck is this?"

"What are you talking about?"

"I was looking through my bag for a lip liner. When I couldn't find it, I dumped everything out on the table . . . This fell out." She reached out her hand and opened up her palm. She was holding a tiny round object, the size of a button, resembling a camera battery. She handed it to him.

General Zhou walked across the verandah to a candle. He held up the object to the light and studied it. To paraphrase Androshka, he knew what the fuck this was: a tracking device that someone had planted in her bag; he had a good idea who that somebody was.

"Tell me again about the prisoner exchange in Gibraltar," he said to Androshka.

"We've already been over that a hundred times."

He became furious when she didn't immediately do what he wanted. That was the trouble with Russian women. They had no respect for their men. He felt himself losing his temper. "Listen, you dumb bitch. This is important. Just answer my question."

"Okay. What do you want to know?"

"You rode in the back of the car with Craig Page. Correct?"

"That's right. Just the two of us. I told him what a great man you were. He treated me with contempt. Called me a whore."

"While you were worrying about what he called you, he slipped this little object into your bag. How could you have been such a stupid cunt?"

She began crying. "I hate when you talk to me this way."

"How would you like me to talk now that you've messed up our lives?"

"It's a tracking device. Isn't it?"

He sighed. "At least, you're not brain dead."

"Then Craig Page knows where we are."

"Probably."

She walked toward the door. "I'll start packing. Maybe we can get out of here before he comes for us."

General Zhou shook his head. "We're not leaving Bali. Go into the house and let me alone. I have to think."

When he had been a student in the Military Academy, General Zhou had read so many times that he practically had committed to memory, "The Art of War," by Sun Tzu. Master Sun's statements were indelibly stamped on his brain. He recalled some of them now. "Draw them in with the prospect of gain, take them by confusion . . . Take advantage of the ground . . . Stay on the heights . . . On steep terrain await the opponent."

General Zhou knew what he had to do.

*   *   *

Early the next morning, General Zhou, accompanied by Captain Cheng, took his car and driver into Singaradji. There, he met with Ahmed, a stout, disagreeable man in his fifties, with a thick, bushy mustache and a long scar on his right cheek.

General Zhou expected this to be a difficult conversation. In their two prior meetings, Ahmed had made it clear he didn't like being directed by the Foreign Ministry in the Indonesian capital of Jakarta to provide hospitality to General Zhou. "I don't even like you Chinese," Ahmed had said. "You think you're superior to us, and you're always taking over."

General Zhou came right to the point with Ahmed. "I want you to provide me with armed guards, eight or ten, at the compound. Around the clock. I'll pay for their salaries and any expenses."

Ahmed looked alarmed. "You're bringing trouble to my peaceful island. That wasn't part of the deal."

"I'm not expecting trouble. I just want to be prepared."

"I should contact the foreign office. Tell them to expel you."

General Zhou gripped the arms of the chair tightly. The discussion had taken an ominous turn. If he were forced out of Bali, where could he and Androshka go until President Li's death? Almost everyplace had an extradition treaty with Spain.

"I don't think that's justified," Zhou said.

Ahmed reached for the phone. Zhou didn't know whether his brother's clout was enough to carry the day. He wanted to kill Ahmed, but that wasn't an option. Ahmed picked up the phone, but didn't dial. Instead, he fiddled with his mustache and looked at Zhou. "Perhaps we could work this out between us," he said.

Then it struck Zhou. Of course, Ahmed wants money. Corruption was endemic in Indonesia.

"Let me make this proposal to you, Ahmed. I estimate costs for your soldiers and their expenses to defend my compound might be as much as five hundred thousand euros a month. Suppose I were to pay that amount to you personally and I flew in Chinese troops for my defense. Would that be acceptable?"

A slight smile appeared at the edges of Ahmed's mouth.

"In principle, that is fine. But I will also have some costs. For example, payments to immigration agents to get your troops and equipment into the country."

"I understand. Suppose we settle on seven hundred thousand euros."

Ahmed was nodding.

"Good. Provide me with the number of a bank account. I'll arrange an electronic transfer."

Ahmed was writing numbers on a piece of paper. As he did, he said, "Bring your men and materials in via Benpasar Airport. I'll have everything arranged."

As soon as General Zhou left the building, he took the phone from his briefcase and called General Yang Gon, the head of the Chinese Air Force in Beijing. General Gon had been a firm ally of General Zhou. Before Zhou left China in exile, General Gon had told him, "I'll do anything to help you. Any time."

Now General Zhou was ready to accept that offer. "Keep this extremely confidential," General Zhou said.

"For sure."

"How quickly can you send ten of your best commandos to Bali for an assignment that may take a month?"

"For you, they'll be on a plane in an hour."

"Excellent. Fully armed with automatic weapons. Grenade launchers. Surface to surface missiles. Surface to air missiles. And anything else to defend a fortress."

"Yes, sir."

"Good. Call me when you have an ETA at Benpasar Airport. I'll meet them there."

Once he was in the back of the car, returning to his compound, General Zhou exhaled deeply. Craig Page had outsmarted himself. General Zhou was confident the American would be in the invading party, and General Zhou would be waiting for him.

This time you're a dead man, Craig Page.

Madrid and Skies over the Ocean

"Are you sure that four of my men are enough?" Carlos asked Craig in an anxiety-filled voice. "I can get more volunteers."

They were standing on the tarmac at a Spanish Air Force base outside of Madrid, waiting for the fueling of the unmarked plane that would take them to Broome, Australia.

"Thanks, but I like to work lean and mean."

"Okay, it's your call."

Carlos's cell rang. Craig heard him say, "Good. Send the men out. Take off in fifteen minutes."

Craig thought about the six volunteers Carlos had sent him early this morning—all of whom had seen action in the recent battle for Southern Spain launched by Musa Ben Abdil. Craig had spent an hour alone with each of them, hearing about their experience before making his selection of four.

Now, standing next to Carlos in the hot midday sun, Craig watched the four with their heavy equipment laden backpacks pass him on the way to the plane.

What struck Craig was how young they were. All between twenty and twenty-five. They could easily have been the children of forty-six year old Craig. In fact, when Craig handed out the equipment an hour ago, Juan, now leading the way to the plane, had called Craig, "Papa." At first, Craig had been irritated, but then he thought, what the hell, he'd take it as a sign of respect.

Juan, at twenty, was the youngest. His baby face, with black curly hair, made him look even younger. As Craig spoke with Juan, Craig quickly realized he was a tough kid. Juan was the youngest of four, born in a Madrid slum to a mother who worked in a laundry and turned tricks at night to support herself and her children to get away from their father who constantly beat her and the children. Juan had learned to fight with older boys in the slum who called his mother names. With her encouragement, he lied about his age and joined the army at sixteen to escape from his domestic situation. Despite all this, Juan almost always had a smile. Miraculous, how some kids manage to avoid being scarred by their background.

Next was Julio, the pilot, the oldest at twenty-five. Julio was a child of privilege from Barcelona. His father was a banker, but all Julio ever wanted to do was fly planes. His father, who had wanted Julio to be a banker, refused to pay for flying lessons. So as a teenager, he scrimped and saved and snuck out for flying lessons. Over the bitter opposition of his father, Julio joined the Spanish Air Force. In the attack on Southern Spain, Julio had flown a bomber which tried to stop the landing of Musa Ben Abdil's troops.

Fredrico, who followed Julio to the plane, was raised on a farm near Granada. He joined the army looking for a different life than raising crops and livestock. Powerfully built, with a dark, almost olive skin, Craig saw in Fredrico, who must have had Moorish blood, the melting pot that was Southern Spain. Perhaps because he was fighting for his homeland, during the battle with Musa Ben Abdil Fredrico had distinguished himself for valor, rescuing one wounded comrade who had been pinned down by enemy fire and going back to rescue a second when Spanish troops tried to block the advance of Musa Ben Abdil's army. Fredrico was also a crack marksman and had won many awards in training.

Taking up the rear was Manuel, the only one of the four who was married. He had a six-month-old son. Manuel was from the Basque country in the north, the son of a fisherman from a small town near San Sebastian. He was short and stocky with legs that looked like tree trunks. He had the toughness Craig had always associated with Basques. And he had scars from knife wounds that proved he liked to fight. One on his arm and the other on his neck. "Not a good place to catch a blade," he had told Craig in the interview.

When Craig had asked him why he joined the Spanish Army, he had said, "I wanted to fight. It was a close question of whether to join the Spanish Army or the violent Basque separatist movement. I figured that the movement was about finished. They lost their will to fight. What was the point of hooking up with them." Manuel was an expert on explosives. Craig suspected he had learned to make bombs as a kid, hanging out with Basque terrorists. In the battle for the Alhambra, Manuel had been sent in undercover to disable any bombs that had been planted.

Their plane to Broome, a port on the northwest corner of Australia, was being flown by two Air Force pilots who would drop them off and wait for their return . . . if they made it back.

Once they were in the air from Madrid to Broome, Craig gathered the four men in a circle and said, "Let's go over the logistics. Feel free to interrupt with questions."

The four were staring at Craig, listening intently as he continued. "An old buddy of mine from my CIA days, who used to be in Australian intelligence, has purchased a seaplane and flown it to Broome, where he's waiting for us." Craig turned to Julio. "You ever flown a seaplane?"

"Naw, but a plane is a plane. I'll figure it out."

"Well if you need any help, my Aussie buddy is supposed to be knowledgeable."

"No big deal, Papa. Don't worry."

"Okay, assuming Julio gets us to Bali, here's the plan. General Zhou's house is at the top of a hill, on a promontory, on an isolated part of the island of Bali. We want the cover of darkness so we'll land on the southern side of the island at two in the morning when hopefully everyone in the compound will be sleeping.

"Julio will remain in the seaplane. We'll have a small rubber inflatable boat with a powerful but quiet motor. Manual will steer it into shore on a rocky beach just below Zhou's compound. And that won't be easy because there's plenty of coral. Then Manuel stays in the boat while Fredrico and Juan go up to the compound with me."

"Why can't I go, too?" Manuel asked.

"We need you to protect the boat. It's our only way out. And you're the only one who knows about boats."

What Craig didn't add was that waiting with the boat was the least dangerous part of the operation. Manuel had a wife and child. Craig didn't want him to be in the fighting.

"How many are you expecting to be in the compound?" Fredrico asked.

"The most recent satellite photos I have were taken two nights ago. According to those photos, in the main building, only General Zhou and Androshka, his mistress, sleeping in one bed. In a small house off to the left as we go up the hill is a building housing the servants' quarters. Captain Cheng, the General's aide, and two servants from Bali should be in there. At the front west entrance where a road runs into the compound, two uniform guards are in a glass booth.

By coming in from the sea, we'll circumvent the guards. If we're quiet and move quickly, they may never know we're there."

Juan asked, "What do we do with General Zhou and Androshka?"

"Fredrico and I will each have chloroform. We'll knock them out. I'll take General Zhou; Fredrico, Androshka. Then we'll carry them down the hill and into the boat. Juan, you'll be covering us the whole way. We have to take both of them. We can't risk leaving Androshka behind to alert the authorities."

"And if Captain Cheng or General Zhou wake up and start shooting?"

Craig recalled what Zahara had said. "Then we shoot to kill."

Broome, Australia, and Bali

Craig sat in the first row of the seaplane and watched anxiously as Julio tried to start the two engines. They coughed and sputtered, then died.

In the cockpit, Julio emitted a string of curses. He turned around toward Craig and said, "We were close that time. I'm sure I'll get them to kick over."

All this was making Craig extremely nervous. Outside, it was pitch-dark. In the plane, Juan, Fredrico and Manuel, dressed in full black nylon outfits, nothing reflective, were belted in their seats and perspiring heavily because there wasn't any air in the plane.

Craig had instructed them to wait to apply black paint on their faces until they were coming down. Then they'd have to strap on their backpacks.

I'm not getting a good feeling about this mission, Craig thought. If the plane won't start here, how do I know it will start for the return flight with General Zhou and Androshka? Maybe I should abort and get another plane.

Then he heard Julio shout, "C'mon baby." The engines sprang to life.

Seconds later, they were in the air.

Craig thought about his plan. So many things could go wrong. He had learned long ago what worked on paper often hit snags in the real world. Sure, the night was moonless, but what if another plane or boat happened to see them? What if a heavy rain storm erupted that woke General Zhou or Androshka in time to sound an alarm. What if General Zhou had beefed up his guards in the last two days since the most recent satellite photos? Or what if the damn plane's engines didn't start for the return trip? Once daylight came, they'd be sitting fully exposed in the Indian Ocean.

All of these and several more things might go wrong. That's why the operation was so risky. But it was the only chance Craig had of abducting General Zhou.

Before Craig had left Madrid, he called Giuseppe, his Deputy Director of the EU Counterterrorism Agency, based in Rome, to review the plans for General Zhou's abduction. Giuseppe was in complete agreement. That sanity check made Craig feel better. And then Giuseppe added, "If you get into trouble, go to the Italian Embassy in Jakarta and call me. I'll alert the Ambassador."

After initially encountering some stiff headwinds, the flight became smooth. And Julio had no difficulty flying without lights. He had his landing point carefully fed into the instruments. Craig looked down at the water. He didn't see any lights. So far, so good.

"We're landing in five minutes," Julio announced. Craig told the others to put on the black paint. He wanted them to move as soon as they were on the ground.

By the time Julio was ready to touch down, the winds had died. His landing was smooth, the sea calm and dark.

*   *   *

Three minutes after landing, Manuel had the rubber boat in the water. Craig, Juan, and Fredrico had their backpacks with grenades and other supplies strapped on. Their faces were painted black. They were wearing night vision glasses. Each was gripping an MPSK automatic weapon.

As Manuel guided the boat, Craig studied Juan and Fredrico. They had grim looks of self-determination. If either felt fear, he didn't show it.

Craig raised his eyes toward the compound on the hill. He saw the six-foot stone wall encircling the property. The second floor of the house was above that. No guards were visible. The distance from the shore to the wall was about a hundred yards, most of that up a steep hill.

Manuel did a good job of navigating around coral. He pulled up the boat onto a rocky beach. "I'll be right here, Papa," he told Craig. "Ready to put back in the instant you return with the hostages."

Following their prearranged plan, Craig, Juan, and Fredrico, fanned out on the beach. Craig didn't want them to climb the hill in a line. If the guard left the booth and spotted them, he wouldn't be able to hit them all easily.

Craig was in the center, Juan on his left; Fredrico on his right.

Loaded down by the backpacks, they each hit the ground and began crawling, clawing their way up the steep, rocky hill while maintaining control of their automatic weapons.

The rocks were jagged. Craig felt them scraping his knees and elbows. His sleeve was bloody. He shrugged that off and kept going. Perhaps it was their youth or superior conditioning, but Craig quickly fell behind Juan and Fredrico. On the plane, he had instructed them: "Once you get to the wall, hold. We'll all go over together."

Craig estimated he was halfway up the hill when he heard a commotion on the top. He raised his gaze and was horrified by what he saw. Standing on the wall were ten Chinese soldiers in full battle dress. Most were gripping automatic weapons. Two had grenade launchers.

"Holy shit!" he cried out. It was a trap. He had led his men right into it.

For a split second, Craig weighed his options. Retreating down the hill was a nonstarter. They'd never make it back to the boat. And if they did, the Chinese would blow them up in the water. Only one choice: stay and fight. To hell with the odds.

"Enemy troops on the wall!" Craig shouted to Juan and Fredrico. "Fire now!"

All three raised themselves to their knees and opened fire. Craig and his men fired first. Craig hit one of the Chinese; Fredrico another one. Both fell off the wall. Two down and eight to go.

Then the return fire came. Vicious and unrelenting. Round after round from automatic weapons. While shooting back, Craig watched Juan and Fredrico take multiple hits.

From a crouching position, Craig took out one more of the Chinese troops. He tried to stand to get more secure footing to fire.

Rising to his feet, he sensed a shot whizzing at him. Craig ducked. As he did, he tripped on a rock and rolled down the hill. Over and over. His downward movement was stopped by a huge boulder. Craig took cover behind it.

The Chinese kept firing in his direction, but the boulder deflected their shots. Craig peeked up at Juan and Fredrico. Neither was moving or making a sound. They had to be dead with the hits they'd taken. He glanced up at the wall. Six Chinese soldiers were still standing. The odds of abducting Zhou had gotten much worse.

Suddenly, Craig saw two grenades flying over his head. Keeping low, he turned around.

"Oh no," Craig cried out.

He watched helplessly as a grenade tore into the rubber boat, blasting it and Manuel to ribbons. The other was on a line toward the seaplane.

With a sickening feeling in his stomach, Craig watched it score a direct hit. He no longer had a chance of abducting General Zhou. All four of his comrades were dead.

Stupidly, he had led them on a suicide mission. Elizabeth was right. His hatred for General Zhou had distorted his judgment. All he could do now was try to escape.

His arms and legs were bloody from the roll down the hill. He didn't think any bones were broken, but every part of his body hurt like hell.

He figured he had a two-second head start while the Chinese watched the seaplane burn. Off to the left, about ten yards away, Craig saw some trees. He made a dash for them. Craig expected to be gunned down. But no one fired.

This had to mean General Zhou told his troops he wanted Craig alive. Craig didn't want to try and imagine what brutal and sadistic games General Zhou would play with Craig as his prisoner.

Once he was in the trees, Craig reached into the bag, grabbed two grenades, and stuffed them into his pockets. He jettisoned the duffel.

Before he resumed running, Craig looked over his shoulder. Two Chinese soldiers were charging down the hill toward him.

Craig put his head down and ran deeper into the trees. He ignored the sharp branches cutting his hands and face. Birds were gawking. Insects swarming.

The trees turned into jungle, which he knew could happen very quickly in Indonesia. He figured he had an advantage. The Chinese soldiers didn't have night vision glasses. A mistake on their part. He had to take advantage of it.

He kept running until the trees thinned out. He heard the Chinese pursuing relentlessly, firing from time to time, shots that flew over his head, convincing him that he was right. Their objective was to capture him.

Craig came into a clearing. He saw a small mound about four feet high and took cover behind it. Then he fired into the air. As he expected, the Chinese soldiers fired back, their shots giving away their location: right next to each other.

Craig pulled from his pocket a slow burning thermite grenade. It emitted a blinding brightness. Even brighter than a welder's torch.

Craig tossed it in the direction of the Chinese troops, knowing it would blind them. But with his dark glasses, he could still see.

Then he ran in the direction of the bright light. Both Chinese soldiers were rubbing their eyes and standing helpless. He raised his MP5K and mowed them down one at a time. They never even fired back.

He didn't think any other Chinese were pursing him, but General Zhou might call the authorities in Bali. Craig had to get the hell off this island. He had to get to Jakarta and the Italian Embassy. Giuseppe would know how to get him out of Indonesia.

That was easier said than done. Craig had committed the geography to memory. Jakarta was 250 miles away. He was only ten miles from Denpasar Airport. Even if he could make it there, that was too risky. It was the first place the authorities would look for him.

About three miles up the beach was a luxury resort. Chances were there would be powerboats for hire by wealthy resort guests. If the price was right, most of those skippers would take anybody anywhere. No questions asked. No reports filed.

Fortunately, Craig had stuffed wads of euros into his jacket pocket. He learned long ago always to travel with lots of cash.

Despite his pain and aches, Craig forced himself to move fast. He still had an hour or so before daylight.

Gasping, he arrived at the marina. The first rays of sunlight were starting to appear. A European looking man, mid-thirties, thick shock of blonde hair, was hosing down a slick, powerful-looking launch. Craig saw a large plastic trash bag. He grabbed it and stuffed his gun inside.

Craig knew he looked like hell. Nothing he could do about that. He approached the man with the hose.

"What happened to you?" the man said in English with a Dutch accent.

"I had a fight with my girlfriend."

"That was pretty stupid."

"How about taking me to Jakarta for two thousand euros cash."

"Hans is my name. Five and you have a deal."

Hans was a thief. But Craig didn't have a choice.

"Only if you throw in a shower once we're underway and a set of your clean clothes."

"Let me see the money."

Craig handed over half. "The rest when we reach Jakarta."

A secretary was waiting for Craig in the reception area of the Italian embassy. She hustled him upstairs where a good looking nurse treated his wounds. The secretary provided him with clean clothes, a fake ID, and a first class plane ticket to Paris.

Everything he needed to get home. But nothing to alleviate the immense pain, grief, and guilt for the four men who had died.

Beijing

Mei Ling sat in the back of an Audi limousine taking her to a meeting with President Li. She was a petite figure, with short black hair, who no one would have guessed would be celebrating her sixtieth birthday in January.

Her face was virtually unlined as a result, she was convinced, of a herbal compound she diligently applied each evening. What was most striking about Mei Ling was her eyes. They were coal black and when she stared at people, her eyes cut into them like lasers.

The Audi was stuck in gridlock traffic. Nothing Mei Ling could do about that, so she didn't fret. Instead, she closed those coal black eyes and reflected on the long rollercoaster ride which had been her life.

Her father had for decades been a close confidant of Mao's. That made her practically Chinese aristocracy with all the perks she wanted, one of which was two years at Stanford University in California following her Chairmanship of the Party Youth League. When Mao turned on her father, as he did most of his colleagues late in life, her father was sent to prison, tortured, and executed. She became an outcast. Reinstatement came at Mao's death.

Her father's friends engineered a meteoric rise for Mei Ling in the Chinese political leadership. Recognizing the importance of her years at Stanford in terms of understanding the United States, she was given a seat on the Foreign Policy Advisory Committee and was elevated to Chairman a year later. She became a member of the Politburo and the Central Advisory Commission.

With her influential connections, she arranged the appointment of her husband, Admiral Xu, to be Commander of the Chinese navy. She wanted to catapult him to Commander of all the Armed Forces. But General Zhou was too powerful in the military.

With her encouragement, her husband displayed enormous courage in defying General Zhou, the head of the Chinese Armed Forces, when he tried to implement Operation Dragon Oil—a plot with Iran to cut off the flow of foreign oil to the United States. Though she could never prove it, Mei Ling was convinced that General Zhou, every bit as evil as Mao, had her husband murdered and made it seem like a heart attack.

Mei Ling recalled with pride that she had thwarted General Zhou's Operation Dragon Oil. It was only because she had delivered to Elizabeth Crowder a copy of Zhou's agreement with Iran that the Americans were able to foil his plot.

Afterwards, she fled to the house of friends in the country outside of Beijing where she went into hiding to escape General Zhou's wrath. Once she learned that General Zhou had left China in exile, she returned to Beijing and resumed her life, spending time with the country's political elite.

The car began moving again, only to stop thirty seconds later. Normally, she would have been cursing the traffic, but today she had something else dominating her thoughts. How odd the call was that she had received this morning from President Li. "I want you to come and see me," he had said. "It's quite urgent and confidential." She had no idea what he wanted.

An hour later, the interminable drive ended. After she was ushered into President Li's office, overlooking Tiananmen Square, all of his aides quietly withdrew. It was only Mei Ling and President Li.

He looked pale, ashen, and was moving slowly. He's a sick man, she thought, trying to remember the last time she'd seen him. It must have been two weeks. He looked bad then, but nothing like this.

He pointed to a sofa in a corner of the office. She sat while he slumped down in a leather chair facing her. His skin seemed chalky white. She was afraid for him. She wanted to say, "What's wrong?" But it wasn't up to her. It was his meeting and he was the Chinese president. She had to be patient.

"I've been diagnosed with colon cancer," he said.

"I'm sorry to hear that."

"Actually, the doctors made the diagnosis some time ago." He paused and took a deep breath. "Perhaps I didn't want to believe it. I thought by ignoring it, I could make it go away."

"I've done that from time to time myself with medical issues," she said, sounding sympathetic.

"Well at any rate, it's become aggressive. My primary doctor has wanted to do surgery for some time. But I found another doctor who thought he could treat it with herbal medicine. So I tried that in an effort to avoid surgery. It hasn't helped. I've run out of options. I'm having the surgery in five days. The surgeon believes they can save my life."

"I'm very happy to hear that."

"I've kept all this confidential. Even my top aides don't know."

She wondered why he told her. She had never considered herself close enough that he would confide information like this.

As if reading her mind, he said, "I'm afraid I won't survive the surgery."

"But you just told me that your surgeon believes he can save your life. You should accept his judgment. He's the expert. Of course you'll survive. And recover."

"You don't understand." President Li's voice was weak.

She leaned forward to hear him.

"Or I'm not making myself clear."

"I don't understand."

"I'm convinced something will happen to me in the surgery. That I'll die."

She was stunned. "What do you mean?"

"We both know General Zhou. He'd give anything to become president of China."

"But he's in exile."

"His brother's here. And extremely powerful."

"Put soldiers in the operating room."

"I will, but they'll be useless. That's not how Zhou and his brother will do it. They're too smart. There will be a medical accident. An unexplained cause of death. The same way your husband supposedly had a heart attack. That's how they do things."

"You should thoroughly check everyone who will be in the operating room."

He smiled faintly. "I've thought of that. It can't be done exhaustively."

"Then have the surgery done abroad. In the United States, Paris, or London."

"Do you know how bad that would look from a PR standpoint?"

"Then please tell me what you want me to do. How I can keep such a dreadful thing from occurring? How I can save your life? I'll do anything."

He closed his eyes and leaned back for a long moment. When he opened them, his face was distorted. "Sorry, sometimes I have waves of pain."

"What can I do?" she repeated.

"Nothing about the surgery. But afterwards."

"Afterwards what?"

"I've spoken with members of the Central Committee. I'm convinced that if I die during the surgery . . ."

"You won't die."

He ignored her words and continued. "That a majority of them will support you to be the next president of China."

"They would never accept a woman."

"I thought that initially. But I realized from these conversations that I was wrong. People on the Central Committee admire your work on the Politburo and the Foreign Policy Advisory Committee. Also, I've let them know privately what a key role you played in thwarting General Zhou's Operation Dragon Oil. They would prefer you to General Zhou."

"Has he been talking to members of the Central Committee about the Presidency?"

"His brother has. And spreading around money. Should I die, a group within the Central Committee wants to bring General Zhou back from exile and make him president. Right now, I believe they are a minority, but . . ."

She finished the thought for President Li. "I've learned never to underestimate General Zhou and his brother, Zhou Yun. They are capable of anything."

"I agree. If you challenge him for the presidency, you should have armed guards around the clock. You'll be putting your life at risk. Are you prepared to do that?"

She nodded her head vigorously. "Anything to prevent General Zhou from becoming president."

Paris

Before the plane from Jakarta touched down at Charles DeGaule, Craig went into the lavatory and looked into the mirror. Dreadful, he decided.

He had bandages on his forehead and chin. One eye was almost closed. His face, like most of his body, was every possible shade of black and blue from the roll down the hill. And he was limping from bad bruises on his upper thigh.

Half an hour later, when he walked off the plane at four in the afternoon, he immediately saw Elizabeth standing at the gate. She didn't rush forward, but stood stone-faced, gaping at his bruised face.

He approached her and pulled her off to the side. "You're still angry."

"It wasn't just that what you did was stupid." Her tone was sharp. "You didn't give my opinion the least bit of consideration."

"Will it help now if I tell you I'm sorry? That you were right? I should have listened to you." He lowered his voice to a whisper. "We walked into a trap. I'm the only one who made it out alive."

"I was sure you would never come back." Her voice had softened. Tears were running down her cheeks.

"Look, I'm sorry. I really am. In my obsession to get Francesca's killer, I lost my judgment. I don't want to lose you, too. I hope you'll forgive me."

"You look awful."

Ignoring the stares of bystanders, he kissed her passionately. Then he pulled back. "I couldn't call you from Indonesia. I was afraid the government was monitoring all calls. I assume the Italian Embassy informed Giuseppe of my travel plans under an alias, and he called you."

They began walking as they talked. "That's exactly what happened. Your car and driver are at the curb. Giuseppe and Carlos are waiting for us at your office. When the meeting's finished, they're both flying home this evening."

"After that," Craig said, "let's head back to the apartment. I can't wait to get into bed with you."

"We'll see about that."

"Okay, maybe dinner first."

He wrapped an arm around her. To Craig's pleasant surprise, she didn't pull away.

When Craig walked into his office with Elizabeth, he saw Giuseppe pacing and a grim-faced Carlos.

"You were the only one who made it to the Italian Embassy," Carlos said. "I assume my four men were killed."

"Zhou set a trap. We walked right into it."

Craig explained what had happened in meticulous detail. At the end, he said, "All four of your men performed bravely. I couldn't have asked for more. Please convey to Prime Minister Zahara and their families my deep appreciation and regret."

Craig got a knot in his throat as pictures of the four flashed into his mind, and he thought of Manuel's six-month-old son.

"Thank you," Carlos replied.

"How come we didn't know about the Chinese troops?" Giuseppe asked.

"You're being kind, my friend," Craig replied, "by using the word *we*. What you mean is how come I didn't know. How could *I* have screwed up so badly."

No one responded.

"On the long plane ride to Paris," Craig continued. "I've asked myself that over and over. What I've concluded is that the latest satellite photos I had of the compound were two days old. My friend Betty at the CIA was operating offline. Unfortunately, she couldn't get later ones. The Chinese troops must have moved in after the last set of photos was taken."

"But knowing you," Giuseppe said, "you're not giving up on General Zhou. I'm sure you have some other way of getting at him."

"Maybe you want to go back to Bali again with four more Spanish soldiers," Elizabeth said sharply. "This time, all five of you can perish."

"I don't think I'll try that again. But General Zhou's not planning to spend his whole life in Bali. Once he moves, we may be able to get at him."

"And how will we know that?" Carlos asked.

"I think we have the technology here without having to involve the CIA. At least, I hope so."

Craig hit the intercom. "Get me Marie," he told his secretary.

Two minutes later, a statuesque blonde in a powder blue sweater and tight navy pants walked in holding a small computer. Craig introduced Marie to the others. Once they were all seated around the table, Craig said, "I have precise coordinates for a residential compound on the island of Bali. I want to monitor all cell phone conversations between anyone in the compound with anyone on the outside. Can you do that?"

"Absolutely," Marie said without hesitation. "We have satellites I can use to do precisely that. I'll be able to tell you who is on both ends of the call."

"Will you be able to record the calls?"

"Yes."

"It's likely they'll be speaking Chinese," Elizabeth interjected.

"Glad you told me that. I have a machine that does simultaneous translation from just about any language. I'll hook it up."

"Sounds like what we need," Giuseppe said.

"Exactly. One other thing, Marie," Craig said. "Besides sending me a recording of the calls, can you have a written transcript prepared?"

"I also have a machine that will do that."

"Isn't modern technology wonderful?" Giuseppe said.

"Only when it works," Craig responded.

*   *   *

Taking deep breaths periodically during another marvelous dinner in the Hotel Bristol dining room, Craig finally relaxed by the time the waiter brought a plate of chocolates along with the espresso. Craig savored the last drops of the 2005 Chambolle Musigny by Dujac before turning to the chocolates and espresso.

During the meal, as they talked about many different subjects, Elizabeth's book, rivalries and infighting at her newspaper, new restaurants to try in Paris, anything other than General Zhou, he sensed her anger dissipating.

But then, without any warning, she looked worried again. He knew he wouldn't like what was coming next.

"You know, Craig," she said sternly, "You're almost fifty."

"I haven't even had my forty-seventh birthday."

"Let's not quibble. Don't you think it's time to let the younger people do the field work. Put their lives on the line while you direct operations from headquarters."

"You think I'm too old for a young man's game?"

"I didn't put it that way. But let me ask you this. Twenty years ago, would Craig Page have walked into that trap?"

He started to respond by telling her that he couldn't get up to the minute photos from Betty and that was the problem. But he swallowed the words. Perhaps she had a point.

"Listen, Craig," she continued. "I love you so much. I don't mean to hurt you. I just don't want to lose you."

"I know that."

"Better to quit too early than too late. You have to know when to hold 'em and when to fold 'em."

"I'll think about it," he said. "I really will."

He wanted to change the subject. "Let's go to Corsica for a few days. Neither of us has ever been. I hear it's beautiful in the spring. Flowers will be in bloom."

"Now that's an idea."

"Can you get away from the paper?"

"You bet. I won't even take my stuff for the book. We both need a vacation."

He signaled the waiter for the check.

Once they entered the apartment, she raced to the hall closet. "What are you doing?" he asked.

"Deciding what to take to Corsica."

Though his whole body ached, he snuck up behind her, wrapped his arms around her, clutching her breasts, and kissed her on the back of the neck.

"Packing can wait," he said softly.

She pulled away and said, "I shouldn't even let you have sex with me. I'm so angry at you for going off to Bali and almost getting killed."

"But I did suggest a vacation in Corsica."

She smiled. "Well, okay." Then she kissed him, pressing her body tightly against his.

He winced from the pain. She pulled away and said, "You're not going into bed. You're going to soak in a warm tub with some bath salts."

"It's large enough for two."

After he soaked alone for fifteen minutes and was feeling better, she came in and sat behind him. He leaned back against her.

"You're a damn fool," she said.

"But you love me."

"I guess so."

He desperately wanted to make amends for the pain he had caused her. But not if it meant foregoing a chance to get Zhou—if he ever had another chance.

Moscow

Orlov was an impatient man. He hadn't heard from Androshka in days and he was becoming concerned that the great plan he had devised and presented to Kuznov would never get off the ground. Perhaps Androshka had been puffing when she told him how General Zhou, her lover, would be the next president of China. Or perhaps, Zhou, even if he did succeed President Li, would never take his Russian mistress back to Beijing.

If either of these occurred, Orlov knew he was in deep trouble with Kuznov. The Russian leader was cruel, vicious, and vindictive. Not someone whose hopes could be raised only to be dashed.

Orlov recalled his meeting at Kuznov's country house. He had killed a guard to gain entry to the Russian president. That was all the pretext Kuznov needed to order Orlov's arrest and a long prison term under the so-called justice system in the new Russia.

Kuznov might not even waste his time with a choreographed prosecution. One day, Orlov might step off a curb in Moscow and be mowed down by a beer truck.

Orlov refused to be a sitting duck. If Androshka couldn't come through for him, he intended to get some false papers and head off to Chile. Once he'd heard Sukalov, his former boss, say that Russians with money were welcome there.

Time to find out whether he was staying or going. He called Androshka on her cell. "Can you talk?"

"Zhou's out on the verandah. Thank God you called."

She sounded hysterical.

"What's wrong," he asked.

"We're still in Bali. We were attacked by the Director of EU's Counter Terrorist Agency, Craig Page, and some Spanish soldiers. There was a terrible shoot-out in the middle of the night."

"Are you okay?"

"It was awful."

"Are you hurt?"

"No. I hid under the bed until Zhou and his men drove them off."

"And Zhou?"

"Not hurt either, but angry that Page got away. He's also furious at me. He's convinced I gave away our location to Page."

"Did you?"

She hesitated. "Of course not."

He knew she was lying. He could always tell. "When will Zhou be going back to Beijing to become president?"

"I ask him that every day."

"What's he say?"

"Soon. He can't wait to get out of this hellhole. And I can't either."

"I heard Bali was supposed to be a paradise."

"Don't believe everything you hear."

Orlov felt relief. At least their plan hadn't been derailed. "You'll call me as soon as you know something."

"For sure."

After ending the call, Orlov returned to his research. He had succeeded in KGB projects because he was thorough. He always knew whom he was dealing with. In this case, he had to learn as much as he could about General Zhou. Androshka had supplied recent information when they met in March in the South of France at Zhou's villa.

She explained to him how Zhou, as Commander of the Chinese Armed forces, operating without the knowledge of President Li, had joined with Iran in a plot to cut off the flow of imported oil to the United States. Zhou's discussions with Iran had taken place in Paris, which was where Androshka had first met Zhou. When Craig Page, working with Elizabeth Crowder, had foiled his plot, President Li had banished Zhou from China.

He moved to Paris and the south of France and asked Androshka to live with him. He was biding his time until, with his brother's help, he became president of China.

In the meantime, Androshka told Orlov, Zhou was searching for another opportunity to get revenge on Craig Page. She had explained that Zhou had joined with Ahmed Sadi, a French Muslim, calling himself Musa Ben Abdil, intent on retaking a part of Southern Spain for the forces of Islam and defeating Page, who was then EU Director of Counterterrorism.

Page managed to thwart that plot as well. Orlov learned this in a brief, surreptitious call which Androshka had made soon after she and Zhou arrived in Bali.

That was Zhou's recent history. To learn about his earlier life before Androshka, Orlov turned to Mikhail Primokov, a friend and former Deputy Director of the KGB Research Department. Obtaining information about Chinese leaders was difficult, but Mikhail managed to compile a dossier for Orlov.

He had learned that Zhou's father had been a close confidante of Mao as well as being the Chinese Director of Energy. During the Cultural Revolution, Mao turned on the father and banished him to the countryside where Zhou's mother died.

Meantime, Zhou and his older brother Zhou Yun, both teenagers, remained in Beijing and formed a tight bond as they survived. Eventually their father was reinstated by Mao and became head of the Chinese National Oil Company, and later, following Mao's death, a powerful industrialist in the new, economically booming China. When their father died, Zhou Yun took over his industrial empire while his younger brother, by two years, pursued a military career, eventually becoming Commander of the Chinese Armed Forces.

At the end of the dossier Mikhail wrote, "General Zhou is arrogant, driven, and power hungry, but at times creative and brilliant. You deal with him at your own peril."

Bali

General Zhou was angry.

He rarely disagreed with his brother. Even when Zhou Yun had urged him to accept President Li's offer to leave China in exile after Craig Page uncovered his plan with Iran to cut off the flow of foreign oil to the U.S. and President Brewster threatened military action, General Zhou had followed his brother's advice and gone to Paris. Albeit reluctantly.

And he couldn't remember being angry at Zhou Yun. But today, he was furious. General Zhou was still in Bali. They were talking on an encrypted cell phone. General Zhou had just told his brother about Craig Page's attempt to abduct him from Bali and the bittersweet victory he had achieved with his Chinese troops. Bittersweet because Page had somehow escaped.

At the end of that discussion, General Zhou asked his brother when President Li was having his surgery for colon cancer. Zhou Yun had said, "I don't want to discuss this topic on the phone."

That infuriated General Zhou. He had to know what was happening in China. And he had to know now.

"But these encrypted phones are state-of-the-art," General Zhou protested. "One of your companies manufactured them. You told me the code can't be cracked."

"Correction. I told you it was extremely unlikely. That's the most that can be said about any encrypted system."

"Fine. I'll take the chance."

"With so much riding on what happens, that's not a wise decision. We have to assume Page is picking up all your conversations. This one included. And the CIA has the highest deciphering capability."

General Zhou was trying to keep his anger in check. His brother couldn't be intimidated. He was capable of simply hanging up the phone.

In a calm voice, General Zhou responded, "Page isn't with the CIA. His EU agency has relatively few high-tech resources."

"He could go to the CIA."

"Norris hates him. We know that from our own source within the United States."

"It's too risky."

"That's my decision," General Zhou said forcefully.

"If you lose, then I lose."

"That's not right. You'll still be one of the wealthiest and most powerful industrialists in China, regardless of who the president is. But my whole life is on the line."

General Zhou heard a deep sigh at the other end of the phone. A good sign. He's coming around.

"President Li's surgery is scheduled to take place next Monday morning, ten o'clock."

"What have you arranged?"

There was a long pause.

"I want to know," General Zhou insisted.

"The anesthesiologist has been paid off. He will mix potassium chloride with the anesthetic. Then he'll appear to be doing everything he can to save President Li. No one will suspect him. The medical examiner is with us as well. He'll conclude it was one of those unfortunate situations that sometimes occur in surgery."

"Excellent."

"Now tell me what's happening in the Central Committee. For their selection of the next president."

"I'm having more difficulty than I imagined."

"Who's opposing me for the presidency?"

"Mei Ling."

General Zhou was incredulous. "That wench?"

"Don't underestimate her. She has President Li's backing."

"But can't you pay off enough members to lock up a majority of the votes?"

"I'm close. But not there yet."

"Well, offer more. You only have three days to get it done."

"It may not be possible. Not everyone's for sale. We need an alternative if she has more votes."

General Zhou was thinking.

"Have Mei Ling murdered," he finally said. "Make it look like an accident."

"You sure you want me to do that?"

"Absolutely. We can't let the Presidency get away. Meantime, I'll have Captain Cheng fly back to China. He'll talk to my closest friends in the military. He'll line up their support. With Mei Ling out of the way and support from the military, the Central Committee will have to pick me as president."

His dream was almost a reality.

Corsica

Craig couldn't remember the last vacation he'd had, and he thoroughly enjoyed the first day he and Elizabeth spent on Corsica.

Ah, Corsica. France's Isle of Beauty. A hundred and ten miles long and fifty miles wide, plunked down in the Mediterranean nine miles north of Sardinia, located between Southeastern France and

Northwestern Italy. The place that savvy, wealthy Parisians went to avoid the crowds in the south of France.

Corsica. The birthplace of Napoleon. Ruled by one power after another for more than two thousand years until Napoleon asserted French control in 1796.

With so much to see and do on the island that had everything—beaches, mountains, ruins, and great food—Craig and Elizabeth decided to start in the north, spending a couple of days in Calvi at La Villa, a small luxury hotel with forty rooms. On Saturday, they rented a car and explored mountains, stopping for lunch. Then they returned to Calvi and walked along the beach. They had a superb dinner at La Villa in the veranda dining room overlooking the Bay and the Citadel, which had resisted the onslaught of foreign armies over many centuries.

When they returned to the suite, Craig dimmed the lights and reached for Elizabeth.

"You'll have to wait," she said. "I left my purse in the dining room. I have to go back and get it."

He didn't remember her having a purse, but he wasn't observant about those things. "Listen, call over there. They'll hold it for you."

"I'll feel better if I get it now. Only be a minute. Why don't you take off your clothes and stretch out on the bed."

When she made up her mind to do something, there was no point arguing with her.

Five minutes later, she returned. She was carrying a bowl and a spoon. "What's that?" he asked.

"Chocolate mousse."

"Yeah. We had it for dessert. It was great."

"Well, I want some more." She put the bowl down and was undressing. "I intend to get your cock hard, spread mousse all over it, and lick off every bit."

And she did just that. Licking and sucking him until he came in her mouth.

Afterwards, to get cleaned up, they took a double bubble bath. Back in bed he returned the favor, going down on her. They spent another hour making love until neither one could move.

As she fell asleep, the last words out of her mouth were, "That mousse was sure good."

At six the next morning, Craig woke up and left a note on his pillow for the sleeping Elizabeth. "Went for a run. Be back for breakfast." He tucked his cell phone into his pants pocket and ran half a mile down the hill, to the sea. They planned to spend a week in Corsica unless one of their jobs called them back to Paris. He hated dragging the phone everywhere, but he had to know if anything happened with General Zhou.

His bruises had stopped hurting. And he was feeling marvelous. He was running barefoot on the deserted, soft, sandy beach enjoying the breeze and cool air when the damn thing rang.

Craig stopped and yanked the phone out of his pocket. As he did, he was a mixture of emotions. He hated having his vacation interrupted. But he knew no one would call, certainly not at this hour, if it wasn't important. And they might have a lead on General Zhou.

Craig saw from caller ID that it was Marie.

"Sorry to disturb you," she said.

"Don't worry about that. What do you have?"

"General Zhou had a phone call an hour ago with his brother Zhou Yun in Beijing. It lasted twelve minutes and forty three seconds."

Craig was bursting with excitement.

"Can you forward a transcript to my Blackberry?"

"Unfortunately not. The words were encrypted. I have two of our top techies on the way to the office now to try and decipher it."

"Let me know as soon as you have something."

For a few seconds, she didn't respond. Then she said, "You should know they're not optimistic, but I promise they'll try everything."

Climbing the hill back to the hotel, Craig thought about the call. His instinct and experience cried out: this is important. Something must be happening, or about to happen involving General Zhou in China.

And he wouldn't be able to find out. The CIA experts would probably be able to decipher the call, but that wasn't an option.

Dammit! Dammit!

He had to find another way.

Elizabeth was just stirring when he returned to the suite. He waited until they were having breakfast on the patio to tell her about the call from Marie.

"I guess our vacation just ended," she said glumly. "Oh well, it was fun. All twelve hours. I'm not surprised. And if I'm dumb enough to be disappointed, well, that's my fault."

He raised his hand. "Whoa. Whoa. We're not going back to Paris. Not because of this. But I would like you to make another one of those calls to Carl Zerner, your reporter friend in Beijing. Be sure to make it sound like nothing more than one reporter calling another, in case his calls are being monitored."

"Sure. What do you want me to tell him?"

"You're doing an article on the top leadership in China. Ask him if there are any major developments on the horizon. "

"Sounds innocuous enough."

She finished a cup of coffee and went into the suite for her cell phone. Back outside, she placed the call on speaker so Craig could listen.

"Liz, good to hear from you," Carl said. "You're lucky you found me in China."

"Why? What's happening?"

"I was supposed to be reassigned to New York, which I desperately want. I'm sick of China, but then I stupidly told my editor that I've heard unconfirmed rumors that President Li is seriously ill. That provoked an immediate response. 'You're staying until you can clarify his health situation.' So here I am. What can I do for you?"

Craig was mouthing the word, "Yes."

She repeated Craig's question about major developments in Chinese leadership.

Without missing a beat, Carl replied, "Nothing so far, but if President Li is really seriously ill, then anything's possible."

"Who's his likely successor?"

"None of my sources has coughed up a name. So I haven't been able to write an article on the subject."

"Will you let me know when you do?"

"Absolutely."

When she hung up the phone, Craig said, "That call was very worthwhile. President Li being seriously ill is valuable information."

"I don't believe Carl."

Craig was puzzled.

"About what?"

"He's heard who's being considered by the Central Committee as a possible successor to President Li. He won't tell me until he's written his own story on the subject, which gets past the censors and appears in print."

"But he's your friend."

She laughed. "Among reporters who work for different newspapers, friendship only goes so far."

"Fair enough. But we still learned plenty. I'll bet anything General Zhou and his brother are mixed up in the question of who the next Chinese president will be if President Li is forced to resign for health reasons. They have to be manipulating the process for General Zhou to succeed President Li."

"You think General Zhou would be able to grab the Presidency?"

"With that scum, anything's possible. And if he succeeds, it would be a disaster."

Bali and Beijing

General Zhou hadn't been able to sleep. All night, he lay in bed staring at the cell phone he and his brother used for encrypted calls, willing it to ring. Next to him, Androshka was snoring softly. Finally, at five a.m. he heard the "Beep . . . beep . . ."

He grabbed the phone and raced with it into the other room. His brother said, "Everything is all set. President Li's surgery is firmly set for ten this morning. I've sent a plane to pick you up at Denpasar Airport. It should be there in an hour."

"Good. I'll wake Androshka. We'll leave now for the airport."

After a pause, his brother said, "Why do you want to bring her?"

"Because I do."

"Leave her there with some money. That's all she wants."

General Zhou was boiling. This wasn't his brother's business. "End of discussion."

"I'm afraid she'll be worse than excess baggage. Detrimental to you."

"I've decided. She's coming."

"Alright," Zhou Yun said with a tone of resignation, "But move fast. I want you to be in Beijing, ready to take charge once word leaks about President Li's death."

*   *   *

Mei Ling used her friendship with Yin Shao, the Health Minister, to gain access to the glass enclosed observation tower overlooking Operating Theater Number 3 in the Beijing hospital. Typically, this observation tower was used by medical students watching an operation. But this morning, the patient was President Li. Mei Ling and the Health Minister, a physician, were the only ones in the observation tower.

The two of them were seated immediately in front of the glass when President Li was wheeled into the operating room on a gurney. Mei Ling thought the Chinese president looked pale. Fear was written on his face.

Armed soldiers were standing in each of the four corners of the room, tightly gripping automatic weapons. That was good, Mei Ling thought. But then she recalled what President Li had told her: "That's not how they'll do it."

As she looked down at the medical team moving around, doing their jobs, a shiver ran up her spine.

In the next few seconds, a team of ten, doctors and nurses, all Chinese, assembled around a table. Mei Ling watched them prep President Li. He was given anesthesia, which put him to sleep. He was hooked up to several monitors. The entire surgical field was exposed and swabbed with Betadine to sterilize the site.

The primary surgeon made an incision in his stomach, and Mei Ling, glancing at each of the members of the team, thought everyone looked tense but fully in control. This must be going okay, she thought. She glanced at the Health Minister who was nodding. Perhaps President Li's fears were unjustified, she wanted to believe.

Then suddenly, in the flash of an instant, the operating room turned to chaos. The surgeon was screaming at the anesthesiologist. Some of the nurses and doctors began rushing around. Others were watching monitors anxiously.

The Health Minister shot to his feet.

"What's happening?" Mei Ling cried out, rising as well. The Health Minister pointed to a large monitor next to the operating table.

"You see those wide complexes on the monitor?" he asked.

"What's it mean?"

"Venticular Tachycardia."

"I'm not a doctor. That means nothing to me. Explain it in words I can understand." Her voice was cracking with emotion.

"President Li's gone into cardiac arrest. Look at the monitor. It's a V tach. He has no pulse."

A nurse handed the surgeon a defibrillator and he pressed the plates against the chest wall. He announced "Clear," in a loud voice. Everyone stepped back. He shocked the patient. "Now ventricular fibrillation."

They tried for several more minutes. They gave three more shocks and three rounds of epinephrine.

Finally, they gave up.

It was obvious to Mei Ling that President Li was dead.

She was terrified. "General Zhou killed President Li," she stammered.

The Health Minister looked appalled and nodded his acquiescence.

The door to the observation tower opened. Mei Ling turned and stared at Wei Fuzhi, a member of the Central Committee, a close friend and supporter of hers for the Presidency. Wei was carrying a black leather briefcase.

"President Li is dead," she told Wei, who didn't seem surprised.

"I have to talk to you," Wei said. "Alone. Please."

She nodded to the Health Minister who quietly drifted out of the room.

"President Li's dead," she repeated. "General Zhou killed him."

"I know that, but we have another problem. One we have to deal with immediately."

"What's that?"

"I'm confident that a majority of the Central Committee would support you if there were a free vote."

"Won't there be?"

"General Zhou has the support of the military. A few days ago, he sent Captain Cheng to firm up that support. General Zhou's in a plane right now on his way back to Beijing due to arrive at an air force base in three hours. The military won't let anyone else be chosen president."

Mei Ling stood erect. Her face tightly drawn. "I'll fight him all the way. Let the people finish what they started with Tiananmen Square. They want freedom from domination, from people like the Zhous. They'll rush to support me."

His mouth drawn tight, Wei was shaking his head.

"Why not?" she said.

"General Zhou has given an order for you to be murdered before he arrives. He doesn't want any opposition. He's demanding that the Central Committee rubber stamp his appointment as president. If not, the military will take over the state and appoint its own designees to the Central Committee."

"How do you know all this?"

"I have a source within the top military command."

"Who?"

"I'd rather not say. And it's better for you if you don't know."

Mei Ling thought about what he said. "You're right. But surely you and your colleagues won't permit General Zhou to take over the government."

Wei held out his hands, palms open. "What choice do we have? The military is too powerful."

In despair and frustration, she ran her hands through her hair.

"Then what do you think I should do?"

He handed her the black briefcase. "In the bag I have a false ID for you, a passport, credit cards. A wig and eyeglasses. Also a roundtrip plane ticket to Paris with a return flight in one week to make it look like you're going for a vacation. Tear up the return ticket when you get to Paris."

Mei Ling was stunned. She couldn't respond.

Wei continued, "My driver is waiting outside the hospital in my car. He'll take you to the airport. And he's completely loyal. You don't have to worry about him."

"I have to go home and pack."

"No. No!" Wei looked terrified. "You don't have time. In the trunk I put a small suitcase stuffed with some of my wife's clothes. Every second is precious. You have to go immediately. Once General Zhou's thugs can't locate you, they'll give the order to passport control at the airport to stop you. But you may get out before that happens. And even if not, the fake ID may be sufficient."

She took the case and raced for the door.

The driver, hunched over the wheel, eyes straight ahead never saying a word, pushed his speed to close to a hundred miles an hour. Mei Ling was tightly belted in the back, her eyes closed, gripping the armrest with one hand and a door handle with the other.

The driver pulled up to the curb at the Air France departure area. He handed her a suitcase from the trunk, seeming as relieved to be rid of his passenger as Mei Ling was to have arrived.

The Air France check-in went smoothly. Passport control was the tough one. Mei Ling found it ironic that in most countries it was far more difficult to get in than get out. But not China. The regime was afraid of dissidents leaving and causing damage to their rule.

Mei Ling was sorry she drew a sour looking obese woman with a red, pockmarked face as the agent to review her documents. She slid her passport under the glass window.

"Lily Fei," the woman said, pronouncing emphatically the name on Mei Ling's passport.

"Yes," Mei Ling said politely, trying to keep her knees from knocking.

"Why are you going to Paris?"

"For a vacation. To see the sites."

"You don't like our sites here? You think Paris has more to offer?"

"I like our sites. It's just for a change."

"You have some people to meet in France? Other Chinese who don't like our country?"

Mei Ling shook her head. "I don't know anyone in Paris."

Once the words were out of her mouth, Mei Ling wanted to take them back.

"And you're going alone?"

"That's right." Mei Ling tried not to sound defensive.

The agent reached for a phone on the counter.

Uh-oh, Mei Ling thought. I'm in trouble.

The agent was staring hard at Mei Ling, who didn't flinch.

Suddenly and inexplicably the agent let go of the phone, stamped Mei Ling's passport and waved her through. The incredible power of these agents was astounding, literarily holding people's lives in their hands. Equally amazing was the arbitrariness with which they exercised it.

In the boarding area, Mei Ling bought a newspaper and sat close to the point at which passengers would form a line. She concealed her face behind the newspaper, pretending to be reading.

She was the third passenger to board the plane. She didn't feel safe until they were in the air. And really safe until the pilot announced, "We're leaving Chinese airspace."

She vowed to defeat Zhou and to return one day.

Corsica and Paris

The ringing cell woke Elizabeth out of a sound sleep at La Villa in Calvi. The red digital numbers on the clock on the nightstand read 4:10 a.m. That damn Craig, she thought. Why doesn't he turn off his phone at night? Then she realized it was her phone. She grabbed it and took it into the living room. She couldn't believe Craig was still sleeping. But he'd drunk at least a bottle of wine at dinner.

She stubbed her toe on an oversized chair and found the green button in the dim light. "Yes. Elizabeth here."

"Listen, Liz. It's Carl in Beijing."

About noon there, she thought.

"I'll talk fast because we could get cut off any second. Something big has gone down here. They've barred all journalists from communicating with their papers or media bosses. They're trying to impose a news blackout. A communication wall around the country. I kept calling foreign contacts, including all the people at my newspaper. I also tried email. Nothing got through until now. Somehow this call wasn't blocked. Only thing I can figure is those systems aren't foolproof."

"What happened?" she said anxiously.

"President Li died during surgery. Cause not known. Meantime, the army is out in the streets. Very visible. Tanks in Tiananmen Square, which is roped off. The works."

"Why?"

"Nobody knows."

"A military coup?"

"Looks like it."

"What do you want me to do?"

"Run the story in your paper. But don't attribute it to me. I don't want to land in a Chinese prison. Certainly not when I'm so close to coming home."

"Can you give me any more facts?"

"You can say that . . ."

The phone went dead. Elizabeth was staring at it when she realized Craig was standing in the doorway.

"Who was that?" he asked.

She told him what Carl had said.

"We called it right, yesterday," Craig said. "General Zhou is trying to grab the presidency. He's probably in the air on his way back to Beijing. He has the military out in a holding operation until he gets back. To prevent the Central Committee from naming someone else as the president."

She reached for her laptop and opened it.

"What are you doing?"

"Writing up the story for the Herald. I'm too late for the print edition, but it'll still make the online version. If Carl's right about the news blackout, I'll have a helluva scoop. We may be the only ones with the story."

"Don't you want to call Rob, your editor, first?"

"Let him sleep a little longer. He gets grumpy when reporters wake him. How would you like to get us seats on the first plane to Paris this morning?"

"I was waiting for you to say that. I didn't want to be the one."

She walked over and kissed him. "Thanks for a great vacation. A little short, but . . ."

"Let's come back when this is all over. We still have a lot of Corsica to explore."

"I'd love that. We'll start at La Villa in Calvi. They have great chocolate mousse."

He smiled.

As he called Air France, he looked over her shoulder, watching her typing. "Chaos in China," was her title.

With the scant information Carl had given her, she finished the article in fifteen minutes, lingering only on the last paragraph. "There are indications that General Zhou, exiled from China by President Li a year and a half ago, is en route to Beijing to seize the presidency. Could this be the beginning of a period of military rule in China?"

Elizabeth asked Craig to read the article while she packed.

After she was finished, she asked him, "What do you think?"

"Perfect. I particularly like the last paragraph."

"Figured you would. I'll call Rob."

As she expected, Rob sounded grumpy. "I thought you were on vacation. That I wouldn't have to deal with you for a whole week."

"Sorry. This couldn't wait. I have your lead story for today's online version. And you'll love me for it. There's a news blackout in China. We'll be the only ones who have it."

"Okay." He yawned. "Send it to my computer and stay on the phone until I read it."

"It's on the way."

After a pause of several minutes, Rob said, "What's your source for all this?"

"I can't disclose that."

"You're kidding, right?"

"No. I'm serious."

"There's a news blackout. You got the info. And you won't tell me your source?"

"That's right."

"Hold on, Elizabeth. I'll call Jeremy, our reporter in Beijing."

"You won't be able to get through."

"Just hold on."

A minute later, Rob was back on the phone. "I can't reach Jeremy on any line. My email to him was marked undeliverable."

"Told you so."

"Okay. I'll run your article with your byline. I'll add upfront, 'Sources in Beijing have disclosed . . .' How's that?"

"Good."

"You won't like this, but I'm cutting the last paragraph. That's pure speculation about General Zhou."

She fought hard for several minutes, but Rob wouldn't budge. And he had the last word.

*　　*　　*

On her return to Paris, Elizabeth was a media star. No one else had the story about President Li's death and Chinese troops in the streets and Tiananmen Square. CNN was complaining about the Chinese news blackout.

She spent the first couple of hours at her desk ducking questions from government officials and others in the media about her source.

At five in the afternoon her phone rang. The caller was speaking English. "This is Mei Ling. I hope you remember me. We met once in Beijing."

Mei Ling sounded frightened.

Elizabeth's heart was beating rapidly. Mei Ling was one of the most heroic people Elizabeth had ever met. She had the courage to defy General Zhou and deliver to Elizabeth a copy of his agreement with Iran which enabled Elizabeth and Craig to block his plan to cut off the flow of imported oil to the United States.

"Of course, I remember you. Where are you?"

"In Paris. I saw your article today. I must talk to you."

"Where can we meet?"

"I'm staying at the Hotel Le Burgundy. Number Six Rue Duphot."

"Shall I meet you in the lobby?"

"No. No. Come to my room."

"Number?"

"Six ten," she replied in a halting voice. "I'm using the name Lily Fei. But please don't mention this to anyone. I'm in great danger."

Elizabeth called Craig and told him about Mei Ling. "Do you want to come with me," she asked.

"No. You're better to go alone. She might not confide in you if I were there."

Elizabeth asked the cab driver to drop her in front of the Madeleine with its large, gray, stone columns. She wanted to walk the last few blocks to make sure she wasn't being followed.

She used Craig's system of three rapid left turns.

Confident no one was there, she entered the six-story, white stone building with red awnings on the front windows and rode the elevator to six. Softly, she tapped on the door. When she heard Mei Ling call from the inside, "Who's there?" she said, "Elizabeth." She heard two locks unsnap. The door opened quickly. Once Elizabeth was in the room, Mei Ling closed it equally fast. The two of them sat down across a small round table in front of the window covered by thick curtains drawn tightly.

"I called you," Mei Ling said. "Because I was convinced when we met in Beijing at the Summer Palace that you were someone I could trust. And I was right. You needed my help in China and you never betrayed my confidence. Now, I need yours."

Elizabeth was leaning forward, hanging on to each word.

Stopping occasionally for a breath, Mei Ling poured out her story about President Li's death, the support she had within the Central Committee to be the next president, General Zhou's plan to kill her, and finally her escape from China. "He wanted to kill me just as he killed President Li."

"How can you be sure President Li was murdered?"

"Even Yin Shao, the Minister of Health, a doctor himself, had no other explanation for what happened in the operating room."

She paused to take a deep breath. "Now I'm scared," she continued. "Even here in Paris. General Zhou will be the next president of China. If he learns where I am, he'll send someone to kill me. He's a vicious man."

After hearing her story, Elizabeth concluded they had to keep Mei Ling safe. To begin with, she and Craig owed a great obligation to Mei Ling for the help she had given them in blocking Operation Dragon Oil.

And if Craig ever found a way to bring down General Zhou, it would help to have Mei Ling in the wings, ready to succeed him.

She called Craig and explained everything to him.

Craig immediately responded, "I'll call Jacques, the Director of French Intelligence. Ask him to arrange for an armed French policeman to be in front of her hotel twenty-four seven. If Mei Ling goes anywhere, the policeman will follow her."

"What about secrecy?" Elizabeth asked.

"I'll have Jacques specify in the records that we're providing protection to Lily Fei, not Mei Ling. Now let me get off the phone so I can call Jacques. I'll tell him to have someone there within the hour."

Elizabeth explained all this to Mei Ling who took a deep breath and exhaled with relief. "Thank you so much."

Though Mei Ling told Elizabeth she could leave now, she remained until they heard a knock on the door. Elizabeth opened it and saw a powerful-looking French uniformed policeman, a gun holstered at his side.

Elizabeth introduced him to Lily Fei. "I'll be out on the sidewalk in front of the hotel, Madam Fei. I'm part of a three man shift. Eight hours each. You don't have to worry. You'll be safe."

When the policeman left, Elizabeth removed a wad of euros from her bag and handed them to Mei Ling. "To help you get settled in Paris."

"No. No. I can't possibly take this."

"Please. You can repay me later."

Mei Ling took the money and thanked Elizabeth profusely. She left after giving Mei Ling all of her phone numbers as well as Craig's, and telling her, "Call me any hour of the day. And I'll keep in touch with you."

From the hotel, Elizabeth went to Craig's office. As she entered, she saw the widescreen television was on. He was staring intently at it.

"This is CNN," Craig said. "The news blackout is over. They're expecting a representative of the Chinese government to make a statement."

Elizabeth pulled up a chair and sat next to him.

Seconds later, a familiar face appeared on the screen: Wang Shi, the Deputy Premier under President Li. He was standing behind a lectern speaking to a room full of reporters.

"The last twenty-four hours," Wang began in a sober tone, "have been significant for the People's Republic of China.

"Our beloved and revered President Li went to a Beijing hospital for a serious surgery. I have the sad task of informing you with great sorrow that he died during this surgery. The medial examiner has concluded that the cause of death was a heart attack brought on by the surgery. The physicians had no basis to believe his body would go into cardiac arrest. It was one of those unfortunate events that sometimes occur during surgery."

"Bullshit," Craig shouted at the television screen.

"He can't hear you," Elizabeth said.

"I know, but I feel better venting."

Wang continued. "The Central Committee met as soon as they learned of this tragic occurrence. I am pleased to tell you that they have selected the new President of the People's Republic of China. And he was a unanimous choice."

Elizabeth was holding her breath.

"The new President of the People's Republic of China is General Zhou, former Commander of the Chinese Armed Forces. A hero. A great man. I am confident, as are all the members of the Central Committee, that General Zhou will continue China's advancement in the world."

"Boo," Craig called out. "Wang's a gutless traitor. He was supposed to be Li's man."

"He's doing what politicians do the world over. Whatever is necessary for their own survival."

Wang didn't take a single question. Instead, he gathered up his notes, walked away from the lectern, and left the room while reporters were shouting after him.

"Our nightmare scenario," Craig said to Elizabeth. "God help us."

"What can you do about it?" Elizabeth asked.

"Well, I certainly can't remove General Zhou from the Chinese presidency. But at least I can make sure Washington understands his perspective and his hatred for the United States. There have been so many changes since President Brewster was in the White House."

"Good luck doing that with President Dalton and CIA director Norris. They won't even talk to you."

"No, but Betty will. And at least she's on the inside."

Craig picked up the phone and dialed. Elizabeth heard him say, "Betty, I know you need a vacation. Spring is a wonderful time in Paris. How about coming over for a few days? You can stay with me and Elizabeth."

He was smart to make it sound like a social invitation, Elizabeth thought. Someone's probably monitoring her calls because they know she's Craig's friend.

Elizabeth watched Craig give a thumbs-up. Then he called out, "Elizabeth, we're having a visitor. Betty will be here in the morning."

Craig was working himself back into the CIA, Elizabeth realized. Norris's days were numbered.

Moscow and Beijing

In Moscow, Dimitri Orlov was also sitting in front of a widescreen television watching Wang Shi announce the selection of General Zhou as president of China.

Once he heard those words, Orlov pumped his fist in the air. "Yes," he cried out. "Our time has come."

To celebrate, he downed half a tumbler of vodka, picked up his cell phone, and dialed Androshka's cell."

"Where are you?" he asked.

"In Beijing with General Zhou."

Orlov was pleasantly surprised. He was afraid General Zhou would ditch Androshka when his exile ended.

"Congratulations. I heard the news on television."

"It's a great day for General Zhou. For me. For all of us."

"I'm ready to implement the plan we discussed in the South of France. Have you told General Zhou about me?"

After a long hesitation, Androshka replied, "Not yet."

"What have you been waiting for?" Then he understood. "You were afraid he'd toss you aside if he thought you wanted something from him."

"I don't like being talked to that way," she said raising her voice. "I'm now the first lady of China."

He wanted to laugh and blurt out, "You mean the first whore of China," but he didn't dare. Androshka had pride and she could get stubborn. So he calmly said, "I'm correct. Aren't I?"

"Yes," she said weakly.

"But you have it all wrong." He was speaking slowly as if he were talking to a schoolgirl. "Being the link to Kuznov and Russia will enhance your value to General Zhou. You can tell him that I am close with President Kuznov and that I have spoken with him about General Zhou. You can also tell him that I want to come to China to meet with him as the official representative of President Kuznov."

"Is all that true?" she asked. "Have you really spoken with Kuznov? And will you be coming as his official representative?"

Orlov recognized the skepticism in her voice.

"Absolutely. We had a conversation on this subject at his home on the lake outside of Moscow. I intend to meet with him in the Kremlin this afternoon now that I've heard about General Zhou's selection. I'm unhappy that you doubt the accuracy of what I told you."

"Sorry, Dimitri. I will talk to General Zhou. I forget, he's now President Zhou. I'll call you with his reaction."

"What I really want is for you to schedule a meeting for me with President Zhou."

"I'll do my best. I promise."

*　　　*　　　*

After an intensive day of meetings with aides and decisions about transition issues as well as personnel for his new administration, President Zhou traveled to his brother's mansion for a quiet celebratory dinner. Just the two of them.

They began with Krug 1990 champagne and Russian caviar in the marble-floored den.

"To your success," Zhou Yun said, raising his glass.

"No. To our success," President Zhou replied. "I could never have done it without you."

"We are a good team. Father would have been proud of us."

Half an hour later, they sat down at the heavily polished wooden dining room table. Waiters brought in platters with shark fin soup, steamed abalone and ginger, spicy Szechuan eggplant with tangerine beef, and seven-spice roast duck. Then they poured 1982 Lafite Rothschild. Afterwards, they departed, leaving the two brothers alone.

President Zhou raised his glass. "To Chinese world domination."

"How do you intend to achieve that?"

"With nothing else to do in Bali, I thought about it a great deal. I have a three stage plan. First, strengthen and upgrade our military. The United States still has a qualitative edge with their Air Force and Navy, but the fools in Washington have reduced their military budget. We should be able to close that gap quickly. Five years. No more. Maybe less."

"And after that?"

"Second stage, we move to achieve military dominance in Asia. We provoke a war with Japan over islands or oil rights under the sea. Our annihilation of the Japanese armed forces will persuade all of the other nations of Asia to accept Chinese domination. They will do our bidding economically and politically. If they refuse, we'll change their governments."

"What makes you think the United States will let you prevail over Japan. Washington has defense commitments to Tokyo."

President Zhou paused to eat some of the delicious food. His brother employed one of the best chefs in all of China. He enjoyed making his brother wait for the answer to this critical question.

Finally, he said, "After Iraq and Afghanistan, the American people are sick of foreign wars. They'll never honor their commitment to Japan.

Zhou Yun looked worried. "And if they do?"

"We'll be ready for them. In this part of the Pacific, we'll have a huge advantage, being so close to home."

"What's your third stage?"

"We challenge the Americans everywhere in the world for natural resources. We strong-arm third world countries to do business exclusively with China. We'll dominate the oil and copper markets as well as other commodities. That will deal a fatal blow to the American economy."

"All of that may be good years from now, but right now we have an immediate economic problem with the Americans."

"What's that?"

"For the last several months, President Dalton has been threatening trade sanctions, which would cripple our economy, unless we do something about human rights."

President Zhou snarled. "That again. Why don't they mind their own business and worry about their problems at home, which are many?"

"I don't know. But Dalton won't let go of it."

"We've heard the same talk from every American president for as long as I can remember."

"True. But this time Dalton sounds serious. He's demanding tangible steps. If not, he'll impose trade sanctions."

"Doesn't he understand we could dump our U.S. government bonds? And not buy new ones? That we make and supply the products which keep his country running?"

"He's convinced that any possible economic action on our part would be too detrimental to China."

"What do you think?"

"Dalton does have a point. I'll have a couple of my economic experts evaluate the issue."

His brother sipped the wine. Zhou Yun's wrinkled forehead told President Zhou his brother was concerned about something. "What's bothering you?"

"I'm still troubled by your attack on Japan in the second stage. The Americans could respond with a missile attack against Beijing and Shanghai from their ships in the Pacific. Unfortunately, we don't yet have the technology to launch a long-range missile attack against the United States. If we had it, we would be in a standoff with Washington. They wouldn't dare attack us even if we attacked Japan."

"Well, can't we develop that long-range missile capability?"

"One of my companies has a contract with the Ministry of Defense to develop that technology. We're working closely with Jiang Hua, the Director of the Technical Branch of the Ministry."

"When will you have it?"

"Unfortunately, we're still years away."

"Push the engineers harder?"

"Believe me, I am."

"Do the Americans have the technology for missiles that can reach China from the United States?"

"They're very close. We believe they've solved all the technical problems. They have designed an extremely precise system. It's just a question of constructing and implementing it."

"Again, the Americans are ahead of us," President Zhou said gruffly.

An hour later, dinner was over. President Zhou walked toward the front door where his aide Captain Cheng was waiting patiently.

"Have you moved into the Presidential House?" his brother asked.

"Yes. With Androshka."

"And your old house?"

"My old wife can stay there." President Zhou laughed. "An old house for an old wife."

*   *   *

Though it was past midnight when Zhou arrived at the Presidential House, as he expected, Androshka was waiting for him. She followed him up the stairs to the sitting room, off the master bedroom, poured two glasses of Armagnac, and handed him one. "To our new life," she said, raising her glass.

Then she pulled one of his Cuban cigars from the humidor, snipped off the end, lit it, and handed it to him.

He puffed deeply. "I remember the first time you did that with a cigar . . . in Paris. No woman ever had. I liked it then. I like it now."

"My aim is to please you."

"I'm glad you came to Beijing with me."

"Thank you for bringing me. I think I can be valuable to you."

"You're always valuable in bed." He gave a short laugh.

She was blushing. "There is something else. I received a call from my brother, Dimitri, in Moscow this evening."

He thought she seemed nervous. "I didn't know you had a brother."

"He was working for another oligarch. A rival of Mikail Ivanoff, the man whose murder you arranged in Morocco. Before that, Dimitri was a high ranking KGB official. Very close with Boris Kuznov, who was then with the KGB."

She raised her hand and pressed the first two fingers together.

"What did your brother say?"

"He wants to come to Beijing and meet with you as an official representative of President Kuznov."

President Zhou recalled his conversation with Zhou Yun that evening. He was intrigued by what she was telling him. An alliance with Moscow could greatly strengthen his hand in dealing with the United States. Since Russia had one foot in Europe, a bellicose regime in Moscow, working with Beijing would force the United States to divert part of its military forces and attention from Asia to Europe in defense of its allies there whose own military resources were meager at best. With reduced forces in Asia, this would minimize the likelihood that the United States would defend Japan in the event of a Chinese attack.

All of that was true, but President Zhou couldn't seem too eager to get into bed with the Russians. He had learned long ago, in dealing with Moscow, you have to make them believe they need you more than you need them.

"Call Dimitri back," Zhou said. "Tell him to come to Beijing in one month. I'll see him then."

He could tell she was pleased.

"So I am valuable to you in other ways," she said.

He stood up and began undressing. "Now show me how valuable you really are."

In bed, she massaged his back using lotion. "Your muscles are so tight. Lots of tension."

He wasn't surprised. He'd had a tough day. Being president was stressful. So much he wanted to do, and quickly. He was concerned about Dalton and Japan. While she stroked the backs of his legs, he was thinking about long-range missile and economic sanctions.

She reached in between his legs and played with his balls, grabbing his cock from the back. That always got him hard, but tonight nothing was happening.

"Time to flip over," she said.

After he did, she went to work on him with her mouth. But he remained limp. He wanted sex with her in the worst way. She was trying everything. All of her tricks with her tongue. But nothing happened.

Finally, she said, "I'll bet you had a lot wine at dinner. That often causes this problem."

She sounded understanding and sympathetic. He appreciated that even though it had never happened to him before. Maybe it was the tension of the Presidency. He had read that Mao had this problem as well.

She put her head on the pillow next to his. "I'll hold you in my arms. We'll fall asleep that way."

This shouldn't happen. He was a strong virile man.

He hoped it was a one-time thing. That it would never happen again. And if it did, what good was Androshka to him? And what was the point of keeping her?

Paris and Moscow

Craig and Elizabeth were in Craig's office, waiting for Betty to arrive. He glanced out of the window.

A cab pulled up and Betty got out. She wheeled a suitcase toward the building and stopped by a bench. As he expected, she sat down and lit up a cigarette.

"You see her?" Elizabeth asked.

"She'll be here in two cigarettes," he said with a smile.

When Betty walked in fifteen minutes later, after freshening up in the lavatory, she kissed both of them on each cheek.

"Isn't that what I'm supposed to do over here?"

"Not necessary," Craig said. "We're still Americans."

"Can you get me a cup of good, strong coffee?"

Craig hit the buzzer. Waiting for the coffee, Betty said, "I'm too old for overnight flights. I didn't do it for you, Craig. I did it for Elizabeth."

Craig smiled, "You did it because you know why we wanted to see you."

"General Zhou—sorry, President Zhou."

"For sure."

"You know what this reminds me of?" Betty said.

"I can't imagine."

"When your daughter Francesca was a little girl, I took her to the movies. Sometimes in those days they showed cartoons at children's matinees."

"I remember," Craig said.

"I don't," Elizabeth said.

"I didn't expect you to. Craig's a lot older than you are."

"Ouch. That stung," he said.

They all laughed.

"Well, anyhow," Betty continued, "Francesca's favorite cartoon was one in which a cat was trying to capture a mouse, but the mouse always managed to escape."

"Zhou's only gotten away from me twice," Craig protested. "Three will be the charm."

"I hope so."

Coffee arrived. Three double espressos. Betty took a gulp, then put the cup down. "Let's talk," Betty said.

"You know," Craig responded, "the world has become a much more dangerous place with Zhou as president of China. And you can be sure he'll be gunning for the United States."

"You're preaching to the choir."

"The U.S. will have to increase its vigilance vis-à-vis China. And President Dalton should stop baiting Beijing with threats to impose trade sanctions. They would be counterproductive. Even if Congress went along."

"You want to come to Washington and deliver your message to Dalton and Norris?"

"They'd never see me."

"Fact is," she said sadly, "neither of them has the competency to deal with challenges like this."

"That's what I figured. But I want to know if you can make an end run around Norris. Deal with people on the China desk in Langley. At DIA and NIA. Then shoot me any information you obtain about Chinese plans or troop movements. I could try to get England,

France, and Germany to lean on Dalton for action. Or even take action themselves. What do you think?"

She pondered his request for a minute.

"Let's do it," she said. "I'll have stuff e-mailed to you from a location outside of the Agency. Less chance of detection."

"What about the risk to you?" Elizabeth said. "The information could be classified."

Betty shrugged. "The most they'll do is fire me. They'll never be able to cut off my pension. I'll take my chances. Nothing is more important now than blocking whatever scheme Zhou next hatches."

*   *   *

With a swagger, Orlov entered the Kremlin. He walked into the office of the secretary to the Secretary, who immediately passed him through to the Secretary to President Kuznov. There, he waited only thirty seconds before the Secretary led him into the inner sanctum of Kuznov's huge office.

The Russian president was alone. He was studying a document on his red leather topped antique desk and frowning.

"I have good news," Orlov said.

"I need good news. Everywhere in this great country, the Muslims are making trouble. What's wrong with those people?"

Orlov took a seat in front of the desk. "We should have killed all of them in Chechnya."

"I agree. And elsewhere. I assume you came to see me about your sister's friend, Zhou, the new president of China."

"Precisely. She called a couple of hours ago to say that General Zhou will meet with me in one month in Beijing."

Kuznov looked irritated. "Why not now? Why in a month? Gamesmanship?"

"She said he wants to get his government solidified. She told him I'll be coming as your official representative. She's confident he'll agree to work with us."

Kuznov perked up. "If that's really true, it would be a good development. An alliance with China would help us do battle with the United States and also assist a Russian resurgence."

"I'll do my best to develop that alliance."

Kuznov got up and walked over to the window. He was staring out. Orlov saw wet snowflakes falling. Doesn't winter ever end in Moscow? Orlov could tell Kuznov was deep in thought. He didn't interrupt the president.

Finally, Kuznov wheeled around and said, "Since you last spoke to me, I had our intelligence people do some research on Zhou. He's smart and cunning. He'll realize that an alliance with China is important for me. He may impose some conditions for a meeting. Do you know what I mean?"

Orlov nodded.

"Listen carefully to what Zhou says to you," Kuznov continued. "Tell him that you have to report back to me. Do you understand?"

"Yes sir. I do."

In truth, Orlov didn't understand what Kuznov was talking about. Though Orlov was clever, he feared that he might be in over his head. Being used by two savvy statesmen with their own agendas, he didn't want to get hurt himself. And he didn't want to hurt Androshka.

"Are you sure you want to do this?" Kuznov asked, as if reading Orlov's mind.

"For sure. It was my idea."

"Zhou plays rough. This could be a zero-sum game. There could be winners and losers. We can't afford to be the losers."

"I understand about Zhou."

What Orlov didn't add was: I also understand about you. I'll have to protect myself. You'll call the shots, but if Zhou gets the best of us, you'll throw me to the wolves and walk away as if you played no role. I won't let that happen.

PART TWO

One Month Later

Beijing

Orlov's plane arrived in Beijing at noon. In the car on the way to the St. Regis, Orlov was astounded by the incredible number of skyscrapers and builders' cranes everywhere. Having never been to China before, he didn't know what to expect. Certainly not the vast metropolis that was modern Beijing.

But economic progress had a price. A cloud of brown smoke hung over part of the city and the traffic was insane. This was something he was used to in Moscow, which is why he opted for his Harley.

Looking out of the cab window, Orlov was struck by the miles and miles of roses that filled the median strip. His Russian mind couldn't grasp why anyone would put beautiful flowers on something as ugly as a highway. The Chinese were clearly different.

In the hotel, he was treated as a visiting dignitary. He smiled, thinking how powerful Adroshka had become. Bellmen and clerks were practically doing somersaults on the white marble floor to serve him.

After viewing his passport, an assistant manager led Orlov to a gigantic suite on the penthouse floor with three bedrooms and baths and a dining room. A sign on the front door identified it as "The Presidential Suite."

Once Orlov's bags were delivered and the assistant manager left, he called Androshka on her cell.

"I've arrived," he told her.

"I hope they treated you well."

"Like royalty."

"Good. Your meeting with President Zhou is at ten tomorrow morning. Just the two of you. No need for an interpreter. You both speak French."

He had thought she might be at the meeting. It could be a sore subject for her. He didn't raise it.

She continued, "You and I should have dinner this evening. I'll arrange to have the it brought to your suite at nine. I'll be there at eight thirty."

Again, he was surprised. He expected they'd be dining at one of those good Beijing restaurants he'd read about or even at the Presidential House. She must want them to have privacy to talk. Before she arrived, he would check the suite for bugs.

Orlov spent the afternoon walking around Beijing, marveling at the shops, at the megamalls with their myriad stores for luxury goods of all types, and at the buildings everywhere. Beijing was such a lively, vibrant city. Flowers and trees were in bloom. What a contrast to dull, gloomy Moscow. He admired the Chinese for advancing so far so quickly, leaving Russia behind. He was hopeful that an alliance with China could lead to renewed Russian development.

Promptly at eight thirty, Androshka arrived accompanied by two waiters, who wheeled in a cart with three kinds of vodka, two bottles of champagne, and Russian caviar.

When they each had drinks, vodka for Orlov, vintage Krug for Androshka, she dismissed the waiters with a wave of her hand.

"We can talk freely," Orlov said. "I've checked the suite for listening devices. Nothing here."

"That's one of the advantages of having a former KGB agent for a brother."

"You've done well for yourself," Orlov said. "I can see why you like it here."

A mask of gloom descended over her face. "But I don't. I can't believe I wanted to live in China. How stupid of me. I'm miserable."

He choked on his drink. When he recovered, he said, "Are you crazy? Look at all you have."

"You don't understand. He has a wife and four children."

"They live in the Presidential House with you?"

"No. In his old house. On an army base. He never sees them."

"Then what's the problem?"

"Everybody here hates me because of his wife and children and because I'm not Chinese. I know they call me his 'Russian whore.' Behind his back of course. If they ever said anything against me to his face, he'd have them executed."

She paused to drain the glass of champagne, then refilled it. She looked sad. He thought she might cry.

"And that's not all," she continued. "I don't speak a word of Chinese. The language is impossible to learn. He's away working every day and most evenings. I'm not included in social functions. So I have nothing to do all day and most nights. I can't watch television. English and French shows are blocked. Even my servants hate me," she said bitterly.

"I'm astounded."

"I'm planning to leave President Zhou and Beijing. To return to Moscow to live."

"What? You can't be serious."

"But I am. I was just waiting until you had this meeting."

Orlov was on the verge of panic. He viewed tomorrow's meeting as the beginning of a process. Perhaps lengthy, leading to a close alliance between Russia and China. Androshka's continued involvement with President Zhou was essential to expedite that process. Smoothing the way as rough edges developed.

Even worse, if she were to leave Zhou, the Chinese president, no doubt a proud man, in anger, might cut off his Russian relationship while in its embryonic stage.

He had to talk Androshka out of leaving. But he had to choose his words carefully. He knew very well from childhood how stubborn she could be. Particularly if someone was telling her to do something she didn't want to do. He vividly recalled the shouting matches she had had with their mother as a young girl.

In a soft voice, Orlov said, "It would be very unfortunate for me personally and for the Russian nation if you were to leave."

He held his breath waiting for her response.

Instead of dismissing him out of hand, she said, "Tell me why."

For the next hour, while eating a wonderful banquet including hot and sour soup, shellfish in a clay pot, West Lake fish in vinegar, and braised Shanghai egg noodles with roast pork accompanied by a 2000 Lafite Rothschild, he told her what his objective was: the resurgence of Russia as a world power. He told her how critical she was, as a direct link to Zhou, to that process.

"If we accomplish this," he said, "we'll be famous. You and I. Revered throughout Russia. And I'll have power. Kuznov will give me what I want. I'll demand to be head of a new revitalized KGB. I'll make sure you share in my power. You'll be a Russian heroine," he added, playing to her vanity.

"That's ridiculous. You're flattering me to get your way."

"I'm not. Have I ever lied to you?"

"No, but . . ."

"I'll tell President Kuznov about your important role. He'll give you a medal. History books will mention you as the linchpin for the alliance."

"Really?"

He could tell she was pleased at the possibility. She was weakening. She looked at him wide-eyed. "For how long do I have to do this?"

"Several months. That's all."

She was shaking her head. "Forget it."

Oh oh, I blew that one, Orlov thought. Better try again. "I really meant one month at most. After that, you can move back to Moscow."

She wrinkled up her forehead. "I can do that," she said reluctantly. He exhaled with relief.

*   *   *

Androshka had left an hour ago, and Orlov lay in his plush, king-sized bed tossing and turning, unable to sleep. In convincing Androshka not to leave Beijing, Orlov had so inflated the importance of his mission that he was now tremendously excited. He now saw himself as an historical figure, not merely a KGB operative and an oligarch's goon.

In the last month, Orlov had read several history books that discussed the bizarre and tortuous relationship between China and Russia since the Bolshevik revolution. Among the many incidents, two were embedded firmly in his mind.

In 1934, during Mao's so called Long March, in which Mao was carried much of the way, Chiang Kai-shek could easily have killed Mao and wiped out his followers. But one factor prevented Chiang from doing that: Stalin was holding Chiang's son, his only child, hostage in Moscow. Stalin made it clear to Chiang: you kill Mao; I'll kill your son. In that sense, Stalin, ironically, was the midwife to the new China Mao created.

Then in the late 1950s, Russia's grain crop was a disaster. Mao sold huge quantities of grain to Russia in return for the technology to build nuclear weapons. Russia not only supplied the blueprints to China, but sent thousands of nuclear engineers to help in the development and construction. An ideal scenario, but for one fact: China didn't have any excess grain. Shipping it to Russia meant millions of Chinese would starve. But in Mao's view, a small price to pay for China, thanks to Russia, becoming a nuclear power.

Years from now, Orlov was confident historians would describe how Dimitri Orlov forged an alliance between Russia and China and changed the world.

*   *   *

With considerable ambivalence, President Zhou waited in his office for Orlov to arrive. Except for Androshka, General Zhou had never met a Russian he liked. The intensity of his animosity was so great that when he realized the classy and sensual looking prostitute who arrived in his Paris hotel room calling herself Bridgette was a Russian, he nearly tossed her out before she even took off a stitch of clothing.

But not quite. He was so sexually aroused that his brain was over-ruled. Something that had never happened before.

Still, he agreed to see Orlov, not as a favor to Androshka, but because Orlov could be useful to President Zhou if he truly was a representative of President Kuznov and if the Russians were anxious to form an alliance with China. How useful, he would see shortly.

Precisely at ten, an aide led Orlov into President Zhou's office and quickly departed.

General Zhou pointed to a chair in front of his desk. He didn't bother with pleasantries. No offer of coffee or tea. He decided on an all-business approach. Show Orlov he was a busy man. He was in charge. And he wasn't particularly anxious for a Russian alliance.

"You wanted to see me," Zhou said gruffly.

Orlov didn't seem flustered. He replied, "I'm an official representative of President Kuznov. He sent me to rekindle a famous old alliance. We have a common enemy: the United States. We both have powerful armies and we have dreams of expanding our influence. We should work together."

That was a fine speech, Zhou thought, but it could have been written by someone else in Moscow. And Orlov memorized it. He decided to test the former KGB operative. "Dreams, you say. I'm not a dreamer. I create realities on the ground."

"Perhaps an unfortunate choice of words. From what Androshka told me, I understand that you are both bold and pragmatic."

"A good answer. You say we should work together."

"That's correct, President Zhou."

"But for what purpose?"

"Our mutual objective should be for China to destroy the Japanese and American navies in the Pacific, cutting off supplies of oil and materials to the United States and Japan. At the same time, Russian tanks should be rolling into Eastern Europe, once again reestablishing our empire. In the Libyan war, the Western European countries showed how pathetic their militaries are. Together, we will deal a powerful blow to the United States and their Western European puppets."

Zhou liked what he was hearing. His instinct had been that he could use Orlov. Everything he had heard so far confirmed that.

"You're certainly not modest in your objectives," Zhou said.

"Those who are daring make history. They don't simply read about it."

"And you see yourself as one of them."

"Yes," he said without flinching.

The man's ego was gigantic. That offered enormous opportunities for Zhou.

"And how do you propose to achieve your objective?"

"As the initial step to advance the Chinese-Russian alliance, I believe that you and President Kuznov should meet. The two of you and interpreters. I will be there, of course. President Kuznov has asked me to invite you to Moscow for that meeting."

"When?"

"As soon as possible."

Pretending to be considering the invitation, General Zhou left Orlov's words hanging. In fact, he knew exactly how to respond. After a full minute, he said, "I'm not prepared to move up on something this significant so early in my Presidency."

He watched a mask of disappointment appear on Orlov's face. Then he added, "I need a little time to solidify my armed forces and my power at home. Then I'll be ready to meet with Kuznov."

Orlov was smiling. He believes he has achieved his goal, Zhou thought. He'll be getting his meeting. Now's the time to exploit his ambition and hubris. To gain something I want. Something I need.

"But," Zhou said looking into Orlov's dark blue eyes that were staring at him. "Before such an important meeting, I'd like you to take some action against the United States which will show your sincerity and President Kuznov's commitment to the proposed alliance. Without that, I can't risk wasting my time and sending the wrong signal to other world leaders by going to Moscow."

"Certainly. What would you like me to do?"

Zhou recalled that his brother had told him in their celebratory dinner after he assumed the Presidency that U.S. President Dalton was a problem for China with his threats to impose trade sanctions unless China changed its policy on human rights. Calmly, Zhou said to Orlov, "Assassinate President Dalton."

He watched Orlov's head snap back.

Zhou continued. "And I don't want my government to be involved in any way."

Orlov was hesitating. Zhou decided to press him. "Dalton has been threatening trade sanctions against China. I can't tolerate that. And Dalton's made it clear that he has no love for Russia. His assassination will benefit both of our countries."

"I know that, but . . ."

"You told me a few minutes ago that those who are daring make history. I'm providing you with the opportunity."

Orlov seemed to be shell-shocked by Zhou's request.

Zhou pressed Orlov. "I heard from a former KGB official that your agency periodically planned the assassination of American presidents."

"Yes, that's true."

"Then, with your KGB training, you should have no trouble doing it."

"I'll have to speak with President Kuznov before I can commit."

"Of course. Talk to him and let me know."

Once Orlov left the room, Zhou smiled. Orlov's coming was truly good fortune. Orlov was someone Zhou could manipulated for his own benefit, with no risk. And as long as Androshka was in his bed, Zhou had a personal hold over Orlov.

Moscow

"He asked you to do what?" Kuznov said with incredulity to Orlov. They were alone in Kuznov's office.

"Assassinate President Dalton."

"That's what I thought you said."

"I told him I'd have to talk to you about it."

"And you want to do this?"

"Yes, because it will lead to an alliance between you and Zhou. Besides, Dalton hasn't exactly been a friend of Russia. You made two attempts at joint ventures and he rebuffed you both times. Even publicly."

Kuznov walked over to the sideboard and poured a generous portion of vodka into a glass. Orlov followed his example.

"It's only eleven in the morning," Kuznov said. "I can see how Yeltsin became an alcoholic. The pressure of the office."

"I'm sorry if I've added to those pressures. But an alliance with China could be the basis for a Russian resurgence. And it was clear to me that Zhou hates Dalton and believes he might do serious damage to the Chinese economy. If we can pull this off, Zhou will be in our debt."

"What do you mean, *we*? You should have said that if *you* pull this off. I won't be involved in any way. You better understand that."

"I do. Then you approve?"

Orlov was anxious to obtain Kuznov's blessing and to get on with it.

"I don't know."

"Can I ask what's worrying you?" Orlov sounded deferential. He and Kuznov weren't equals.

"Does Zhou really want an alliance with Russia, or does he just want you to do his dirty work? You were with him. You heard him. What do you think?"

Kuznov was asking a good question. Orlov had been worried about the same issue. Yet, he had brushed that concern aside, wanting to believe Zhou was sincere.

"I honestly don't know," Orlov said.

"Good. I'm glad to hear you're not taken in by your sister's lover."

"Not at all."

"Getting rid of Dalton would be a plus for Russia. How do you intend to kill him?"

Orlov hesitated, then said, "I'm still thinking about it. I don't have a plan finalized yet, but I will."

"Meaning you don't have the faintest idea. Right?"

Orlov couldn't lie to Kuznov. "That's right. But in my KGB days, 'Yes I can' was my creed. I'm confident that I'll find a way."

"I'll give you a suggestion."

Orlov was ecstatic. He needed help desperately. "Sure."

"President Dalton likes to go to Camp David, the presidential retreat, most weekends. When I visited Washington last year, we had a Friday morning meeting at the White House. Then in the afternoon, we took the helicopter to Camp David."

Kuznov paused to sip his drink.

"And?" Orlov asked anxiously.

"In that chopper, I felt incredibly vulnerable. We were flying over woods and sparsely populated areas. Someone with a rocket on the ground could have easily hit us. Do you understand what I'm saying?"

"Absolutely, President Kuznov."

"But you can't be on the ground firing the rocket. And it can't be anyone else who's a Russian."

"That's not a problem," Orlov said, now sounding excited. "I have intelligence contacts around the world. So many people hate the United States. I'll be able to find someone."

"Good. I'll put a plane and pilot at your disposal, but remember one thing," Kuznov raised his hand and pointed a finger at Orlov. "Your shooter can't survive the assassination. He has to die as well. Dead men don't talk."

"For sure. We have the perfect model. The assassination of President Kennedy."

"Exactly. The precisely conceived operation. Even after fifty years, Americans can't be sure who was responsible for the death of their president. And one other thing."

"What's that?"

"Dalton's assassination can't be attributed to Russia."

Orlov recalled Zhou telling him that the Chinese government couldn't be involved in any way. Both Zhou and Kuznov were setting him up. And if the mission went to hell, they'd want him to swing alone. But he wouldn't let that happen.

Paris and Berlin

Craig was in his office at ten in the morning when his cell phone rang. He checked caller ID. It was Betty, at five am Washington time.

"I'm calling from home," she said. "I'll talk fast. Less chance of our conversation being picked up."

"What do you have?"

"I just spoke to Wayne Nelson, our station chief in Beijing. He succeeded your friend Peter Emery."

"Don't remind me about that bastard."

"Well anyhow, Wayne and I go way back. I asked him to call and tell me about anything unusual President Zhou did."

Craig was pressing the phone tight against his ear as if that could give him the information faster. "And?"

"He told me that two days ago Zhou had a meeting one-on-one with a Russian, Dimitri Orlov."

"How'd Nelson learn about it?"

"That I better not put over the airwaves. Even on an encrypted phone. Don't worry. It's reliable information."

Craig was tearing his memory, trying for any recollection of Dimitri Orlov. He came up empty. "Who the hell is Dimitri Orlov?"

"I ran him through our database. Nothing."

"Thanks for letting me know. This could be valuable."

"That's what I figured. Definitely worth chancing the call, but keep the guestroom free in your apartment. If Norris finds out I'm funneling information to you, I'll need a place to lay low."

"It's yours any time. We'll even let you smoke on the patio."

Craig hung up the phone, closed his eyes, and leaned back in his chair, deep in thought. As he told Betty, this could be valuable information. One month into his Presidency, Zhou had to be a busy man, his time limited. Yet, he had a meeting with an unknown Russian.

Dimitri Orlov had to be an emissary of President Kuznov. That was the only explanation.

Craig had to find out who Dimitri Orlov was.

Kuznov had been powerful in the KGB. Chances were he'd have selected one of his former KGB cronies to send off to Beijing on a mission. By checking KGB files in Moscow, it was likely Craig would locate Dimitri Orlov. Not an option.

Second choice was Germany. Most KGB operatives spent some time in East Germany where the Stasi, the secret police, kept meticulous records. If Dimitri Orlov had been in East Germany, Stasi would have recorded that fact and information about him. Those Stasi files ended up in the German Intelligence Agency files in Berlin after unification.

Craig called Kurt Dieter, the Director of German Intelligence, to arrange a late afternoon meeting. Then he booked a flight to Berlin.

*   *   *

Kurt Dieter was a short man with a small, bald head and one of the most brilliant minds of anyone Craig had ever met. And Dieter was one of the relatively few sixty year olds who had a total mastery of computers and other technology. Unlike Craig, who relied on technological assistants like Marie known as techies, Dieter did his own work.

Dieter's office was on the top floor of a starkly modern, twelve-story glass and steel structure constructed a year ago.

Craig was only half way through the explanation of what he wanted when Dieter interrupted. "Okay. I've got it."

Dieter turned ninety degrees in his chair to his computer and began pushing buttons.

"I thought we'd be down in a dusty file room searching through crumbling documents," Craig said.

Dieter gave a deep belly laugh. "You underestimate our technological capability. All the files have been scanned and entered into our computer data base. Even those of the Stasi. We're light years ahead of others in the EU, and I won't even talk about Washington."

After two minutes, Dieter looked up from the computer. "Dimitri Orlov was in East Germany for about six months when Kuznov was there. In fact, he did an operation for Kuznov, something about disinformation with the Americans."

Dieter hit a couple more buttons and the printer spit out four pages. Dieter handed them to Craig. A picture and a three page bio.

"Here's your man."

Craig began reading Orlov's bio. He stopped on the second paragraph entitled "family background." The words "holy shit" came out of Craig's mouth.

"Is that a Russian or a French intelligence term?" Dieter asked, while laughing.

But Craig wasn't paying attention to Dieter. He had just learned that Orlov had a sister Androshka. He stopped reading and turned to the photo. The longer he studied Orlov's picture, the more convinced he became that Orlov and President Zhou's Androshka bore a striking physical resemblance.

Craig was certain he'd hit pay dirt. Orlov had to be the emissary of his old KGB boss, Kuznov. He was perfect for the role because of Androshka.

But what were they discussing in their Beijing meeting? President Zhou and Orlov?

Knowing Zhou and his hatred for the United States, Craig would have bet anything that Zhou wanted to use Orlov in some action against Washington. He realized this was a leap based on the little he knew, but Craig's instincts rarely let him down in matters like this.

"Can I keep these?" Craig asked Dieter while clutching the photo and bio.

"Of course. I can print additional copies of you'd like."

"No, these are enough. Thanks for your help. I really appreciate it."

"How about dinner this evening?"

"I'd like to, but I have to be back in Paris."

Dieter was shaking his head. "Unfortunately, you're still more American than European. I give Paris another year to corrupt you."

*　　　*　　　*

Craig took an evening flight back to Paris and went right to his office. There he called Norris, the CIA Director, on a secure line.

Before he had a chance to tell Norris what he wanted, the CIA Director tore into him. "I'm really pissed at you for going over my head to President Dalton when you wanted U.S. Air Force help to save the Pope and the Vatican."

Craig had no intention of taking this crap from Norris. "To be honest, if I'd have gone to you, the Pope would be dead and there'd be a hole in the side of St. Peter's Basilica large enough to drive a train through."

"That's ridiculous. We always cooperate with the EU, and I always work with you. I just need evidence to support what you want to do."

"Okay, I'll give you a chance to prove that."

"What happened now?"

Craig explained everything he had learned about Orlov's visit to Beijing and that Orlov was the brother of Zhou's mistress, Androshka. "I'll send you Dimitri Orlov's photo and bio. I want you to distribute them to all INS agents at U.S. international airports and border points. If he tries to enter the country, arrest him for questioning and call me. I'll come over."

"What am I arresting him for?" Norris sounded skeptical

"I believe he's planning some type of attack against the U.S. If he enters the country, then the attack will almost certainly be within the U.S."

"And exactly what evidence do you have to back this up?"

"I've told you everything I know. My knowledge of President Zhou is a critical component. If you have Orlov in custody, we'll be able to learn more."

"In other words, you don't have a damn thing."

"C'mon, you know intelligence work isn't a precise science. With our experience and instincts, we save lives."

"And you're asking me to trample on this man's rights if he comes to the U.S." Norris sounded hostile.

"Now you're concerned about the rights of a former KGB agent." Craig was raising his voice. "And a Russian mobster. That's absurd."

"Why does every conversation with you turn into a shouting match?"

Craig was past the boiling point. "Because you're an asshole."

"Go fuck yourself."

"Do you want Orlov's photo and the bio, or not?"

"You can stick them up your ass."

Norris slammed down the phone.

Craig would have to find a way around the CIA Director.

Islamabad and Moscow

Orlov decided to call Colonel Khan before flying to Islamabad. Now that the Colonel had been promoted to Director of ISI, the Pakistan military intelligence agency, Orlov wasn't sure he'd be willing to talk to an old Russian crony. Orlov knew that lots of Pakistanis hated the Russians because of the way they cut and ran, tail between their legs, from Afghanistan, ceding the territory to the Americans.

After Orlov gave his name to the Colonel's assistant, he held his breath. A minute later, the Colonel was on the phone speaking English, which they had used in the old days. "Well, well, Dimitri Orlov, a name from my past," the Colonel said in an ebullient voice.

"Your present and future as well, I hope. Congratulations on your promotion."

"It's a thankless job."

"But somebody has to do it."

They both laughed.

"What are you doing now?" the Colonel asked.

"A little of this and a little of that. I'd like to come and talk to you."

Orlov guessed the Colonel wouldn't ask the subject over the phone—what prompted this call out of the blue. The Pakistanis were convinced that the Americans monitored calls in and out of the ISI.

Even if he had, Orlov wouldn't have provided any information on the phone.

"When?" the Colonel asked.

"Tomorrow afternoon."

"Call my assistant with an ETA. I'll have my car and driver meet you at the airport."

*　　　*　　　*

In the plane to Islamabad, Orlov thought about his prior dealings with Khan when the Pakistani was only a Captain in the ISI. The Russian army was bogged down in a quagmire in Afghanistan. It was a mind numbingly stupid war in a country referred to as the graveyard of empires because it had decimated powerful armies from the Greeks to the British, just as it was chewing up the Russian army.

It was never clear whether the Pakistanis were on the side of the Taliban trying to seize control of Afghanistan or the Russians. Orlov was convinced they were working with both sides, taking payoffs from whoever offered them with the objective of ending up with a weak Afghanistan that Pakistan could control.

Orlov's assignment was to obtain intelligence on the Taliban from Khan. Dollars and Johnny Walker Blue Label would grease the skids.

As the plane descended through the clouds into Islamabad, Orlov fully anticipated that Khan would be playing exactly the same game with the Americans and the Taliban. Only the uniforms of the foreign army had changed.

The one thing Orlov had never been able to determine was where in the world Khan stored all that cash. He'd learned never to underestimate Khan. The man was, in addition to being venal, incredibly savvy with an instinct for survival.

*　　　*　　　*

The dirty gray Toyota sedan with Orlov in the back was mired in heavy traffic on the way to the ISI headquarters. The car was a change. In the old days, the Director of ISI's car was a shiny new Jaguar. The Colonel must have decided it was too attractive a target for terrorists.

What hadn't changed was that Islamabad, the capital of Pakistan, was the same hellhole that Orlov remembered—dusty side streets, open food stands attracting a myriad of flies in the heat, and beggars accosting tourists. Mosques dominated the skyline. And everywhere swarms of people and more people.

Orlov was relieved to enter the cinderblock ISI headquarters. An armed guard in a military uniform met him at the door and rode up with him in the elevator to the top floor. The fourth.

In the reception area, the guard pointed to a cheap plastic chair. When Orlov sat in it, keeping his briefcase between his feet, the guard took a chair across the room facing Orlov.

A woman was sitting behind a desk. Orlov wondered what she was thinking about her visitors, but he had no way of knowing. Her face was covered in black, except for her eyes, hazel brown eyes, Orlov noticed when she stared at him, but then looked away.

As Orlov expected, he had to wait until the Colonel deigned to see him. Obviously a power play. Khan had to show he was in charge. Not too long today. Only half an hour.

When Orlov was summoned, he picked up his briefcase and headed toward the open door. The armed guard remained behind.

Orlov thought the fifty-eight-year-old Colonel had aged markedly since they had last been together. His neatly trimmed black mustache was sprinkled with gray as was the hair on his head. His face was etched with deep creases. The rakish smile Orlov remembered was gone. His black eyes were sunk deep into the sockets. He looked wary.

While the Colonel remained seated at his desk, the receptionist clad in black shut the door. Orlov was now alone with the Colonel, who pointed to a chair in front of his desk. Then the Colonel picked up a gadget resembling a remote. He pushed a button. Orlov heard the lock on the office door click shut.

"Well, talk," the Colonel said impatiently.

"First, let me congratulate you," Orlov said, "on your promotion."

"I have the Americans to thank for it."

"The Americans. How?"

"Heads rolled after they killed Osama Bin Laden. The General searched for someone who couldn't be tagged with complicity. I had the good fortune of being at our border with India at the time."

"Luck is a valuable ally."

"You want something from me. You Russians always do."

This won't be easy, Orlov thought. He reached into the briefcase at his feet, removed a bottle of Johnny Walker Blue Label, and put it on the desk.

"Beware of Russians bringing gifts," the Colonel said.

"Actually, it was Greeks."

The Colonel ignored the correction. He rose, gun holstered at his hip, walked over to the credenza, and extracted two glasses. He poured them each a good measure of scotch and locked up the bottle.

While Orlov sipped, he watched the Colonel savoring the scotch.

"It's becoming extremely difficult to get scotch into this country," the Colonel said. "The Fundamentalists are exerting more and more control."

"A shame. They'll make life intolerable."

The Colonel nodded. "Now tell me what you want."

Orlov reached into his bag again. This time with both hands. He removed a pile of euros. A million in total, placed them onto the desk, and slid them forward as a poker player might do with his chips at a casino.

The Colonel didn't reach for the money. He just stared at it. Then he looked up. Orlov had center stage.

"Once, when we spent a long evening together . . ." Orlov began, recalling a night in Kabul when he and the Colonel, sitting alone together, had consumed so much scotch that the Colonel finally passed out. Orlov had had to revive him and lead him back to his room. "You told me that your government had planted sleepers in the United States."

"I don't recall that."

Orlov was convinced the Colonel was lying. He ignored the response and continued. "I want the identity and location of one of those sleepers."

The Colonel raised his eyebrows. "I didn't think the Russians carried out terrorist attacks in the United States any longer. With the collapse of the Soviet Union, I thought Russia became a nation of pussies. Racing to get out of the way of the Americans."

Orlov felt the bile rising in his body. He kept his anger in check, refusing to succumb to the Colonel's taunts.

All business, he responded. "I want a name and an address."

"For what purpose?"

"You don't have to know."

"A sleeper is a valuable asset. I have to receive something in return. A quid pro quo."

Orlov pointed to the pile of euros. The Colonel scooped them up, carried them over to the credenza, and locked them up.

The Colonel smoothed down the ends of his mustache. "Now we'll talk about compensation."

"You greedy bastard."

"You Russians taught me how to negotiate. What's mine is mine. What's yours is negotiable. One of your generals once told me: negotiations are like cutting salami. You slice some off, take it for yourself, then return to the salami and start over. You keep doing this each time until you have the entire salami."

"I'm familiar with the concept. You have the cash. Now tell me what else you want."

"Engineering assistance. The Americans are terrified that our nuclear weapons will fall into the hands of people they can't control. As a result, our military is afraid the Americans will one day swoop in and seize our nuclear weapons just as they killed Osama Bin Laden."

"That occurred to me, too. The Americans might very well do that."

"But they won't succeed if you bring me a Russian engineer who can design a solution. One that will keep our nukes from the Americans. That lets us get at them to use against India. If you bring me that engineer, you'll get your sleeper in the United States. Do you understand?"

Two could play at this game, Orlov decided. "The engineer you want is a big thing. If I bring the engineer, you'll have to give me something besides the sleeper."

"Yeah, what?" the Colonel said warily.

"A U.S. made rocket-propelled grenade launcher with grenades. You must have lots of them in your weapons warehouses."

The Colonel smoothed the ends of his mustache. "Okay. You'll get it. After the engineer is here."

"Good. Then we have a deal."

The Colonel picked up the remote and pushed the button. The door lock snapped open, signaling that the meeting was over.

*   *   *

Orlov returned to Moscow and reported on his meeting with Khan to Kuznov.

At the end, the Russian president gave a deep sigh. "Your Pakistani friend is a thief."

"For sure. But he's risen to the top because he's succeeded at the way they do business."

"I'll call the Director of Military Engineering. We'll find somebody to go with you to Islamabad and to design the system the Colonel wants. You think he'll return alive from Pakistan?"

Orlov shrugged. "Depends how paranoid the Colonel is about leaks. At our last meeting, you told me 'Dead men don't talk.'"

Kuznov picked up the phone and made the call.

"When he was finished, he turned to Orlov. "I want you to succeed so I'll give you one other nugget of information."

"What's that?"

"How are you planning to learn President Dalton's schedule for flying to Camp David?"

Orlov shrugged. "I figured I'd work on that when I got to Washington."

"You expect the White House to publish it in the *Washington Post?*"

Orlov reddened. "No. But I'm confident I'll find a way."

"I'll make your life easier."

"Go ahead." Orlov was listening carefully.

"When I was a young KGB operative in England thirty-five years ago, I formed a relationship with an idealistic young American student at Oxford. Twenty years old. A child. She was studying history. She thought I was a student in England as well. Valerie Clurman was her name."

"You slept with her?"

"Of course, but that's immaterial. What counts is she had been influenced by the war in Vietnam and the American youth movement in the seventies. She hated her government. I told her I had ties to the

Russian government and that I would be returning to Moscow to take an important position. She offered to help me bring the corrupt U.S. government to its knees. You have to think about what I'm telling you in the context of a turbulent era in American life."

"I understand that. I'm a student of history as well. What did you tell her?"

"To finish Oxford. Then get a job in the U.S. Secret Service that guards the president. One day I would call her and ask for her help. But in the meantime, we would see each other from time to time in Europe when she took vacations."

"So your romance continued?"

"We saw each other two years later in Florence. And three years after that in Venice."

"Was she in love with you?"

Kuznov looked irritated. "Why are you so interested in personal details?"

Orlov decided to back off. He'd pressed a hot button. Perhaps Kuznov had been in love with Valerie. Or maybe she was just a great fuck.

Orlov shrugged. "Sometimes these details are important."

"Well, not here. I never saw her again after that second meeting in Venice. Meantime, I followed her career through American sources. She has risen to a high administrative position in the Secret Service. I checked their website yesterday. She is still employed there."

"What should I tell her to persuade her that I'm your representative?"

"Begin by saying, 'My name is Ivan.'"

"One other thing. Did you record your conversations recruiting her?"

"I wish I had. That was a mistake on my part."

Orlov thought: you were so hot for her that you forgot to do your job. Instead, he said, "Doesn't matter. I can work around it."

As Orlov started toward the door, Kuznov said, "Guard what I just told you with your life. I've never told anyone else about it. Even my bosses in the KGB."

Kuznov was definitely in love with Valerie, Orlov decided. He was anxious to meet this woman.

*   *   *

Four hours later, Orlov boarded a Russian Air Force plane with Captain Nicholas Malinkov, in his fifties, a six foot six beanpole resembling a basketball player, who was dressed in civilian clothes and carried two large bags. They were stuffed with blueprints.

On the plane ride, Orlov went over the assignment again with Nicholas. Patting his briefcase, the engineer said, "I know exactly what's required. An underground bunker carved deep into the rocks with redundancies for access. I already designed a system like that for construction in Volgograd when the Americans were paying us to gather and safeguard nuclear weapons from the former Soviet Republics. I promise you the Pakis will like this."

"Where'd you learn to call them the Pakis?"

"I spent a year at a London Engineering school in England. There they don't just call them the Pakis. They call them the 'fucking Pakis.' The British hate them."

Orlov was alarmed. "But you won't show contempt for them, or use terms like Pakis will you?"

"Of course not. I don't want to get us both killed. Besides, I was told my orders come from President Kuznov. And I should do a good job."

"Well, you better keep it under control."

"Don't worry. I will."

Orlov wasn't sure.

*   *   *

From the moment they entered the Colonel's office, Orlov's concern dissipated. Nicholas was deferential, almost obsequious to the Colonel, who seemed impressed with the qualifications of the Russian engineer and the work he had done in Volgograd. The Colonel turned Nicholas over to Pakistan's Director of Military Engineering.

Once they were alone, the Colonel reached for the phone. Orlov heard him give instructions to have the rocket-propelled grenade launcher with grenades delivered to Orlov's plane.

When he put down the phone, the Colonel said, "You'll be pleased with the weapon, still in the original crate. The Americans delivered it to us last month."

"And the information on the sleeper?"

The Colonel didn't respond. Orlov stared at his poker face, then at the clock on the wall with a black sweep second hand. If he doesn't give it to me in the next minute, Orlov thought, I'll climb over the desk, grab the letter opener and stab out his eyes one by one until he tells me. If he still doesn't, I'll kill him.

The Colonel cracked a tiny smile. He knows he's playing a dangerous game.

Ten seconds before Orlov's deadline, the Colonel reached into his jacket pocket, pulled out a small piece of paper and handed it to Orlov.

Orlov read: "Asif Pasha." Underneath was an address in Manassas, Virginia. Orlov knew that was a far out suburb of Washington.

"Has he had military training?" Orlov asked.

"Two years in the Pakistan Army. A special course on the use of arms and planting bombs."

"How did you recruit him?"

"An American drone attack missed its target, but killed both of his parents and two of his siblings, who lived across the street. They weren't involved in any terrorist activities. He wants revenge. He's prepared to sacrifice his own life to gain that revenge."

"Who's his contact?"

"I am."

"How will I be able to persuade him to do what I want?"

The Colonel reached into his pocket again. This time, he removed a small piece of metal and held it out in his hand across the desk. Orlov took it from the Colonel.

Orlov saw that it was half of a small silver medallion in the shape of Pakistan. "Asif has the other half?" Orlov asked.

"Precisely. He'll obey whoever shows up with this."

While Orlov stared at the medallion, the Colonel continued. "You may be worried that I'm tricking you. That you'll show up in the United States and you won't find this sleeper."

"That thought has occurred to me."

"Then rest easy, my brother. I want you to succeed with an attack on American soil. So don't fail me."

New York and Pennsylvania

Orlov flew from Moscow to New York via London Heathrow. His Russian ID and passport identified him as Anton Dubkin. He was pretending to be a Russian tourist.

In the passport control line at JFK, he felt a twinge of anxiety as the man ahead of him was being put through a rigorous examination by a jowly, tough-looking, no-nonsense, immigration agent with a black sandpaper beard. Orlov hoped it was because the man was olive-skinned. Middle Eastern looking.

Orlov considered switching lines but rejected that for fear his move would be picked up by a concealed camera and raise suspicion. So he decided to tough it out.

Good choice, he realized ten minutes later. The agent yawned, glanced at Orlov's documents and asked, "Purpose of visit?"

Orlov replied, "Tourist." The agent stamped the documents, handed them back, and signaled to the next in line.

At the airport, Orlov rented a gray Odyssey minivan with GPS and New York plates, promising to return it to JFK in a week.

He didn't breathe easy until he was on the New Jersey Turnpike heading south at seven in the evening and confident from lane changes that no one was following. The dicey part would come tomorrow in Pittsburgh.

In Moscow, Orlov personally packed the rocket-propelled grenade launcher and the grenades in a wooden crate marked on the sides to read: "medical equipment." He shipped it from Moscow to Toronto by way of Paris because he knew the French did little or no checking of shipments that were in transit. And since the final destination was Pittsburgh, he was hoping the Canadian airport authorities could care less. For the last leg, from Toronto to Pittsburgh, he decided on an overland freight carrier, figuring that an eighteen wheeler had the greatest chance of avoiding scrutiny at the U.S. border point.

All of that was working as planned. When he checked shipping records on his computer before boarding the plane at Heathrow, he learned that his package had been picked up by Highway Lines at their freight center in Toronto airport on schedule. It had been delivered yesterday to the Highway Lines terminal in Pittsburgh. Orlov thought his choice of Pittsburgh was wise: close to Camp David but outside the Washington area with its heightened security and terrorist checks.

Exhausted, he pulled off the New Jersey Turnpike at a Holiday Inn to sleep. Before leaving the minivan he hooked up an alarm that would alert him in the room if anyone tried to break into the vehicle.

No one did. He was confident that he had avoided detection when entering the United States. No mean feat for a former KGB agent who might be in the CIA database.

At four in the afternoon the next day, Orlov reached the Pittsburgh terminal of Highway Lines on Smallman Street in an industrial part of the city which development had missed. Orlov parked near a small metal finishing shop across from what had once been a booming steel mill, but now was deserted and abandoned. A victim of and testimony to America's manufacturing demise.

He walked two blocks to the Highway Lines terminal. Slowing, but not stopping, he glanced through the double glass door. He saw a pick-up counter with one man behind it. He was short and squat, mid-twenties, red spiked hair, an earring, and a pock-marked face. The sign on the door said, "Hours 8 AM to 5 PM." Orlov didn't see anyone else in the terminal.

He kept walking. The street, with pot holes the size of craters, was deserted. Many of the buildings were boarded up, the paint identifying their former occupants faded and peeling.

Orlov saw a small lunchroom: The M and H. He hadn't eaten since breakfast. He went inside.

The only other customers were two middle-aged men in the back drinking beer and playing a pinball machine. The beige tile floor was covered with decades of scuff marks.

Orlov sat at the wooden counter. A man in his fifties, solidly built, thinning hair in front, wearing an apron that said, "Moe," stopped cleaning a coffee urn and walked over.

Orlov glanced at the menu on a chalk board leaning against the wall. "Liverwurst sandwich," he said. "Chips and a Budweiser."

A few minutes later, Moe brought over the order.

"Where's the accent from?" Moe asked.

Orlov didn't want to answer questions. But he didn't want to be rude. That would have raised alarms. Besides, he had made up his mind to kill anyone who got in his way.

"Russia," Orlov answered tersely.

"My father was born in Russia," Moe answered. "In the west near Poland. He came here in 1912."

He's a Jew. Orlov thought, with contempt. Jews aren't Russians. Jews never were Russians.

To end the conversation, Orlov carried the food and beer to a table along a wall away from the pinball machine. Moe went back to cleaning his coffee urn.

At fifteen minutes to five, Orlov left the lunchroom and went back to his Odyssey. He pulled the minivan alongside the truck terminal and walked into the front door.

The kid with the spiked red hair said, "Can I help you?"

Without saying a word, Orlov pulled the shipping documents out of his pocket and plunked them down on the counter.

"I'll get your stuff," the redhead said.

Maybe I was worrying needlessly, Orlov thought. Perhaps this won't be difficult.

He cautioned himself not to drop his guard. The box could have been opened by United States Customs, which let it proceed to its destination to trap him. The redhead could have been told to call the FBI when anyone came to pick up the package. Orlov had a pistol in one pocket of his black leather jacket. A knife in the other.

The redhead wheeled out a dolly holding a wooden crate. Orlov recognized the markings.

"You'll have to sign," the clerk said, placing documents on the counter.

"Show me where," Orlov replied, trying to conceal his accent.

"And I'll have to see some ID."

Orlov pulled out his Russian passport.

The redhead was frowning. He pointed to the crate. "What's in there?"

"Medical supplies. That's what it says on the box. That's what the documents say."

The kid looked worried. "Suppose I was to ask you to open it."

"You can't do that. You're not a government agent."

"But I could make a call and have them here in ten minutes."

Orlov decided to make one more try at doing this the easy way.

"I'm sorry I don't understand. Why are you interested in medical supplies?"

"I'm not trying to be a hard-ass, but the police came round here a few months ago. They said we have to be diligent about possible terrorist attacks."

"Do I look like a Muslim terrorist?"

The redhead stared at Orlov. "No, but you're a foreigner. You could be working with them. Remember before 9/11—all those signs that were missed. Listen, Mister, it'll only slow you down by a few minutes, but I'm calling the police. He reached for the phone.

Orlov had enough. There must be other trucking company employees in the back. He had to dispose of the kid and get his package without making any noise. Orlov leapt over the counter and wrapped his hands around the redhead's throat.

I can't let him scream.

With his hands still around the kid's throat, he flung the redhead to the floor and landed on top. He was squeezing tighter and tighter. The kid's face was turning pale. He tried to struggle, but Orlov was too strong. In seconds, the redhead was dead.

Orlov grabbed the documents on the counter and stuffed them into his pocket. He wheeled the dolly outside toward the minivan. A young African American employee in a dark green Highway Lines uniform approached.

Orlov was reach to go for his gun.

The employee said, "You need help with that?"

Turning him down might make him suspicious, Orlov decided.

"Sure," he said.

Together they loaded it in the minivan.

Orlov drove away, hoping the employee didn't pay attention to his license plate. No reason he should.

While constantly glancing in the rearview mirror, looking for flashing lights that never came, Orlov used the GPS to get out of Pittsburgh at the nearest Interstate entrance heading east.

Orlov needed a place to store the weapon and a base for his operation. It had to be far enough from Camp David to avoid raising suspicion yet close enough that he could keep control of Asif, the Pakistani sleeper.

He spent another uneventful night at a Day's Inn off the Pennsylvania Turnpike.

The next morning, he drove to Gettysburg, Pennsylvania, and began his search. It struck his sense of irony that while planning the assassination of one American president he would be holed up in a location of such historical significance to another American president who had also been assassinated.

He parked the minivan in a three-story garage on the edge of downtown Gettysburg to keep it out of sight, set the alarm, and walked to the center of town.

Orlov located the main business street and stopped walking when he saw a sign that said, "Sara Burns Real Estate."

He checked photographs in the window of the office. On the far left was what he was looking for: farmhouse for rent.

Orlov entered the office and saw a hay-colored bleach blonde with a weather beaten face and a hard as nails look, sitting behind a desk with a sign in front that said, "Sara Burns." She was alone in the office and stood up. She was wearing a short khaki skirt and cracking gum.

"I'd like to talk to you about renting the farmhouse described in the window."

"Yeah. It's a good property. A small farm. The owner died. His wife moved away. She gave up trying to sell it. Unless of course you'd like to buy the whole farm."

Orlov laughed. "No. I just want it for six months."

"What for?" She was working that gum aggressively.

"I'm from Hungary. In the United States to write a novel. I need a quiet place."

"This is quiet alright. The rent's five thousand a month. One year lease. First two months and the last one in advance."

Orlov was willing to take that, but if he didn't negotiate, Sara might get suspicious. "How about four thousand a month, on a six month lease. First two and last one up front. And I'll pay cash."

"You don't want to see it first?"

"It's only for six months."

She raised her eyebrows. "Okay. Then forty-five hundred a month. Three months in cash up front. And it's all yours."

He guessed if she had any qualms, the possibility of all that cash in her hot little hand overruled them.

He pulled out the money and was preparing to reach for a Hungarian passport, but she never asked for it.

"Give me your name?" she said.

"Lazlo Richter."

"Okay. I'll prepare the contract."

Minutes later she handed it to him. He signed with an unintelligible flourish but Sara was happy. She had her money. She handed him the keys and gave him a map to the place.

He loved dealing with Americans. The profit motive always took priority.

Orlov walked back to the Odyssey. He left town by a circuitous route to avoid passing Sara's office.

The farmhouse was forty five minutes away, but only half a mile from a gas station and a truck stop with a convenience store where Orlov bought food.

He pulled the minivan into the deserted barn adjacent to the house, closed the door and locked it.

The house was a two-floor A-frame with peeling paint. Inside, furniture was sparse. A bed. A table and chair. A refrigerator. Enough for Orlov.

He ate and, exhausted, fell into bed.

The next morning, he walked to the gas station. There he told the driver of an eighteen-wheeler that his car had broken down and he had to get to Lancaster for a funeral.

They settled on two hundred dollars.

In Lancaster, Orlov went into a Hertz office. He produced a Florida driver's license and credit card in the name of Philip Savier. That was enough to rent a maroon Toyota with GPS.

Orlov set his destination as Washington, D.C. and left the Hertz lot.

It was time to meet Valerie Clurman, Kuznov's old girlfriend.

Paris

Craig always tried to put himself in the mind of the terrorist he was tracking. If you can anticipate their moves, you can be waiting for them at their next target.

He was convinced that Orlov's meeting with Zhou in Beijing meant Zhou was using Orlov to launch an attack against the United States. Of course, there were American targets all around the world—embassies, bases, organizations. But the most dramatic strike would be on American soil, and Zhou always tried for something big.

Immediately after his frustrating conversation with Norris, Craig realized that having INS agents detain Orlov when he tried to enter the United States wasn't an option.

No, I have to pick up Orlov before he gets to the United States, Craig decided. Grab him and force him to talk.

How would Orlov get to the United States? Craig asked himself. Not a direct flight from Beijing or Shanghai. Zhou would never countenance that because it would mean leaving a trail back to China. Besides, Orlov probably had to return to Moscow to brief Kuznov.

There were direct flights from Moscow to the United States. Craig doubted Kuznov would permit that. Again, the trail issue. Besides Craig had no way of obtaining the cooperation of Russian airport agents. Even if he could, he'd be tipping his hand with Kuznov and Orlov.

Craig had to assume that Orlov would fly from Moscow to a European city and from there to the United States. It was also likely Orlov wasn't using his own name.

Same appearance or plastic surgery?

Not enough time to alter his appearance, Craig decided.

Craig circulated Orlov's photo and name to the National Police in all the European countries and asked them to provide the information to immigration agents at their airports. "If you see this man, detain him, and call me."

In view of his position as EU Director of Counterterrorism, the National Police were willing to cooperate. After receiving their positive responses, Craig was hopeful. As the days passed, and he heard nothing, he repeatedly emailed them. He kept coming up empty and despaired.

Finally, one week after sending out the information, Craig received a call from Captain Ernest Mason at Scotland Yard. Mason didn't beat around the bush.

"We screwed up, mate," he told Craig.

"What do you mean?"

"Orlov, that Russian fella you were looking for, passed through Heathrow three days ago. Using an alias. Anton Dubkin."

"You're sure it's Orlov?"

"We didn't trust our eyes. We had the photo machine confirm the ID."

Craig felt the anger rising. "Then why wasn't he stopped at Heathrow?"

"Look, mate. People make mistakes. Maybe our agent was tired. Maybe he didn't have the photo nearby. Stuff happens. I don't think it was deliberate."

"Damn . . . damn . . . damn," Craig muttered too low for Mason to hear.

"Then how did you find out about it now, Captain Mason?"

"We were examining video feed from Heathrow searching for a Muslim terrorist when one of our people recognized Orlov. He was calmly walking to his plane. Like I said, that was three days ago."

"Where was the plane going?"

"BA176 to New York JFK."

"Oh fuck. Orlov's in the United States."

"What'd you say?"

"Never mind. Thanks for the info."

Craig hung up and called Detective Patrick Malloy of the NYPD. Three years ago, when Craig was still a CIA agent, Patrick had helped Craig circumvent CIA Director Kirby and break up a planned Al Qaeda suicide bombing at Madison Square Garden, which earned Craig the Medal of Freedom from President Brewster.

Craig's call reached Patrick on his cell, having breakfast at his home. Once Craig explained what he wanted, Patrick called to his wife, "Hey Jill, breakfast just ended."

Patrick told Craig, "I'll get on it immediately."

Two hours later, Patrick called back. "The news isn't good."

"Shit!"

"I figured you'd say that."

"What happened."

"The man calling himself Anton Dubkin, arrived on BA176 three days ago. He cleared Immigration routinely. He had a tourist visa. At JFK, he rented a gray Odyssey minivan with GPS and New York plates from Avis. He's supposed to return the car in a week."

"So he could be anywhere in the United States by now," Craig said glumly.

"Exactly. I'll feed the plates and car ID as well as his photo to law enforcement around the country. But at this point, it's a long shot."

"Very long. We're talking about a former KGB agent."

"Then he no doubt ditched the car."

"That's what I figure."

"You have an idea about his likely target?"

"Not a hint. But I know it'll be a major strike if he succeeds."

Washington

When Orlov reached Washington, he checked with telephone information. There was only one Valerie Clurman. She lived on 3499 Newark Street in Washington. Orlov got her telephone number. He drove past her house, between Connecticut and Wisconsin Avenues in Cleveland Park. It was a three story wood frame, freestanding house that looked to be about a hundred years old.

Orlov checked his watch. Four ten in the afternoon. He parked a block away and dialed the number.

"Please leave your name at the tone." He heard in a woman's pleasant sounding voice. He hung up without leaving a message.

He'd wait until evening to try again. With time to kill, he found a small Italian restaurant on Connecticut Avenue where he ate pizza. Then he walked along the sidewalk, passing shops and restaurants in this pleasant, upper middle class neighborhood.

All the while, he was thinking about Valerie. She should be fifty-five. She hadn't seen Kuznov in thirty years. What would her reaction be to a stranger trying to collect on a commitment she made thirty-five years ago as a foolish and impressionable young girl. Anger? Outrage? Denial?

He didn't care. He was holding all the cards. He had her life in his hands.

At seven thirty, he dialed again. A woman answered. "Yes?"

"Is this Valerie Clurman?"

"Who's calling?"

"My name is Ivan."

Silence for a moment. Then the phone slammed down.

He dialed again. It kicked over to the answering machine.

Orlov began speaking. "I received your name from an old friend of yours from Oxford. For your own sake you should talk to me. If not, I'm prepared to . . ."

She picked up. "Who are you?"

"I want to come to your house and talk to you."

"What about?"

He detected fear in her voice.

"I think we should do this in person."

Silence for several seconds. Then she gave him the address, which he already had.

"I'll be there in fifteen minutes."

*   *   *

Valerie Clurman was a petite brunette who reminded Orlov of a once beautiful rose which had faded in the summer's heat and with the passage of time. Her skin was wrinkled; her eyes sad, her walk slow and halting. She was dressed simply in a white cotton blouse and navy skirt.

As she moved away from the door to let Orlov enter, she looked terrified. Fear might account for the trembling Orlov noticed in her hands. Or maybe it was something else.

"Who are you?" she asked as he quickly closed the door.

"That's not important. I'm a friend of Fyodor Kuznov. That's all you need to know."

When she didn't respond, he left the words hanging in the air and looked around the living room. No pictures of a husband or children. He guessed that she had never married. Probably lived alone.

Prominently displayed along one wall, was a framed certificate commending her for twenty-five years with the Secret Service. It was signed by President Dalton two months ago. She had been married to her job, he decided.

When she didn't respond to his mention of Kuznov, Orlov added, "You remember Fyodor Kuznov. You first met him at Oxford and you saw him twice after that."

"Oxford was a long time ago."

Through the corner of his eye, Orlov saw a picture resting on the mantle above the fireplace next to a beer mug with the word "Oxford" on the front. Orlov walked over and studied the photo. Standing in front of an Oxford banner was a group of six young people, three men and three women. He recognized Valerie in the center. A young man had his arm draped around her shoulder. Had to be Kuznov. The resemblance was striking.

Before Orlov could ask her about it, she walked over, removed the picture and slid it in the drawer of the desk.

"Oxford was a long time ago," she repeated.

"But promises were made."

"I was young and foolish. Oxford was a wonderful place. So many intelligent people."

"Perhaps you were wise beyond your years."

"What do you want?"

"One small bit of information. That's all. And we'll never bother you again.,"

"What is it?"

"Whether President Dalton is going to Camp David this weekend and if so, when?"

She looked horrified. "You're planning to kill him?"

"Of course not."

"Then why do you want it?"

"You don't have to know."

"And if I don't tell you?"

"Kuznov recorded all of your conversations. I heard them. The technology in those days wasn't as good as it is now, but the words are clear. As I'm sure you're aware, he's become quite an important man now. president of Russia. If I were to deliver the recordings to the Secret Service Security Office, there would be repercussions."

Her face was red with rage. "You're a bastard."

"As I said, I'll never bother you again."

"You're asking me to choose between my life or Dalton's. One of us will be destroyed."

"I guess you could put it that way."

He pointed to the computer. "All you have to do is go over to that computer, access Dalton's schedule, and give me what I want."

"Oxford was a wonderful place. So many smart people. We used to sit around and . . ."

Orlov had to get her to focus. "Just *go* to the computer and give me what I want."

"Tell me again. What is it?"

Orlov was taken aback. "I want to know whether President Dalton is going to Camp David this weekend and if so when."

"I won't give you that information. You don't have clearance for it."

"I'll get you fired. Ruin your life."

"It doesn't matter. I'm retiring in a month. I'm not well. I won't end my career by giving out classified information without clearance."

"What's wrong with you?"

"Have you ever been to Oxford?"

"Do it now," Orlov said in a menacing tone. She walked over to the desk. Orlov was hopeful she'd boot up the computer. Instead, she sat down, removed the Oxford photo from the drawer, and stared at it. "Oxford was a wonderful place."

He cut across the room, grabbed her by the shoulders and shook her.

"Hey! You're hurting me," she cried out.

Orlov weighed his options. He could torture her, but he was convinced she'd never do what he wanted. He'd have to find another way.

He bolted toward the front door. Behind him, he heard her saying, "Oxford was a wonderful place."

*   *   *

Orlov spent the night at a Days Inn on Connecticut Avenue.

At ten the next morning, he called Valerie. As he expected, the phone kicked into voice mail. Good. She must be at work.

In a heavy rainstorm, he drove south on Connecticut, turned onto Newark, and parked a block from her house. He was glad for the rain. The sidewalk was deserted. Given the hour, traffic was sparse.

When he reached Valerie's house, he glanced over his shoulder to make sure no one was watching him, then went around to the back of the house. Large trees blocked the view from neighbors. Orlov climbed the three cracked cement stairs leading to a small wooden porch with decaying wood. He tried the back door by turning the knob. The lock was in place, but he could tell it was old and weak. He leaned his powerful shoulder against the door. The lock quickly gave way.

One more glance behind. Confident no one had seen him, Orlov went right to the living room. He sat down at Valerie's desk and stared at the blank computer screen.

Lots of people, he had learned over the years, were fearful of losing the passwords for their computers or the numbers to gain access to a safe, so they write the information down and hide it. Generally, not very well.

Valerie might even have left the paper with the password in the desk drawer. He began with the side drawers. Just pens and supplies. No paper with the password. He opened the center desk drawer. On top, Orlov found a booklet containing a telephone and email directory for the U.S. Secret Service. He recalled Valerie saying last night, "I won't give you that information." And not, "I can't access it from my home computer." The presence of the directory confirmed what Orlov had deduced from Valerie's words. Like many people, she used her home computer for work.

Under the directory, Orlov found a medical report from Johns Hopkins Medical Center in Baltimore with Valerie's name on top. It contained a date one month ago. Orlov pulled it out and began reading.

"Conclusion:

The patient is displaying the early signs of Alzheimer's disease. At this point, it is difficult to state how rapidly the disease will proceed."

Valerie knew she had Alzheimer's. This medical conclusion strengthened Orlov's conviction that Valerie had written down her computer password.

He rifled through the rest of the center desk drawer. No password. He tried drawers in a couple of chests. Only dishes and silver.

Orlov looked around the room and asked himself: where would Valerie be likely to hide it that she could get at it quickly.

The beer mug above the fireplace caught his eye. Orlov pulled it down and looked inside. He found a small piece of paper. On it, Orlov saw written in pencil the word Oxford. Then a series of numbers 1-26. The first twenty-five had lines through them.

Orlov was now convinced he had what he needed. Valerie's password was Oxford and a number. The U.S. Secret Service, like many organizations, no doubt required that people change their passwords periodically. So she had done it by repeatedly changing the number next to Oxford. He placed the paper back in the beer mug. Excited, he returned to the computer and booted it up. "Welcome to the U.S. Secret Service" appeared on the screen. Orlov entered Valerie Clurman for user and the password Oxford26. Then he held his breath. *Eureka!*

He was in the system.

It took Orlov five minutes to locate President Dalton's schedule. He went to Friday, three days from now. There, he found what he wanted: "POTUS" will be leaving the White House by helicopter at four ten in the afternoon. POTUS will be flying in the second helicopter."

Orlov was amused by the American intelligence community's use of the acronym POTUS for president of the United States. Everyone knew it. Why didn't they just say Dalton?

Well, never mind. He had what he wanted.

He turned off the computer and tried to make everything in the house look like it had been when he entered.

*   *   *

Orlov spent Tuesday night at a hotel near Baltimore airport. The next morning, he bought hiking equipment in Baltimore. Armed with a map on which he had added a line from the White House to the presidential retreat known as Camp David, he drove northwest into the Catoctin Mountains in northern Maryland.

He saw a parking lot for tourists about twenty miles from Camp David on a line from Washington to the presidential retreat. It was the middle of the week. As he expected, the parking lot was deserted. Orlvo got out of the car and trudged through the thick forest, pushing aside branches which scratched his arms. He was searching for an abandoned or deserted hut or cabin. Any kind of abandoned or empty structure he could use to conceal his Pakistani assassin. If he didn't find one, he'd have to settle for positioning the assassin in thick trees and bushes—a much less desirable alternative.

He walked for nearly three hours in the increasing heat and humidity. His shirt was wet with perspiration. He'd been bitten by a dozen mosquitoes. He narrowly avoided stepping on a snake. His two large water bottles were almost empty.

He was beginning to despair, when he saw ahead a small wooden cabin.

He looked up into the clear blue sky. No obstructions on the line from Washington to Camp David.

He approached the cabin cautiously. On the side, was one very dirty window. Orlov wiped it with his handkerchief and peered inside. He didn't see anyone.

Orlov checked the front door. It was locked. With his shoulder, he forced off the lock. Inside, he looked around. He saw a couple of hunting rifles in a case. Above the fireplace, hung a deer's head with a large set of antlers. Every surface was coated with dust. It must have been months since anyone was here. Perhaps not since the last fall hunting season.

Orlov could hardly believe his luck. A deserted hunting cabin. He needed it only for one night. Thursday. The hunters would never be back on a week day this time of year.

Everything was falling into place. Only one more piece was missing. And it was a large one: the assassin.

Manassas, Virginia

At seven Thursday morning, Orlov arrived in Manassas, Virginia. He parked a block from the red brick two-story town house with the address the Colonel had given him in Islamabad.

As he rang the bell, Orlov thought, I have to do this carefully. Asif has been living in the United States. He might have been seduced by the good life here. Now Orlov would be asking him to give all that up. Even to die.

A Pakistani man, tall and thin, with a neatly trimmed mustache, wearing khaki slacks, suspenders, and a white undershirt opened the door.

"Asif Pasha?" Orlov asked.

The man's face showed uncertainty, mixed with fear. "Yes. Who are you?"

Orlov pulled from his pocket the portion of the silver medallion in the shape of Pakistan the Colonel had given him and held it out.

Asif took it. Then closed it up in his hand.

Before Asif had a chance to say a word, a heavy set Pakistani woman dressed in a pink terrycloth robe came out from the kitchen holding a knife in her hand. Orlov wasn't sure if she had brought the knife to use as a weapon against an intruder, or whether she'd been in the middle of cooking breakfast and came out to see what was happening.

She stared hard at Orlov while clutching the knife tightly. She's smart, Orlov thought. And instinctively, she doesn't like me. She knows my presence here means trouble for her and her husband.

Asif looked at his wife. "It's okay. He's a friend of a friend. He just wants to talk to me."

She looked alarmed. Orlov wondered if Asif had explained to her the deal he had made with the Colonel.

"We're going downstairs to talk. Go back to the kitchen," Asif told her. "Don't disturb us."

She didn't seem happy but turned and obediently returned to the kitchen.

"Come with me," Asif said to Orlov. Asif led the way through the living room to a door which opened to stairs going down to the basement.

The downstairs was unfinished. The walls were concrete blocks. A furnace was in the corner. Asif pulled two chairs and a bridge table from a closet and put them against one wall.

When they were seated, Orlov produced a flask from his pocket. "Some plum brandy?"

Asif shook his head. "I never drink alcohol. But you go ahead."

Orlov took a gulp. "Colonel Khan sends his regards."

"I'm ready for my mission."

Orlov was startled by the conviction with which Asif said it. And the Pakistani's eyes were blazing. Orlov realized his fears were groundless. Here was a man hell bent on revenge against the Americans whose drone attack had killed his parents and siblings.

"I want you to assassinate the American president," Orlov said.

Asif didn't flinch. "Good. I wanted something significant. My fear was that my efforts would be of minimal value. When?"

Orlov explained the logistics to Asif. At the end, Asif said, "When I was in the Pakistani military, I used American grenade launchers. That should be no problem."

"Good. I want you to come with me now. I have everything you'll need, including food for two days, in my farmhouse in Pennsylvania. This afternoon, when it's still daylight, I'll take you with the weapon to the hunting cabin in the mountains. You'll spend tonight there alone. Also, until the helicopter comes between four and five tomorrow afternoon."

"Where will you be?"

"Close enough to help if you have a problem. Take your cell phone. I'll give you an emergency number to call me. But don't write it down or program it into your phone. Memorize it."

"I understand."

"One other thing?"

Wide-eyed, Asif looked at Orlov. "Yes."

"You can't let the Americans capture you. The torture would be unbearable. You would prefer to be dead."

Orlov held his breath. This part was key. How would Asif react to the need to kill himself?

"I have already reached that conclusion" Asif said. "Capture is not an option. Will you provide me with a gun I can use to kill myself?"

"My recommendation is a cyanide capsule. Death is faster and a lot less painful."

Orlov didn't add: and it's more certain of achieving the result.

"I will use the cyanide then. I don't know your name, and I don't want to know it, but I want to say that you're a very thorough man."

"Thank you. I appreciate that."

"I'm not asking you to judge me. However, I want you to understand my motivation."

While Asif spoke about the drone attack, Orlov didn't interrupt to say he already knew what had happened. Listening to Asif, Orlov concluded that the retelling was good. A catharsis for Asif. It strengthened his resolve.

"Now you understand," Asif said.

"I would feel the same way."

Asif looked relaxed, displaying an inner peace Orlov hadn't seen before. "Are you ready to go with me?" Orlov asked.

"Give me a few minutes to gather some clothes and other things. Also, to tell my wife I'm going away for a couple of days. Of course, I won't mention the real purpose. We don't have any children."

"Will you be bringing a copy of the Koran?"

Asif shook his head. "I am not a believer. I would never want anyone to think this was part of the Jihad some of my people have launched against the Americans. My motivation is personal revenge. Nothing else."

Orlov nodded. Expecting this might be the case, he had purchased a copy of the Koran in Islamabad and brought it with him to the United Sates. At the time he installed Asif in the hunting cabin, he planned to conceal the Koran behind the chest containing hunting rifles. When the Americans found it, they would conclude this was an attack by Al Qaeda or another Fundamentalist group as part of a Jihad.

Waiting for Asif to talk to his wife, Orlov reviewed his own plans in his mind. He was now confident Dalton's assassination would go exactly as he had planned.

The presidential helicopter would be leaving the White House at four ten on Friday afternoon. At three fifty, Air France flight 39 was scheduled to take off from Dulles Airport for Paris. Orlov planned to be in the business class cabin of that plane. Far from the scene of the assassination. No one would ever tie him to it.

Paris

The trip to Corsica had done Craig a world of good, he believed. Though he and Elizabeth had cut the vacation short and though he was monitoring every bit of information he could get from China, looking for President Zhou's next predatory action, Craig had regained his mental balance. He slept at night. His mind was clear and analytical. President Zhou was his target. Not his obsession.

This Friday evening, Craig and Elizabeth were having a quiet dinner at Le Voltaire, an elegant dark wood paneled restaurant with a clubby atmosphere on Rue du Bac along the Seine. The restaurant attracted an elegantly dressed celebrity crowd. Before they ordered, while they were sipping champagne, Elizabeth had pointed out an actress to Craig, and they both recognized Jean Claude, French Interior Minister, in the doorway who stopped to say hello to both of them on his way to a table. He had in tow a gorgeous black-haired woman, whom he didn't introduce. When they were seated across the room and out of hearing range, Elizabeth said, "That's not Jean Claude's wife."

"I'll never tell."

She slapped him on the wrist. "You men are all the same."

He laughed. "Hey. What'd I do?"

Two hours later, Craig was finishing a delicious rack of lamb. He sipped some of the '99 Vosne Romanee Le Beaux Monts from Rion and looked across the table at Elizabeth. "When your book's finished, I want to take you to Sardinia, to Hotel Cala di Volpe. Giuseppe told me it's the most incredible resort in the world."

"I didn't think Giuseppe was the type for that sort of thing."

"He's not, but the Italian Prime Minister has a house nearby. He hauled Giuseppe down there for a briefing and installed him at Cala di Volpe."

She raised her wine glass. "Good. Count me in."

"What's your targeted completion date?"

"I won't answer that. I don't like pressure."

Before Craig could respond, he felt his cell phone vibrating in his pocket. Craig took it out and looked at caller ID. It was Jacques. He wouldn't be calling at eleven thirty on a Friday evening if it wasn't urgent.

Craig glanced around. The diners on each side had departed; many of the tables were vacant. The Interior Minister and his girlfriend were engaged in an intense conversation. As long as he kept his voice low, no one could overhear him. "Yes, Jacques."

"President Dalton has been assassinated."

Craig's heart was thumping. "Where did it happen?"

Craig saw Elizabeth staring at him.

"He was in a helicopter en route from the White House to Camp David. A rocket from the ground brought it down."

"Thanks for letting me know. Elizabeth and I will go back to my office right now. Want to join us?"

"I can't. We're now frantically checking security for President Duquesne in case this is a multipronged attack to take out more than one Western leader."

Craig powered off the phone, gave a deep sigh, and whispered to Elizabeth what Jacques had told him.

"Dinner's over," he said and signaled the waiter for the check. From across the room, he heard the Interior Minister's phone ringing. The man's romantic evening had just ended. Craig passed the Minister on the way out of the restaurant. "I already heard," Craig said to the grim-faced man.

"I'm sorry," he replied. "For all you Americans."

*   *   *

In Craig's office, they turned on two televisions, one displaying CNN and the other a French news channel.

Both kept replaying the ghastly attack, showing the missile hitting the president's helicopter and turning it into a ball of fire. Craig guessed that one of the reporters traveling in a following chopper or in the motorcade on the ground had a video camera.

Craig thought about his last encounter with Dalton, the president being so pig-headed and difficult before he ultimately agreed to provide American Air Force assistance to thwart the attack on the Vatican. Craig believed Dalton's political agenda was ridiculous and his judgment absurd. But still, he was the President of the United States. This should not have happened.

He glanced over at Elizabeth. Though she didn't like Dalton anymore more than he did, she looked troubled.

CNN cut to Vice President David Treadwell being sworn in as president. Treadwell was standing in the Vice President's house on the grounds of the Naval Observatory along Massachusetts Avenue. He had his hand on a bible. The Chief Justice was administering the oath of office.

"Call your friend Betty at the CIA," Elizabeth said. "See what they know."

Craig placed the call on a secure phone and put Betty on the speaker so Elizabeth could hear.

"It's pretty chaotic over here," Betty said.

"Any idea who's responsible?"

"Personally, I think it's Al Qaeda or one of the other Jihadist groups. The FBI found a Pakistani man dead in a nearby hunting cabin. Appears to have taken his own life with a cyanide capsule. They found a copy of the Koran concealed in the cabin. None of those facts have been released to the media or the public."

"Who took the video of the assassination?"

"A CBS reporter traveling in a following chopper."

"Does Norris agree with your assessment about a Jihadist being responsible?"

"This is weird. He's holed up in his office. Not talking to any-one. He must be expecting to be blamed for this horrific event. He's mumbling that it wasn't his fault. That he can't possibly uncover every planned attack on the president. The assassination pushed him off the deep end."

"*He is responsible*," Craig said.

"What do you mean?" a startled Betty asked.

"About a week ago I called Norris and told him that Dimitri Orlov, a former KGB agent, had met with President Zhou in Beijing, that Zhou's mistress was Orlov's brother, and that I was fearful Orlov might be coming to the United States to launch some type of attack being engineered by Zhou. All I asked Norris to do was to distribute Orlov's bio and photo to all INS agents at U.S. international airports and border crossing points, and to arrest Orlov when he appeared. Norris refused."

Craig paused to take a breath. "Wait, I remember exactly what he said. That I could stick the photo and bio up my ass. Then he hung up. So he is responsible. If he had given the order, we would've arrested Orlov and Dalton would be alive."

"That's a hell of a big leap," Betty said.

"Is it? Really? That bastard Zhou hates the Americans. Dalton was threatening trade sanctions unless China liberalized on personal freedom, which Zhou would never do. You want to reconsider?"

"You remind me of a teenage boy who sees sex in everything."

"Don't dismiss my idea so quickly. Has any Jihad group claimed responsibility?"

"Not yet."

"Don't they always? And very quickly?"

"True, but . . ."

He recognized the doubt in her voice.

"Keep me posted," Craig said

"For sure."

When he hung up the phone, he turned to Elizabeth, "What do you think of my theory about President Zhou being responsible? And using Orlov?"

"Same as Betty. Wild and unsupported speculation."

"The sisterhood at work."

"Do you know Treadwell?"

"Only met him once. When I thwarted the Madison Square Garden bombing, Brewster was president at the time. He kept the incident out of the press, but he told Treadwell who was then a Senator from California and Chairman of the Senate Intelligence Committee. Treadwell called me into his office for a private briefing."

"How did that go?"

"Couldn't have been better. I was tremendously impressed with Treadwell. He's like Brewster was. Smart. No nonsense. Listens to people. Respects expertise. He's a good man. The country is definitely better off with Treadwell in the Oval office."

Craig suddenly recalled that he'd had a second meeting with Treadwell. "Sorry," he said. "I also met him one other time."

"When was that?"

"The day after I turned down Brewster's offer to be CIA Director in favor of the EU job. Treadwell called me down to his office on the Hill and asked me to reconsider."

"You never told me that."

"It didn't matter. I was moving to Paris with you. That was a done deal."

She ran a hand through her hair. "Oh. Oh," she said and sighed.

"What's that mean?"

"We better go home and start packing. I'll bet we're moving to Washington."

"You think Treadwell will ask me to be CIA Director?"

"Of course."

"Yeah. Right. Then we'll buy a house in a Washington suburb with a white picket fence and a dog and live happily ever after."

"I'm telling you he'll offer you the job. It's okay with me. I'm willing to live in Washington even without the white picket fence. It's time to go home."

"But what about your work?"

"I'm far enough along on the book that I can do it anywhere. I'm confident the paper would let me operate from Washington. The important thing is that this is something you would want to do. Something at which you could make a difference to the United States and the world."

"I think you're wrong. Treadwell won't ask me to become Director. He'll stick with Norris."

She reached into her bag, pulled out a hundred euro note and plunked it down on his desk. "You want to cover that?"

He thought about it some more and left her money sitting alone on the desk.

Beijing

With the assistance of a siren and flashing lights, along with a police motorcycle escort, President Zhou's driver threaded his way through heavy early evening traffic. Zhou in the back seat was headed for his brother's house to celebrate Dalton's assassination.

To Zhou's pleasant surprise, Orlov had done exactly what Zhou had asked. He had called his brother and said, "Chill the champagne. I'm coming over this evening."

Zhou could've asked his brother to come to the Presidential House, but he wanted to be free of Androshka, at least for this evening. He was finding her whining increasingly annoying. What did she think she would find when she moved to China? She should have learned the language. Then she would have friends. She was no longer pleasant to be with.

Truth is, he brought her with him to Beijing for one thing and one thing only: she could make his stalk harden and stand up. But since his return, often she couldn't do that. On those occasions when he failed, he was convinced it was her fault. She was too miserable to give him pleasure. Well, she had better improve. China was full of young women with talented mouths and fingers who could succeed and would give anything for the opportunity.

Zhou was so disgusted with Androshka, that if it weren't for her brother, whom Zhou needed for one more mission, Zhou would have Androshka killed. He could never permit her to leave the country. She knew too many of his secrets.

What he would do, he decided, was wait until he was finished with Orlov. Then have her murdered, making it look like an accident.

Euphoric with Dalton's assassination, Zhou's brother opened a bottle of Krug the minute Zhou walked into his mansion. As he raised his glass, Zhou Yun said, "Dalton would have crippled our economy with his sanctions. Good riddance to him."

It had been his brother's words which had given Zhou the idea of assassinating Dalton. Zhou asked, "Will Treadwell be any better for us?"

"I've attended business conferences at which he spoke. He was a businessman in California before he went into politics. He's pragmatic and he understands that his country's economic health depends upon China's economic vitality. I once heard him say, 'For better or worse our economies are joined at the hip. If one catches cold, the other will be sick as well.' He won't be a pushover on military matters though. As chairman of the Senate Intelligence Committee, he engaged in aggressive American defense policy vis-à-vis China."

"Good. I enjoy a challenge," General Zhou said.

His brother looked alarmed. "For now, we should move slowly to develop a firm and friendly relationship with Treadwell. We must not act precipitously to confront him."

"Have I ever done that?" Zhou said, and then he laughed. His brother wasn't laughing.

Zhou couldn't understand why his brother was so hung up on friendship with Treadwell. He guessed it was because his entire focus was on what was good for business and increased profits. He'd lost sight of the larger objective: Chinese political and military superiority, not just an enhanced GNP.

Zhou had no intention of debating the issue with his brother, who could be unyielding on matters like this. Nor did he have any intention of telling his brother what he planned to do next with Orlov. His brother would never have approved. Well, too bad. He was the President of China. Not his brother.

Once the champagne was finished, President Zhou rode back to Tiananmen Square and his office. He had summoned the twenty members of the Central Committee to a ten o'clock evening meeting.

The subject was the assassination of President Dalton. General Zhou had invited Yin Bao, the Intelligence Minister, who had been appointed by President Li to provide his assessment of Dalton's assassination and what the elevation of Treadwell to the American presidency would mean for Chinese American relations.

Zhou waited in his office down the corridor from the ornate large conference room used for Central Committee meetings for the others to arrive.

He removed a Cuban cigar from the humidor, lit it, and took a deep puff. Zhou thought about this evening's meeting and his objective. Zhou had never liked Yin. The man was a lackey for President Li. He never had an independent or creative thought, but merely parroted what staff members told him. Director of Intelligence was too important to be held by someone like that. And besides, Zhou needed total loyalty from the occupant of the position.

In their initial meeting, Yin had told Zhou, "Some physicians have questioned the mysterious circumstances of President Li's death. Perhaps I should launch a comprehensive investigation."

Zhou had told Yin to leave it alone, but he was afraid the issue wasn't closed.

Zhou could have simply replaced Yin, but then, outside of Zhou's control, Yin might have become a lightning rod for those who wanted to question Li's death. No, a more radical approach was needed in dealing with Yin.

Zhou had another objective this evening. He was aware that nine members of the Central Committee had preferred Mei Ling to become president. And he knew who they were. He had no chance of winning their unqualified support. That meant they would constantly be searching for a way to depose him as president and bring Mei Ling back unless he could instill sufficient fear within them that they would abandon Mei Ling. This evening, he was launching his campaign of fear.

Captain Cheng came into the office. "They're all here."

"All twenty?"

"Yes, sir."

"Grumbling about a ten o'clock time for the meeting?"

"Yes. As you expected."

"Too bad. Has Yin arrived?"

"A couple of minutes ago."

"Good. Let's go."

Lit cigar in hand, Zhou strode confidently down the hall. Captain Cheng was two steps behind.

When Li had been president, he had sat along one side of the heavily polished walnut table. Zhou, believing he had to assert his authority, reconstructed the room to place a raised platform at one end with a table and a single chair. Zhou's position.

While Captain Cheng settled into a seat near the door in the back of the room, Zhou moved to the front, while puffing on his cigar, and climbed the three stairs up to the platform. An armed soldier stood in each corner.

Zhou called on Yin, who was also seated near the door, close to Cheng.

"Tell us about the Dalton assassination," Zhou demanded.

The Intelligence Minster rose. Briefcase in hand, he approached the table, pulled out some papers, and sat down. He glanced at Zhou and began speaking. "Dalton's assassination . . ."

"Stand when you speak to me and look directly at me," Zhou commanded.

Yin stood and started again, "Dalton's assassination represents one more example of the continuing war which Muslim fundamentalists, Al Qaeda, and Jihadists are waging against the United States. It follows the model of their 9/11 attacks as being completely unanticipated by the Americans. There will be others. The question for us is how . . ."

The fool had no idea what he was talking about. He had fallen into Zhou's trap. Zhou interrupted and said, "Exactly what evidence do you have to support your conclusion that Jihadists were responsible for the assassination?"

With confidence, Yin replied. "I've learned from intelligence assets in the United States that a Pakistani was the shooter. A Koran was found close to his dead body. He took his own life."

"So what?" Zhou snapped. "Anybody could have hired a Pakistani and put a Koran there. I have good relations with top people in the Pakistan military. So do many others. Any of us could have been responsible. I can't have an Intelligence Minister who leaps to unjustified conclusions. Wouldn't you agree?"

"Yes," Yin said meekly.

"You're an incompetent fool," Zhou shouted, "reaching totally unsupported conclusions and wasting our time with them. I have no idea why President Li appointed you to this important position. I want you to apologize now to me and the members of the Committee for your incompetence."

For a few seconds, Yin was too stunned to respond. Then, red-faced, he stammered, "I apologize for my incompetence."

"Louder," Zhou ordered.

"I apologize for my incompetence," Yin shouted out, his face a picture of humiliation.

"I have no intention of retaining you in this important job."

Zhou signaled to Captain Cheng. "Arrest Yin. I want him taken to a prison and interrogated. His report may not have been the result of incompetence. He may be an American agent."

Following the script Zhou had prepared, Cheng motioned to two of the soldiers. They closed in on Yin, roughly grabbed him, and dragged him out of the room.

"Let me make one other point," Zhou said to the startled members of the Central Committee. "In the United States, the transition from Dalton to Treadwell will be difficult and awkward. This will be a perfect time for China to gain an edge on the American military."

"What do you intend to do?" one of the members asked.

"I'm considering a number of possibilities. You can be sure I'll come back to you before I take any action."

Zhou had no intention of doing that. And he was certain nobody in the room thought he would.

Paris

Three days after Dalton's assassination, Craig picked up the phone in his office and heard, "Mr. Page, please hold for the President of the United States."

Over the years Craig had a number of calls and meetings with American presidents, but dealing with the world's most powerful individual was still exciting for Craig.

"I've been following closely what you've done in Europe," Treadwell said. "Stopping the attack on the Vatican and the takeover of Southern Spain was a tremendous accomplishment."

"Thank you, sir. I was both shocked and saddened to hear about Dalton's assassination."

"These are difficult times here in the United States. I'm calling to ask you to come to Washington and meet with me. Quite frankly, I need your help, and I would like to talk to you about that."

Well there it was, Elizabeth was right, Craig thought. "When would you like to see me?"

"Can you fly tomorrow morning?"

"Absolutely, Mr. President. I'll be on the morning nonstop on Air France. Should arrive in Washington around two in the afternoon."

"Perfect. I'll have a car and driver meet you and bring you to the White House."

Craig immediately called Elizabeth. "I'm glad I didn't bet you. I could have lost a hundred euros."

"He offered you the CIA job?"

"Not yet. Just called to invite me to come for a meeting. I'm flying to Washington tomorrow morning. Can you join me?"

"I'd love to. It'll be nice moving to Washington."

"He hasn't offered me the job yet."

"He will. And I assume you'll take it."

"I'm not sure."

"You're kidding. Right?"

"I've come to like our lifestyle here in Paris. There are plenty of challenges in the job. And I hate the Washington bureaucracy. How do you feel about it?"

"As long as we're together, I'll be happy in either place. My work will be the same. So it's your decision."

As soon as Craig finished the call with Elizabeth, he summoned Marie from his agency's high tech center.

"Have you had any success deciphering the encrypted disc from General Zhou's conversation with his brother in Beijing, made when Zhou was still in Bali?"

She looked chagrined. "We have people working around the clock. The Chinese used a very sophisticated system. So far we're at a dead end."

"You think the CIA could do it?"

"It might take a little while. But they would have a much better chance."

Craig continued to believe in his gut that this conversation between General Zhou and his brother was important. Craig recalled what Betty had said about Norris. If the CIA Director had lost his grip, with Betty's help, Craig might be able to make an end run around Norris and get the conversation deciphered. And if he became CIA Director, he could give the order to the agency's techies to do it ASAP.

That evening while they were at home packing, Elizabeth's cell phone rang. Craig heard her say, "Yes. Yes. Of course. I'll be right there."

She hung up the phone and grabbed her coat. "It was Mei Ling. She has some important information for me."

"You want me to come with you?"

"I better go alone."

*   *   *

Mei Ling was still staying in room 610 of the Hotel Le Burgundy. Elizabeth tapped twice on the door and said, "It's Elizabeth."

She heard the sound of two dead bolts and a chain being removed.

"Are you sure you weren't followed?" Mei Ling asked anxiously.

"Positive. What happened?"

"I received a call from Qua Ping, a friend on the Central Committee. He told me that President Zhou said he has good relations with top people in the Pakistani military and he could have been responsible for President Dalton's assassination."

Her words rocked Elizabeth back on her heels. "Did he elaborate on that?"

"No. But he also announced that he's planning to take advantage of American weakness during the transition to launch a military action against the United States. Meantime, to consolidate his hold on power, Zhou's moving to purge officials who had worked with President Li. He humiliated the Intelligence Minister, Yin Bao, before the Central Committee, had him arrested for being an American spy, and executed by a firing squad. He announced to all the members of the Central Committee that Yin confessed to being an American spy. The man had been tortured so badly that he could barely stand before the firing squad. Zhou's a monster. You and Page have to find a way to stop him."

"I'll report all this to Craig. I know that he'll do what he can."

"Page has to succeed. Zhou has to be stopped."

As Elizabeth rode back to the apartment, she thought about the effect Mei Ling's words would have on Craig's decision. It would make him more likely to take the CIA job if Treadwell offered it because it would give him the best platform for stopping General Zhou and gaining his revenge.

On the other hand, he despised CIA bureaucracy. She had learned long ago that she could never predict with confidence what Craig would do.

Beijing

With pride, Orlov recounted in detail for Zhou everything he did to arrange President Dalton's assassination. The two of them were alone in Zhou's office.

At the end, Orlov said, "In summary, I believe it was the perfect operation."

To Orlov's astonishment, Zhou was smiling. That alarmed Orlov. He had never seen the man smiling before. He was on guard, fearful Zhou's objective was to suck him into some kind of trap.

"You did a good job," Zhou told Orlov. "With Dalton's assassination."

"Thank you," Orlov said. "Now I want to arrange for you to come to Moscow and meet with President Kuznov."

"I intend to do that," Zhou said. "I am interested in forging an alliance with your president."

"Good. Let's set a date."

"I'm not quite ready," Zhou said. "I need you to do one other thing first."

So there it was, Kuznov was right. Zhou was yanking him around. But what could he do about it?"

"I thought we had an understanding."

The smile was gone, replaced by a hard, cruel look. "Then you thought wrong."

"Perhaps you can have the meeting with Kuznov in Moscow. Afterwards, I'll do this additional thing."

"That's not possible. I had you kill Dalton to prove yourself. Now I'll let you and President Kuznov share in something incredibly valuable."

Orlov recalled Kuznov's words when he told the Russian president that Zhou wanted him to assassinate Dalton. "Does Zhou really want to have an alliance with Russia? Or does he just want you to do his dirty work?"

Kuznov would not be happy that Orlov hadn't been able to arrange Zhou's visit to Moscow after the Dalton assassination. He wasn't looking forward to being the messenger for that news. But for now, he had to listen to Zhou. Hear what he wanted.

As if reading Orlov's mind, Zhou said, "This is the last thing I'll ask you to do before I come to Moscow to meet with President Kuznov. And when you hear what it is, you'll realize how beneficial this will be to Russia as well as China."

"What is it?"

"The United States has developed, but not yet built, a new class of sophisticated long-range missiles. If China and Russia had this technology, then China could launch attacks against Japan and Taiwan, and Russia could launch attacks against Eastern Europe, knowing that the United States wouldn't dare retaliate for fear that we'd launch our own long-range missiles against American targets. So this technology is critical to our alliance."

Orlov was puzzled. Zhou continued, "Do you know what I'm saying?"

"I hear you, but what do I have to do with this?"

"I want you to steal the American technology for these long-range missiles. And provide it to Kuznov as well as to me."

"Let me be clear. I have had no education or training in technology."

Zhou interrupted him. "But I presume that your KGB masters gave you lots of training in how to steal American secrets."

"Of course."

"Good. Then I will have you meet with Jiang Hua of the Technical Branch of the Chinese Defense Ministry. He'll explain to you exactly what you need to know to steal this technology. I'll attend this briefing. It's important for me to understand it as well."

Zhou pressed the intercom and said, "Get Jiang Hua over to my office."

While they were waiting, Zhou said to Orlov, "Have you seen Androshka?"

"The last time I was here. Not yet on this visit. I came to you from the airport. I plan to see her after our meeting."

"Is your sister happy in Beijing?"

What an explosive question, Orlov thought. He had spent enough time with Zhou to realize that the man had a massive ego. If Orlov said "no," Zhou would likely expel Androshka from China or perhaps kill her. He couldn't let that happen, not only because he loved Androshka but because having her in Zhou's bed gave Orlov a personal connection, albeit tenuous, with Zhou, and perhaps a source for information if Orlov ever wanted to use Androshka to spy on Zhou.

Choosing his words carefully, Orlov responded, "Androshka told me she was very happy in Beijing. That you've made her feel like a Chinese Empress."

"That's good. I care a great deal for Androshka."

Orlov felt as if he'd dodged a bullet, not just for himself, but for Androshka.

With relief he watched the door open and a short, slight man, barely five feet tall, with a shaved head and dressed in civilian clothes enter. He was carrying a thin laptop.

"Jiang Hua," Zhou said. "Meet my friend Orlov. He's a Russian who failed math in school and now wants to learn about the most sophisticated military technology in the world, dealing with long-range missiles. Can you provide him with what he needs to know?"

"I can do that, Mr. President," Jiang said deferentially.

Zhou pointed to the table in the back of the room and the three of them sat down with Zhou at the head of the table.

Jiang locked his fingers together and began speaking. "This new American weapons system is called Prompt Global Strike, sometimes referred to as PGS. It is capable of reaching any corner of the earth from the United States in under an hour and with such incredible precision and force that they could destroy an Iranian nuclear site, attack a North Korean missile on a launch pad, or kill a terrorist in a cave in Afghanistan. And all from the United States."

Orlov gave a long, low whistle. "Exactly," Jiang said. "It clearly changes the balance of power in the world. The technology has just been completed. Implementation will begin if and when the construction budget is approved by Congress. PGS was developed by Rogers Laughton, a huge U.S. defense contractor located in Gaithersburg, Maryland, outside of Washington. Rogers Laughton has a special unit, called the Epsilon Unit, of five brilliant engineers devoted to the PGS project. We've compiled detailed bios on the five."

"How do you know all this?" Orlov asked.

"We had our military intelligence people sift through information on various websites. Of course, we don't have the PGS technology, but we've zeroed in on the five engineers who developed and have access to it. Four men and one woman."

Jiang opened his computer, punched several buttons and turned the screen toward Orlov.

Displayed was a picture of four men and one woman.

"The members of the Epsilon Unit," Jiang said. "I can pull up bios for each of them."

"Can you print the photos and bios for me?" Orlov asked.

"Yes. Give me a couple of minutes."

Before Jiang had a chance to print them, Zhou slammed shut his computer, narrowly missing Jiang's fingers. "You don't get the bios until I know Kuznov is in."

*   *   *

That evening, Orlov arranged to have Androshka come to his suite at the St. Regis for dinner.

An hour before her eight thirty arrival time, he checked the suite for bugs. He found one attached to the bottom of the frame of a landscape picture hanging on a wall in the dining room.

Orlov was convinced that Zhou, knowing Androshka was coming for dinner, had planted it. At eight twenty, Orlov disabled the listening device. He'd reconnect it when she left. He didn't tell her about it. His objective was to persuade her to stay in Beijing. If she learned Zhou was spying on her, she'd go home, pack, and head to the airport.

Orlov, who was three years older than Androshka, knew very well how impulsive she could be. Growing up, she was always flying off the handle.

After their father's death, their house became a virtual war zone. Their mother, a nervous chain-smoker with aspirations of grandeur, became embittered once her husband died and the Party perks ended. So she declared war on her daughter, jealous of her younger age; and Androshka responded by rarely doing what her mother asked.

Orlov, as the man of the house, took responsibility for Androshka. That meant taking her side in battles with their mother, the despised enemy, which led the two of them to develop a closeness.

In the end, Androshka always listened to Orlov. If he told her to follow mother's command on some issue, she would do it.

He hoped that he still had that kind of influence over his sister. He knew that he'd need it this evening. As soon as the waiters deposited champagne, vodka, and caviar and departed, Androshka said to Orlov, "Can I leave Beijing now and move back to Moscow?"

Oh oh, he thought. "Not quite yet."

"The last time we had dinner, you told me I'd only have to stay a month. No longer. That's my limit."

He gulped down some vodka. "I was unduly optimistic. It'll take a little longer. I'm sorry. Factors beyond my control."

"Screw that!" she said in an emotionally charged voice. "I'm leaving tomorrow." She stood up and bolted toward the door.

He cut her off before she reached it. "Don't go. Please. Let's at least talk."

She relented and slumped down onto a sofa. "Zhou's a changed man since he returned to Beijing to take over the Presidency," she said. "He has no time or interest in me. In Paris, he had an amazing sexual appetite. Here, many times he can't even perform."

"He's under a lot of pressure in his job. You have to appreciate that."

"You don't understand. It's more than that. He had an Intelligence Minister, Bao Yin, whom President Li had appointed. Zhou got rid of him."

"He's entitled to select the members of his own government."

"He didn't simply remove Bao from his job. He had Bao arrested in the middle of a meeting. The next morning at sunrise, after being tortured all night, he was executed by a firing squad without a trial."

"What was Bao's crime?"

"Zhou said that he was not only incompetent, but he was a spy for the Americans. He made Zhou angry."

"How do you know all this?"

"Zhou told me. He's proud of it. Sometimes, when he gets angry, he frightens me."

Her words shook Orlov to the core. If he weren't careful, both he and Androshka would end up like Bao. But for now, he still had to talk her into remaining in Beijing. Just as she had told him about Bao, she might learn other valuable information being with Zhou. Having her on the inside was important to his mission.

"No more than two months," he said.

She sighed deeply. "I don't know if I can."

"Please, Androshka. I'm asking you to do it for me." Those were the words he used when they were growing up and he was trying to persuade her to accede to one of their mother's arbitrary commands.

She ran her hand through her hair, then finally said, "Only for you, Dimitri, but in my mind, I'm planting a calendar and I'll tick off the days one by one. If it hits sixty, I'm gone."

"That's all I ask. Now, let's get the waiters back. Time to eat."

"I have no appetite."

"You'll see the food. You'll be hungry."

Androshka called the waiters. As Orlov looked at her sad face, he realized he was playing a dangerous game, not letting Androshka leave. At some point, she might lose her temper, fly off the handle and tell Zhou what she really thought about him. Just as she had told their mother. That would be in character for Androshka. And having heard about Bao, Orlov was afraid to imagine how Zhou would react.

Washington

Sitting in the reception area outside the Oval Office, Craig thought about the three prior times he had been here. All when Brewster was President. The first, two years ago after he had thwarted a suicide bombing in Madison Square Garden planned by Al Qaeda terrorists. That day, Brewster had awarded him the Medal of Freedom. Then a year later, he was in the Oval Office on a conference call with Brewster, and they were talking to Chinese President Li, to ascertain whether Li was supporting General Zhou's effort to cut off the flow of imported oil to the United States and leapfrog China ahead of the United States in world domination. Fortunately, Li repudiated General Zhou's plot and exiled Zhou.

The third time was two weeks after that conference call. Craig and Elizabeth had exposed CIA Director Kirby and William March, the U.S. Ambassador to China, as being involved with General Zhou. Brewster had invited Craig and Elizabeth back to the Oval Office where he presented them with the Medal of Freedom, as well as Craig's daughter Francesca posthumously. He then offered Craig the CIA Director's job, which Craig subsequently declined, preferring the EU counterterrorism position.

But alas, Brewster had a fatal heart attack two months later, and there arose a new pharaoh who knew not Joseph.

Dalton, who had been Brewster's VP, had no familiarity with or fondness toward Craig. And his CIA Director, Norris, resented Craig, knowing Norris had been Brewster's second choice. Norris, the company man, was perfect to carry out Dalton's neo-isolationist policy.

Now Dalton was dead. Craig wasn't sure what to expect with Treadwell.

His thoughts were interrupted by the shrill voice of Joyce, Treadwell's secretary, whom Craig remembered from Treadwell's office on the Hill when Treadwell was Chairman of the Senate Intelligence Committee. "President Treadwell can see you now."

"Thanks for coming over," Treadwell said, as he pointed to the living area in the center of the office. Craig settled into a leather backed chair, Treadwell on the sofa across from him.

In appearance, Treadwell was California personified. Perhaps not the reality, but the stereotype. Sandy brown hair, still thick at fifty-eight, blue eyes, a good suntan, tall and lanky, with a fit look that came from being a runner. In his youth he had competed in marathons and still ran five miles three or four mornings a week.

"It's a sad time for the country," Craig said. "I'm sorry."

"Dalton wasn't President Kennedy, but it's still a huge blow. Like 9/11, it exposes our vulnerability as a free society. Somehow, we have to do a better job stopping our enemies. That's why I called you. I want you to take over the CIA Director's job."

Well, there it was, Craig thought. No beating around the bush for Treadwell.

On the long flight from Paris, Craig had a chance to formulate his response. "I'm deeply honored, Mr. President. I would be willing to take the job, but I do have three conditions."

"Only three?" Treadwell laughed. "Okay, fire away."

"First, I'd like Betty Richards, the Chief Analyst, to be my Deputy Director."

"Easy. That's your choice all the way. What's next?"

"I want to report directly to you. Not to McCormick, the Director of National Intelligence. Creating that job made no sense. I won't be saddled with a layer of bureaucracy between you and me."

"I'm okay with that," Treadwell replied without hesitation. "I plan to downgrade McCormick's job to glorified record keeping."

"Good. Speaking of personnel, you should be aware that Leeds, the FBI Director, and I clashed at the time of the Madison Square Garden incident. He called me a cowboy, and I told him he was an asshole."

"Will you be able to work with him?"

"I'll sure try."

"You should know that I don't like Leeds either, but he has powerful friends on the Hill. I'll have to wait a while to replace him. What's your third condition?"

"I want to be able to leave Langley and go into the field on an operation if I think it's justified."

Before responding, Treadwell removed a small orange rubber ball from his desk and squeezed it. "That's a biggie. You'd be a helluva a target for kidnappers or assassins."

"I would only do it in an extreme situation if I thought it was warranted by what's at stake."

Treadwell nodded thoughtfully. "I'll trust your judgment on that. But I want to be informed about what you're doing ahead of time. Not read about it in the newspapers."

"I understand."

"Now, when can you start?"

"I'd like thirty days to try and get my deputy Giuseppe appointed to my EU job. I like Giuseppe. He's a good man, and I owe it to the EU."

"I can live with that. Besides, they are our allies . . . or at least supposed to be."

Craig laughed. "Disagreements even happen among the best of friends."

"Now it's my turn," Treadwell said, "to give you my thoughts."

Craig leaned forward in his chair, listening to the President, who continued, "When you take over in a month, your first priority should be finding out which of the Islamic groups was responsible for Dalton's assassination. I not only want the perpetrators brought to justice, I want to destroy those organizations and the Jihadists who are plotting against us. Wherever they are."

Craig took a deep breath. No point concealing his belief from Treadwell. "I don't think Jihadists planned Dalton's assassination."

Treadwell's head snapped back in surprise. "Run that by me again."

"I don't think Jihadists were responsible."

"But the shooter was a Pakistani. A copy of the Koran was found in his cabin."

"Anybody could have hired him. The Koran could have been a plant."

"Then who?"

"I think President Zhou of China was somehow responsible."

"Based on what?"

Craig explained what Mei Ling had told Elizabeth.

"I have a law degree," Treadwell said. "You know how far a case based on that would go."

"I also have my own instincts."

Treadwell's eyes bored in on Craig like lasers. "What you just said worries me."

"Why's that?"

"I know about your history with General Zhou, now President Zhou. And both of your run-ins with him. Also about what he did to Francesca and to Elizabeth."

"Zhou's a despicable human being. And he hates the United States."

"All of that may be true. But he also happens to be the leader of the second most powerful nation in the world. We have to get along with him . . . I can't have my CIA Director engaged in a personal vendetta, using the resources at his disposal to gain his personal revenge."

"I understand what you're saying, Mr. President. If you want to withdraw my appointment, then . . ."

Treadwell cut him off. "Dammit, Craig. You're far and away the best man for the job."

"But I have baggage . . . which you spelled out very well."

Treadwell sighed deeply and shook his head. Craig wasn't sure what the President would do.

"Let me ask you," Treadwell said. "And think about it carefully before responding."

"Sure."

"Do you honestly believe you can compartmentalize your feelings toward Zhou and do the job as CIA Director in an objective manner?"

Treadwell certainly did have a law degree, Craig thought. That was a tough cross examination question. Craig took a full minute to weigh the issue. As he thought about it, Treadwell paced.

Finally, Craig stood up. "I do, Mr. President."

"Good. Then the job is yours."

As soon as Craig left the Oval Office, he called Elizabeth.

"Well, you didn't win a hundred euros, but I'll buy you dinner at Tosca. That's worth even more."

"He offered you the job?" She sounded excited.

"Yep."

"And you took it?"

"I decided you were right. I could make a difference."

"Alright!" She gave a victory cry.

"What are you doing now?"

"House hunting."

"But I already own a house in McLean, not far from the CIA."

"You can always sell it. We'll have more fun living in the city. Besides, I'm not the type for the 'burbs. And neither are you."

"So where are you looking?"

"Georgetown."

He laughed. "That's for the rich and famous."

"True. But you're famous. And with the royalties from my book, I'll be rich."

"Okay. See what you find. We'll talk about it when I meet you back at the Four Seasons. Meantime, I'll make a nine o'clock dinner reservation."

Craig's next call was to Betty. "We have to talk."

She met him at the greasy spoon diner they liked on Route 123, not far from the CIA headquarters.

He told her what had happened in his discussion with Treadwell. At the end, she lifted her glasses with thick lenses up on her head and said, "Damn right. Let's shape this place up."

He reached into his bag and removed the disc of the encrypted call Zhou had with his brother from Bali. He explained the background, then said, "My people in Europe haven't been able to decipher this."

"I'll get our techies on it. High priority. The highest."

"Good. Meantime, what have you learned about Dalton's assassination?"

"Not a thing. Norris froze me out. But by the time you come back to Langley in thirty days I'll have a complete handle on everything any U.S. or state agency has been able to learn. Don't worry, we'll find out who was involved."

Craig decided not to tell Betty what Elizabeth had learned from Mei Ling. He preferred to let Betty dig on her own. See what she discovered.

Treadwell had been right. Craig had a theory about Zhou and Orlov, but he needed hard evidence to back it up.

Moscow

On the plane ride from Beijing to Moscow, Orlov thought about his upcoming meeting with Kuznov and how to handle what would be a very difficult encounter. Kuznov would be angry that Orlov wasn't delivering a meeting with Zhou. Even worse, Zhou's insistence on the PGS theft before he would schedule a meeting played into Kuznov's suspicions that Zhou, with no intention of having a meeting, was merely getting Orlov to do his dirty work.

Kuznov had a furious temper and he hated being taken advantage of. All of that pointed toward a Kuznov blow-up. No way to avoid that. The question was how to diffuse it.

Their meeting took place outside of the Russian President's country house. Orlov and Kuznov were walking along a dirt trail that climbed into the hills in a wooded area adjacent to the house. Two beefy security agents were following behind far enough back so they couldn't hear the conversation.

Orlov began by recapping how he had arranged the Dalton assassination, leaving out his killing of the trucking company clerk in Pittsburgh and the fact that the Pakistani shooter's wife had seen Orlov when he went to the man's house. Those were loose ends that could lead back to Orlov. Kuznov didn't have to know about them.

Instead, in an effort to put Kuznov on the defensive, Orlov dwelled on Valerie and the fact that she refused to honor her commitment to Kuznov.

"Well it was a long time ago," Kuznov said, sounding as if he was willing to forgive her. Did the brutal spy master have a soft spot for this young American he'd slept with, Orlov wondered. Was Kuznov human after all? Kuznov continued. "But I figured you'd find a way around her unwillingness to help. Breaking into her computer was a good move."

"What have you heard from our intelligence people in Washington?"

"The Americans have bought the story that the assassination was the work of Jihadists, perhaps Al Qaeda. Using the Pakistani and leaving the Koran in the cabin were good moves. Also, they've no doubt traced the grenade launcher to one of their shipments to Pakistan. As of now, *you* are in the clear."

Orlov noticed Kuznov's choice of the word you, not we, and his emphasis on it. Distancing himself personally from the assassination.

"True," Orlov said. "And I believe we are better off with Treadwell in the White House than Dalton. So the operation achieved something beneficial from our point of view."

"Agreed. Have you spoken to Zhou since the assassination?"

Oh, oh, Orlov thought. Now comes the tough part. "I was just in Beijing. I flew to Moscow from there yesterday."

"What's the date for my meeting with Zhou? When's he coming to Moscow?"

Might as well put it on the table, Orlov thought grimly. Try to put on a positive spin. "He wants me to do just one more thing. Then he'll come to Moscow."

As Orlov expected, Kuznov exploded. "That fucking liar," he shouted. "Zhou promised you that if you assassinated Dalton, we'd have the meeting and the alliance. He has no intention of meeting with me or forming an alliance. He's just yanking me around. Mao always pulled the same crap with Stalin and Kruschev." Kuznov reached into his pocket and pulled out a cell phone. "Tell Zhou I said to go fuck himself. You can even use my cell phone."

Orlov felt like a tennis ball being slammed back and forth between Kuznov and Zhou. This wasn't what he had in mind when he forced his way in to see the Russian president at Kuznov's house along the lake. Although it was a small comfort, he recalled what his brutal taskmaster had said in KGB training. "In real life, things rarely go as planned." In an effort to mollify Kuznov and get the project back on track, Orlov decided to focus on PGS. "Let me explain what Zhou wants."

"Okay. Go ahead," Kuznov snarled.

"Have you heard of the new long-range missile system the Americans are developing? Prompt Global Strike, or PGS, they call it."

Kuznov looked interested. He put away his cell phone. "On my last visit to Washington, when Dalton took me to Camp David, he told me about it. He did it in a threatening way, telling me that just because he was pulling troops out of distant locations didn't mean the United States was dropping its guard. He explained that with the Prompt Global Strike system, the U.S. had the capability of hitting any spot on the globe, even a specific room in my country house, with a powerful bomb; and they would do that from California. 'A game changer,' is what he called the PGS weapons system."

Kuznov's words were music to Orlov's ears. "What did you tell him?"

"I said, 'Don't threaten me. If you move forward and construct this system, you'll be starting a new arms race. We'll expand and enhance our nuclear arsenal. And if you dare to unleash PGS, we'll respond with nuclear weapons against American cities.'"

"Our planes would have to get through their air defense systems."

"True."

"But if we had the PGS technology, we'd be at parity with the United States."

"Correct. As soon as I returned from Washington, I appointed Vladimir Drozny, one of our top aerospace engineers, to begin work on our version of PGS."

"How close is he?"

"Still years away. Why?"

"Zhou wants me to steal PGS from the Americans. He offered to help me by providing detailed bios for the five American engineers working on their development project in the Epsilon Unit of Rogers Laughton. Once I have those, I'll zero in on one of the five and make him disclose it. For Russia to have PGS would be an incredible boost to our military capability."

Kuznov slowed his pace. "I'm well aware of the value of PGS. What troubles me is whether Zhou will share it with us, or whether he'll keep it all for himself."

"I can understand your suspicions," Orlov replied. "But if I steal PGS, I'll be in control of the technology. I won't turn it over to Zhou until he comes to Moscow to meet with you. He'll be begging you to share it with him. You'll be in the driver's seat."

"You make it sound so easy. It won't go that way. Not with Zhou."

Orlov, now on a roll, was feeling more self-confident. "Sure there are risks. But with PGS as the prize, the stakes are now huge—the payoff great."

Kuznov stopped walking and turned toward Orlov. The security agents halted as well.

"For you, the stakes truly are huge," the Russian president said. "If you don't succeed, if I don't get the PGS technology and my meeting with Zhou, I'll have you arrested and thrown into a jail cell. And then . . ."

At a distance of twenty yards, a deer with large antlers came into a clearing and nibbled some greens on the ground.

Kuznov removed a pistol from the holster at his waist, aimed at the deer, and fired. Wounded, the deer staggered back into the forest. Kuznov fired another shot and brought it down.

"I'll come into your cell," Kuznov told Orlov. "I'll fire the gun myself. And one shot will be all it will take."

Orlov's blood ran cold. He knew that Kuznov meant it.

Beijing

President Zhou played tennis with the same incredible intensity that he did everything. Today, on a brutally hot and humid Beijing day, he was playing with a lieutenant thirty years his junior and a member of the Chinese army team. Zhou liked playing with this lieutenant. Unlike Androshka, whom Zhou easily defeated, the lieutenant was a formidable opponent. Zhou always won, but just barely. Usually six-four or seven-five. Zhou was convinced that the lieutenant took enough off his game to let Zhou win, but he didn't care. That was still preferable to losing.

The court, which Zhou had constructed in back of the president's house immediately after his return to Beijing, was red clay which he had imported from France. He had grown fond of playing on red clay at Cap d'Antibes because it was so much easier on the knees and joints. The expense involved was irrelevant.

They were in the second set. Zhou, having won the first, seven-five, was leading five-four and serving at deuce. Through the corner of his eye, Zhou saw Captain Cheng, dressed in civilian clothes, a suit and tie, approach the side of the court. Cheng sat down on a chair at courtside.

Zhou now wanted to end this match as quickly as possible. He had to find out what Cheng had learned in the United States, but he refused to stop until it was over.

Zhou hit a strong first serve to the lieutenant's backhand. The return was a short ball. Zhou moved up quickly and blasted it toward the corner. The lieutenant hit the ball in the air, firing it back directly at Zhou, who raised his racket, as much from self-defense as to make a shot. The ball bounced off Zhou's racket, hit the net cord, and landed on the other side. The lieutenant made a furious charge to get to it. Too late.

"Add in," Zhou called.

Zhou's next serve was perfect. Just nicking the center line. The return was high, coming down close to the baseline. Zhou let it bounce. Too close to call in or out with any certainty. Zhou shouted, "Out!" The match was over.

Zhou, sweating profusely, shook hands with the lieutenant at center court. "Tomorrow, same time," Zhou said.

"I'll be here, sir." The lieutenant headed toward the exit.

Zhou approached Cheng, who tossed him a towel and held out a bottle of water.

Zhou dropped his racket and collapsed into a chair next to Cheng. While Zhou drank greedily, security guards and tennis court maintenance officials moved away.

Zhou finished the bottle of water. Cheng held out another one. Zhou took it and clutched it in his hand. "Tell me about your trip."

"I had no difficulty getting in and out of the United States. I used a phony passport and wore civilian clothes, pretending to be a Chinese investor. I've just come from the airport."

"Did you meet with our American friend?"

"In San Francisco. He flew out from the east. We both stayed at the Mandarin Oriental Hotel. I'm sure no one saw me when I went to his room at three a.m."

"Good. What did he tell you?"

"First, he wanted me to pass along his congratulations to you for becoming the president of China. He would have preferred to come to Beijing and express this personally, but he thought under the circumstances, it was better not to."

"He's right about that."

"Still, he hopes to see you again soon."

"What did he tell you about Dalton's assassination?" Zhou asked impatiently.

"He said that the Americans are convinced a Muslim group, probably Al Qaeda, was responsible for Dalton's assassination. The words China or Russia have not even surfaced in Washington, and our friend has access to the highest levels in the American government."

Zhou drank some more water. "Excellent."

"But I did learn something else from our American friend."

"What's that?"

Cheng looked around as he spoke.

"Craig Page will be replacing Norris as CIA Director. Treadwell has decided on the appointment. He'll announce it any day."

"You sound concerned."

"Well I thought . . ."

"You thought wrong," Zhou said emphatically. "I'm glad Page will have the job."

Zhou was confident that if he monitored and supervised Orlov, then he and Orlov would be able to steal the PGS technology from under Page's nose. Once and for all, he would soundly defeat his nemesis. As CIA Director, Craig Page would be disgraced.

Yes, that was what Zhou wanted: to thoroughly disgrace and humiliate Page in front of his American countrymen. The whole world. Zhou had learned well one of Mao's lessons: disgrace is more damaging to your enemy then death. He must live with it and face others.

But apart from his victory over Page, Zhou would have the PGS technology. With it would come military superiority over the United States. No one could stop him from launching the war to establish China's world dominance.

PART THREE

One Month Later

Washington

For Craig, it was a great thrill to be sitting in the Director's corner office on the seventh floor of CIA headquarters with the floor to ceiling windows looking out over the bucolic Virginia countryside. He could still recall when he started at the agency and was in awe of the Director. Today was a heady experience. At eight this morning, his first day on the job, he received greetings from everyone he saw beginning with two men on the reception desk who simultaneously said, "Good morning, Mr. Director," as Craig passed through the marbled floor lobby to the elevator.

All that was fine, but now the work began.

His first meeting was with Betty.

"I'm ready for you, boss," his one-time mentor said as she entered his office, a smile on her face.

"You can call me Craig," he replied, laughing.

"Okay, now, we have to talk about the Dalton assassination."

"What have you learned?"

"I've combed through the files of all the law enforcement agencies involved," she said, as she took a seat in front of his desk.

"Good. Can you give me some bottom lines?"

"Sure. The weapon used was a grenade launcher manufactured in the United States. Based upon serial numbers, we know that it was shipped to Pakistan as a new weapon six months ago."

"A wonderful expression of gratitude on their part. Why didn't we just leave it here and save them the cost and trouble of transporting it."

"The Koran found in the cabin was published in Pakistan."

"What do we know about the assassin?"

"Man by the name of Asif Pasha. He lived in Manassas, Virginia. Moved to the United States from Pakistan about a year ago. Married. No children. To our knowledge, no known Jihadist connections. We have his wife stashed at a CIA protective house outside of Leesburg."

"How'd you manage that?"

"She wanted it. When I sent two of our agents to interview her, she refused to tell them anything about her husband but said her life had become a living hell since this happened. She couldn't go outside. People were screaming at her. Putting up signs with obscenities in front of her house—by the way, she speaks very good English. When she said, 'I have to get away from all this,' the agents called me. I told them to take her to the safe house."

"Good move."

"That evening, I went out to talk to her. She wouldn't say a word. You want to give it a try?"

"You mean the strong domineering male might succeed?"

"No. Actually, I was thinking of you as a used car salesman."

"Very funny. You want to go with me?"

"I think you're better to go alone. But don't try and bludgeon this woman. I don't think that will work."

"Okay. I'll go out this afternoon. Any success yet in decoding the encrypted message between Zhou and his brother?"

"The techies are still working on it. The Chinese are good. Our people think they'll eventually crack it, but they don't know when."

"That's what they kept telling me in Europe."

"Speaking of which, did Giuseppe get your old job?"

"I had to bring around the Germans and French, who wanted it to be one of their intelligence people. And Jacques is pissed at me. He believed the job should be his. But the answer's yes."

"Good. I like Giuseppe. Good luck this afternoon."

"Thanks. I'll need it."

*   *   *

Craig sat down in the living room of the safe house with Asif's widow, who was dressed in western clothes, a navy skirt and white blouse, her black hair uncovered. She was scowling and glaring at him.

"My name is Craig Page. I've just been appointed Director of the CIA."

"I read that in the newspaper," she responded curtly. "I should be honored that you came yourself."

Craig ignored the sarcasm. "I think we can help each other."

"I don't see how."

"I want to find out who persuaded your husband to fire that grenade at President Dalton's helicopter, and I think you do, too."

"What difference does it make to me? I had absolutely nothing to do with it. I had no idea Asif was planning to kill the president."

She paused to take a breath. From the way she said it, Craig believed her. She continued, "Yet my life is ruined. I can't live here. I can't return to Pakistan."

"But," Craig was speaking softly, "if I find out who planned the Dalton assassination, the attention will shift to them away from your husband."

"That sounds good. However, you can't possibly believe it. Asif Pasha's name will be carved into history and vilified like Lee Harvey Oswald and Sirhan Sirhan. I'm his wife. People will spit on me when I walk into a supermarket." She sounded depressed. He couldn't blame her.

If he wanted to persuade her to talk, Craig decided his only chance was to offer her a way to change her life." If you cooperate with me, I promise to relocate you with a new identity at the government's expense in California. You will be able to start a new life."

She looked at him with suspicion. "Why should I believe you?"

"I'll put it in writing."

"How do I know I can trust you?"

"I could have the paper signed by the Attorney General of the United States."

"I don't know him. This could all be a trick."

Craig was losing patience. He'd have to change his tack. "Listen, Mrs. Pasha. I can only give you my word. There are no ironclad guarantees. But right now, your situation is hopeless. Either you cooperate with me, or I'll have my men drive you home to Manassas. We'll send you right back to the people who will spit on you in the supermarket. Either you cooperate with me or face them. Take your pick."

For a moment, a heavy silence settled over the room. Finally, she said, "Put it in writing. If you sign it, that's enough. I'll take my chances."

Craig breathed a sigh of relief. Then he took a pad and pen from his briefcase and wrote out exactly what he had promised. He handed her the paper.

She was nodding. "What would you like to know?"

Craig decided not to record the conversation. He thought she'd talk more freely that way. "How did your husband get involved in this? Did he belong to a terrorist group? Did he meet someone in a mosque? Whatever you know."

"Asif was a secular man. He never went to a mosque. He despised the Jihadists."

"Could he have become religious recently?"

She shook her head vigorously.

Craig continued. "But they found a Koran in the cabin."

"It wasn't his. He never read it. He didn't own a copy."

"Then how did he become involved in Dalton's assassination?"

"I blame a cousin of his back in Islamabad."

"Who was that?"

"Colonel Khan. He's a big deal in the Pakistani military intelligence."

Craig nearly fell off his chair. A big deal, Craig thought. That's an understatement. The man's now the head of ISI. "Did Asif see the Colonel frequently before he moved to the United States?"

"For the first several years we were married, Asif rarely saw the Colonel. Then something happened. An American drone fired missiles to attack a terrorist living close to the house occupied by Asif's parents and siblings. The missile struck their house, killing all of them. Asif was enraged. I'd never seen him like that before. He began spending time with the Colonel. Shortly thereafter, we moved to the United States. Asif is a skilled electrician. He learned that in the army. He was able to get a visa to work with an electrical firm. So we moved."

Craig was getting the picture: the Colonel had planted Asif as a sleeper in the United States, planning one day to use him for a terrorist attack. So was Craig wrong about Zhou being responsible? Perhaps it was the Pakistanis who had reasons of their own to eliminate Dalton. He never concealed his hatred for them.

"Was Asif happy in the United States?"

"The only thing he was unhappy about was that we couldn't have children," she said reluctantly. "We had tests here. Something was wrong with his sperm. My husband was a good man." Her voice was cracking with emotion. "If we had a child, I don't think he would ever have done this."

She began crying. Craig handed her his handkerchief and got her a glass of water.

"What else do you want to know?" she asked.

"Did Asif communicate often with the Colonel when he was in the United States?"

She shook her head.

"In the days before Asif's death, to your knowledge, did he meet with any other Pakistanis?"

"No," she said with hesitation in her voice.

"You're thinking of something else."

"Yes. Thursday morning, the day before the attack on President Dalton, Asif had a visitor at our house. A little after seven in the morning. A Russian."

Craig was on the edge of his chair. "How do you know he was a Russian?"

"From his accent. I heard plenty of them back in Pakistan when they were at war in Afghanistan."

"Do you know what this Russian and Asif talked about?"

She shook her head again. "They went downstairs. I couldn't hear them. After they were finished, my husband said he was going away for a couple of days. He wouldn't tell me where. But surprisingly . . ." she hesitated.

"Yes?"

"When Asif left with the Russian, he had an inner calm that he hadn't since his parents and siblings had been killed. I should have suspected something."

Craig reached into his bag and pulled out Dimtri Orlov's picture which he had gotten from German intelligence. He handed it to her. "Is this the Russian who visited Asif that morning?"

She studied it for a few seconds and said, "Yes."

"You're sure?"

"Very sure. I'm good at remembering faces."

Craig felt as if he had scored a touchdown at a critical part of a game. Now he was even more confident that Zhou, who had met with Orlov in Beijing, was responsible for Dalton's assassination.

"I appreciate your help," Craig said.

"When will I be able to move to California?"

"It will take a little time. No more than six months. I promise you. Meantime, we'll keep you safe and comfortable in this house."

He wrote a telephone number on a piece of paper and handed it to her. "This is my personal cell phone number. You can call me any time."

*   *   *

From the car, he phoned Betty. "Did anyone take fingerprints in the assassin's house?"

"The FBI tested for prints in the cabin near Camp David and found only the shooter's. I don't know about his house. I'll call the FBI. I'll get right back to you."

"If they haven't, have them do it ASAP, particularly downstairs."

*   *   *

Three hours later, when Craig was back in his office, Betty charged in.

"The FBI found three sets of prints in the house. The shooter's. A woman's. Must be the wife. And an unidentified male. The FBI is running that last one through their database and state databases. I'm waiting for a call back."

Her cell rang. She put it on speaker. Craig heard. "Betty, this is Bill Harrison at the FBI."

Betty replied, "I have Craig Page with me. What'd you learn?"

"Pittsburgh, Pennsylvania police have a match. Someone strangled a clerk at the pick-up counter at Highway Shipping Lines in Pittsburgh a few days before Dalton's assassination. They haven't been able to apprehend the killer. No car license plates, although the owner of a lunchroom next door may have seen him."

Craig said, "I want the Pittsburgh police to show the lunchroom owner Dimitri Orlov's picture. We'll send it to you. I'm certain he'll ID Orlov."

"Will do."

When they hung up the phone, Craig told Betty, "So Orlov killed the clerk at the truck company. He probably asked too many questions about the package Orlov was picking up. Must have been the grenade launcher."

"Makes sense," Betty said. "The package came overland from Toronto. Listed as medical equipment. Prior to that, it came from Paris. Before that, Moscow."

Betty paused for a moment, then she continued, "I could go back in the chain, try to get some info in Moscow."

Craig was shaking his head. "Orlov's former KGB. It'll be a dead end. Besides, we don't want to tip off the Russians. Orlov must be taking orders from his former KGB boss Kuznov. "

"So what do you want to do next?"

"Fly to Islamabad. Talk to the good Colonel."

"What do you hope to learn?"

"I'm not sure. But we know the Colonel is in this up to his eyeballs. The weapons and the assassin are both linked to Pakistan."

Betty looked concerned. "That could be a dangerous trip."

"A chance worth taking. How soon can you arrange an Air Force flight for me to Islamabad? And a couple of security people dressed in civilian clothes?"

"I'll get on it immediately. You planning to report any of this to Treadwell?'

"Not yet."

"I hope you know what you're doing," she said in a concerned voice.

Washington

"My house in Georgetown," Craig said to his driver when he climbed into the back of the car at

CIA headquarters at ten thirty in the evening.

Those words had a strange ring to Craig. The only place he had lived in the Washington area was the house in McLean. But Elizabeth had pushed hard for Georgetown, telling him, "You'll be working all the time. I don't want to be stuck in the burbs. When you are around, there's always so much more to do in the city evenings and weekends."

Finally, he had yielded, using the money from the sale of the McLean house to finance Georgetown.

He realized for Elizabeth it wasn't simply the advantages of living in the city. The McLean house had too many memories for him, having lived there with Carolyn, his only wife, who died of bacterial meningitis, and his daughter Francesca, whose murder Zhou and Kirby had arranged. Ironically, he and Elizabeth first met in that McLean house following Francesca's funeral. He could understand that she wanted to start over with a clean slate and he had to move on as well.

It was almost eleven in the evening when the car pulled up in front of the house on P Street, a block east of Wisconsin Avenue. Climbing the stone steps, Craig looked up and saw lights on in the second floor room that Elizabeth used as an office study. No doubt, she was working on her book or preparing an article for the *International Herald*.

As soon as Craig entered the house, she bounded down the stairs. "How was the first day of school?" she asked.

"If you have about an hour, I have lots to tell you."

"Sure. I even cooked some beef bourguignon to show you that my time in Paris wasn't only spent writing. I'll warm it."

"Sounds fabulous."

Craig opened a bottle of Chevillon Nuit St. George, and they sat down at the dining room table.

He took a bite and said, "Hey. This is delicious."

"You sound surprised."

"Not at all."

He described his meeting with Betty, with the Pakistani assassin's widow, and what they learned about Orlov.

"Great. So you now have every law enforcement official in the country looking for Orlov."

"I decided not to do that."

"Why not? Orlov could still be in the United States."

"Even if I caught Orlov, that wouldn't give me Zhou."

"You could cut an immunity deal with Orlov."

"That wouldn't give me Zhou. I'd have the word of a former KGB agent that the Chinese President was involved. That and a quarter . . ."

"So what do you want to do?"

"If Orlov doesn't know we're on to him, sooner or later he'll surface. He and Zhou are no doubt planning to do something else. Then I follow Orlov and he leads me to Zhou."

"I guess."

He could tell she was unconvinced.

"It's our best shot."

"Does Treadwell agree?"

"He doesn't know yet."

She stopped to sip some wine. "Okay. You're going to tell him tomorrow."

"No. Tomorrow I'm going to Islamabad."

"As in Pakistan?"

"Correct. Colonel Khan, the head of ISI may have some information linking Zhou to Dalton's assassination. China and Pakistan have gotten much closer. It's possible General Zhou hatched Dalton's assassination with the Colonel, then used Androshka's brother Orlov to do his dirty work."

"Are you insane? Going alone to Islamabad to confront the Colonel with allegations that he was involved in Dalton's assassination and doing it without Treadwell's knowledge?" She raised her voice, charged with emotion. "It's madness."

"Don't hold back. Tell me what you really think."

"Your obsession with Zhou is skewing your judgment."

He thought about his conversation with Treadwell when he took the Director's job. Could he really be impartial? "I don't think so."

"At least, you should let Treadwell know what you're doing."

"I'll tell him when I get back."

"I think you're making a big mistake. You promised Treadwell that you'd keep him informed."

"I'm doing it anyhow," Craig said stubbornly.

"Because you're afraid Treadwell will order you not to go. That's why you won't tell him. Isn't it?"

"I suppose so. The opportunity is too good to pass up."

"Opportunity!" she cried out. "What opportunity? What could you possibly learn in Islamabad about Zhou's involvement?"

"The Colonel has a nasty habit of secretly recording his conversations. So if he met with Zhou, then . . ."

She raised her hand. "Stop. Given the state of relations between the United States and Pakistan, do you really think he'd give you his recordings of those conversations?"

"The Colonel likes to play both sides. That's why he's been so successful."

She was shaking her head. "It's obvious I can't talk you out of going. Still, I'll say it one final time. "You're out of your fucking mind. Going to Islamabad. You'll never get out alive."

"I'll arrange a security detail. They'll protect me."

"Protection for Americans in Pakistan is impossible. The place is a cesspool of violence. If they ship your body home, and that's a big if, I'll bury you next to Francesca."

Los Angeles

Orlov, who had entered the United States by car from Canada after a flight to Vancouver, walked into the bar at the Four Seasons hotel in Los Angeles and looked around. At seven on a Sunday evening, the place was busy. Most seats at the bar were taken and about two thirds of the tables. As he scanned the room, he saw several women who appeared to be by themselves—high class-prostitutes, he guessed. Exactly what he wanted.

He sat down at an open table and ordered a vodka on the rocks. By the time he had his drink, he decided on his first choice: a tall, busty blonde sitting three tables away, dressed in a pale pink tank top that showed half of her boobs. She had a glass of champagne in front of her, but wasn't sipping it.

Orlov noticed her glancing his way a couple of times. He picked up his drink and walked over. "Can I join you?" he asked.

"Sure. My name's Angie."

"I'm Val."

He didn't know what perfume she was wearing, but she smelled damn good.

"Where's that accent from?" she asked.

"Prague, in the Czech Republic."

She smiled, showing perfectly white teeth. "I know where Prague is. I was even there a couple of years ago on a tour of Eastern Europe."

"Did you like it?"

"Great city. I still remember that exotic clock in the tower in the old city. I met lots of nice people in Prague. What are you doing in Los Angeles?"

"I work for a bank. We're looking at some investments here. What about you? Where are you from?"

"Australia. Sydney."

"Down under."

"The end of the world is a more apt description."

"I gather you're glad to be out of there."

"You better believe it. The most overrated and provincial place in the world. Ever been there?"

"Not yet. I was hoping to get there one day, but if I spend time with you I might reassess."

Angie was a good talker. That made her even more valuable for the job.

Casually, she reached down and touched his knee. Then left her hand resting there. She had long fingernails. Polished bright red.

His plan had been to hire Angie to pick up Paul Walters, one of the five engineers in Rogers Laughton's Epsilon Unit who developed the PGS technology. But based on Walters's behavior last evening, he wouldn't be in the Marriott bar until eleven. That left Orlov almost four hours. He could easily go off with Angie and still have her pick up Paul at eleven. He couldn't remember the last time he'd had sex. And Angie was an incredible turn on. Looking down her tank top, he saw that she wasn't wearing a bra. He felt his prick stiffening.

As if reading his mind, she moved her hand over to his erection.

"Wow," she said softly. "I like having that effect on men."

"What else do you like?"

"We could go to my place, and I'll show you."

"That sounds good."

"Two thousand."

"I can handle that." He finished his drink in a single gulp, paid the bill, and followed Angie out of the bar. She was wearing an incredibly tight pair of Armani jeans. Looked like they were painted on.

She drove a white Audi convertible, top down, too fast for Beverly Hills. Seat belt on, he closed his eyes and let the breeze whip through his hair. He was in LA, baby. Ain't no place like it in the world.

Her apartment was on the twelfth floor of a luxury high-rise on Wilshire Blvd. near Beverly Glen. Business was good, Orlov thought.

When they entered her apartment, she said, "Want something to drink?"

"I don't think so. I want you now."

She held out her hand. He reached into his bag, extracted two thousand in hundreds, and handed them to her. She tucked them into a desk drawer.

"Now we can play," she said.

She looped an arm around his back and led him into the bedroom. He was standing close to the wall. She kicked off her shoes and pressed her body against him. Then she unzipped his pants, reached in and pulled out his hard cock.

"Wow," she said. "That's something. I got so wet talking to you in the bar," she whispered and nibbled his ear.

"Let me see."

She wiggled out of her jeans and pale blue silk panties. He reached down and touched her blond bush. Her pussy was soaked.

She was unbuttoning his shirt while he yanked off her tank top and played with her breasts.

"I can't wait to feel your hard cock inside," she said.

She pushed him down on the king-sized bed and removed a condom from the end table, which she slipped on him with her mouth while she stroked his balls.

"I want to ride you," she said.

"Whatever you want, honey."

She climbed on top. Sitting, she slid him inside. Then she leaned her arms back. With her hands anchoring her, she moved up and down. He watched the rising and falling of her breasts. She was moving faster and faster.

God, she was good, driving him wild. Pleasure filling his whole body. He wanted to make it last as long as possible but he couldn't. He felt himself exploding.

"Yes," she cried out. "Yes, I'm coming, too."

He was convinced she was lying, but he didn't care. She had made him feel so damn good.

She climbed off and headed off to the bathroom. He heard water running. Sated, he closed his eyes and lay back on the plush pillows.

"Can I take you back to the Four Seasons?" she said. "Or drop you somewhere else?"

He watched her putting on her clothes. She was all business now. A working girl. She had to move on to the next client. That was how she had gotten the apartment and the Audi.

"I have a financial proposition for you," he said.

"I'll listen to anything. Get dressed first."

When he came out to the living room, she handed him a glass. "Vodka on ice," she said. "I heard you order it at the Four Seasons."

He sat down in a brown leather chair facing her on the sofa. She was perfect for what he wanted. With enough money, he was confident she'd do it.

"Okay, what do you have in mind?" she asked.

He removed a man's picture from his bag and handed it to her. "His name is Paul Walters. He's in Los Angeles on business, staying at the Marriott in Century City. Last night at eleven he went to the bar in the hotel. He spent about an hour eyeing various women, but he never made a move. My guess is that he was thinking about trying to pick them up, but he's too shy, and none of them went for him.

"He's supposed to be at the hotel for three more nights. Tonight, Monday, and Tuesday. Chances are he'll be in the bar tonight. If he is, I want you to bring him back to your apartment and give him the wildest sex of his life. Stuff he couldn't even imagine. But I don't want you to accept any money from him. Make him think you're attracted to him. I'll pay you."

She looked wary. "Why are you doing this?"

"You don't have to know."

"There's more to it. What else? I don't want to end up in jail."

The woman was no dummy. "While you're having sex with him, I'll be hiding in your bedroom closet and filming it through a crack between the door panels."

She stood up, fixed herself a glass of ice water, and sat back down. "Why should I do shit like this? I'll get into trouble."

"I won't film your face. Just his."

"You're going to put this on the Internet."

"Quite the opposite. He'll want to keep it quiet. And I'll agree to do that."

She was nodding. "Okay, I get it. But it'll cost you."

"I'll pay you ten thousand in cash."

"Twenty."

He thought of negotiating with her, but decided against it. "Okay, twenty."

"Ten now, and ten when he leaves."

"If I give you ten now, how do I know you'll do it?"

"You know where to find me. I imagine you'd know how to get your money back."

"True."

"And I'll throw in a blow job when you give me the second ten."

"That's good. But wait. There's more to it."

"What else?"

"The next two nights, Monday and Tuesday, Walters will still be in Los Angeles. I want you to make dates with him for dinner and sex. Both nights. I won't be filming. Let him think you're in love with him. As the Americans say, fuck his brains out. Really get him hooked so he doesn't think tonight was a one-night stand. Tell him you'd like to see him whenever he comes to Los Angeles."

"If I have to have dinner with Walters, that means I won't be able to see anybody else tomorrow and Tuesday. My time is money. So my price goes up when somebody wants to do dinner."

"I understand that. I'll pay you six a night for each of those two nights."

"Eight."

She was a greedy little bitch. "Okay, it's a deal. Call your broker. Figure out how to invest the money."

"I only buy bonds. I'm risk adverse."

He laughed. "By the way, I want you to know Walters doesn't have any money. So don't get hooked on him. I'm the one you have to satisfy."

Islamabad

C raig's Air Force plane arrived at a Pakistani airbase outside of Islamabad. Betty had arranged with the American Ambassador to have an armor-plated, bulletproof car with a driver and two security agents take him into the city for his meeting with the Colonel. She had also arranged to have a Marine helicopter standing by at the airbase. "Just in case," Betty had told him.

"How'd you pull that off?" he asked.

"Ostensibly, in case you decide to tour Pakistani installations. They are supposed to be our ally. As you might imagine, it took a hefty payoff to the officer in charge of the base. It helped that he hates ISI and the Colonel."

Craig rode in the back with one security agent. The other rode up front with the driver. All four were constantly looking around, but Craig's guess was that if the Colonel set up an attack, it would come after his meeting with Craig, not before. The Colonel had to be curious about why Craig made the trip.

Craig had met the Colonel twice when he had been stationed in the Middle East. Both times, Craig was tracking Al Qaeda terrorists who had escaped to Pakistan. And both times, the Colonel gave them sanctuary and denied they were in the country. Not a damn thing Craig could do about it. Craig would have given anything to wipe the smirk off the Colonel's face when he mouthed the denial.

When Craig entered the Colonel's office, he saw that same smirk.

"In a strange quirk of fate," the Colonel said, "We both became the head of our intelligence agencies at the same time."

"Congratulations to you."

"And you as well."

The Colonel motioned to a chair in front of his desk and Craig sat. He watched the Colonel lean back in his desk chair, putting his feet up on the desk, blatantly showing his disrespect for Craig. "To what do I owe the honor of this visit?" Sarcasm was dripping from the Colonel's voice.

"I would like to move our relationship from mutual suspicion and animosity to cooperation."

"I don't think it's possible."

"Why not?"

"First, the United States would have to apologize for invading our sovereignty to kill Osama Bin Laden. "

Craig had anticipated the Colonel's words. He was ready with his response. "You mean after you apologize to us for giving Osama Bin Laden sanctuary and lying about what you knew about his location."

"See, I'm right. A grand rapprochement is not possible."

"Then let's start with something simple."

"What's that?"

"Your role in President Dalton's assassination."

Craig felt as if he had thrown a live grenade on the Colonel's desk. The Pakistani flinched. "We had no role," he said, raising his voice.

"Let me tell you what I know. The assassin was a cousin of yours. Asif Pasha. You arranged for him to move to the United States and become a sleeper. There, a former KGB agent, Dimitri Orlov, planned the assassination and persuaded Asif to fire a grenade launcher which you supplied."

The Colonel was gripping the arms of his chair tightly. The smirk was replaced by a grim expression.

Craig continued, "Come on. You can't be surprised that I know this. The grenade launcher had a serial number. You received it from us six months ago. No doubt you shipped it to the United States in the original crate."

"If you know everything, why did you bother to come this far?"

"Because I'm missing one piece to the puzzle. Who persuaded you to supply the weapon and shooter? Was it President Zhou or someone from Chinese intelligence?"

"I have no idea what you're talking about."

"Are you telling me it was only Orlov and the Russians?"

"This is all a fairy tale."

"I'm willing to compensate you for the information. Personally. With a considerable amount of cash. Or an electronic deposit in an account of your choice. Anywhere. No one will ever know."

The Colonel looked indignant. "I don't do business that way."

"Since when?'

Craig decided to take a different approach. "Let me lay my cards on the table. At this point, President Treadwell doesn't know about your involvement and that of your government. When I go back to Washington and tell him and key congressional people, they'll cut the funding and arms we supply to your government."

"Your president would never do that. He knows we could not defend ourselves from terrorists or safeguard our nuclear weapons. We'd have no choice but to turn to the Chinese. You can tell him that."

"They would not be as generous."

"We'll see about that."

The Colonel picked up the phone, placed a call, and phone in hand, turned away from Craig, while speaking so softly that Craig couldn't hear him or read his lips. He may be giving the order to attack me, Craig thought. But meantime, Craig took advantage of the situation. He removed a small black object the size of a button. A very powerful transmitting device and attached it to the bottom of his chair.

When the Colonel hung up the phone, Craig, though feeling frustrated, decided to take one more stab. "We can avoid all this acrimony. Just tell me about President Zhou and Chinese involvement in the Dalton assassination."

The Colonel stared coldly at Craig without saying a word.

Craig pressed on. "I know that Orlov and Zhou are working together. I need you to complete the picture."

The Colonel stood up. "If you have nothing else to say, Mr. Page, our meeting is over."

As Elizabeth had predicted, Craig had struck out in his meeting with the Colonel. His only chance was picking up something from the listening device if the Colonel called Zhou or another Chinese official to tell him about Craig's visit.

But what if he didn't? It was possible that Zhou had sent Orlov to deal with the Colonel, and the Colonel had no idea Zhou was involved. Another possibility was that Zhou hadn't been part of the assassination. Craig refused to believe that. But now Craig had another concern. If he was right about the call the Colonel had made, then the Colonel had no intention of permitting Craig to leave the country alive.

Craig climbed into the back of the car and told the three men, "Odds are great they'll be attacking us. Arms out and high alert."

Craig removed his gun from the chest holster and gripped it tightly. The two security guards did the same.

The driver started the engine. As he did, Craig pulled the audio receiver from a box concealed beneath the center arm rest. He activated the device and listened. The reception was clear. He heard the Colonel barking orders, but nothing involving Zhou or China.

They were in heavy traffic on a road leading out of town when Craig, who was both watching the road and listening to the Colonel's conversation, suddenly felt a powerful jolt from behind. He looked around and saw that a pickup truck had rammed into the back of their car. Two men jumped out of the truck and opened fire on Craig's car. The bullets bounced off.

Craig glanced through the tinted side window on the left. Two more gunmen were racing toward their car. On the right, three more were coming. Behind them, on the right, Craig saw a grassy cricket field. Cars in front had driven forward and moved to the side of the road to get out of the way of the shooting.

Craig shouted to the driver. "The cricket field on the right. Get there."

"Okay. Tighten seatbelts."

He cut the wheel hard to the right, clipping the sides of two cars and barreling toward the wooden fence surrounding the field. The driver blasted through it, scattering the wood panels.

Meantime, Craig was on his cell calling the Marine helicopter.

"We need you now," he called out.

"We're on our way. We can pinpoint your location from the tracking device we installed in your car."

"Good. We're in the middle of a cricket field."

Craig told the driver to stay behind the wheel while he and the two security agents scrambled out. Craig was holding a gun in his right hand and the listening device, which he viewed as his line to Zhou in his left.

Men in civilian clothes were running toward the cricket field and firing. Fortunately, they were all coming from one direction.

Craig and the two security agents took cover behind the bullet proof car. Using that for protection, they returned the fire. Craig counted six Pakistanis down so far, but more were coming. One of Craig's guards took a bullet in the upper arm. Craig crawled over to the man, ripped off his shirt, and tied it tightly around his arm to stop the flow of blood.

Craig glanced skyward. Where the hell was that chopper?

The other agent kept firing, but the Pakistanis were getting closer. All of them were in civilian clothes. No military or police. No doubt the Colonel wanted to say it was spontaneous. Craig resumed firing. He hit two more.

Then Craig heard the most beautiful sound in the world. The inbound chopper. The pilot put it down about ten yards from their car.

Two Marines, automatic weapons in hand, jumped out and sprayed fire at the onrushing Pakistanis. Some were hit, screamed, and fell to the grass. The others turned around and ran.

Once the firing ended, the Marines grabbed the wounded man. With Craig providing cover, they ran toward the chopper. The driver and the other security man followed.

They all climbed into the chopper which took off leaving the car alone in the field. As they flew, the Marines were manning guns, knowing well that they'd be no match for a Pakistani air force plane or even a surface to air missile. Craig thought about how vulnerable Dalton had been in his helicopter going to Camp David. Craig hoped the Colonel didn't have enough clout or didn't dare risk the response that would come if it was clear the Pakistani military killed the CIA Director. As it was now, the Colonel could apologize for those lawless elements beyond the government's control. Maybe even say it was the Taliban who opened fire.

Over the roar of the chopper, Craig held the listening device up to his ear. He heard lots of Arabic chatter, but no mention of Zhou or the Chinese.

That chatter continued even when Craig boarded the U.S. Air Force plane and took off. Then suddenly, the listening device went dead.

Craig pressed the troubleshooting button. The response was immediate. "Transmitter deactivated."

Shit, the Colonel had found the listening device and destroyed it.

Craig's mission to Islamabad was a complete failure. He didn't breathe freely again until they were out of Pakistani airspace.

After the shootout, Craig knew that word of his jaunt to Pakistan would reach the Oval Office. Craig would have hell to pay with the president.

Los Angeles

I should be a professional cameraman, Orlov thought, as he drove from the Four Seasons to the Marriott at five thirty on a chilly morning. The video was perfect and the stills he had made from it at a shop in the Valley that specialized in porn films, were crisp and clear.

Briefcase in hand, he knocked on the door of Paul Walters' hotel room.

"Who's there?" he heard Walters shout.

"The bellman. I have an important fax from your company."

"Just a minute."

The door opened. Walters, with shaving cream on his face, was dressed in a pair of boxer shorts. He was five foot eight and twenty pounds overweight, his stomach protruding over the elastic band, with thinning brown hair and bulky black glasses. Orlov knew from Angie that Walters's plane back to Washington was leaving at nine twenty this morning.

"You're no bellman," Walters cried out. He raced toward the phone. "I'm calling hotel security."

"Not a smart move, Paul. I was a witness to your fun and games with Angie Sunday night. Three times. I'm impressed. For a fifty-one year-old man, you should be proud of yourself. And then, you had a great time with her Monday and again last night. You must be exhausted."

Walters grabbed a white terrycloth robe from a chair and hastily put it on. "Who are you? What do you want?"

Orlov pointed to two chairs next to a desk. "We have to talk, Paul. You better be sitting when you hear what I have to say."

"I have a plane to catch."

"I know. You're on the nine twenty to Washington on United. You have plenty of time."

When they were both seated, Orlov reached into his bag and removed a folder and a DVD.

"This DVD," Orlov said, turning it over in his hand, "Contains a video taken from a closet in Angie's bedroom Sunday night. In the folder are some stills that I made from scenes on the DVD."

Walters appeared too stunned to speak. Orlov pressed on. He opened the folder, removed the top three photos, and spread them out on the desk, close to Walters, who was leaning forward, looking through those heavy black glasses.

In the first, Walters, naked, was standing up and Angie was on her knees sucking his cock. Her face was blocked by her blond hair. Walters' expression was contorted with pleasure.

In the second, naked Angie was on the bed on all fours, her face away from the camera, her rear end facing toward the side of the bed. Walters was standing on the floor at the side of the bed. He had entered her vagina from the rear, his hands at her waist. He had a wild expression on his face.

In the third, Walters and Angie were both on the bed. She was stretched out on her back. Her face wasn't visible. Walters' head was over her bush; he was licking her.

Orlov looked at Walters. He was as white as a sheet and trembling. Orlov hoped he didn't have a heart attack on the spot.

"I have more pictures if you'd like to see them."

Walters shook his head weakly.

Orlov continued, "Looks like you had a good time with Angie."

"What do you want, you bastard?"

"To help preserve your marriage. I know you're happily married to Claire with two children, Paul Junior at Penn and Linda at Cornell. It would be unfortunate if any of them received these pictures or the video. Even worse, if your boss at Rogers Laughton saw them and knew how you were spending time on a business trip."

"What do I have to pay you?"

"You have it backwards. I'm willing to pay you one million dollars, deposited into a Los Angeles bank so you can wine and dine Angie when you come out here. Also pay down the hefty mortgage on your Potomac, Maryland, house and cover tuition for Linda and Paul Junior."

"And in return for that?"

"I want the CDs with the technology for PGS, Prompt Global Strike. And I want them delivered to me at Great Falls in Maryland, outside of Washington, tomorrow at midnight."

Walters' jaw dropped. "You're not serious."

"Oh, but I am."

"Get the hell out! Right now! I'm no traitor."

"No. Of course not. You're just a man who made a mistake. I'm helping you avoid damage."

"And if I don't do it?"

"I'll destroy your life. I'll not only deliver these photos and the video to your wife, children, and boss, I'll put them on the Internet on aerospace sites."

Walters closed his eyes.

He's thinking it over, Orlov decided. The brilliant engineer is trying desperately to find a way out. But there is no solution to this problem. He has to give me the CDs.

Orlov reached into his bag and removed a map with a penciled x in the center. "Here's the meeting point tomorrow at midnight. You better be there with those CDs. Oh, and open a Los Angeles bank account. A soon as I have the CDs, I'll transfer the million to your bank account."

"I'll be there," Walters said weakly.

Orlov stood, then added, "Don't even think about going to the police or the FBI. I'll sense that when I approach Great Falls and I won't show. Then I'll distribute the photos and video. And if I'm caught, I'll deny everything. You don't have any evidence. Also, before tomorrow night, I'll make a copy of the photos and video. If you try to trick me, one of my colleagues will anonymously distribute them. You're up shit's creek without a paddle. So be there."

"I will," Walters replied in a faint hoarse whisper. "But I'll want all the copies of the photos and the video."

"Of course, I won't need them anymore. We'll be finished with each other."

Orlov said it with such conviction that Walters seemed to believe him. The truth, Orlov thought, was quite different. Once Orlov had the CDs, he couldn't risk leaving Walters alive.

Beijing

President Zhou sat in his office brooding. He had finished reading for the second time the report that State Security forwarded to him on Mei Ling's activities.

He was astounded to learn how close she had come to capturing the presidency when she had challenged him. He was also amazed to read the transcript of a telephone call Qin Ping, a member of the Central Committee, had with Mei Ling, prepared pursuant to Zhou's directive to record all calls which Central Committee supporters of Mei Ling conducted. The call didn't last long enough for State Security to pinpoint Mei Ling's location. Only that she was somewhere in France. But the substance of the call astounded Zhou. Ping told her that Zhou had boasted that he was responsible for President Dalton's assassination and that he planned to launch a military action against the United States.

Ping had also told her about the arrest and execution of Bao, the former Intelligence Minister. Ping had called Zhou a monster and Mei Ling promised to enlist Craig Page's help to stop Zhou.

When he finished the transcript, Zhou was spitting bullets. The nerve of those two traitors.

Though Zhou despised Mao for destroying his parents, he still had studied Mao's methods to preserve his rule. When advantageous, Zhou was prepared to emulate Mao. One thing Mao did was eliminate all of his adversaries.

That meant killing Ping and Mei Ling. In the case of Ping that would be easy. He was in Beijing. Captain Cheng could easily arrange for him to have an accident.

With Mei Ling, there was a problem. France was a large country. Zhou had to locate her. There had to be a way.

Then it struck him. She had a son in the Chinese navy who was currently at sea. He might know where his mother was.

The power of the Chinese president was awesome. In five minutes, Zhou had on the phone the Captain of the ship on which Mei Ling's son was serving.

Zhou gave the Captain an order to arrest Mei Ling's son. "I want you to interrogate him, using extreme torture if necessary, whatever it takes to get his mother's location. Then toss him overboard. Call me back as soon as you have the information."

While waiting for the ship Captain's call, Zhou studied a report Jiang Hua forwarded to him "for your eyes only," describing in detail the American PGS system and its schedule for implementation. The Pentagon was formulating a proposal to install it in California, outside of Los Angeles. Cost analyses were being prepared by Rogers Laughton.

"I need that technology," Zhou said aloud. "Orlov had better get it for me or . . ."

The intercom rang. Zhou's secretary said, "Captain Cheng is here to see you. He says it's an important matter."

"Send him in."

Cheng looked worried.

"What is it," Zhou asked."

"I was just informed by one of our military intelligence people stationed in Pakistan that Craig Page traveled to Islamabad for a meeting with Colonel Kahn, the head of ISI."

At the mention of Page, the veins began protruding in Zhou's neck. "Do we know what happened?"

Cheng nodded. "The Colonel gave our man a complete report. He said that Page has proof that Orlov was responsible for arranging Dalton's assassination. Page also has information that Orlov met with you in Beijing."

That damn Mei Ling, Zhou thought. That must be how Page found out. She must have a line of communication with him. Probably through Elizabeth Crowder. He should have killed Crowder in Marbella.

"What else did he say?" Zhou asked.

"That Page was anxious to have the Colonel implicate you in the Dalton assassination, but he refused to do that. So Page only has Orlov."

Zhou thought of tipping off Orlov, but decided against it. Orlov might break off his effort to get PGS and go into hiding. Zhou couldn't risk that.

"I want you to do two other things for me," Zhou told Cheng. "In the next couple of days, arrange for Qin Ping to have a fatal accident."

"I can do that," Cheng said. "What else?"

"I'll let you know shortly."

Four hours later, Zhou received a call from the ship captain. "Mei Ling son's broke after only mild torture. He's now food for the sharks."

"Where is his mother?"

"Paris, France. Room 610 at the Hotel Burgundy on Rue Duphot."

Zhou gave Captain Cheng the information about Mei Ling's location. Then he added, "After you dispose of Qin Ping, I want you to go to Paris and kill Mei Ling."

Great Falls, Maryland

Expecting it to be deserted at midnight, Orlov had selected an observation point adjacent to the Potomac River for his meeting with Walters. The air was unseasonably cool after two days of heavy rain. A full moon shone between the clouds.

Orlov had learned long ago that people in Walters' position sometimes do foolish things. He had to make certain Walters didn't enlist the aid of the police or the FBI. Orlov arrived in the area an hour early and parked fifty yards from the observation point. No other cars were in the lot.

Orlov climbed a rock and flattened himself down out of sight. With night vision binoculars, he had a clear view of the gazebo in the observation point as well as the surrounding area. He couldn't see anyone. No signs of a trap. Whew, he let out his breath with a sigh of relief.

He focused on the river. With the recent rain, the flow was fast. Orlov checked his watch. Forty minutes to midnight. He removed a chocolate bar from his pocket and ate it. Then he waited.

Thirty minutes later a dark blue Toyota pulled into the parking lot for the observation point. Through the binoculars, Orlov watched Walters, wearing a navy windbreaker with zipper pockets large enough to hold CDs, exit the car and walk slowly and hesitantly toward the gazebo. Orlov waited five more minutes to make certain no one else came. Walters was sitting alone on a bench in the gazebo. Satisfied, Orlov climbed down the rock and headed toward Walters. Orlov was holding a cell phone in his hand. He planned to tell Walters that as soon as he had the CDs with PGS he'd use his Swiss bank's automatic transfer system to send the money to Walters' account. He had no intention of doing this.

As soon as Orlov stepped into the gazebo, Walters stood up on the dirt floor. With his back toward the river, Walters was facing Orlov.

"Give me the PGS CDs." Orlov said. His jaw was set tight, his eyes bearing in on Walters like lasers.

"I didn't bring them," Walters replied, his voice quavering.

"If you're trying to hold me up for more money, you're playing a dangerous game."

"It's not that."

"What's the problem?"

"I don't want to do this."

"You don't have a choice. I'll deliver the photos and videos to your wife. To Linda at Cornell and to Paul Junior at Penn. Also your boss at Rogers Laughton. I'll put them on the Internet."

Hunched over, Walters looked away from Orlov's relentless stare. "I'll take the humiliation. Rather than be a traitor."

"No, you won't. That's not an option. Tomorrow morning, you'll get the CDs. Then we'll meet again tomorrow night, right here at midnight."

"No. I won't do it," Walters said, straightening up.

Orlov hadn't anticipated this response from Walters. His face displaying a cold fury, Orlov moved in close to Walters. But Walters didn't cower.

Orlov slipped the cell phone into his jacket pocket and pulled out a hard black rubber truncheon. "I'll beat you with this. Not on the face so anyone can see, but on your stomach and your genitals. I'll beat you until the pain is so great that you'll think you're going to die. You'll never have sex with Angie or anyone else again. Then you'll agree to get the CDs. Or I'll go up to Philadelphia and beat your son the same way. I'll destroy your manhood. Then I'll destroy his."

When Walters didn't respond, Orlov raised the truncheon in his right hand high above his head. "This is your last chance."

Still, Walters remained mute. Orlov lunged for him, trying to grab Walters with his left hand. At the same time he pulled back his right arm to swing the truncheon.

Orlov was concentrating on aiming his blow. He never saw Walters' foot viciously swinging at his groin until it was too late. A muddy, black-pointed shoe smashed into his balls. Orlov almost passed out. He gave a loud cry. "Au...Au..." He dropped to his knees.

"You'll pay for this, bastard," Orlov growled.

Expecting Walters to race for his car, Orlov, in excruciating pain, was too stunned to react immediately when Walters turned and bolted for the river. Orlov crawled, then staggered after him, but he was too slow. In horror, he watched Walters standing at the edge of the swiftly moving muddy river.

Orlov removed a gun from his pocket. "Don't do it, Paul," he called. "You'll drown."

Walters ignored Orlov and plunged in. Orlov fired, but had no chance of hitting Walters.

Orlov went up to the edge of the river. In the moonlight, he saw the current tossing Walters around and carrying him fast. He was bobbing up and down. Going under. Not coming up.

Shit. He's a dead man, Orlov thought. And I may be as well, when I have to explain this to President Zhou.

Washington

President Treadwell looked angry. Real angry, Craig thought.

"When I appointed you," Treadwell said to Craig, "people told me that you were a cowboy and a loose cannon. I thought they were exaggerating, but after what I heard from General Thomas about what happened in Islamabad, I realize they were right."

It was eight in the morning. Craig and the President were alone in the Oval Office. Treadwell had summoned Craig for a briefing about his trip.

"Dammit," Treadwell continued. "You should have told me about it ahead of time."

Craig thought about Elizabeth's warning. Time to suck it up. "I'm sorry, Mr. President. I was wrong. I won't do it again."

"And you expect me to believe you?"

"Please. I mean it. I hope you will."

"Humph." He shook his head in dismay. "Okay, now tell me about this sudden trip of yours to Pakistan."

Craig took a deep breath and began talking. "I now have almost a complete picture of who was responsible for Dalton's assassination."

Treadwell sat up straight. "Go ahead."

"A former KGB agent by the name of Dimitri Orlov approached the Pakistani shooter, Asif Pasha, took him to the cabin near Camp David, and supplied him with a grenade launcher. Asif was a cousin of Colonel Kahn, the head of ISI, who planted him in the United States after one of our drones accidentally killed Asif's parents and siblings. Orlov hid the Koran in the cabin; it didn't belong to Asif, who was a secular man. The grenade launcher was supplied by Colonel Kahn. It was manufactured in the United States, shipped to Pakistan, and never used by the Pakistanis."

"And you can prove all of this?"

"Yes, Mr. President. Most of the information I got from Asif's wife. She identified Orlov as the man who came to see her husband."

Treadwell's face was taut and red. "For all the money we give those fucking Pakistanis, this is what we get."

"With all due respect, Sir, these are the people who hid Osama Bin Laden."

"Humph. You said that you had almost a complete picture."

"That's right."

"What are you missing?"

"I don't know who was pulling Orlov's strings: Russian President Kuznov, Chinese President Zhou, or both of them."

"What makes you think Zhou was involved?"

"Orlov had a meeting in Beijing with Zhou a little over a month ago. Before Dalton's assassination. No doubt arranged by Orlov's sister, who is Zhou's mistress."

"You're certain of that?"

"Yes, sir. When I was still in Paris in my EU job, Betty Richards, who knows of my interest in Zhou, told me that Wayne Nelson, our CIA Station Chief in Beijing, reported that Zhou met with a Russian by the name of Dimitri Orlov. I obtained Orlov's bio from German Intelligence. I was worried that Orlov might be planning a terrorist attack in the United States so I called Norris, offered to give him Orlov's photo and bio, and asked him to circulate it to all border entry points. That way we could pick up Orlov before he entered the United States."

"And Norris told you to go pound sand?"

"More precisely, he told me where I could stick the photo and the bio."

Treadwell's face was beet-red with rage. "That explains why Norris went off the deep end after Dalton's assassination. He must have realized that he could have avoided it. That Dalton would still be alive."

"I'm afraid that's right. Orlov was the linchpin for this Zhou-Kuznov operation."

"So why don't we find this Orlov, arrest him, and make him tell us whom he was working for? Is he still in the United States?"

"I don't know."

"I should call Leeds at the FBI and have him launch a full-scale manhunt. Do you have a photo or fingerprints?"

"Both. Orlov also killed a trucking agent in Pittsburgh when he picked up the grenade launcher. His prints were on the man's throat. The owner of a lunchroom next to the trucking company remembered seeing Orlov in his place right before he killed the trucking agent."

Treadwell reached for the phone. I can't let him do that, Craig thought.

"Can we discuss this a little more, Mr. President?"

"Okay." Treadwell let go of the phone.

"Orlov's a former KGB agent. It's extremely unlikely that he'll talk. A better approach might be not to let him know that we're on to him. Chances are Orlov, Kuznov, and Zhou will do something else. Then we may be able to catch all of them with their hands in the cookie jar. At that time, you can take firm action."

"Suppose I agree with you. What do I do about Pakistan?"

"Let's hold on them, too."

Treadwell raised his arm and rested his head in his hand. "I don't know, Craig."

There was knock on the door. The president's secretary entered, holding a note. She walked over and gave it to Treadwell. He nodded and picked up the phone. Craig heard Treadwell say, "Absolutely, Bill. I'll see you in ten minutes. I'll have Craig Page with me."

As the secretary left the Oval Office, Treadwell put down the phone and turned to Craig. "We'll have to table our discussion about Dalton's assassination. Bill Merritt wants to talk to me about an urgent matter of national security. You know Bill?"

"I've never met him, but I know he's the CEO of Rogers Laughton Aerospace. Our largest defense contractor."

"Bill's also a good friend. I got to know him well when I was a senator from California. Even though their headquarters is in Gaithersburg, Maryland, up the I-270 corridor from Washington, they have several large facilities in California. At the time, Bill was based in Rogers Laughton's Los Angeles office with the job of Director of Strategic Planning. After that, he became the CEO and moved east. He's very much of a hands-on leader."

Treadwell removed a small orange ball from the desk drawer and squeezed it. "I'm having circulation problems," he told Craig, as if an explanation was needed. "Doctor Lindsay, my primary doctor, says it's no big deal. Goes with the stress of the job. If he thinks it's anything more, he'll send me to Bethesda Naval for a cardio workup. Anyhow, Rogers Laughton is working on our most important military contract."

"Prompt Global Strike," Craig said.

"Exactly. Nothing is more vital than PGS. Rogers Laughton finished the development work here in Gaithersburg. Dalton never moved forward with implementation. One of the first things I did as president was to give the green light to move aggressively with installation at Vandenberg Air Force Base in California. Construction of parts will be done at one of Rogers Laughton's Los Angeles area plants. I hope to hell Bill isn't having a problem with PGS."

The intercom rang. Treadwell picked up and told Craig. "Sorry, I have to take this. You can stay."

For the next ten minutes Craig listened while Treadwell argued and cajoled the House Speaker about budget issues. Craig was relieved that he and Treadwell had gotten off the subject of Dalton's assassination and Craig's trip to Pakistan.

As soon as Treadwell put down the phone, there was a knock on the door. His secretary opened it and Bill Merritt walked in. The pictures Craig had seen didn't do justice to the fit looking, tall, trim fifty-five year old with a thick head of brown hair who was known for his outdoor exploits: mountain climbing, kayaking, and triathlons.

"Thanks for agreeing to see me, Mr. President," Merritt said.

"Forget the Mr. President, Bill. I already told you to call me Ed."

"Sorry. This office is intimidating."

"To me, too," Treadwell said and smiled. "I want to introduce Craig Page."

Merritt was holding a briefcase with one hand. He shook Craig's with the other. "I've heard a great deal about you, Craig."

"I hope you didn't believe it."

Treadwell chimed in. "He's even worse than you heard. He owes his life to one of your helicopters which whisked him out of Islamabad yesterday. Right Craig?"

"Yes, sir. I do."

Treadwell pointed to the living area in the center of the office, and three of them sat down. Merritt began. "Ed, I know you're familiar with our PGS work. Craig, how much do you know about it?"

"I've read a fair amount."

"Good. Then our starting point is that the technical development work for the system was done by five brilliant engineers: four men and one woman. The smartest people in our company, in a special group called the Epsilon Unit based here in Gaithersburg. The Unit is in our R&D Division, headed by Bruce Colbert, retired Air Force General, our VP for Science and Technology. Last night one of the five, Paul Walters, died under mysterious circumstances."

"What happened?" Treadwell asked.

"At about five this morning, someone found his body washed up along the banks of the Potomac, not far downstream from an observation point at Great Falls. Walters lived in Montgomery County, which is where his body was found. The Montgomery County Police immediately went to his home and notified his wife, Claire. As you might imagine, she was very distraught, but she showed them a handwritten note Paul had left on the kitchen table. He apparently slipped out of the house while she was sleeping."

"What did the note say?" Treadwell asked.

Merritt removed a tablet from his briefcase and turned it so Craig and Treadwell could see the screen. The note said: "Claire: Please know that I love you, Paul Junior, and Linda, even though I've done something stupid. An evil person is after me. But I'd never betray my country. Love, Paul."

"So it was suicide," Treadwell said.

"Looks like it, but here's another wrinkle. Once the Montgomery County Police found out from Claire Walters that her husband worked for us on a top-secret national security project, they called the FBI, who sent two agents to the area. The FBI agents found in the gazebo, just upstream from the point at which Walters' body landed, fresh footprints of two men. One matched Walters. The prints showed evidence of a struggle. Also there were fresh tire tracks from two cars nearby."

"So Walters met someone in the gazebo," Craig said.

"That seems logical. I got a call from FBI Director Leeds about half an hour ago. He has agents headed out to Gaithersburg. They want access to Walters' office and everything he worked on. We can't possibly permit that. This is all top-secret information. I have no idea what clearance these people have. So I told our security people at headquarters to admit no one other than employees. Not even police or FBI. Then I called you."

Treadwell resumed squeezing his hand. "I'm glad you did. Let's establish one ground rule right now. Walters note and his work establish that this is a national security matter. I want Craig to go out to Gaithersburg and conduct the investigation at your facility. No one else."

"Good," Merritt said. "What do I tell Leeds and the Montgomery County Police?"

"You don't. I'll call Leeds and tell him. The FBI and the County will focus on Walters' house and the Potomac River. Craig is handling your facility in Gaithersburg."

Craig was sure Leeds would scream when he got the order. The man was always trying to expand his turf. And Craig was right. Though Treadwell didn't put the call on speaker, Craig heard Leeds' surly voice on the phone. After listening to his pleas and rants, Treadwell said, "I'm the President, and that's how it's going to be."

When Treadwell put down the phone, Craig said to Merritt, "Have your security people made an investigation?"

"Good question. That's where I was going next."

Jim Paxton, retired Army Major, is the head of security. Claire Walters called him as soon as she learned about her husband, and Paxton called me. The critical PGS technical information is contained on a set of CDs maintained in a metal lined vault in our Gaithersburg headquarters. Those CDs could be duplicated. However, access to the vault is strictly limited to certain specified individuals. Walters is one of them. But to do so, he'd have to pass both fingerprint and iris ID. Each entry to the vault is automatically recorded. Time and date."

"Did Walters enter the vault recently?"

"Paxton told me that he entered it yesterday. His last prior entry was two weeks ago. Last Sunday, Walters went to Los Angeles for a business trip to work with our plant people about PGS implementation. He returned from Los Angeles Wednesday evening. Thursday, yesterday, he was in the office and he did enter the vault at ten fifty a.m. He remained in there for thirty-three minutes."

"Long enough to copy the CDs," Craig said. "And deliver them to whomever he met at Great Falls before that individual pushed Walters into the river."

"But he didn't do that," Merritt replied firmly.

"How do you know?"

"With my approval, about six months ago, Paxton installed a hidden camera in the vault that constantly films the room. Except for the technician who installed the camera, no one else knows about it."

"What's it show for Walters' entry yesterday?" Treadwell asked.

"Paxton forwarded the key portion of the tape to my computer."

Treadwell looked amazed.

"Although we build airplanes and missiles," Merritt said, "We're basically a high tech company."

Merritt placed the screen between Treadwell and Craig. The video depicted Walters entering the vault. He walked over to a metal cabinet that had "CDs" on the front. He punched in two numbers of a code. He was preparing to punch in a third. Then he stopped. The cabinet door remained closed.

Walters walked away from the cabinet and sat down in a chair. He put his head into his hands. He appeared to be crying, his body shaking.

Merritt said, "You can continue to look if you like. But Walters remained this way the rest of the time he was in the vault."

"I've seen enough," Treadwell said.

Craig nodded and said, "So whoever Walters was meeting expected him to bring the CDs, and he didn't. Then either that man pushed Walters into the Potomac, or he jumped when he realized they wouldn't leave him alone and probably had a way to blackmail him."

"That's pretty much what I thought," Merritt said.

"Makes sense," Treadwell said glumly.

"What do you want to do in Gaithersburg?" Merritt asked Craig.

"Talk to Walters' boss, Bruce Colbert. Also, the four other people in the Epsilon Unit."

"I want you to be in charge of that investigation," Merritt said. "Not Colbert or Paxton. It has to be someone outside the company. We can't risk bias that could influence the results. Give me your email address. I'll forward the bios of the other people in the Epsilon Unit to you, as well as Colbert's. Also Walters. You can read them in the car on the way out."

Craig gave Merritt his email and cell phone contacts.

Treadwell said, "Send the bios to me as well."

"Will do," Merritt said. "Whoever Walters was involved with may contact one of the other four. We have to let them know."

"I agree," Craig replied. "I will do that."

"Remember," Merritt cautioned, "these people are brilliant scientists, but quirky people."

"Thanks. I'll tread carefully. What about the media? To your knowledge, have they gotten hold of the story yet?"

"I don't think so. I asked Leeds to impose a media blackout. Also, I asked Jane Porter, the Chief of Police in Montgomery County, with whom I have good relations, to do the same. Is there anything else I can do?"

Craig shook his head and looked at Treadwell who said, "Thanks Bill. We now have everything. I'm grateful for what you've done. We'll keep you in the loop."

Merritt rose to leave. Treadwell turned to Craig. "Will you stick around for a minute before you go to Gaithersburg?"

"Sure."

When Merritt had gone, Treadwell said to Craig, "You won't like this, but I'm setting up a Task Force to deal with the issue. The first meeting will be here in the Situation Room at six this afternoon. I'll ask Leeds to come and report what he's learned. I'll want you to do the same. Jeannie is in the Middle East, so I'll get someone else from State. The Chairman of the Joint Chiefs and a rep from DOD."

Treadwell was right. Craig didn't like the idea of committees, but he knew opposition was futile. Treadwell was the President.

Craig had something else on his mind. As he thought about what Merritt had said, he was rapidly concluding that the other shoe had dropped in the Zhou, Orlov, Kuznov operation. This effort to obtain PGS must have been engineered by Zhou using Orlov and Kuznov. This time, Craig would nail the Chinese President.

As Craig stated toward the door, Treadwell said, "I know what you're thinking."

"What's that?"

"You believe this is another scheme developed by President Zhou."

"You're a very good mind reader, Mr. President."

"Actually, I won't argue with you. China has the most to gain from having PGS. It fits with their rapid military buildup."

"And the most to lose if we have it, and they don't."

"Then you have to make sure they don't get it."

Gaithersburg, Maryland

Once the car pulled away from the White House, Craig yanked out his laptop. He focused on the bios with photos Merritt had forwarded: Bruce Colbert and the five members of the Epsilon Unit.

Colbert, an Air Force Academy graduate in engineering, had been an Air Force General in charge of R&D who retired five years ago at the age of fifty and stepped right through the revolving door to assume his present position at Rogers Laughton. His Air Force career had been exemplary. Nothing stood out in his bio.

The three other men in the Epsilon Unit, Darrell Perkins, the Unit's Director, Gus Morse, and Roy Slater, had similar backgrounds. All PhD's in aeronautical engineering, the first two from MIT; the third from Georgia Tech. All three had joined Rogers Laughton after receiving their PhDs and rose through the ranks of the company's R&D division. Darrell and Gus were in their forties. Roy was thirty-nine. All three were married with children. Nothing in their bios jumped out at Craig.

When he finished reading Roy's bio, Craig asked himself: "What am I looking for?"

Then it struck him. He had to get ahead of these people. He couldn't simply be reacting. He had to put himself in their heads.

Walters didn't turn over the CDs, so their likely next move would be to approach another member of the Epsilon Unit. To catch them, Craig had to place one of the other members of the Epsilon Unit out as a dangle, hoping someone approached the dangle to get the CDs. Certainly a high-risk operation for the member of the Epsilon Unit, but Craig was convinced this was his best shot.

As he turned to the remaining member of the Epsilon Unit, Jill Morgan, Craig thought that selecting a woman would be advantageous. It would totally change the dynamics. But she had to be right for the role.

Looking at Jill's picture, he was stuck by how much she resembled Elizabeth. Similar facial features. Another brunette, although with shorter hair. Good-looking, but not beautiful. She had an athlete's figure accompanied by a serious, intense look.

He expected that Jill would be another PhD in aeronautical engineering, but all she had was a bachelor's degree in computer engineering from the Air Force Academy, where she had graduated first in her class having gotten an A in every course. She also had a photographic memory, the bio said. Jill was Air Force all the way. Her father, a pilot, was shot down over Vietnam and died in a POW camp. Following graduation from the Academy, she became a pilot, flying F-16s for two years. Then she developed Meniere Syndrome, an inner ear problem, which grounded her. She was assigned to an Air Force R&D Unit at Edwards Air Force Base in California.

A year later, Jill married Hank Morgan, also a pilot. They had one child, Tracy. When Tracy was eight, Hank's plane was shot down by Afghan insurgents, and he died in the crash. Immediately after that, Jill left the Air Force and joined Rogers Laughton. That was four years ago.

The bio also said that Jill had expertise in martial arts and boxing, which she acquired in high school. When she was a freshman at the Air Force academy on a date, a classmate tried to rape her. She beat him up and walked away. Two nights later, three cadets attacked her planning to gang rape her to avenge their buddy. First she kicked two of them in the head so hard they lost consciousness. The third came at her with a knife. She took it away from him, then yanked down his pants and informed him she planned to cut off something and shove it in his mouth. Before she could do that, two upperclassmen, who happened to be in the area, raced over and pulled her off. In response, she organized the female cadets into a group called "The Sisterhood," and convinced the administration to arrange martial arts training for members of the group.

Jill is Elizabeth's soul mate, Craig thought. Both brilliant and tough. From her bio, she sounded as if she would be perfect to be the dangle.

Craig's cell phone rang. It was Bill Merritt. "Bad news," Merritt said. "WTOP Radio had the story of Walters' death. With the espionage implications, I'm sure it'll be on the networks and CNN in minutes."

"Shit!"

"My sentiments exactly."

"What'd they say?"

"I'll read it from my computer. One of the PR people at the company sent it to me."

"Go ahead."

"Paul Walters, a top engineer at Rogers Laughton, died this morning. His body washed up on the shore of the Potomac downstream from Great Falls. Police are investigating the cause of death. Walters was engaged in classified work for the U.S. government."

"Whoever leaked it knew what they were taking about."

"Any guesses?"

Craig's instinctive reaction was to suspect Leeds because the FBI Director was angry at Treadwell for taking him off the critical part of the investigation. Craig decided not to share that with Bill Merritt.

"I don't know," Craig said. "I'll inform the President."

"He won't be happy."

"You're right about that. But he's been around long enough to know that Washington leaks like a sieve."

Dulles Airport

Orlov was anxious as he sat in a restaurant at Dulles Airport. It was nine thirty in the morning, and he was waiting for his plane to San Francisco where he was scheduled to connect to Beijing. He dreaded the idea of having to explain to Zhou what had happened with Walters and that he would not be able to get the PGS technology, but he knew that he had to do it in person.

Zhou had control over Androshka. Trying to avoid the Chinese president would put her at risk and Orlov didn't want to do that. Orlov not only loved his sister, but he felt responsible that she was still in Zhou's clutches. If it weren't for Orlov cajoling her, Androshka would have left Beijing and returned to Moscow.

He sipped some awful tasting, watery black coffee. Why couldn't Americans make decent coffee?

Orlov raised his head and glanced at the TV above the bar, set to CNN. Paul Walters' picture appeared on the screen. Orlov nearly flew out of his chair.

He moved close to the set so he could hear the announcer. "Walters, an engineer with Rogers Laughton, was engaged in highly classified work for the U.S. government. The cause of death is unknown. Police and the FBI are investigating . . . In Egypt, the government continues to battle Islamic protesters . . ."

Orlov returned to his seat. All he could think of was Angie.

Once she saw Walters' face on the television or in a newspaper, she'd freak out. She'd be panicked that she'd be implicated in his death. And she'd be right. It was only a matter of time, and not much, until the FBI got to Angie. She would tell them how a man claiming to be a Czech banker had arranged everything. She would provide a description of Orlov, which the FBI artists would convert into photos for distribution around the world. Somebody in Europe would undoubtedly recognize Orlov. And even if he managed to avoid arrest and extradition, he'd have Kuznov's fury to deal with.

Don't involve Russia, Orlov had told him. That also meant: don't get caught. Suddenly, an operational failure had turned into a disaster.

Angie was a loose end that couldn't be tolerated. He had to take care of her. As he thought about it some more, he realized that he had been stupid, not planning to deal with Angie even before Walters' picture was on the television.

When Walters had surprised him by jumping into the Potomac, Orlov had panicked. He hadn't slept at all last night. And he hadn't been thinking clearly.

He went to the men's room and splashed cold water over his face. "Get a grip," he told himself.

He knew what he had to do. He went to the United Airlines customer service desk and changed his flight to one to Los Angeles; then Beijing that evening.

Fortunately, it wasn't even seven o'clock in Los Angeles. Angie would still be sleeping. Orlov called her cell and woke her.

He told her what she'd see if and when she turned on the television.

Sounding groggy, she said, "Run that by me again."

So he repeated it. At the end, he said, "Don't worry," trying to sound reassuring. "Nobody knows about you."

"Don't worry?" she shouted hysterically. "Jesus, that's easy for you to say. You won't become a household joke. Having your picture flashed around the world on the Internet and YouTube."

"And nether will you."

He had to make sure she didn't do anything rash. Like go to the police or the FBI to bargain for anonymity. "Listen," he said. "I'm about to board a plane to Los Angeles. I'm bringing you a million dollars in cash. You'll be able to go home to Australia for a while until this blows over."

"A million dollars in cash." She had calmed down.

"Yes, all in hundreds. I have them in my suitcase."

"Okay," she said sounding mollified.

"Meantime, call the airline to book your flight to Australia this evening, but stay in the apartment until I get there."

"And what do you suggest . . ." she was raising her voice again, "I do when the FBI knocks on the door?"

"Those people never move fast. I'll get there before that happens. Don't worry. I'll take care of you."

Gaithersburg, Maryland

Craig was greeted in the white and black checkered marble floor lobby of the Rogers Laughton headquarters building by a heavyset woman, mid-forties, with short black hair, wearing a dark brown suit and white blouse.

"Hi. I'm Wendy Greene, the company's General Counsel. Bill Merritt asked me to make sure you get everything you want."

He imagined she had a nice smile. But not today. She looked somber. This was a serious matter for the company.

"Thanks, I appreciate that."

"Bruce Colbert, I should say General Colbert, because that's what he likes to be called, our VP for R&D, is waiting in a conference room upstairs. I figured the three of us should talk first. Then you can decide how you want to proceed."

"Sounds like a plan."

Craig, who was accustomed to forming instant judgments about people, took a liking to Wendy. That was offset by the dislike he took to General Colbert. He was a tall, imposing figure, barrel-chested with lots of gray hair and blue eyes that bore in on Craig. He was seated at the head of the conference room table and didn't bother to stand when Craig walked in with Wendy, who made the introductions.

Wendy poured coffee for herself and Craig.

Once they were seated, Colbert, looking stern, said, "Bill Merritt asked me to hold off talking to the other members of the Epsilon Unit until you arrived, Craig. So I did that." He sounded annoyed. Then he continued. "However I've isolated all four of them in separate offices. I've taken their cellphones and cut off their landlines. Also no computer access. As you might imagine, their anxiety levels are high. One of their colleagues is dead. Maybe even murdered. I think it's critical to learn whether any of them have been approached by the people whom Walters was involved with and what, if anything, they told these people. I intend to keep them separate and question them one at a time while hooked up to a polygraph."

Craig couldn't believe Colbert. He was not only arrogant, but adopting a ridiculous counterproductive approach. He wasn't running an Air Force unit. All he would do is alienate the other members of the Epsilon Unit whose cooperation was critical and whose loyalty he had no reason to doubt. As far as learning whether anyone had contacted them, Craig believed that he was a good enough interrogator to determine that in informal questioning. Craig realized he was about to make an enemy in Colbert. But he didn't care. Merritt had told Craig he was in charge of the investigation.

"I don't want to do it that way," Craig said.

Colbert looked at Craig in disbelief. The General wasn't accustomed to having people disagree with him. "How then?"

"We'll bring the four into this conference room. I'll make a brief statement. Then I'll take them off one at a time for separate one-on-one conversations. I've found that's the best way to get people talking in a situation like this."

"I want to be present in those interviews," Colbert said.

"That would be a mistake," Craig replied, politely but firmly. "You're their boss. It wouldn't work."

"You may think that, but I'm still in charge of the Epsilon Unit. I'll decide how we do it."

Wendy broke in before Craig had a chance to respond. "I'm sorry, General Colbert," she said respectfully, "but Bill Merritt said that Craig is in charge. We're doing it his way. If you don't agree with that, we can get Bill Merritt on the phone."

The lawyer carried the day. The general became red-faced and looked ready to spit nails, but he didn't say a word.

After this outburst, Craig considered barring the general from the group meeting, but decided he could get what he wanted from the one-on-one interviews.

Wendy said, "I'll have someone get the four members of the Epsilon Unit."

Moments later, Craig watched them file in, dressed casually in slacks and jeans with sports shirts. No suits and ties for this crew. They took seats at the conference table as Wendy made the introductions. Craig tried to read their body language: they were all scared. And being introduced to the CIA Director, not surprisingly, did nothing to allay their anxiety.

Craig stared at Jill. In person, her resemblance to Elizabeth was even more striking.

Wendy began, "Craig is here at the request of President Treadwell and Bill Merritt. Craig, do you want to take it from here?"

I have to level with these people, Craig decided. They're too smart to mislead. He remained seated. Speaking softly, he said, "Paul Walters died last night . . . under mysterious circumstances. His body entered the Potomac at Great Falls on the Maryland side and was swept up on the rocks a couple of miles downstream. Cause of death appears to be drowning. At the time he went into the water, we believe someone was with him. Another man. We don't know whether Walters jumped in or was pushed."

Craig's eyes moved from one of the four Epsilon engineers to the other. He could guess what they were thinking: was Walters a spy for a foreign government? Did he disclose PGS before it was installed in the United States? Jill was the closest to Craig. He saw goose bumps on her arms. All too horrible to contemplate. But what else could explain Walters' death?

Craig continued, "At this point, we don't know whether Walters was working for another country, foreign individuals, or a competitor of Rogers Laughton. The answer may be none of the above. Our best information is that someone wanted him to turn over the CDs for PGS, but he didn't do it."

Craig sensed a collective sigh of relief. "In order to round out our information, I'll be talking with each of you. One-on-one. Informally. No tape recorders. Nothing like that."

He glanced at the General, who was fuming. "Before we do that," Craig added, "do any of you have questions?"

Darrell asked, "Are we being suspected of espionage?"

Craig answered. "None of you is being suspected of anything. As I said, we want to understand what happened to Walters and whom he may have been involved with outside the company."

Darrell followed up. "Then can we get our cell phones back and use the company's phones?"

Colbert responded. "Not until we conclude our investigation."

"Some of us have personal issues," Darrell replied.

The others looked angry.

Craig had to head this off. "At two o'clock, everybody gets their phones and computer access back unless I learn something from one or more people that suggests this would be unwise."

Roy said, "Should we get a lawyer before we talk to you?"

Wendy responded in a kindly voice. "I honestly don't think that's necessary. As Craig said, none of you is suspected of anything. Speaking for Bill Merritt, I hope you'll cooperate with us."

Craig admired how she said that. The subtle, unspoken threat that failure to cooperate would put a black mark on your employment record.

Jill said, "I have a twelve-year-old daughter. She has a baseball game at three this afternoon. I was planning to attend. Can I still do that?"

"Absolutely," Craig said.

Gus spoke up. "If we wanted to, could we leave the building now?"

Through the corner of his eye, Craig saw the General planning to jump in. Before he had a chance, Wendy said, "Of course. This is your place of employment. Not a prison."

That evoked nervous laughter. Wendy added, "If you get calls from the press, I would urge you to pass them along to me so I can have the company's press people respond." Then she turned to Craig. "Why don't you start with Darrell. He's the Epsilon Director. I've reserved conference room E, three doors down the hall."

Darrell had a shaved head and thin, wire frame glasses. He was 6'2" and skinny. Craig noticed that his fingernails were bitten down.

"Thanks for agreeing to talk with me," Craig said.

Darrell shrugged. His expression conveyed: what choice did I have?

Craig decided not to take notes. He'd remember anything significant. He didn't want to risk intimidating them. If he needed formal statements later, he could get those.

"How long have you been the Director of the Epsilon Unit?"

"About two years. Ever since it was formally organized. The five we have now—I mean four, since Paul Walters is dead—are the group we started with."

"How well did you know Walters?"

"Just as a work colleague. We don't socialize as a group outside of work. Jill spent the most time with Walters because they often traveled together to California in connection with the implementation of PGS."

"Did you ever observe anything in Walters' behavior that, as you think about it now, might make you believe he was involved with a foreign government?"

Darrell thought about the question for a moment. Then he said, "Nothing."

"Did anyone ever approach you about divulging information?"

"Absolutely not."

Craig spent the next ten minutes going over some of the same ground with Darrell with different formulations. At the end, he was convinced Darrell was telling the truth and didn't know a thing.

Craig's questioning of Gus and Roy followed the same pattern as Darrell's. Then he was ready for Jill.

"What position does your daughter play in baseball?" he asked.

"Pitcher. I missed the last couple of games. I really want to go today."

"That won't be a problem. I played football in high school and college. It always meant a lot when my dad came."

"Where'd you play?"

"Quarterback for Carnegie Mellon. Not exactly a football powerhouse."

"Quarterback is still quarterback."

Jill had a nice way. He was impressed with how she overcame her nervousness to talk casually with him.

"Paul Walters," Craig said. "How well did you know him?"

"In Gaithersburg, we both worked in the Epsilon unit. We didn't socialize. In the past six months, we've taken three trips to California together. We were the only ones from the unit. We stayed at the same hotel. Not surprisingly, we spent time together. Some breakfasts. Dinners, too."

"When was your last trip?"

"This week. And I'm really glad to talk to you about what happened with Paul. I wanted to tell someone."

"Why don't you start at the beginning."

"We had meetings scheduled in Los Angeles Monday and Tuesday related to the installation of PGS. One of our California plants is doing the construction at Vandenberg Air Force Base. Paul and I were supplying the knowledge of the system and the technical input to aid in the installation. I flew out Sunday evening. Paul said he wanted to fly out Saturday. We returned together on a Wednesday morning flight."

"Why'd he want to go Saturday?"

"He didn't say. I didn't ask. We were both staying at the Marriott in Century City. I called his room when I got in Sunday evening to suggest meeting for breakfast, but he didn't answer. He called me at seven the next morning and we met."

"Did you notice anything peculiar about his behavior in Los Angeles?"

"Actually, yes. Based on our prior trips, I expected to have dinner with Paul and perhaps plant people Monday and Tuesday. But both evenings, he said he had other plans and we should go without him. Then Monday evening, we had a mild earthquake in Los Angeles about two a.m. I called Paul's room to make sure he was alright. No one answered. He also seemed a little tired, sluggish, during the meetings. I chalked it up to jet lag. But then he slept on the plane almost all the way home."

"What'd you think then?"

"When I put it all together, I decided Paul was seeing someone. A woman in LA, which really pissed me off."

"Why?"

"Because he's a married man, and his wife was back in Maryland. I was on the receiving end of this adultery shit. I would have divorced Hank once I found out, but he never came back from Afghanistan."

Craig agreed with her deduction about Walters. He must have been seeing another woman and Craig's guess was that's how he had been recruited: the honey trap.

Craig asked her: "In LA, did you see Paul with any people you didn't know from the company?"

She shook her head.

"Did anyone approach you to discuss PGS?"

"No one."

"Do you have any basis for believing that Paul may have been involved with a representative of a foreign government?"

"None at all."

"Did Paul discuss with you his going to Great Falls last evening?"

"He didn't say a word. But speaking of going, I'm scheduled to present a paper next week at an international aerospace conference in Las Vegas. I'll cancel that if you think I should stay here."

"No need to do that. What's your paper about?"

"Accuracy of long-range missiles. But of course, I won't be divulging any secrets. Only summarizing publicly available information."

"Your country means a great deal to you, doesn't it, Jill?"

"Absolutely. That's why I wanted more than anything to be a pilot. To follow in my father's footsteps. He was a hero in the Vietnam War. I wanted to do the same. To serve my country. Hey, the United States isn't perfect. But it's a helluva lot better than any other place in this world."

"I couldn't agree more."

"I figured as much or you wouldn't be in your job."

"Anything else you want to tell me?"

"Yeah. I hope you find the bastard who sucked Paul into this. Who found some pussy to ring the bell of this dull, nerdy, middle-aged engineer who was a decent human being." Her voice had an emotional edge. "As you can tell, I really have a hatred for spies."

"Based on what, if I can ask."

"I loved my father a lot. I learned many years after his death, when I did some digging as a student at the Air Force Academy, that someone had given the Vietcong his flight plan. Nobody knew who. But that's why he was shot down and subjected to years of torture in a POW camp before he eventually died. So I'll do whatever I can to help you."

As she left the room, one thought kept running through Craig's mind: this woman would be perfect to be the dangle.

But he couldn't raise it at the six o'clock Task Force meeting at the White House. If he did, Leeds and perhaps others would find a thousand ways to kill an idea that wasn't theirs. The "not invented here" syndrome. Instead, he'd have to sell it to Treadwell after the meeting. The members of the Task Force would learn about it later.

He couldn't risk one of them disrupting his plan.

Paris

Sitting in her room on the sixth floor of the Hotel Le Burgundy on Rue Duphot in Paris, Mei Ling was terrified. She had scheduled times for telephone conversations with her son, who was at sea with the Chinese navy, but he hadn't called today. Under normal circumstances, an adult son failing to call his mother wouldn't be cause for alarm.

But these weren't normal circumstances. Ever since she had tried to coerce Zhou, who was then head of the Chinese armed forces, to appoint her son commander of the Chinese navy in return for her silence regarding Zhou's plan to cut off the flow of imported oil to the United States, Mei Ling realized that she had let Zhou know how much she cared for her son. That evil bastard would have deduced, now that he was in power, that killing her son was a way of gaining revenge against Mei Ling for helping to thwart his Operation Dragon Oil and for challenging him for the Presidency. And she feared that's what he had done.

Mei Ling grew weary of staring at her cellphone, resting on the desk, waiting for it to ring. She picked up the phone and called her son's cell. The call went into voice mail. She tried again ten minutes later. Same result. And a third time, ten minutes after that. More voice mail. Her mother's intuition told her something terrible had happened to him.

With trembling fingers, she dialed the cell of Qua Ping, her close friend and ally on the Central Committee. She explained the problem to Ping, who had known her son from birth. "What ship is he on?" Ping asked.

"The Empress of China."

"I'll make some discrete calls for you. Stick by the phone."

An hour later the phone rang. It was Ping.

"Well," she said anxiously.

There was a pause. Then a cough at the other end of the line. She feared the worst. Finally, she heard, "I spoke with one of the top naval commanders, whom I've known for many years, and who was a friend of your husband's. While he kept me on hold, he called an officer on the ship. After a few minutes, he told me there had been an accident."

Her hand was wet with perspiration. "What kind of accident?"

"He said that your son slipped on the deck and went overboard. He drowned. I'm so sorry."

A bloodcurdling scream spewed out of Mei Ling's mouth.

"I pressed him to tell me about the accident. At first he wouldn't say anything. Finally, he told me that Zhou had ordered the captain to have your son killed. That's all he was able to learn."

Mei Ling screamed again. "No . . . No."

"I'm sorry."

"One day I'll make Zhou pay for this."

"You have to find a way to come back to Beijing and take the Presidency from him. That would be your revenge."

"Believe me, if I ever have the chance, I will."

"Opposition is growing against Zhou for his increasingly outrageous behavior. Business colleagues have told me that even Zhou's brother is upset."

She thanked Ping and hung up the phone.

Her grief was too overwhelming to bear alone. She had to tell someone, but in Paris she had no one. If she called someone in China, they might press her about her location.

Elizabeth. That's who she'd call. Elizabeth would not only be comforting, but she'd tell Craig. He was now CIA Director, Mei Ling had read. It would give the Americans one more example of Zhou's outrageous behavior. One more example of why this venal man should be ousted from his position.

With tears running down her cheeks, she picked up her cell phone and dialed Elizabeth.

Please help me, Elizabeth. Help me!

Washington and Los Angeles

Craig was in the car riding from Gaithersburg to CIA headquarters when his cell phone rang. It was Elizabeth.

"Mei Ling just called with horrible news."

"What happened?"

"Zhou arranged her son's death. Her only child. He was in the navy at sea."

Her words cut through Craig like a knife reminding him that Zhou had killed Francesca, his only child. "That seems to be what Zhou is good at—killing children."

"She really wants us to find a way to get rid of Zhou."

"I'm working on it. Believe me I am. I have my own score to settle with that bastard."

He explained to her about Walters' death, what he had done in Gaithersburg, and the Task Force meeting. "The PGS business may be a way to snare Zhou, but it won't be easy."

"Please, do what you can."

"Oh, I will. You can count on that. I just have to survive dealing with that asshole Leeds."

"I know what you think of him, but you better take it easy with Leeds at the meeting. You don't suffer fools easily, but you don't want to lose credibility with Treadwell. I imagine that he already skewered you today over your little jaunt to Islamabad."

"Let's just say he wasn't happy."

"I'm not sure you want to piss him off twice in the same day."

"Thanks, Mom."

"You know I'm right."

"Maybe, I should take two Valium before the meeting."

"Either that or a beta blocker."

"Okay. Okay. I got it. I'll behave. How about a nine o'clock dinner this evening at Tosca?"

"Sounds good. I'll meet you there."

*　　　*　　　*

At five minutes to six, Craig entered the Situation Room and looked around. Already seated at the heavily polished conference room table were Air Force General Braddock, Chairman of the Joint Chiefs; Colonel Rhodes from DIA; Ed Grayson, Secretary of Defense, and P. J. Hennessey, the Deputy Secretary of State for National Security Affairs sitting in for Secretary of State Jane Porter, who was in the Middle East. Missing was George Leeds and anyone he might be bringing from the FBI. And of course President Treadwell. The President never entered the room until everyone else was there. That was protocol.

*　　　*　　　*

Orlov was wheeling a black rollerboard suitcase when he entered Angie's apartment. He saw three large suitcases piled up in the entry way. Angie was dressed in a gray designer suit, hair tied up in a bun.

"I took your advice," she said. "I booked a flight to Australia."

"When is it?"

"Eleven thirty this evening. That was the next one. I got a seat in first class. Nonstop to Sydney."

"Great. We have time to go to bed. One more fuck for the road."

"Do you have my million dollars?" She sounded anxious.

"Of course," he patted his black wheelie suitcase.

"Can I see it?"

"You don't trust me." He sounded annoyed.

"Please, just a little peek."

"To hell with this. I'm taking my money and leaving."

He reached for his bag.

"No. No," she pleaded. He was standing close to the wall. She leaned against him, forcing his back against the wall. She opened her jacket and pressed her breasts against him. Then she unzipped his pants, reached in and pulled out his cock. The instant she got her hands on it, his prick started to swell.

"You're right," she said, running her fingernails along the shaft. "We have to take care of him first. The money can wait."

He left the suitcase in the living room and let her lead him by his cock into the bedroom.

*   *   *

At ten minutes past six, Craig decided that Leeds was coming late to emphasize his importance. A moment later, the FBI Director filed in with a smug expression on his face, followed by a good-looking young woman carrying a computer. Craig was struck by how short Leeds was. He doubted if the FBI Director broke the five foot line, even with his platform shoes. Leeds' assistant, whom he introduced as Maureen, dropped the screen along one wall for a PowerPoint presentation. A minute later, Ralph Donovan, the president's Chief of Staff, entered the room long enough to make sure everyone was there. Then he left to bring the President.

Treadwell began. "I appreciate all of you coming on short notice. I'm going to let Craig Page, who's chairing this Task Force, tell you what this is about.

Craig glanced at Leeds whose lips were pursed together and whose face was turning red.

"This morning," Craig said, remaining in his seat, "Paul Walters, an engineer with Rogers Laughton, was found dead along the Potomac just below Great Falls. Walters was a member of Rogers Laughton's Epsilon Unit which developed the Prompt Global Strike system, PGS. As I'm sure you're all aware, PGS is our most sensitive and most critical new weapons system."

Time to be a team player, Craig thought.

"George Leeds and I split the investigating work. I went to the company's headquarters in Gaithersburg. George focused on the Great Falls area and Walters' house. We want to summarize what we've learned. Bottom line: my opinion is that Walters was recruited in Los Angeles this week by a representative of a foreign government. But he did not turn over the CDs with the PGS technology."

Craig decided to keep his theories about Orlov, Kuznov, and Zhou to himself. At this point, they were still supposition. "I don't know who did the recruiting or which government is involved. I believe the recruiter, let's call him R, used a woman to snare Walters. The old honey pot."

Leeds jumped to his feet. "Craig, I'll take over at this point."

Craig held out his hand.

Leeds signaled to Maureen working the computer. On the screen flashed a picture of a jigsaw puzzle with some pieces together, others scattered.

"Thus far, *I've* managed to put together a major portion of a complex puzzle."

The next slide read, "FACTS."

Then a puzzle piece with the words, "DEATH OF PAUL WALTERS."

Listening to Leeds, who was aiming his talk at the President, Craig recalled that the FBI Director had no idea Merritt had briefed Treadwell and Craig this morning. And he never called to exchange information before the meeting. Should be real interesting to see how he spins the story.

"What we know for certain," Leeds said, "is that Paul Walters drowned early this morning in the Potomac River. His body washed up on rocks half a mile downstream from the point where his car was parked at Great Falls. From the tracks and footprints, we've established that Walters met another man in a gazebo at an observation area in the location. No evidence to determine whether Walters was pushed or jumped into the river. No marks on his body to indicate a struggle."

"Unfortunately, the story of his death has already been in the media," the President said irritably. "I hoped you would have imposed a news blackout."

"We tried, Mr. President," Leeds said. "We did everything humanly possible. We believe the leak came from the Montgomery County police."

Good old George, Craig thought. Always steps right up and blames someone else.

"Too bad," the President said, emphasizing his displeasure with a wave of his hand.

"We're investigating the source."

"Lot of good it'll do us now. What else do you have?"

Leeds' face was becoming flushed. "Meantime, we've made certain that the official story is that Walters drowned, and the police are investigating."

"Okay. Next."

Up on the screen flashed a puzzle piece with the words, "ANGIE RYAN."

Leeds continued. "FBI agents obtained two critical facts from Paul Walters' wife, Claire. First, that Paul returned home Wednesday evening from Los Angeles. Thursday, he opened a Los Angeles bank account. His wife learned this from a voice mail a clerk of the bank left at their home. When she asked Paul about it, he told her it would be convenient because he expected to be spending lots of time in Los Angeles on business. Claire Walters became suspicious and checked through the items he brought back from Los Angeles. In his shaving kit, she found a small piece of paper concealed in a zipper compartment with a Los Angeles phone number. She turned that number over to our agents. We established that it is a cell phone for a woman by the name of Angie Ryan."

The next slide appeared. A busty blonde in a skimpy bikini.

"This is Angie Ryan." Leeds sounded proud of himself for digging this up. "The photo is from her escort website. We have her address on Wilshire Boulevard. I have agents in Los Angeles prepared to question Angie Ryan, but I asked them to hold up until after this meeting."

"You did what?" Craig blurted out.

"I asked them to hold up . . ."

"I heard you, but why?" Craig was raising his voice. "Once Angie saw Walters' picture on the television, she could have gotten scared or run away. Christ, whoever used her to recruit Walters could have killed her. You've got to move up on this woman right now. Interview her and take her into custody."

Leeds looked flustered. "I will right after this meeting."

Craig couldn't stand it. "No. Dammit it. Now. Leave the meeting and give the order to your Los Angeles agents."

Treadwell was nodding. "Craig's right."

Leeds yanked the cell phone from his pocket and left the room.

*　　*　　*

"You're the best," Orlov said to Angie.

Naked, they were on her bed. He was stretched out on his back. Her head was between his legs. She was sucking his cock.

"I can't believe it," he said. "I already came once and you've got me hard again."

She pulled her head away. "For a million dollars, you're entitled to the best."

"I want to be on top this time."

"Whatever you want."

She lay on her back and spread her legs. He climbed on top and slid right inside.

"Oh God. That feels so good," she cried out. "Yes. Right there. Please. God. Right there."

He doubted if she felt a thing. But he didn't care. He was moving back and forth inside of her getting a rhythm. He was straining. Sweating. The second time was always difficult. Drops of sweat were falling onto her chest. Her eyes were closed. At last, he felt himself coming. As he did, he clutched her neck, grabbing her tightly with his hands.

She opened her eyes.

"Hey, what are you doing?" she cried out.

He was squeezing tighter and tighter. She tried to yell, but he had cut off her vocal cords. She twisted, straining to get away, but he was too strong. She swung her arms but the blows bounced off his body without any impact.

At last, she was still.

Calmly, he pulled away from her dead body. He dressed, grabbed his suitcase and left the apartment.

Riding down in the elevator, he felt satisfied. He had accomplished his mission and had some fun. How could she have been such a fool to think he would be giving her a million dollars? Or even that he had it in the suitcase. Looking away from the doorman, he walked through the double glass doors onto Wilshire Blvd. toward his car parked a block away. As he did, two unmarked black sedans pulled up in front of Angie's building. Four men jumped out of each. Orlov heard one shout to the doorman, "FBI. Move aside."

You're a little late, Orlov thought

*   *   *

After placing the call to Los Angeles, Leeds returned to the Situation Room.

"FBI agents are on the way," he said meekly and sat down.

General Braddock, the Chairman of the Joint Chiefs, asked Craig, "How certain are you that Walters didn't turn over the CDs with PGS?"

Craig replied, "Let me show you what I base this conclusion on."

He put on the screen the video of Walters in the vault at Rogers Laughton which Merritt had shown him and Treadwell this morning.

At the end, Braddock said, "I'm satisfied."

Hennessey interjected. "Which government do you believe is behind this?"

"That is the sixty-four thousand dollar question. Unfortunately, I have no evidence pointing to anyone."

Hennessey followed up. "You think it's Iran?"

"Certainly a good candidate."

"Let me play the devil's advocate," Hennessey said. "Isn't it possible that all of this involved only Walters' love life? A middle-aged man having a fling. So before we go off on a witch hunt that damages our foreign relations, shouldn't we eliminate that possibility?"

Craig couldn't believe Hennessey. This was typical State Department bullshit.

Calmly, Craig replied, "The presence of a second man at Great Falls negates the romance-only possibility."

"That makes sense," Treadwell said. "But let's be fair to Craig. He hasn't even had this for twelve hours."

Leeds' cell phone rang with a piercing noise. All eyes turned toward the FBI Director.

Craig heard him say in a pathetic voice, "Yes . . . Yes . . . I understand . . . Strangled . . . body still warm. Get prints and forward them to Washington." He hung up the phone and said sheepishly, "Angie is dead."

That was too much for Craig. His promise to Elizabeth went out the window. Leeds' stupidity had cost them their only hope for blowing this open. He shot to his feet and screamed at Leeds. "You fucking idiot. How could you have done this? You're so busy puffing yourself up with your cute little slide presentation, with pieces to a puzzle and ass-kissing the president that you didn't do your job."

The president was on his feet as well. The other seemed stunned.

"That's enough, Craig," Treadwell said. "Angie's dead. We'll move on from here. Anyone have anything else?"

No one said a word.

"Good, we're finished," Treadwell said.

The president left first, heading toward the Oval Office. Craig raced up and fell in alongside. "Could I please talk with you privately," he said in a calm voice.

Treadwell looked angry. "To apologize for your behavior?"

"That and to tell you some things about the Walters matter that I couldn't say in the meeting."

"Okay. Meet me upstairs in the living quarters in thirty minutes."

While waiting to go upstairs, Craig called Betty and told her what had happened in the meeting. At the end he added, "When the FBI gets those prints, call someone over there and have them forward the prints to you."

"You figure they'll be a match for Orlov?"

"I'd bet my house on it. I just want confirmation."

"Will do. And I won't tell a soul."

"Good. I'm afraid I made an enemy for life."

"Don't worry about it. Leeds never liked you before this. He'll destroy you if he has the chance."

Washington

C raig found the president in the White House living quarters, sitting on a sofa, his shoes off, a drink in his hand. "Fix yourself one," Treadwell said, pointing to the bottle of McCallum's on the credenza. "You need it."

Craig poured two fingers of scotch in a glass and added some ice.

"You better start with the apology," the president said sternly.

Craig took a belt of scotch. He felt like a school boy called to task by the teacher. "I was horribly wrong, Mr. President, to scream at Leeds that way. Regardless of what happened, there was no justification for what I did."

"I hope you mean it. Really, I do. For your sake. And for the sake of our relationship."

"I do. It will never happen again. I assure you."

"You mean I don't have to sign you up for anger management counseling?"

Treadwell smiled.

That was good, Craig thought. "No sir. That won't be necessary."

"Look, I know Leeds is an ass. I'm appalled by what happened today. If I could fire him, I would immediately. But for political reasons, I can't. I'm stuck with him for this term. I also know you didn't like the idea of the Task Force, but I have to build a consensus on tough issues like this. "

"I understand."

"And one other thing I want you to understand is that if you and I are going to work together, you'll have to level with me. Tell me what you're thinking and what you're doing. Will you be able to do that?"

"Absolutely. I do want to have that kind of relationship with you."

"Okay. I'll let the trip to Pakistan go, but I won't do it again. And I'm willing to put your behavior at the meeting behind us."

"Thank you, sir. I appreciate that."

"What do you want to talk about?"

"First, the Walters matter. I'm waiting for fingerprint ID, but I'm confident Orlov killed Angie."

"Based on what?"

"Strangling is part of his MO. He did it to the clerk in Pittsburgh in connection with the Dalton assassination.

Treadwell sighed deeply, "If you're right, this confirms that we're dealing with the Orlov, Kuznov, Zhou group again."

"Exactly."

"But how the hell can we catch Kuznov and Zhou?"

"I start with the premise that Zhou and his partners really want PGS. They didn't get it from Walters so they'll try again. This time we don't wait for them and be reactive. We take the lead. Select another member of the Epsilon Unit and put that person out as a dangle. Zhou and his partners will make a move to get the PGS CDs from the dangle, and we catch them."

The president finished his drink in one gulp. "It's dangerous. You better pick the right man to be the dangle."

"Actually, I want to use a woman . . . if she'll do it."

"I read the bios Bill Merritt forwarded. You mean Jill Morgan?"

Craig nodded. "I like the idea of using a woman. It changes the dynamic. Also she's the only one who could do it. The other three are nerdy engineers. They would crumble under pressure. Jill's not only brilliant but tough enough for what we'd be exposing her to."

Treadwell stood up. He looked woozy and grabbed an end table for support. Alarmed, Craig sprang to his feet. Treadwell waved him down. "I'm fine. Just a little light-headed. I get that sometimes with the new medicine Doctor Lindsay prescribed to deal with my circulation problem."

Treadwell walked around the room for a few minutes, then turned to Craig, "I agree with everything you've said, but I won't let you use Jill."

Craig was flabbergasted. "Why not?"

As he sat down, Treadwell said, "She lost her father serving the country. She lost her husband that way too. She's paid enough of a price. Also, she's a single parent with a twelve year old. We can't subject her to this . . . and I won't."

Craig decided to try another approach. "Jill's very patriotic. Perhaps we should give her the choice."

Treadwell was shaking his head. "She probably would say yes, but that's not the issue. It's a question of humanity and decency. Do you understand what I'm saying?"

"I do. And I can't disagree. I just don't like the result."

"Nor do I. The idea of a dangle is a good one. Reevaluate those three male nerdy engineers and pick one of them."

"Will do," Craig said glumly.

"Anything else?"

"Yes sir, there is."

Craig told the president that Zhou was responsible for killing Mei Ling's son. "I wanted you to know about it."

"You think it's related to the Walters matter?"

"No. Just one more example of Zhou demonstrating that he's a monster."

"I know that, but let me ask you something? If we ever found a way to get Zhou out of the Chinese presidency, any chance we could help Mei Ling move into that position?"

"Now that's a helluva good idea."

"Occasionally, I come up with one."

Craig reddened. "I didn't mean that."

With a grim expression, Treadwell ignored Craig's words and said, "Make it happen."

*   *   *

Craig felt depressed as he rehashed for Elizabeth what had happened. They were having dinner at Tosca. The restaurant was crowded, but the tables well-spaced, letting them talk as long as they kept their voices low. She was eating grilled baby octopus; Craig a delicious rack of veal.

"The President's right about Jill," Elizabeth said.

"I know it."

"Tell you what. When we get home, give me the bios of the people in the Epsilon Unit. I'll look at them. Maybe one of the three men will be okay."

"You weren't listening. What you'll find is that Jill would be perfect for the job. The three men would be a disaster."

"Okay. Okay. I hear you, but I still want to look for myself."

"Did I ever tell you that you're stubborn."

"Coming from you, that's the supreme compliment."

When they reached the house, Elizabeth took the bios into her study. Craig was planning to unwind in the bath when his cellphone rang. It was Betty.

"You were right," she said. "We got a match on the prints. Orlov strangled Angie."

"Good. Now we have confirmation that Zhou and Kuznov are behind the Walters affairs and the attempt to steal the PGS."

Craig hung up the phone and ran in to tell Elizabeth. After he did, he noticed that she was holding Jill's bio and staring at it. "Now do you agree with me on the four Epsilon people?" he asked.

"Absolutely. The three men wouldn't work. Jill would be perfect."

"Yeah. Well, Treadwell counted her out."

"That's true. But he didn't count me out."

Craig knew immediately what she was thinking. "No. There is no way I'll let you become the dangle, pretending to be Jill Morgan. Forget it."

"Why not?"

"Because I said so."

"That's not an answer. It's the perfect solution. The two of us have enough of a physical resemblance. I'd have to get my hair cut. Touch up my eyebrows. Use makeup to get rid of some of my lines . . ."

"The answer's no. I won't expose you to that."

"You think I'm not as tough as Jill. I may not have beaten up Air Force cadets, but I fought with a thug from the Taliban and won. Not to mention what I've done with you the last couple of years."

"I love you and care about you. Don't you understand that?"

"And you don't care about Jill?"

"Not in the same way. Of course not."

"Dammit, Craig. Don't be so pigheaded. You've exposed yourself to all kinds of danger to get Zhou. Remember your attack in Bali."

"I know, but . . ."

"Besides, I have my own score to settle with Zhou. He held me as a prisoner in a dungeon in that awful house in Marbella. Apart from my own motives, this country and the world can't afford to have Zhou as president of China. And certainly not in possession of PGS. He has to be stopped. I care about my country, too. There's no other way to bring down Zhou."

He sighed deeply. Sat down on the sofa, closed his eyes, and thought about what she'd said. Unfortunately, she was right on everything. "Okay, I'll present it to Treadwell in the morning . . . on one condition."

"What's that?"

"Nobody can know, other than you, me, Treadwell, and Jill that you're out there doing this rather than Jill. In other words, we tell the Task Force that it's really Jill as the dangle."

Elizabeth looked puzzled. "What's worrying you?"

"I don't trust Leeds. I'm convinced he leaked the Walters story to the press. After today, he hates me even more. He'd disclose that we're using a dangle and that it's you, not Jill, just to get at me. That would put you at greater risk."

"You think he's that evil and vindictive?"

"I do."

"Alright. Present your condition to Treadwell along with the proposal."

Washington and Gaithersburg

At eight on Saturday morning, Craig walked into the Oval Office. Treadwell was waiting for him behind the large green leather-topped desk, empty except for a cup and saucer.

"I have some news, Mr. President," Craig said.

Craig told him about the match of the fingerprints on Angie's neck and those of Orlov.

"So you were right. Now we know what we're up against. We have to get that dangle out there. Have you decided which of the three men to use?"

Craig coughed and cleared his throat. "Actually, sir, I have another idea. Are you familiar with Elizabeth Crowder?"

"Sure. She's your whatever. That newspaper reporter who helped you stop Zhou's plot to halt the flow of imported oil to the United States. President Brewster told me about her after he gave her the Medal of Freedom along with you and Francesca. Brewster said she was clever and feisty. His words."

"Well, she looks a lot like Jill Morgan and . . ."

Treadwell cut Craig off in mid-sentence. "I love the idea of passing Elizabeth off as Jill and using her as the dangle."

Breathing a sigh of relief, he replied, "It was Elizabeth's idea."

"Good for her."

"I have only one condition."

"What's that?"

"We don't tell anyone. Not even the task force. As far as they will know, we're using the real Jill Morgan."

Craig didn't want to share his concern about Leeds with the President. So he simply added, "Less risk to Elizabeth that way."

Treadwell squeezed his hand. He'll agree to it, Craig thought. And he did.

"What'll you do with the real Jill? Hide her?"

"I'm still working on that."

"How soon do you want to get started?"

"Now that you've given me the green light, Elizabeth and I will head out to Jill's house and tell her."

*   *   *

Jill lived in a modest two-floor red brick colonial in a subdivision about two miles from Rogers Laughton headquarters. When Craig had called to say he wanted to come out with a friend and meet with her, she had replied, "Sure. I'm just sorry Tracy won't be here to meet you. She's at baseball practice."

When they walked toward the house, Jill came out to meet them. She was dressed in white shorts and a powder blue tank top. Craig had to remind himself that this suburban looking mom was a top aeronautical computer engineer and a former fighter pilot.

The sprinkler was running on the front lawn. It was a gorgeous summer day, bright sun, low humidity, one of the few Washington has every year.

Inside, Jill poured coffee and they settled in the living room. The end tables were cluttered with models of United States Air Force planes. Her father's Medal of Honor hung above the fire place next to a picture of him in his Air Force uniform, standing beside his plane.

Elizabeth broke the ice, telling Jill that she, too, had been a baseball pitcher. "As a girl, I had to fight like hell to pitch for my all boys high school team. It didn't matter how many strikeouts I had. The hardest part was getting accepted."

Jill laughed. "Nothing's changed. I hope you'll meet Tracy sometime. Maybe you can give her some tips."

"I'd like that."

As they were talking, Craig was thinking: how do you tell someone you want to take over their identity? With Jill, he decided to lay it right out and use President Treadwell for support. Craig had no idea how Jill would react.

"I had a meeting with President Treadwell yesterday afternoon. I told him how helpful you were in the interview, and he said to express his appreciation." Jill was smiling.

Craig continued. "The president believes, and I concur, that we have to catch whoever recruited Walters before they find a way to obtain PGS and do damage to the country."

"I couldn't agree more."

"We've settled on a strategy. We want to put a dangle out there, hoping the people who recruited Walters will try to recruit the dangle. Then we can catch them."

"And you want me to be the dangle."

Craig raised his eyebrows. She had cut to the bottom line fast. "You're close. We want Jill Morgan to be the dangle, but Elizabeth to pretend she's Jill Morgan."

Jill was frowning. "Why do that? I can be the dangle . . . I want to be the dangle," she said forcefully.

"Actually, it was President Treadwell's decision."

"But why?"

Craig could tell Jill was upset. When all else fails, he had learned long ago to tell the truth. "The president believes strongly that you've sacrificed enough for the country. Losing a father and a husband in the line of duty. You're a single parent. He won't expose you to the risk."

"Perhaps I could speak with President Treadwell personally."

"The President was quite firm in his conclusion."

Jill winced, but didn't argue. Treadwell was the Commander in Chief. In her military training, Craig knew she'd learned to accept the commander's decision even when she disagreed.

"Okay," she said albeit reluctantly. "How will this work?"

"You told me yesterday that you have a speech scheduled at an international aerospace conference in Las Vegas next week."

"That's right. I'm planning to fly to Vegas on Thursday morning. My speech is scheduled for Friday morning."

"Is the conference being widely advertised among people in your field?"

"Absolutely. It's one of the top two annual conferences. This one draws the largest international attendance. "

"Is there any way you could get the group to put out a blast of publicity announcing your presentation?"

"All it would take is a sizeable contribution by Rogers Laughton to the Association."

"Good. I'll talk to Bill Merritt and have it done."

Jill was staring at Elizabeth. "You kind of look like me."

"I'd have to get my hair cut. Maybe you can tell me who does yours."

"Sure. And the eyebrows."

"Agreed."

"We're probably the same size. I could lend you some of my clothes."

Craig was pleased that Jill was completely on board. "What about the voice?" he said. "Elizabeth, you do not sound like Jill, and you'll have to give a speech."

"I've been thinking about that," Elizabeth said. "Medical people can spray my throat with something, that'll make me sound hoarse. As if I have a bad cold or laryngitis. Before the speech, I'll apologize for that. So nobody will focus on the difference."

"That will have another advantage," Jill said. "There's usually a brief Q and A after the speech. I don't think you'll want to respond to technical questions. So you can beg off because of the throat."

"Perfect. I'd like to do something else," Elizabeth said. "I know it's an imposition, but . . ."

"Go ahead," Jill said eagerly.

"From now until Thursday morning, I'd like to move into your house. You'll still go to work Monday, Tuesday, and Wednesday, but this weekend, evenings and early mornings, I'd like to be here with you. If I'm going to be Jill Morgan, I want to get to know her."

"That's okay with me. The only ones in the house are Luz, my housekeeper, and Tracy. Luz has Saturday's off. She sleeps here as well."

"What will you tell Luz and Tracy?" Craig asked.

Elizabeth had a response. "That I'm a journalist and I'm doing an article about Jill. Top female engineer in a male-dominated field."

"I only want one thing from you," Jill said, looking at Elizabeth.

"What's that?"

"Help Tracy with her pitching."

"I'd love to."

Suddenly Jill looked worried. "What happens to me and Tracy, starting Thursday when Elizabeth assumes my identity?"

"I haven't decided," Craig said. "We could take you, Tracy, and Luz off to a safe house until this is over, or you could stay here with a couple of my agents, armed and living in the house."

"If I have a choice, I'd prefer the latter. I could stay in the house twenty-four seven, but I'd like Tracy to live her life normally. She has school and she has baseball. That means a lot to her."

"Perhaps Tracy could stay with a friend," Elizabeth said.

"No," Jill replied. "I want to keep my daughter with me except when she's at school or playing baseball."

They all looked grim, focusing on this issue which underscored the danger that Elizabeth, Jill, and Tracy were facing.

"Okay," Craig finally said. "We'll do it that way."

Craig felt as if he owed Jill this much. She wanted it, and he had to give her something.

As soon as the words were out of his mouth, Craig regretted the decision. If Orlov wanted to, he could assemble enough of a force to overpower the agents Craig installed to watch Jill and Tracy.

Beijing

As Orlov related what happened with Paul Walters. Zhou listened in stony silence while seething. When Orlov finished describing the debacle, Zhou couldn't take it any longer. He picked up a half full ceramic water pitcher resting on his desk and flung it across the room. It smashed against the wall soaking a chair and the wooden floor.

"I don't tolerate failure," Zhou shouted. "And I hate fucking incompetents. That's what you are."

Orlov was trembling. "I'm sorry. I didn't think . . ."

"That's just it. You didn't think."

"Perhaps we should abandon the effort to get PGS."

"Never."

"Maybe you should use someone else."

"I've come too far with you. Either you continue and try again, or I kill you."

Zhou said it in a hard, cold, steel voice.

Before Orlov had a chance to respond, Zhou added, "And don't try to trick me by saying you'll do it, then abandoning the effort once you leave China. Don't forget your sister, Androshka, is still my guest here in Beijing, and I won't let her leave until I've gotten PGS."

"I'm prepared to try again," Orlov said weakly.

"Good. This time I'll help you with the planning. Leaving you on your own was a disaster. Also, I'll give you an encrypted cellphone so you and I can communicate if we have to."

Zhou called Jiang Hua, the director of China's military technology branch. "I want you in my office. Right away."

"I'll be there in twenty minutes."

"Fifteen."

"Yes, sir."

While waiting for Jiang, Zhou banished Orlov to a windowless room down the corridor and stationed one armed soldier in the room and another outside. Let him feel like my prisoner, Zhou thought. It'll motivate him to make a better effort to get PGS.

Jiang arrived twenty-five minutes later. No apologies. He was one of the few people, Zhou had noted, who were not intimidated by him. For that and Jiang's technical expertise, Zhou gave him grudging respect.

When Orlov joined them, Zhou told Jiang, "At the last meeting, you gave Orlov the bios of the five Epsilon Unit engineers working on PGS."

"Yes, I recall."

"One of them, Paul Walters, is now dead."

Jiang raised his eyebrows.

"Did you know the man?" Zhou asked.

"We met once at an international aerospace conference. He was a competent engineer. No more. Seemed like an unhappy man. What happened?"

"He took his own life. Plunged into the Potomac River."

"I see."

Jiang's words and expression conveyed the sense that he had a general idea of what had happened.

"Well, at any rate, Orlov wants to meet another member of the Epsilon Unit to obtain the CDs for PGS. What would you suggest?"

Without hesitating, Jiang responded, "Next Friday in Las Vegas, Jill Morgan, one of the four, will be presenting a paper at the International Aerospace Association conference. I know that because I'm planning to attend. That could be a good opportunity for Orlov to meet her."

"Could you get Orlov credentials so he can attend as a Russian delegate?"

"Easily. I'm friends with the British head of the organization. If Orlov gives me a Russian name, I'll get him the credentials."

Zhou turned to Orlov. "I'll have some make-up people change your appearance before you go back to the United States so they don't recognize you from this Walters fiasco."

Zhou asked Jiang, "Is this Jill Morgan married?"

"A widow with a twelve-year-old daughter."

"Perfect. I'll tell them to make Orlov better looking. Perhaps he can romance Jill Morgan." Then Zhou looked squarely at Orlov. "Talk to your sister, Androshka, she knows how to use sex to get what she wants."

Zhou watched Orlov roll his hands into fists. He'd like to attack me, Zhou thought, but he doesn't have the balls to try.

PART FOUR

The Endgame

Las Vegas

Following Jill's advice, Craig arranged with Bill Merritt for Rogers Laughton to make a large contribution to the International Aerospace Association in return for a blast of publicity advertising Jill's presentation entitled "Cutting Issues in Long-Range Missile Development." Craig was hoping to lure Orlov to Las Vegas to meet with Jill. It made sense. This was a high visibility aerospace conference. Chinese and Russian delegates would be there. Jill would be speaking on a topic related to PGS.

Rogers Laughton's interface with the Association fed Craig information. Eight Russian delegates were registered for the conference. All were staying at the Hotel Sienna, the conference site. Working with the hotel management, Craig obtained copies of the passports of all eight, which were made when they registered Wednesday and Thursday morning for rooms. None of them looked exactly like Orlov. That didn't dissuade Craig. He expected Orlov to change his appearance. Three bore a slight resemblance to Orlov.

Craig also studied the video from the camera in the registration area which operated twenty-four hours a day by focusing on the times the three registered. He concluded that only two of them had a height and weight resembling Orlov's.

Craig had a CIA agent dressed as a maid take fingerprints from the rooms of the two. The prints were sent electronically to Betty in Langley. Moments later, he saw her return email: "Eureka!"

Before Elizabeth's anticipated arrival at the Sienna at three, Thursday afternoon, Craig had matched Orlov's prints with the delegate claiming to be Vladimir Drozny, an aerospace engineer from RSR Industries in Volgograd.

Craig then fired off an email to Jill in Gaithersburg asking her, "Does the name Vladimir Drozny mean anything to you? Attached is a picture of a delegate with that name."

With her photographic memory, Craig was confident she'd remember if she ever met him.

Back came an immediate response: "Vladimir Drozny is an engineer with RSR, a Russian aerospace firm. That is not his picture."

Craig then turned to the Chinese delegation. He knew that Zhou was a control freak. After Orlov's failure with Walters, Zhou might have insisted that one of the Chinese engineers team up with Orlov. Craig obtained the identifying information and photos of the Chinese delegation and forwarded them to Jill.

A minute later, she responded: "Jiang Hua is the head of R&D for the Chinese military. I've never met him."

Craig's guess was that if Zhou had recruited anyone to work with Orlov, it would be Jiang. He'd have to watch Jiang, too, to see if he contacted Elizabeth, thinking she was Jill.

As soon as Elizabeth arrived in the suite, registered in the name of Jill Morgan, Craig explained all of this to her and showed her the photos of Vladimir and Jiang. She was stripping off her clothes.

"What are you doing?" he asked.

"Changing into my bikini. I'm off to the pool. I want to see if Vladimir is looking to make new friends."

"Just be careful. Remember he's dangerous. Don't get over confident."

Three hours later, Elizabeth returned looking glum.

"What happened?" Craig asked.

"Nobody talked to me. A real blow to my ego, but I got a good suntan."

They had dinner alone in the suite. Once the room service waiter left the food and departed, Craig began talking. "I've been working with hotel security. It's amazing how they have every inch of this hotel, except for the inside of guest rooms, covered with hidden cameras. I have Dale, one of my people, down in the hotel's video control room where he can pull up live feed from any camera in the hotel in real time. The hotel security people are willingly working with us. Orlov is in room 1015. He's now in his room. We followed him there with cameras. Room service arrived with his dinner half an hour ago."

"This is all incredible."

"I agree. When he leaves the room, we'll follow him with the cameras. If he exits the hotel, we'll pick him up as soon as he returns. The more likely scenario is that he'll go to the casino. When he does, I want you to go there as well. Give him a chance to make contact with you there."

"Okay."

"Let's review the plan for the casino again."

"We've been through it a dozen times."

"One more won't hurt."

She sighed. "Okay. I play craps and lose. Making it look like it hurts. When I'm cleaned out, I go to the bar."

"Precisely. I'll be watching it all on video and giving you info about Orlov via a tiny device you'll have in your ear."

Elizabeth looked annoyed. "Why do we need that?"

"It's a micro receiver. Even with your shorter hair, to resemble Jill, your hair covers the ear. He'll never notice it."

"That's not the point. It's overkill, Craig. You don't have to keep such tight control over me. Orlov won't expect me to have the CDs in Las Vegas. What can he do to me?"

Craig was ready with his answer. This was something that worried him ever since he had agreed to substitute Elizabeth for Jill. "Don't forget. Jill has a photographic memory. If they've done their homework, they'll know that, too. Which means they don't need the CDs. They can force Jill to divulge all of the technical components in her mind."

"I guess so."

Craig could tell she wasn't convinced. He didn't care. He wasn't taking any chances with her.

Craig's cell rang. It was Dale in the video control room. Craig had given Dale instructions to watch Orlov/Vladimir and Jiang. Craig put it on speaker so Elizabeth could hear. Dale said, "Russian subject is on the move . . . Left his room . . . En route to the elevators . . . Pressed down button . . . Entered elevator three . . . Two other women inside . . . Lobby floor is lit . . . Subject didn't press any other buttons."

"Talk about big brother," she said.

Dale continued, "Russian exited the elevator and is in the lobby en route to casino. He's wandering around the casino. Appears to be deciding where to play."

"What about the Chinese target?"

"Just entered the dining room with three other members of the Chinese delegation. They're having drinks. He's in no hurry."

"I'm on my way down to your position. I'll watch with you."

Craig ended the call and turned to Elizabeth. "Showtime. I'll leave the suite first. You go five minutes later. Make sure you wear your delegate's ID badge. We want Orlov to recognize you and make his move."

*   *   *

With his eyes glued to the screen streaming live video from the casino, Craig watched Elizabeth walk around for a few minutes, then settle at one of the craps table. Orlov was eyeing her. He moved over to the same table. Standing across from her. Craig watched Orlov watching Elizabeth.

She reached into her purse, removed five thousand in hundreds, and converted them into chips. Across the table, Orlov bought five thousand in chips as well. In forty minutes, Craig watched Elizabeth's pile shrink to a handful of chips, while Orlov's remained about the same. Elizabeth placed her remaining chips on the come line. The point was eight and the shooter tossed the dice against the back of the table. Elizabeth strained to look. It was a seven. Her chips were scooped away. "Damn dice," she muttered loud enough for everyone at the table to hear.

Looking distraught, she converted another five thousand. "Now I'm playing for my daughter's college tuition," Elizabeth said loudly, as she piled up her chips.

"Easy, Elizabeth, don't overplay it," Craig said sotto voce.

Elizabeth had the dice. She was betting heavily. Two thousand on each roll. Craig watched in dismay as she scored two points, recouping much of her losses for the evening.

A beefy red-faced man at the table shouted in a Texas drawl, "Lady has a hot hand."

Unbelievable, Craig thought. She's the only person in history who didn't want to win, but suddenly was. Luck couldn't be that cruel.

Orlov was betting with Elizabeth and winning, too. Craig saw him smiling. With a reckless wave of her hand, Elizabeth left her winnings on the table.

All the bets were down. She rolled the dice in her hand then tossed them. They came up as a six and a four, establishing the point. Another round of bets was placed on the table. Elizabeth put down another thousand on the come line.

"Come one ten," somebody yelled.

She rolled again. Even from the screen, Craig felt the tension. He held his breath.

"Seven and out," said the tuxedo clad Hispanic croupier who swept up her chips and all of those who bet with her.

"Damn! There goes my winter vacation," Jill called out.

The dice passed to someone else.

Five minutes later, Craig saw a very sad looking Elizabeth place her last two chips on the come line. The point was an eight. The shooter tossed the dice against the back of the table. She strained to look. It was a seven. Her two lonely chips were gathered up.

Across the table, Craig saw that Orlov had about as many chips as he'd started with. Perhaps a few more.

Elizabeth grabbed her purse, left the table, and headed for a bar in the corner. Craig and Dale picked her up on another camera.

Only two people were seated at the bar. In the center, a tired looking gray haired man in his seventies, Craig guessed, with a drink in front of him. On the right end, a buxom blonde in a tight-fitting, low cut, short black dress that exposed most of her thighs and half of her boobs. A glass of champagne in front of her. Craig thought the blonde resembled Angie, based on the picture in a bikini that Leeds had put on the screen during the Task Force meeting.

Elizabeth sat down on a bar stool on the left side. Moments later, Orlov headed toward the bar.

He's taking the bait, Craig thought, feeling a surge of excitement. Elizabeth's back was toward Orlov. Craig expected Orlov to sit down in the empty chair next to Elizabeth, but he didn't. He eyed her for a few seconds, then passed her and sat down next to the blonde at the far end of the bar. He's playing with us, Craig thought. He must suspect something.

Eyes bulging, Dale said to Craig, "Look at the headlights on that blonde."

"You're supposed to be working."

"Sorry, boss."

Ten minutes later, Orlov left with the blonde, his arm around her waist. Elizabeth looked dejected.

Craig didn't see any sign of Jiang in the casino. He said to Dale, "Go back to the dining room. See if the Chinese target is still there."

A minute later, Dale said, "He and his buddies are still eating."

Craig said to Elizabeth over the two-way, "Time to shut down for the evening. Meet you back in the suite."

Craig got there first. When Elizabeth arrived, she kicked off her shoes. "I feel like a total failure," she said. "Maybe I should have gotten those breast implants a couple of years ago. That's all you men are interested in."

"You're kidding, right?"

"No, I'm serious. You're not a woman."

"The hooker he picked up looked like Angie. You want to compete with that?"

"I guess not."

She rifled through the mini bar. Found a bottle of cheap chardonnay and opened it.

"You want a glass?" she asked, holding up the bottle.

"Bad wine gives me a headache."

"Snob."

She poured herself a glass and gulped down half of it.

"I'm afraid Orlov suspects something," Craig said.

"I don't think so."

"What is it then? Orlov didn't come all this way to get laid with a prostitute. He could have done that in Russia. He came to meet Jill Morgan and talk to her about PGS."

"The problem is the atmosphere in this damn Las Vegas hotel. It's spooking him. With his KGB background, he has to know there are hidden cameras everywhere. After what he did to Paul Walters and Angie, I'll bet he's afraid to be caught on film making contact with me."

Craig thought about it for a minute. "You've got a point. But how do we get around it? This is the setting we have to work with."

She drank some more wine, then said, "Tomorrow, at the end of my speech, I'd like casually to throw in that next week I'll be going to

Monte Carlo for a vacation. If Orlov doesn't approach me tomorrow, let him make his move on me there. Plan B. What do you think?"

Craig was frowning and shaking his head. "I hate it."

"Why?"

"Do you know how tough it would be for me to protect you in Monte Carlo?"

"Use your friend Giuseppe. He could enlist Jacques. Together, they could provide all the bodies you need."

When Craig didn't respond, she pressed him. "C'mon Craig. It's the only way. You know that. We have to get Zhou for what he's done to both of us. Not to mention what that lunatic will do to the United States if he gets his hands on PGS."

"Okay. Okay. I'm convinced. But hopefully, he'll make contact with you tomorrow and we won't need Plan B."

*   *   *

Sated from sex, Orlov lay in bed in his hotel room watching the woman called Terry dress. He had paid her three thousand up front.

Before leaving, she came over and kissed him on the forehead.

"Thanks," she said.

He reached into the night table drawer, pulled out five hundred and handed it to her. "A tip."

She gave him a card. "My cell and email address. Call me."

When she was gone, Orlov got up and poured himself a glass of vodka to clear his head.

He had never been in Las Vegas before, and he'd always wanted to see it. Vasily Sukalov, the Russian oligarch he'd worked for, had told him that Vegas had the most awful heat, but the women were not to be believed. "Once they know you have money, you can't keep them away. They'll swarm over you like bees over honey. They'll do anything you want. For one week, I fuck my brains out. I thought it would fall off. The next time I go, I'll take you along."

That never happened. But Orlov had to admit that Vasily was right on both counts. In terms of the weather, the place was a hot air oven. Walking from the air-conditioned airplane terminal to the cab, and later to the hotel, Orlov thought he would pass out from the heat.

This place was hell without the flames. Terry, or whatever her name was, had given him one of the best times he'd ever had in bed. And he'd even won a few dollars in the casino because he bet a lot smarter than Jill Morgan.

All of that was fine, but it wasn't why he'd come to Las Vegas. His objective was to establish contact with Jill. She wasn't at all bad looking. In fact, he found her attractive. Nice face. Good body. Tight ass. He'd come to Vegas with the idea of getting her in the sack and winning her over that way. He was confident that he'd be so good in bed she'd do whatever he wanted, including turning over the CDs from PGS. It had worked for him in the past; it would work for him again.

Yeah, that was the plan he'd developed on the long plane ride to Vegas. The trouble was there were so goddamn many hidden cameras in this fucking hotel that he couldn't make a move without one of them picking him up. People might have seen him entering or leaving Angie's apartment building when he killed her. That place might have had hidden cameras as well. He knew that Americans were enamored with the damn things.

Though the Chinese had changed Orlov's looks, his physical characteristics, like his walk and how he carried himself, were the same. The FBI or CIA could have made an ID from the cameras. He couldn't take a chance of someone concluding that the man who killed Angie was now hooking up with Jill Morgan. If that happened, they'd pick him up before he even got started with Jill, and his whole PGS project would go into the toilet.

Orlov finished his drink and poured another. But that didn't mean, Orlov thought, that this evening was a total loss. It wasn't.

In the casino, Orlov had learned something very valuable: Jill Morgan needed money. That was the hook he'd use to recruit her. Money, not sex. It might not be as much fun, but it was a lot easier.

*   *   *

At nine thirty the next morning, Craig was back in the hotel's video control room. The video stream he and Dale were focused on was coming from the cameras in the Grand Ballroom—set up in a theater format with a raised platform in front for speakers. Twelve hundred delegates were seated in chairs in the audience.

Looking for Orlov, Craig scanned their faces. After a minute, he saw the Russian seated in the back row wearing his Vladimir Drozny credentials, and looking bored. In the middle of the room, Jiang sat with the other members of the Chinese delegation.

Craig turned toward the screen showing the front of the room. Seated at the table on the dais, Elizabeth was listening to the polite applause from the audience. The first speaker, from Carlton Industries in the UK, a manufacturer of advanced sensors, had just finished his prepared speech. "Now I'll take a few questions," the speaker said.

After ten minutes, the speaker returned to his seat. Cecil Weinright, the moderator, was back at the lectern.

"As you know," Cecil began in a British accent, "this morning's session is devoted to technology with particular applicability to military uses. No company in the world has been on the cutting edge of this technology as much as Rogers Laughton. And we're fortunate to have today as our speaker Jill Morgan from Rogers Laughton. Jill is a graduate of the Air Force Academy where she was at the top of her class. She was a fighter pilot before joining her company. Her topic today will be technology related to long-range missiles.

"Jill has asked me to tell you to bear with her. She is suffering from laryngitis following a nasty cold. Just another sickness rampant in Washington, D.C."

That evoked laugher from the audience.

Cecil waited for it to die down before continuing. "Jill absolutely refused to cancel her speech so cut that scratchy voice some slack. However, she may not be able to answer questions. Now please welcome Jill Morgan."

The audience gave a large round of applause as Elizabeth, dressed in a navy blue Ann Taylor suit with a white cotton blouse that belonged to Jill, stood and walked to the lectern. She signaled to one of the administrators on the association's staff who dimmed the lights and prepared to follow the speaker's directions with slides for the PowerPoint presentation.

Craig shifted screens to glance at Orlov who was now on the edge of his chair, staring straight ahead, looking as if he'd be hanging on every word. The same for Jiang.

Five minutes into the fifteen minute talk, Craig was impressed with Elizabeth's mastery of the text. She sounded self-confident, completely at home with the material. All those hours practicing the presentation definitely paid off. Elizabeth was totally in control of the words and the slides. Silence reigned in the ballroom except for Elizabeth's voice. The delegates were focused on her. Everyone had to think she was Jill Morgan. If there were differences in facial features between Elizabeth and Jill, they would have been impossible to pick up in the dim light with the delegates at a distance from the lectern. With the spray the doctor had administered that morning, Elizabeth sounded hoarse but could be easily understood.

She was now coming to the end of the speech. "We are just engineers. We are not statesmen or politicians. But never forget the lesson from the development of nuclear weapons in the 1940s. We engineers have the power, for better or for worse, to change the way in which nations make war and thereby conduct their foreign affairs. Long-range missiles are the cutting edge of military technology. Those who have the technology to hit a small target thousands of miles away will have an incredible advantage. Today I've summarized for you some of the early work we've done in this field. As you might imagine, we are continuing this development. Thank you for listening."

The audience responded with a burst of applause.

Elizabeth downed a glass of water, then said "With this throat, I'm afraid I can't take questions today, but please send them to me at my office via e-mail at Jill.Morgan@Rogers Laughton.com.

"Don't expect an answer too quickly. Next Thursday I'm off to Monte Carlo for a little vacation with my boyfriend. I have to win back in the casino there what I lost here." A large round of laugher from the audience.

"Certainly my luck can't be any worse than it was last night."

More laughter.

Then applause as she moved back to her seat on the dais.

Five minutes into the next speaker's presentation, Craig watched Elizabeth get up from her chair carrying her bag, exactly as they had planned. She was heading toward the nearest side exit from the ballroom. That opened to a side hallway which ran to the main corridor from which delegates entered and left the ballroom.

Once she reached the main corridor, Elizabeth headed toward the nearest water fountain.

Craig was watching her intently. Dale, meantime, was watching the screen with feed from a camera in the ballroom. Dale said to Craig, "The Russian is leaving his seat in the ballroom and heading toward the exit."

Craig asked Dale, "What about the Chinese man?"

"Not moving."

Craig said to Elizabeth on the two-way, "Orlov is headed out. Not Jiang. I repeat. Only Orlov. Hold you position near the water fountain until he appears."

*　　　*　　　*

Orlov had gone running on city streets early that morning. When he had seen a small tumbledown diner in a seedy part of town, he stopped, went inside, and bought a bottle of water. The diner would be the perfect place to meet with Jill later today, he decided. No cameras. No security people. No other aerospace delegates would be there. After finishing the water, he had snatched a grease-stained card that said, "Duchess Diner," with the address and phone number from the counter next to the cash register, and shoved it in his pocket.

As he had resumed running, the rest of his plan had fallen into place.

He'd ask her to meet him at the Duchess Diner at three that afternoon. "I'll give you some gambling tips to win back your money and much more."

But he had to deliver that message outside of the view of the hotel cameras. How?

After five more minutes of running, he decided. Following her speech, she was likely to go to the restroom. Speakers often did. He'd follow her into the ladies' room. There wouldn't be cameras inside. He'd claim he'd made a mistake. "Wrong door, sorry." Then deliver his message for a three o'clock meeting.

When he saw her leave the dais, Orlov thought everything was falling into place. She had to be on her way to the ladies' room.

He exited the ballroom swiftly, looked down the corridor toward the nearest restrooms, expecting her to be en route, but she was standing near the water fountain, drinking water, not moving.

What to do now? Hand her the Duchess Diner card and give her his invitation in the corridor? It would all be picked up on camera. Too risky.

But shit, it was the only chance he had. Take the risk?

"No, don't be an idiot," he chided himself. She's going to be in Monte Carlo next week. Meet her there. Still, he wanted make casual contact with her, one delegate to another, to make sure she'd remember him when they met in Monte Carlo. So he made a beeline for the water fountain. Before he had a chance to open his mouth, she said, "Hi Vladimir. How're you?"

That was good, he thought. She remembered him from their prior meetings. Monte Carlo would be easier.

"Excellent speech, Jill," he replied. "I'd like to talk to you about it someday, but right now I have a plane to catch."

*   *   *

With the microphone concealed beneath Elizabeth's jacket, Craig heard her exchange with Orlov. After Orlov said, "Right now I have a plane to catch," Craig watched him turn and head toward the elevator. Craig said to Elizabeth, "I'll meet you in the suite." Then he turned to Dale. "Stick with the Russian and keep me informed."

When Craig entered the suite, Elizabeth was already there. He heard from Dale: "Subject just left his room, wheeling suitcase toward elevator. Appears to be checking out."

Craig had a tough decision: to arrest Orlov or not. After all, the man was responsible for the deaths of President Dalton, Paul Walters, Angie, and a trucking company clerk in Pittsburgh. Craig could try to cut a deal with Orlov and hope Orlov gave him Zhou and Kuznov.

Or he could let Orlov leave the hotel and probably the country, hoping that Orlov made a move on Elizabeth in Monte Carlo to obtain PGS. But if Orlov didn't approach her in Monte Carlo, then Craig might never get his hands on Orlov again.

"Orlov's checking out," Craig said to Elizabeth. "What are the chances of him making contact with you in Monte Carlo?"

"Sixty-forty he will."

"Shit. I'd like better odds."

"Sorry. I'm being honest. That's as much as I could get from his body language."

Dale said, "Orlov is at the checkout desk. He's paying the bill."

Now or never, Craig thought.

Close call.

I'll take a chance.

"I'm letting Orlov leave," Craig said to Elizabeth.

"It's your call. For what it's worth, I would have, too."

"Okay. Let's talk about Monte Carlo. Why in the world did you say you'd be going with a boyfriend?"

"No woman goes by herself. I wanted it to sound real."

"It can't be me. Orlov would recognize me."

"I know that. I figured you'd find me a boyfriend."

"You want me to run an ad on the Internet?"

"Call Betty. The CIA must have lots of attractive single men."

"Many of whom are in the Russians' database and might be recognized." Then it occurred to him. From time to time the agency hired contract agents to do odd jobs off the books when they didn't want to use an employee for one of a variety of reasons.

He called Betty and explained the problem.

"I'll get right on it," she said. "How likely is it that whoever we use will get caught up in a fire fight or other rough stuff in Monte Carlo?"

"I don't know. At this point, my bigger concern is that this is all a fool's errand. That Orlov will never contact Elizabeth in Monte Carlo and all our work has gone down the toilet."

Paris

In the days since she had learned of her son's death, Mei Ling was sleepwalking through life. She wandered the streets of Paris aimlessly, followed by the French policeman who was part of the protection Elizabeth had arranged. She forced herself to eat, to maintain her strength, so that one day she could gain her revenge, but that was easier said than done because she had no appetite. She slept ten or twelve hours a day because she had no desire to get out of bed.

After days of grieving, her mind began to focus again. She forced herself to think: why would Zhou have killed her son now? What did he have to gain?

Then the answer came. Her son was one of the few people who knew where Mei Ling was. If Zhou wanted to locate and kill the person who challenged and almost defeated him for the Presidency, then forcing it out of her son would be the logical way to proceed.

It was afternoon in Paris. She walked over to the window overlooking Rue Duphot and looked out from a break in the curtains. She could hardly believe her eyes.

On the sidewalk in front of the hotel was the French policeman protecting her, but standing next to him was a Chinese man dressed in a suit and tie who was talking to the policeman. She thought she recognized the Chinese man.

No. It couldn't be. Her eyes must be deceiving her.

Mei Ling snatched the binoculars from a desk drawer and looked down. Her eyes weren't deceiving her. It was Captain Cheng, Zhou's personal aide and henchman. There was only one reason Captain Cheng was here: *to kill her*. She needed help and she needed it fast. She knew Jacques was the head of French Intelligence and Craig's friend, but she didn't have his number. The only person she could call, Elizabeth Crowder, was thousands of miles away in the United States. It was probably hopeless, but Mei Ling had nowhere else to turn.

While keeping her eyes focused on the sidewalk below, she frantically dialed Elizabeth's cell.

She heard, "This is Elizabeth. Who's calling?"

"It's Mei Ling. I need help. I . . ."

Holding the phone to her ear, Mei Ling watched in horror as Captain Cheng whipped out a knife. He stabbed the policeman in the chest and knocked him to the ground. Then Captain Cheng stepped over his bleeding body and walked into the hotel.

"What's wrong?" Elizabeth cried out.

"Zhou sent somebody to kill me. He just killed the French policeman outside the hotel. He's coming into the hotel now. What should I do?"

"Get out of your room fast. There's an inside staircase two doors away. Leave your room; lock it. Then hide in that staircase. Don't go out on the ground floor. He might see you."

"What if he comes in the staircase?"

"I'll get help for you before that happens. Only listen to someone who tells you: 'Jacques sent me.' Now stop talking and move."

*　　*　　*

In Washington, Elizabeth had been at home working on her book when Mei Ling called. She would have liked to call Craig and have him call Jacques, but there was no time for that. Besides, Craig was at the White House for a meeting with Treadwell. She'd have to deal with this herself. She dialed Jacques. Fortunately, he answered the phone.

As soon as Elizabeth spit out her story, Jacques said, "I'll get on it. Call you right back."

"Thanks. Make sure your men tell her, 'Jacques sent me.'"

*　　*　　*

The staircase was dimly lit and dusty. Straining her eyes to see and holding onto a railing to avoid falling, Mei Ling took baby steps down three flights to the midpoint; then stopped. She could go up or down depending on which direction he came from.

She felt stupid. She should have brought a knife with her into the staircase. Even a bottle she could have thrown. Anything she could use as a weapon, but she didn't. You fool, she berated herself.

She remained still. Trying to breathe softly.

Then she heard it: a series of blasts coming from the sixth floor, like a car backfiring. But she knew it was gunfire. One . . . two . . . three . . . four shots. Then silence.

The door to the staircase flew open on the sixth floor. Mei Ling held her breath. The bright beam of a flashlight zeroed in on her face.

"French police. Jacques sent me."

"Yes," Mei Ling called out with relief.

Her knees wobbling, she walked up the stairs to the policeman who told her, "Your assailant is dead. You're safe."

She walked back to her room. Two French policemen were lying on the floor not moving. Across the room was Captain Cheng in a pool of blood. Dead!

Mei Ling called Elizabeth and told her what happened. "I can't thank you enough."

"It was all Jacques, the Director of French Intelligence. He's coming now to your hotel room. He'll take you to a safe house in Paris where you'll be heavily guarded around the clock. You don't have to worry anymore. And I'll tell Craig what happened."

"How long will I have to stay in that safe house?"

"A month or two. By then, hopefully, we'll bring down President Zhou."

Washington

"Run that by me again," a visibly upset President Treadwell said to Craig. The two of them were alone in the Oval Office at ten the next morning.

Craig repeated his words. "I didn't stop Orlov when he checked out and left the hotel."

"That's what I thought you said. Orlov was responsible for President Dalton's assassination. What the hell were you thinking?"

"That Orlvo will take the bait with Elizabeth in Monte Carlo."

Treadwell was squeezing his hand. "From everything you've told me about Orlov's behavior in Las Vegas, I doubt that. I think he's on to us."

"As I said, Mr. President, it was a close call. I used my best judgment."

"Humpth."

Treadwell stood up and paced around the office. Finally he said, "You're the intelligence pro. I have to respect your judgment . . . I guess . . . I just hope you're right."

"I do, too, Mr. President," Craig said, without much confidence.

"What about the Task Force? Have you had a meeting with them where you told them about the dangle?"

Oh shit, Craig thought. Accustomed to being a solo player, he'd forgotten all about the Task Force. "It all moved so fast with Las Vegas, that I haven't had a chance. I'll set up a meeting for this afternoon. What is your schedule?"

"Completely booked. Go ahead without me."

"I'll set it up for six in the Situation Room."

"Good, if my schedule changes, I'll join you."

Craig had turned off his cell phone when he was in the meeting with the president. Walking through the White House corridors to his car, he turned it back on and checked for missed calls. One from Elizabeth. He called her back.

Once she began telling him about Mei Ling and Captain Cheng, he stopped walking and sat in a chair in the corridor. He didn't want to miss any of this. At the end, he told her, "Well done. What shape's Mei Ling in?"

"She's tough. She'll be okay. Jacques will take good care of her. How'd it go with Treadwell?"

"He thinks I made the wrong call letting Orlov leave Vegas, but he didn't beat me up too badly."

"Because he respects your judgment."

"That's what he said. I'm not sure he meant it. He's pragmatic. What's done is done. Or as my dad used to say, 'Mrs. Murphy already had her drink.'"

"I never heard that one before."

"See you tonight. I have to get back to my office at Langley to see if Betty has found you a boyfriend."

"I'd like one tall, dark, and handsome."

"I'm sure you would."

As soon as Craig walked into his office, his secretary said, "Betty wants to see you."

"Good. Have her come over."

Minutes later, Betty entered the office and said, "I found a boyfriend for Elizabeth for Monte Carlo."

"Who?"

"Jimmy Palmer."

"I've heard that name," Craig couldn't remember when.

"Anyhow, he's forty-two years old. Graduated from Michigan where he was starting forward on their basketball team, went to the NCAA finals his senior year."

"Okay. That's where I heard it."

"Then spent a year at Georgetown Law. Dropped out and joined the CIA. We had him hunting Al Qaeda operatives in Africa for two years. He got very good reviews. His father, who owned and ran a huge electronic import business in Detroit, developed cancer. Jimmy quit and went back to take over the family business. The old man died, and it took Jimmy a couple years to put it on automatic pilot. By then, he was wealthy and bored. Living in Detroit as a wealthy playboy bachelor. So he cut a deal with the agency. They'd use him from time to time for special assignments—often taking advantage of his cover from the import business. They love the idea here in Langley because he provides the type of cover they would have to spend millions to create."

"Sounds perfect. Is he available?"

"Ready to go. I didn't tell him the assignment. Just that it meant going to Europe for a week or so."

Betty reached into a folder, pulled out a photo and handed it to Craig. "This was taken of Palmer a year ago."

He did look like the wealthy playboy Betty had described. Dressed in a sport jacket, striped shirt, and Hermes loafers with big gold H's on the front. He was a little chunky. Definitely not his basketball weight. Gray hair at the temples. A good smile.

"He's good-looking," Betty said. "I hope Elizabeth doesn't fall for him."

"Just what I need right now is humor. Palmer will work. Have him come to Washington so Elizabeth and I can brief him. Meantime, I have to get ready for a root canal."

"Sorry. I didn't know you were having trouble with your teeth."

"I'm not. I have to attend a Task Force meeting."

Beijing

President Zhou was angry at his brother, Zhou Yun, which almost never happened. The two were having dinner alone at the President's house. Androshka had wanted to join them but President Zhou told her "positively not." His brother had said he had something important to discuss.

As they approached the end of dinner, Zhou Yun delivered his message: "Ordering the humiliation of Bao Yin, the Director of Intelligence, in front of the Central Committee and his execution, was not a wise move."

"The man was incompetent. We can't tolerate failure among our top leaders. Certainly not in a position as important as this. I intend to take China to the next step. To lead it to world domination. We can't surpass the United States with fools and incompetents."

"I don't disagree with that. And I won't defend the man's competence. But a summary execution like this smacks of Mao's methods. People are starting to talk."

"What people?" President Zhou asked, sounding enraged.

"I hear it from business leaders, my brother. We can't afford to lose their support. They want stability, not turmoil or erratic behavior."

"Who used those words? Who accused me of erratic behavior?"

Zhou Yun was staring at his brother. "Who isn't important. Word is also circulating that you had Mei Ling's son killed on his ship and also Qin Ping, who was not only on the Central Committee, but a close friend of Mei Ling's."

"He was feeding Mei Ling lies about me," Zhou protested.

Shaking his head, Zhou Yun looked very unhappy. "You may not know this because you were in Bali, but I had an incredibly difficult job persuading a majority of the Central Committee to select you over Mei Ling for president. Even with all the millions I spent in payoffs."

"That's why I tried to have Mei Ling killed."

Zhou Yun seemed flabbergasted. "You did. Where?"

"In Paris. I didn't want to risk leaving her alive to lead a coup. Captain Cheng failed. He died in the attempt. The damn French have now hidden Mei Ling. It must have been Craig Page's doing."

"Who else knows what happened in Paris?"

"Nobody in Beijing."

"That's good. Keep it that way. If people find out, they may turn against you and look toward Mei Ling to lead the country. She still has a great deal of support. It will grow if your attempt to kill her became common knowledge."

Zhou gripped the arms of his chair tightly to keep from shooting to his feet with a furious diatribe against his brother. "That's ridiculous." Then he clenched his teeth to keep control.

"Believe me, brother, I talk to business people. You are isolated. You spend your time with lackeys who pander to you. And with the military leaders who have a narrow focus."

President Zhou had planned to tell his brother about the efforts he was making to obtain the Americans' top weapon, PGS, for the Chinese military. But he was so angry at everything he'd heard that he decided against it.

Besides, he now worried that after the Paul Walters incident, Orlov might not succeed. He hadn't heard from the Russian for days. That was not a good sign.

Zhou Yun said, "All I'm asking is that you think about what I've said. I only want the best for you. Believe me."

"I need your support. I don't want you listening to my enemies."

"You'll always have my support."

His brother's words didn't mollify General Zhou, but there was no point prolonging the discussion. He had barely kept his rage from boiling over. He'd never been so angry.

President Zhou's brother left and he went upstairs to the bedroom suite. Androshka was pouting. "I don't see why I couldn't have been included at dinner. You could have had your discussion afterwards."

Just what he didn't need now was whining from that Russian bitch. "Because that's what I wanted."

"Perhaps I should go back to Moscow."

"To do what?" He was shouting. His rage from the last hour exploding. "Be the whore of a Russian gangster . . . or the stooge for that incompetent brother of yours?"

"Orlov's a good man." Her eyes were blazing.

"He can't do anything right. The worst thing I ever did was getting involved with your brother. And that was all your fault." He was pointing a finger at her, yelling "I pulled you out of the gutter and made you an Empress here. You've changed and I don't like it. All you do is complain."

She began to cry.

"Get out of my sight," he told her with a wave of his hand.

Screaming, she ran from the room.

Now alone, Zhou poured a glass of Armagnac and sat down in a leather chair. Upset by what his brother had said, he was mulling over Zhou Yun's words. His critics lacked vision and courage. They didn't understand or appreciate that Zhou was planning to lead China to world dominance.

He knew how to silence his critics. All he had to do was steal the PGS technology. Unlike the Americans, China had plenty of money to construct the system immediately. He would parade the new PGS missiles through Tiananmen Square and the streets of Beijing. China would then be able to take any military action it wanted. That would be his vindication.

Androshka walked into the room dressed in a sheer pink negligee. "I put on your favorite," she said, her face still red from crying. "I'm sorry for what I said. I'd like to make it up to you." She walked over and unbuttoned his shirt then unzipped his pants. "Come to bed. I'll relax you."

"I need that."

When they were both naked in bed, he stretched out on his front. She took some lotion and massaged his back. "Oh, that feels good. So good."

She worked her hands down over his legs then up to his buttocks. She reached in and played with his balls, grabbing his limp penis.

He flipped over. She caressed him, then took him into her mouth. Dammit, he wanted sex more than anything, but his stalk wouldn't stand up. Except for a couple of nights, this is how it had been since he returned to China.

She was playing with him while sucking, but nothing happened.

He pushed her away. "You're no good," he said. "You can't get me up. You're not even good for that."

She looked angry. "You're blaming me? You're the one with the problem. You can't perform. You haven't been good for weeks."

"How could anyone be interested in you," he shouted. "Somebody who does nothing but whine and complain."

"I'm bored here," she shouted back. "There's nothing for me to do."

"How about being grateful. I rescued you from your life as a whore. Killed Mikail Ivanoff before he killed you. And this is what I get from you in return."

"I've done everything to please you."

"Don't make me laugh."

"I should have gone back to Moscow long ago."

"And go back to being a whore."

"At least I'll get sex. With you nothing. You have a problem. You should see a doctor. I'll only stay if I can find a young Chinese man. I heard they stay hard forever. Not like you."

That was too much for Zhou. First his brother heaped scorn on him. Now this Russian tramp insults his manhood. He'd had enough.

He reached over to the end table, opened the drawer, and pulled out a gun. She looked at him wide-eyed with astonishment. Then terror. She jumped out of bed and ran toward the open bedroom door shouting. "No, Zhou. No."

Before she reached the door, he fired, hitting her in the center of the back. She turned around facing him and collapsed to her knees. "Please. No," she moaned.

He fired two more time. Hitting her in the chest.

Calmly, he walked over and checked her pulse. She was dead.

He threw a blanket over her head. Then, he shouted for Liu, one of the servants whose orders were to remain close by at all times in case Zhou needed anything.

Liu ran into the room. "Yes sir," he said.

Zhou pointed to Androshka's bloody body. "Get her out of here. Bury the body secretly and clean the carpet. I don't want any sign that she was ever here."

Washington

President Treadwell couldn't attend the Task Force meeting. But the rest of them were there when Craig arrived ten minutes late because of insane traffic on the Theodore Roosevelt Bridge coming into the city. Washington in rush-hour traffic was the worst in the country.

The others were all seated around the table. To paraphrase the movie *Casablanca*, he had rounded up the usual suspects. Ed Grayson from DOD, General Braddock, Chairman of the Joint Chiefs, Colonel Rhodes from DIA, R.J. Hennessey from State, and George Leeds, the FBI Director, accompanied by his young assistant, Maureen. Craig couldn't understand why Leeds needed her. His guess was that Leeds felt having her tag along wherever he went enhanced his own importance.

"I want to bring you all up to date," Craig said, "on recent developments."

All eyes were focused on the CIA Director.

Without PowerPoint, Craig reported that he had made the choice of Jill as a dangle. He then distributed her bio. He explained what happened in Las Vegas, omitting that Jill was in her house with guards around the clock and Elizabeth was pretending to be Jill. He told them he would be going to Monte Carlo with Jill and a CIA contract hire to try and catch whoever was trying to get their hands on PGS.

The instant Craig finished, Leeds pounced. In a surly voice he said "I can't believe you let that Russian, Vladimir, or whoever the hell he was, leave Las Vegas. You should have arrested him."

"I'm hoping we can move up the food chain in Monte Carlo."

"*Hoping.* That's the operative word." Leeds voice was dripping with sarcasm. "Perhaps *praying* might be more accurate. And to think of how you chastised me for not arresting Angie. What you've done is ten times more stupid."

Craig tried to remain calm. "I'm sorry you feel that way. The situations are not analogous."

"And when your Russian pal doesn't show in Monte Carlo and you're standing around with your dick in your hand, you'll know then that you screwed up your chance to blow this wide open."

Craig had the same concern. Which he had no intention of sharing with members of the Task Force. Looking around, he saw troubled faces. To some extent, he thought, they no doubt shared Leeds' misgivings.

"What's worse," Leeds continued in his harangue. "These people will now go underground only to surface months from now when we least expect it."

Hennessey spoke up. "Why didn't you bring the dangle idea to the Task Force before you launched it?"

"There wasn't time."

"That's bullshit," Leeds shot back. "Of course you had time for a brief meeting or even a conference call. You wanted to act on your own."

Hennessey picked it up. "The process point bothers me. President Treadwell appointed a Task Force to run the operation, responding to Paul Walters' death. He made you Chairman, but we weren't supposed to be bystanders. We were intended to have meaningful roles. You've essentially disenfranchised all of us. You're flying solo on this."

"Amen," Leeds said.

Craig decided he'd better smooth this over before it got out of hand. "You make a good point, R.J. Even if there wasn't time for a meeting, I should have convened a conference call. I'll do better in the future. Okay?"

Hennessey was shaking his head. "I'm also troubled by the substance.

"What do you mean?"

"With all due respect, Craig, I don't like the dangle idea." He sounded worried. "I've read Jill's bio. You're putting the life of a single mom at risk. Someone who lost her father and husband in the service of our country. It's just too dangerous. You'll never be able to protect her in Monte Carlo. I propose that we cancel the operation right now."

Craig responded. "I have already secured the assistance of Giuseppe, the Director of the EU Counterterrorism Agency, and Jacques, the head of French intelligence. You can be sure that we will protect Jill."

"You're dreaming," Hennessey said. "It's a terrible idea. "Too dangerous."

"Jill is aware of the risks," Craig replied.

Hennessey was looking around the room. "Do any of you share my concern?"

"I certainly do," Leeds said.

Of course, you're opposed, Craig thought, because it was my idea.

General Braddock spoke up. "To be honest, I am concerned about Jill Morgan. But nothing means more to the defense of our country and its military superiority than PGS. I would do just about anything to safeguard this weapons system. That includes finding out who's trying to steal it."

Ed Grayson was nodding. "Exactly what I was thinking. And besides Craig, you're very experienced in the espionage business, and you've gotten great results over the years. If you tell us that using Jill as the dangle is the right way to go, that's good enough for me."

"And me," Colonel Rhodes added.

Craig looked at Leeds and Hennessey. They had nothing further to say.

"Alright, I'll move forward with Monte Carlo," Craig said, wrapping up the meeting.

As Leeds left the room, he glared at Craig with a menacing look. He's planning something, Craig thought.

Monte Carlo

On Wednesday, Orlov arrived at the airport in Nice and rented a black Mercedes for the drive to Monte Carlo.

Behind the wheel, with the sparkling blue Mediterranean on the right, he was having doubts about what he was doing. His gut told him that this whole operation was increasingly likely to turn to shit. He couldn't define precisely why he felt that way; but he'd had enough operations go south on him over the years to feel it happening now. The sensible course was to break it off. Go back to Moscow and tell Kuznov that Zhou was too deceitful and he'd never give Kuznov what he wanted. Kuznoz wouldn't object. The Dalton assassination was a plus for Russia and Kuznov never trusted Zhou. As for Orlov, he had enough money in Swiss banks from what Sukalov had paid him and what he had skimmed to live comfortably the rest of his life. So why not do it?

Orlov was in the left lane driving 120 kilometers per hour when some maniac in a red Audi was flashing his lights from behind. Orlov moved over to the right lane.

Grimly, Orlov thought, walking away wasn't a choice. If he did that, Zhou, who was desperate to get his hands on PGS, would kill him. Hiding from a man like Zhou with the resources at his disposal wasn't possible. The world wasn't large enough. Zhou would hunt him down and kill him if it was the last thing he ever did.

Besides, Zhou had Androshka and he'd kill her in a minute if Orlov abandoned the project. And Orlov loved his sister. He couldn't let that happen.

No, skipping out wasn't an option. He'd better forget about that and concentrate on doing the job: recruiting Jill and having her turn over the CDs for PGS.

Orlov arrived in Monte Carlo on a gorgeous day. The sun was beating down on the sea and the town with its incredible number of modern high-rise apartment buildings sprouting up from the rocks surrounding the city, inhabited by the rich and famous who took advantage of Monaco as a tax haven. Tourists were milling around the streets. The harbor was crowded with large yachts and sailboats.

Orlov checked into the hotel Metropole in the heart of the town, across a grassy square from the casino. Then he went to work. The first thing was to find out where Jill was staying. She said she'd be flying Thursday. That meant a Friday arrival.

He called one of his former KGB colleagues in Moscow who was an expert at hacking into commercial computer systems. In thirty minutes, Orlov had Jill's itinerary. On Thursday, she'd be leaving Washington with James Palmer, flying into Paris on Air France and connecting to Nice arriving at noon. Jill and Palmer were staying at the Hotel de Paris, the luxury watering hole adjacent to the casino.

Somehow, Orlov had to split Jill away from Palmer so he could talk to her and make his proposition. She would no doubt be in the casino, trying to win back what she'd lost in Las Vegas, but again too many cameras.

In search of a better venue for his meeting, Orlov visited her ostentatious but classy hotel which reminded him of the expression, "everything to excess." He could hang out in the new baroque lobby with its gold decorated walls, huge mirrors, and chandeliers, and make contact with her there. She thought he was Vladimir Drozny, a professional colleague, so he was confident he could convince her to leave Palmer and go off with him to discuss an aerospace matter. He could make their encounter seem like a chance meeting. If he played it right, she wouldn't be suspicious. It wasn't ideal because the hotel lobby was a very public place and someone might see them together. Also where to take her to talk? His hotel was probably best. It all seemed so awkward. There had to be a better way, but he couldn't think of it.

Out on the street, he walked to the back of the Hotel de Paris, past Gucci, Valentino, and other luxury shops, then down the hill to the port area. All the while, he was thinking about how he could arrange his meeting with Jill and take her off to talk. He kept coming up empty.

As Orlov walked along the Quai Albert 1er, he gazed at the yachts in the harbor, some of them huge. His eyes focused on a sleek two-hundred-foot luxury yacht custom built by the Dutch company Feadship. On top, it had a helipad with a helicopter. The name OLI-GARCH was printed in large black letters on the side.

Orlov knew that yacht belonged to Yuri Rosnov, one of the wealthiest men in Russia, who controlled a huge industrial empire. Orlov had met Yuri a couple of times. Even more significant for Orlov was that Yuri's chief assistant, performing the role Orlov had for Sukolov, was Boris Verely. A close friend of Orlov's from their KGB days. Maybe Orlov could enlist Boris's help.

As Orlov walked down an incline path that led to the Oligarch, he thought about Kuznov's warning: don't involve Russians in this operation with Zhou. Well, that was easy enough to for Kuznov to say, seated in his plush office in the Kremlin. But Orlov was out in the field. He had to get the job done. There was no other way.

Orlov walked up the ramp to the deck and asked one of the crew in Russian if Boris was on board. The crewman asked Orlov's name and used his cellphone. Minutes later, he led Orlov down to a richly wood-paneled office. Boris stood up. He was a tall, elegant man, dressed smartly in a white polo shirt, trimmed in blue, with Boris monogrammed on the pocket, and tight fitting khaki slacks. The last time Orlov had seen Boris he was almost bald. Now he was sporting a toupee that looked very much like his own hair. For money, you can get anything.

"You're living well, my friend," Orlov said.

"Who would have ever thought you and I would have ended up the way we are now when the Soviet Union collapsed and the Communists lost control?"

"One door closes. Another opens."

"Exactly. Something to drink?"

"Why not? A small vodka."

Boris fixed two vodkas over ice and handed one to Orlov.

"To the continuation of good times." Boris said.

"I'll drink to that."

After they each took a large gulp, Boris said, "I heard you split with Sukalov. What brings you to Monte Carlo my friend?"

"I'm freelancing. And I could use a little help."

"You've hit me at the right time. Yuri is off in Brazil for a business deal. I'm on my own for another week or so. I'd like doing something with you."

Orlov's mind was now clicking on all cylinders. "Do you have many friends in Monte Carlo?"

"Lots. There's a large Russian émigré population here as well as in the south of France. They come with suitcases filled with cash. And I don't mean rubles. Dollars or euros."

"How would you like to have a party on this yacht, Saturday evening?"

Boris was smiling. "You have a babe you'd like to impress?"

"You guessed it. And I'd also like to separate her from her boyfriend. I want to spend a little private time with her."

Boris winked. "Same old Orlov. Always chasing pussy."

"That's not it. Believe it or not."

"I don't, but regardless, I'd be happy to help out. I have to tell you, though, that parties like that are expensive here. And Yuri has a finance guy who's always checking on what I spend. He's a real pain in the ass."

"How about if I delivered a hundred thousand euros to you in an hour. Would that cover the costs?"

"As I said, Monte Carlo is an expensive place."

Same old Boris, Orlov thought. Always trying to skim from any operation.

"How about a hundred and fifty thousand euros?"

"That would cover a nice party."

"Good. Now I have something else I'd like you to do with me Saturday in addition to the party. I'll pay you well for your time."

"I'm listening," Boris said.

Orlov laid out his plan for snaring Jill Morgan. At the end, he said, "If I pull this off, I'll become the second most powerful person in Russia. And I'll find a place at the top for you. You'll be your own master. Not somebody's gopher."

Boris raised his glass to that.

*   *   *

At four on Friday afternoon, Elizabeth left the suite in the Hotel de Paris and went with Palmer for a walk in the area around the hotel. Playing the tourist, she gazed into shop windows, then wandered into a Louis Vuitton boutique, then Valentino and Gucci.

All the while she was thinking: I hope Orlov is here and approaches me. If not, this is all a wasted effort. Even worse, it will be a terrible blow for Craig for not grabbing Orlov in Las Vegas.

No sign of Orlov around the shops.

"Let's go down to the port," Palmer said.

They turned and headed in that direction. After they had walked fifteen more minutes and were passing the Mandarin Restaurant in the Hotel Port Palace overlooking the water, she heard a voice from behind calling, "Jill."

She whirled around to see Orlov looking at her. He said, "It is you, Jill Morgan? I thought so."

"Vladimir. What a coincidence."

She made the introductions. "Jimmy, this is Vladimir Drozny, a famous Russian aerospace engineer. He heard my speech in Las Vegas last week."

"And it was a very good speech."

"I'm not surprised," Palmer said.

"Vladimir, this is Jimmy Palmer, a friend of mine from home."

"How long will you be in Monte Carlo?" Orlov asked.

"A few days," Palmer responded. "Our plans are fluid."

"Good. Then listen, Jill," Orlov said. "Tomorrow evening, Boris, one of my Russian friends, is having a party on his yacht which is docked here. Why don't you and your friend Jimmy Palmer come?"

Don't seem too eager, Elizabeth cautioned herself, while concealing the excitement she was feeling. Finally they had gotten what they wanted. She looked at Orlov warily. "I don't know. I was planning to spend my time in the casino. Besides, I don't like going to parties with strangers. I'm just an engineer. Not very social and Jimmy isn't either."

Orlov smiled. "You Americans are so uptight. It's a party. You'll have a good time. Meet some new people. Live a little. Boris is incredibly rich. He has great parties. Afterwards, you can go to the casino."

She looked at Palmer. "What do you think, Jimmy?"

"Sounds like fun. I made a dinner reservation Saturday at Ducasse, but I'm sure I can change it to Sunday."

"We'll have plenty of food," Orlov said.

"I don't have anything to wear," Jill said.

Palmer took the cue. "That's okay, honey. We'll go shopping."

She wrinkled up her nose.

"Oh, go for it," Orlov coaxed.

"Okay," Jill said. "We'll come. What time?"

"It's called for nine. Come at ten. The boat is the Oligarch."

Orlov provided directions to the dock. "You won't be sorry. I promise you."

*   *   *

"You agreed to do what?" Craig said. They were in the hotel suite which was registered to Jimmy Palmer. It connected with a single room registered to Jill Morgan. The arrangement was for Palmer to have the single room. Craig and Elizabeth had the suite bedroom for sleeping and the living room as an operation center. Craig planned to remain in the suite, out of sight from Orlov.

Elizabeth and Palmer had finished describing their meeting with Orlov and the party on the Oligarch.

"You agreed to do what?" Craig repeated.

"It's very simple," Elizabeth replied. "We're going to a party on the yacht of Orlov's friend, Boris. All of which is perfect. He wants to talk to me. He's taken the bait. Reached for the dangle. That's what you've been hoping for. You should be pleased. Instead, you look like you just bit into a lemon."

Palmer laughed. Craig ignored him and looked at Elizabeth. "You should have told him you wanted to think about the invitation and then talked to me before accepting. You're the one always giving me lectures about being a team player."

"I was afraid that would have compromised my cover. What the hell's bugging you?"

"I'm worried about your safety."

Palmer jumped in. "I'll be there to protect her."

Craig brushed aside the comment with a wave of his hand. "A boat like this is the worst possible place for a meeting. The two of you will be completely at their mercy. Jacques has people on standby in a villa up in the hills," Craig said pointing in that direction. "For a party on a yacht, I won't be able to call for back up from Jacques' people. And suppose while you're having a merry time at this party, your new friends," he said sarcastically, "decide to untie the boat and head out to sea. What do you do then? Call in the Marines . . . ? Unless of course they have a bunch of goons on board who take your cellphones away."

"I can't believe you're being so negative," she said, her voice cracking with emotion.

"And I can't believe you're being so naïve. You're a babe in the woods in this business." Craig paused, went over to his computer and did a search on the Oligarch. Two minutes later, he looked up, staring hard at Elizabeth, and said, "Just as I suspected. The Oligarch is owned by Yuri Rosnou. Boris Verely is his aide."

"So what?" she replied stubbornly.

"Do you have any idea whom you're dealing with? Yuri, the Russian gangster, who owns the Oligarch, and his stooge, Boris, are both former KGB people. The same as Orlov. They may know that Jill has a photographic memory. If they do, they could try to force you to divulge the information on the CDs. Has it ever occurred to you that I don't want you to end up like Walters and Angie?"

"You know what I think?"

"I don't have the faintest idea. I doubt that you're thinking at all."

"This is all about ego. Yours! You have to call every shot."

That stopped Craig. "Tell you what. I'll call Jacques. We'll see what he says."

"Fine. But don't lead the witness."

Craig got the Frenchman on the phone. After he explained the situation, Jacques said, "Let her go to the party."

Craig was flabbergasted. "How do we protect Elizabeth and Palmer?"

"I'll have unmarked boats near the marina exit. If the Oligarch makes a move to leave the slip, we'll stop it and board the yacht."

"What about protecting them on the boat?"

"We'd have the same problem in a locked hotel room. It's Elizabeth's and Palmer's call. If they want to do it, you should let them."

This wasn't the answer Craig was looking for. It had been his idea to call Jacques. He was stuck. He looked at Elizabeth. "You and Palmer are good to go."

"I won't wear a wire. With high tech equipment, they'd pick it up the second I walked on the boat."

Craig didn't argue with her. Elizabeth was one gutsy person. Mixed in with his love for her was his admiration. They'd come through a lot together. He didn't want to lose her now.

*　　*　　*

Elizabeth gave a long low whistle.

"That's some helluva boat," she said to Palmer, as they turned from the Quay to the path leading to the Oligarch. The night was crystal clear. A full moon and a star-laden sky.

"More precisely, it's called a yacht," Palmer said.

"How much does something like that cost?"

"In the neighborhood of a hundred million. If you have to ask, you can't afford it."

She wouldn't admit it to Palmer or to Craig when she left the suite, but she was more than a little nervous. Her knees were trembling. She reminded herself that she'd gone up against some pretty tough people in the past. Like the Taliban in Afghanistan, but no KGB agents. Craig had called her a babe in the woods. Damn you Craig, she wasn't that. But she was still a newspaper reporter, not a spy.

Approaching the Oligarch, Elizabeth saw that the party was underway on the deck. About thirty people were crowded together, milling around, drinks in hand. A small combo playing music. Tuxedo-clad waiters in white jackets were passing trays of food. The men were dressed in sport jackets and shirts open at the neck; the women mostly in short black cocktail dresses.

"Showtime," Palmer said. "You ready?"

"Absolutely."

"By the way, you look great in that magenta Valentino number I bought you today."

"I think it broke Craig's budget."

"Don't worry about that. You have to look like my girlfriend. Now remember the plan. We stick together. If Orlov wants to take you off for a discussion or to meet with Boris, you try and bring me if you possibly can without blowing the meeting."

"You've told me that a thousand times. You're starting to sound like Craig. I'm not an idiot."

As soon as they were on the Oligarch, Orlov came rushing over. "Hello, Jill," he said. "So good to see you."

"Happy to be here."

Palmer spoke up. "Some yacht your friend Boris has."

"You'll meet him later."

A waiter approached with a tray containing six champagne glasses. He first held it out to Jill, who took the one closest to her, to be polite. She had no intention of tasting a drop. She wanted all of her reflexes to be as sharp as possible. Behind her, she heard people talking Russian and French.

The tray was offered to Palmer, who said to the waiter, "Is it possible to get a Perrier?"

"But of course, monsieur," he answered. Then he offered champagne to Orlov, who took one. The waiter headed off to the bar for the Perrier.

"I've always wanted to be on a yacht like this," Palmer said. "I'm in the electronics business myself. I can imagine how sophisticated the electronics are."

"Well, please feel free to look around. Do you manufacture?"

"Actually, I sell televisions and toys like that."

Once the waiter handed Palmer his Perrier, Orlov raised his glass. "To making new friends," he said as he took a long drink. Palmer did the same. Elizabeth just wet her lips.

"Let's talk about betting on craps," Orlov said to Elizabeth. "For an engineer who's an expert at math and computers, you didn't give yourself the best possible odds in Las Vegas."

"Tell me what I should have done."

A waiter passed caviar on blinis. Elizabeth took one. Palmer and Orlov as well.

While Orlov was rattling on about probabilities at the craps table, Elizabeth glanced at Palmer. He looked bleary-eyed. She was about to ask him if he was okay when a Chinese man walked over accompanied by a statuesque blonde six inches taller than he was and wearing a low-cut white dress, showing half her breasts the size of those luscious green melons that grow in France. Amazing what a skillful plastic surgeon could do. The man positioned himself between Palmer and Elizabeth, who was listening to Orlov.

"Jack Wilson," she heard the Chinese man say to Palmer. "I never thought I'd see you again."

"Sorry, you're mistaken," Palmer replied. "I'm not Jack Wilson."

"But you're kidding. I know you're Jack Wilson."

"Personally," Orlov was telling Elizabeth, "although I made an exception for you in Vegas, I prefer to bet against the roller, putting my money on the "DON'T COME" line. Do you know why?"

"Because you think you get better odds."

"No. Because I'm Russian. We're always contrarians. As a people, we always fly in the face of history."

"You're putting me on, Vladimir. Right?"

He laughed. "You're very smart, Jill. Now I want you to meet my friend, Boris. He'll make you a rich woman, as well as a beautiful and smart one."

"That, I'd like. I sure didn't accomplish it in the casino in Vegas. And I doubt if I'll do it here."

"That's probably true. Now follow me."

He led the way to a staircase with a polished brass railing that went below the deck. Before taking a step down the stairs, she whirled around to look for Palmer. You were so anxious to join me for this meeting, she said to herself. Where the hell are you?

What she saw totally astounded her. Palmer was seated on a deck chair in the back of the Oligarch. Leaning over him, practically on his lap, was the blonde who had been with the Chinese man. A wild fury gripped Elizabeth.

Is this your idea of protecting me, she thought. Well to hell with you. I can handle this on my own. Great job of finding someone to protect me, Craig.

With a glass of champagne in one hand and her purse in the other, she walked behind Orlov down the stairs, then along a corridor covered with oriental carpets to a closed wooden door. Orlov knocked twice. From inside the cabin, she heard a man call out, "Entrée."

Following Orlov inside, she saw a handsome man in his fifties seated behind a desk with hair so thick and brown, she wondered if it was his own. He was dressed in a double-breasted navy blazer from Brioni as the gold buttons embellished with a B attested, a powder blue shirt, and white slacks. As they entered, he had been making notes on a document. He shoved it into the center desk drawer and stood up.

"You're even more beautiful than Vladimir told me," Boris said.

And you're as full of shit as he is, she thought. "Thank you," she replied demurely.

"Please sit down," Boris said, pointing to three brown chairs that belonged in an executive's office, not on a boat. His English was spoken with an accent obviously Russian, just like Orlov's, she decided.

Elizabeth took one chair. The two men, the others, which they rolled on, sandwiching her in the middle of them.

"I'd offer you a drink," Boris said. "But you seem to be taken care of."

She had forgotten about the glass of champagne she had been holding, but never sipped. She put it down on a small table, leaning forward as she did and showing them enough cleavage for their eyes to follow her. Meantime, she was studying the layout of the room. If either of these two Ruskies made a move for her, she would punch him out and make a dash for the cabin door, which Orlov hadn't locked. Not a good option. Even if she could handle one or both of them, escaping like that would save her, but blow the mission. No, she had to use her brains and talk her way around to what Craig wanted. He was such a control freak that he'd given her a script to follow in case she and Palmer became separated, but she knew that would only go so far. At some point, she'd be on her own.

"I'm sorry I didn't get your name," she said to their host.

"It's Boris."

"Boris what?"

"Just Boris. That's what my friends call me. I'm expecting you to be my friend when you leave here tonight."

She decided to get right down to business, which Craig's script called for, consistent with the notion that she was hurting for money and possibly desperate. So she looked at Boris. "Vladimir said you wanted to make me a rich woman. I'm willing to listen, but not if it involves sex. I'm no prostitute. If that's what you want, I'm out of here."

Boris smiled. "As I said, you're a beautiful woman, but in that department, I have as many as I can handle and then some."

Russian pig, she thought.

"Then what do you want with me?"

"Vladimir said that you're an engineer at Rogers Laughton in the United States working on long-range missiles."

"Yeah," she said warily. "The whole world knows that. I just presented a paper on the subject in Las Vegas." Her voice had a hostile edge.

Orlov jumped in. "Ah, but the whole world doesn't know that your Epsilon Unit has just completed Prompt Global Strike, or PGS, as you call it, and is preparing to implement it."

Elizabeth stood up and looked horrified. "Why are you telling me this? What do you want with me?"

"We have a business arrangement to offer you."

"I'm no traitor to my country if that's what you mean." She sounded indignant. "I was an Air Force pilot. My father and my husband, too."

"Please sit down and listen," Orlov said. "If you don't like what we're proposing, you can say 'no' and walk out of here. If you ever report the conversation to anyone, we'll deny it. On the other hand, you stand to make a lot of money. Now will you listen?"

Elizabeth acted hesitant, giving the appearance of a woman who was torn between her country and the money.

Orlov said, "As an example of our good faith, Boris will give you ten thousand euros just for listening. No strings attached. No commitments on your part."

Orlov motioned to Boris, who reached into his jacket pocket, extracted a wad of Euro notes, and plunked it down on the small table next to her champagne.

"That's yours," Orlov said, "whether you agree to work with us or not."

Without reaching for the money, Elizabeth sat back down. "Okay," she said skeptically. "I'll listen."

"Boris and I are working for an international consortium which wants to acquire PGS from you."

"Who's in the consortium?"

"We can't tell you. And you don't have to know. In fact, you are better off not knowing."

"So what do you want me to do?"

"Deliver the CDs for PGS to me next Thursday evening at midnight at the Adams Mill in Rock Creek Park in Washington. And in return, I will electronically transfer to your checking account one million dollars."

She looked offended. "It's a joke. An insult to me."

Orlov was taken aback. "Come again."

"I could be executed or put in jail if I'm caught. You want me to risk all of that for a puny one million dollars. And for the most important new military system in the world? I'm going back to the party."

She stood up and walked toward the door. As she did, she kept thinking: I hope to hell I'm not overplaying my hand. If I walk out of here without a deal, Craig will kill me. She had her finger on the doorknob when Orlov called to her. "What is it you want?"

Great, she thought. Now she had credibility. She'd have to keep it. Negotiating wasn't something she'd ever done much. She thought about how Harold, her book agent in New York, had successfully negotiated her contract with the publisher and decided to follow his approach. Start high and stay there.

She wheeled around, looked Orlov in the eye, "One million transferred electronically to my account tonight as a good faith payment. Then twenty million on Thursday when I turn over the CDs."

"You're insane," Orlov responded.

"I'm a young woman. It has to be enough for me to live on for the rest of my life because once you get PGS, I intend to leave

Rogers Laughton and disappear from Washington and my present life. Maybe move to Brazil. I can't take a chance of sticking around if it ever comes out. Starting a new life this way is expensive."

"But you have a daughter, Tracy," Orlov said.

Mentioning Tracy almost threw Elizabeth for a loop. She didn't like them bringing Jill's daughter into it. She struggled to keep her composure. "Precisely my point. I'll take her with me. I'll need more money."

Orlov walked over to the bar and poured a vodka for himself. He took a sip. Finally, he said, "I want to be fair. I'll split the difference. Five hundred thousand; then ten million."

"The answer's no."

"You can't be serious. You're willing to turn down that much money?"

"What part of 'no' don't you understand? The n or the o?"

Boris laughed. Orlov's face turned beet-red with anger. Elizabeth knew she was playing a dangerous game. She was on a roll now. There was no turning back. Harold's approach had worked in New York. Hopefully, it would work now.

"It was your idea to do this deal," she said calmly. "Not mine. I'm perfectly happy with my life at Rogers Laughton."

"You're in trouble financially."

She laughed. "Don't underestimate me. I can borrow money and stop gambling. Interest rates have fallen. I'll refinance my house. That'll put me back on my feet."

"Seven-fifty and fifteen million," Orlov said, again trying to split the salami.

"One and twenty is my position," she fired back without any hesitation. She picked up her arm and looked at her watch. "You have thirty seconds to accept." Then she sat still.

Orlov finished the rest of his drink in a single gulp. "Fine. I'll take your terms."

"Good."

"I assume you don't want it in writing."

"No, of course not. I think I can rely on your word."

She reached into her handbag and removed Jill's checkbook, which she had asked to borrow and Jill's cellphone. She tore off a blank check and showed it to Orlov. "Copy down the routing info and account number. Then transfer the one million dollars. I'll use the automatic call in service at the bank. Once I learn the million is deposited, I'll know you're serious."

Five minutes later, it was done.

Looking very satisfied, Elizabeth picked up the pile of euros Boris had put down next to her champagne. "I'll take this for spending money in Monte Carlo."

She tucked the money into her handbag and lifted the champagne glass. She turned to Orlov and said, "I'll see you Thursday in Rock Creek Park."

"Just give me your cell phone number if we have a change of plans."

She gave him Jill's. Then she strutted out of the room. Orlov made no effort to take her back to the deck of the boat.

Very proud of herself, she was now ready to deal with that jerk Palmer. When she climbed the stairs, she observed that the party was still going full blast. Not seeing him, she headed for the back of the boat, where that busty blonde had been fondling him.

To her astonishment, Palmer was all alone, sitting on a deck chair, his head slumped over to one side. He looked like he was asleep. No sign of the blonde.

At that moment, she realized what had happened. They had somehow drugged Palmer to isolate her for the meeting with Orlov and Boris. Probably with the Perrier he'd asked for. He hadn't been doing anything with the blonde. She had just been moving the woozy, drugged Palmer to an out of the way place.

With a struggle, Elizabeth managed to get Palmer to his feet. One of the other guests, a young man speaking French, saw her plight and helped her take Palmer off the boat. He signaled for a cab and assisted her in loading Palmer into the back seat.

She thanked the man and told the driver, "Hotel de Paris."

She was confident that Palmer would be alright in the morning. Since Orlov wanted to do business with her, he wouldn't dare kill the man he thought was her boyfriend.

*   *   *

Craig was so furious at Palmer that Elizabeth was convinced he'd punch Palmer if Palmer had been fully conscious. Craig was mimicking Palmer. "I'll be there to protect her."

"Forget it," Elizabeth said. "Shit happens. Let him go to bed. I want you to hear what an amazing job I did."

Craig was smiling as she gave her report.

"Damn. You did a great job, Elizabeth."

"Don't sound so surprised."

"I just don't like the fact that the exchange will take place in Rock Creek Park at midnight. It'll be tough to protect you."

"God, you always find something to complain about. I did alright on my own. Let's worry about your end now. How do you intend to handle this?"

Craig said, "Okay, here's the plan. I'll have Jill give us two sets of CDs containing technical info for long range missiles. Not PGS, but an earlier version that's in the public domain. You'll take the two sets to your meet with Orlov. Each set will have a micro tracking device that will let us follow its movement throughout the world."

"Why two sets?" she asked.

"Hopefully, we'll track one to Beijing and one to Moscow. By the time they figure out the CDs are phonies, we'll have all the proof we need that Zhou and Kuznov are manipulating this. They're both going down."

Beijing

President Zhou was in his office meeting with the Minister of Finance when the encrypted phone he had given Orlov rang. Zhou answered and told Orlov, "Wait a minute." Then he dismissed the Finance Minister and returned to the call. "What do you have for me?" he asked.

"We hooked our fish," Orlov said, sounding ecstatic.

"How'd you do it?"

"Easy. 'A piece of cake,' as the Americans say. I watched Jill Morgan gambling in Las Vegas. She was unhappy about losing. So I figured money was the key. She agreed to turn over the PGS CDs next Thursday night in Washington. There's only one complication."

"What's that?"

"I had to pay her a million dollars, which I had, and I've agreed to pay her another twenty million on Thursday, which I don't have."

"Are you out of your fucking mind? Twenty-one million. That's ridiculous."

Zhou's voice was cracking with anger. "You're supposed to be so good. This girl took you to the cleaners."

"It's small change for the world's most valuable weapons system. But if you don't want to send me the money, I'll call it off."

"I can't believe you'd agree to that. You should have found a way to bring her down to a lower price."

"You weren't there. You have no idea what happened."

"That doesn't matter. I would never let a woman push me around like that."

"Fine. Then I'll contact her and tell her the deal's off. Is that what you want?"

Zhou was fuming. "No. No. Don't do that. I'll wire you twenty million, but if I find out that you're skimming and she doesn't get all the money, I'll cut off your balls."

"I wouldn't dream of it."

Of course you would, Zhou thought. All you Russians are thieves.

When Zhou hung up the phone, the intercom rang. His secretary said, "Your visitor is here."

"Good. Send him in."

Zhou stood up and came forward to greet the American. He normally sat at his desk and waited for visitors to come to him as supplicants. But William March was special.

March, who at the time was the U.S. Ambassador to China, had helped Zhou, then Commander of the Chinese Armed Forces, to plan and to implement a daring plot for Operation Dragon Oil to cut off the supply of imported oil to the United States, enabling China to leapfrog over the Americans to world dominance. They almost succeeded and would have, except for Craig Page and that asshole Kirby, the CIA Director. Zhou never blamed March, an old friend and New York investment banker for the Zhou family businesses before he became the

United States Ambassador to China. Zhou was relieved when President Brewster decided not to prosecute March because of the damage it would do to Chinese American relations. That was a year and a half ago. Zhou had not seen March since, although Captain Cheng had met with March in San Francisco recently at a meeting arranged by Zhou. Then yesterday, Zhou received a call from March saying, "I'd like to see you about an urgent matter. I'll fly to Beijing."

Zhou immediately made time for March. This could involve PGS.

"Congratulations on becoming president," March said. "I hope we'll be able to work together in the future."

"I do as well. What are you doing now?"

"I've gone back to Hansell Gray, my investment banking firm in New York."

"Happy to hear that. I'll let my brother and our Finance Minister know. They are planning many large transactions in the United States. Your advice would be valuable." Zhou paused for a minute. Enough about business. He was anxious to hear what information March had. "You said you wanted to speak with me about an urgent matter."

"Yes. I've learned that some foreign power, and I deduced it might be you, is making an effort to obtain an advanced United States weapons system known as Prompt Global Strike, or PGS. If I'm mistaken, and you're not involved, then I made this trip for nothing and I apologize for wasting your time."

Zhou pointed to the chairs in a corner of the office. "Let's sit down." Zhou had no hesitation confiding in March. In their prior venture, March never betrayed a confidence regardless of the risk to himself.

When they were seated, Zhou said, "You're supposition was correct. How do you know about it?"

"A man by the name of Hennessey worked for me at Hansell Gray before I became Ambassador to China. We've stayed close, though he no longer works with me. Hennessey is now in a senior position at the State Department. He's also part of a Task Force headed by our old nemesis, Craig Page. They're trying to find out who was responsible for the death of Paul Walters, a Rogers Laughton engineer, and who is trying to obtain PGS."

March coughed and cleared his throat.

"Does Page suspect me?" Zhou asked.

"Hennessey told me that Page hasn't said whom he suspects. He's playing his cards close to the vest. But that's not what I came to warn you about."

"What then?"

"Page is trying to trick you, or whoever is working for you. He's put out a dangle, Jill Morgan, an engineer with Rogers Laughton. Page wants you or your people to take the bait and focus on her. In fact, she's working for Page. His hope is that by using her, Page will be able to get to who's controlling this operation."

March's words delivered a jolt to Zhou. "How confident are you of this information?"

"One hundred percent. Hennessey sat in on a Task Force meeting when Page discussed it. Hennessey was upset that Page had used Jill as a dangle because she's a single mother with a twelve-year-old daughter. Exposing her to this danger, in Hennessey's view, is unjustified. Also, Page infuriated Hennessey, with his autocratic style. In Hennessey's words, 'Nobody elected Page to be president or anything else.' He was so upset that he told me about it at dinner two days ago. I listened. Didn't say a word and called you."

Zhou was stunned by what he had heard. Page had totally manipulated Orlov. The Russian fool, so pleased with himself, had no idea. Zhou would love to get rid of Orlov for his ineptitude, but at this late date changing horses wasn't possible. Zhou was grateful to March for coming to him with this information, but he was also worried Page knew of Hennessey's relationship with March and might be using Hennessey in an effort to reach Zhou via March. Zhou refused to underestimate Page. "How did you happen to have dinner with Hennessey?"

"We had set it up before the Task Force was formed. Hennessey wants to leave the government and come back to the investment banking firm."

"Will you take him back?"

"Probably. I have to talk to my partners."

Zhou was now satisfied he wasn't being set up. "I appreciate your bringing this information to me."

"I'd also be happy to give you some advice about how to proceed if you'd like."

"First, tell me about Jill Morgan, the dangle."

"She's a genuine patriot. Father was an Air Force pilot and hero in Vietnam. She flew fighter jets for a couple of years before a medical condition grounded her. Prior to that, she went to the Air Force Academy. She's quite smart. Graduated top of her class in engineering. Has a photographic memory."

"What did you say?"

"She's quite smart."

"No, I mean at the end."

"Jill Morgan has a photographic memory."

"Tell me about her personal life."

"A widow. Husband was an Air Force pilot. Killed on a mission over Afghanistan."

"Children?"

"A daughter, twelve. Now let me ask you a question."

"Go ahead."

"Who have you been using to recruit Jill?"

Zhou hesitated for a second.

"If you don't want to tell me, I could understand that."

He didn't have to worry about telling March. March could only help him. "A former KGB agent. Dimitri Orlov. He's convinced Jill will deliver the CDs for PGS to him in Washington next Thursday evening in return for money."

"Page has done a good job tricking Orlov. My guess is that Page knows about the Russian because Orlov killed a prostitute, Angie, in Los Angeles. Page must have Orlov's prints. You can't let Orlov come to the United States for his rendezvous with Jill. Page can arrest him and force him to testify against you. Page won't hesitate to use torture."

"So what are my choices?"

"You could shut down this operation now. It's likely that neither Jill nor Page have information about anyone higher in the chain than Orlov. You could pay off Orlov to buy his silence. Or you could kill him."

Killing Orlov was an attractive option for Zhou, but as he told March, "Then I won't get PGS. And I want it more than anything in the world right now. Not only for China, but because I want to steal it from under Craig Page's nose."

"Okay. Another option is to tell Orlov to switch his rendezvous point with Jill to a location outside the United States where he can isolate her."

"You think Page would allow those CDs to leave the United States?"

"Probably not. But it doesn't matter. As I told you, Jill Morgan has a photographic memory. She'll be able to give the information on the CDs to Orlov from memory."

"And we'll be able to convince her to do that with torture or because she has a twelve-year-old daughter."

"Precisely."

"Suppose Page doesn't let Jill leave the United States?"

March thought about it for a moment, then said, "Based on what Hennessey told me, I'm confident Page will do anything to find out who's trying to get their hands on PGS."

Zhou paced for a moment trying to make up his mind what to do now that he knew Jill was a dangle and working for Page. His first instinct had been to abort the whole operation, but March was right. In view of Jill's photographic memory, he could still get what he wanted from Jill. All he had to do was shift the rendezvous point outside of the United States where Page couldn't control Jill.

But Zhou couldn't let Orlov know that Jill was a dangle. Orlov had no need for that information. The Russian might become frightened and cut and run. Instead, Zhou would make up a phony story to persuade Orlov to move his rendezvous point with Jill outside of the United States. And Zhou intended to make certain Orlov knew that Jill had a daughter and a photographic memory. Those could be useful.

Zhou stopped pacing and turned to March.

"Okay, you've convinced me. Sit here while I call Orlov."

Zhou placed the call on the encrypted phone. First, the lie. "I've heard from an American source that the FBI is doing surveillance in the United States on the other members of Paul Walters' Epsilon Unit. So, I want you to shift the exchange with Jill Morgan to a location outside the United States."

Zhou was pleasantly surprised when Orlov didn't challenge him. "I'll call Jill and change it." The Russian almost sounded relieved.

Now for the truth. "Are you aware that Jill Morgan has a photographic memory and a twelve-year-old daughter?"

"Thanks," Orlov said. "The second I knew. The first might be useful."

"So where do you want do to the exchange?" Zhou asked.

There was a pause. Orlov must be thinking. Zhou let him take his time. Finally, he responded, "The Czech Republic. I have friends there from the good old days when we controlled the country."

Zhou hung up the phone and turned back to March. "I'm grateful for your help. I'll make sure you are rewarded with work for your investment banking business."

March shook his head. "That's not why I came. I will admit that when I worked with you on Operation Dragon Oil, my motive was the financial benefit that I would gain from being on the winning side in China's competition with the United States. But now there is something else."

"What's that?"

"I hate Craig Page for wrecking Operation Dragon Oil and doing his best to have me prosecuted for treason. I won't rest until I get even with him."

Zhou rose to his feet and rolled his hand into a fist. "That makes two of us who want to destroy Page."

Paris

Ever since Captain Cheng's effort to kill her, Mei Ling didn't answer her cell phone and rarely returned calls because she worried the call was a ploy by Zhou to determine her location and to send someone to kill her. But when the caller ID showed that Yin Shao, the Chinese Health Minister, was calling, she made an exception. Mei Ling and Shao were longtime friends. She knew that Shao despised Zhou. She doubted whether Shao would be working with the Chinese president. While there was a chance that Zhou's security people were eavesdropping on the call, unbeknownst to Shao, Mei Ling was willing to risk it. Weary from being cooped up alone in the safe house, interacting only with French security people, Mei Ling desperately wanted contact with one of her countrymen.

"Yes," she answered in a halting voice.

"This is Yin Shao. I'm in Paris for an international health symposium and I would like to see you."

She hesitated. Was it a genuine social visit? Or a trap? Something Shao had been coerced by Zhou into doing? Then she recalled that Shao had been with her in the observation booth above the surgery theater when President Li had been assassinated; and he had been appalled. He knew what had happened: That Zhou had killed President Li. It was possible that Shao was bringing her information: maybe a message from one of her friends on the Central Committee. Attending an international health conference was the perfect cover.

She had to risk it and meet Shao. She was confident that Jacques would agree to let her do it with sufficient security. If not, she'd call Elizabeth.

"I can meet you this afternoon," she told Shao.

"Tell me where and when."

Mei Ling couldn't let Shao come to this house. Too dangerous if she was making a mistake. She had to call Jacques and get his consent. Also ask him to set a place. "I'll call you right back with the details," Mei Ling said.

She then called Jacques. "This could be an important meeting for me. I need your help in arranging it. I'd like a place that would be natural for a Chinese tourist to visit yet easy for you to defend."

When he didn't respond, she said, "I could call Elizabeth or Craig and get their approval if you'd like."

"You're in France," Jacques said gruffly. "This is my turf. I call the shots."

"I'm sorry," she replied demurely.

"Okay. Okay. Call your friend, the Health Minister, back. Tell him to meet you at three this afternoon in the Sculpture Garden in back of the Rodin Museum on the Left Bank. At noon, I'll clear out the museum and have the large metal gates in front closed. No other visitors will be permitted until you both leave. We'll post a 'private event' sign."

*　　　*　　　*

Mei Ling arrived first, walked through the Museum and into the bright sunlight of the garden, and took a seat on a bench in front of

Rodin's Thinker. As she opened a small umbrella to shield her face from the sun, she glanced up at the museum roof. Three French sharpshooters were lying flat on their stomachs, their guns raised. Ten minutes later, precisely at three, Shao arrived.

Approaching her, he was looking around anxiously, his gait unsteady. While the day was warm, it didn't justify the perspiration that dotted his forehead.

A terrible thought ran through her mind. What if I'm wrong? What if he reaches into his pocket, pulls out a gun, and shoots me?

She closed her eyes and took a deep breath. It might be her last.

Then she felt the bench vibrate as someone sat down. She opened her eyes to see Shao staring at her. "Are you alright?" he asked.

"Yes. And very glad to see you."

"I hope you've been well."

"Thanks. The French are taking good care of me."

"Is this place secure for us to talk?"

No one else was in the Sculpture Garden. "Absolutely," she replied.

"I know that Zhou sent Captain Cheng to assassinate you, but the French killed Cheng."

"How did you learn that?"

"A group of us, including supporters of yours on the Central Committee, share information about Zhou and the outrageous things he's doing."

"He had my son murdered. Didn't he?"

Shao looked down at his feet. "Yes, I'm sorry to say. Zhou ordered your son's Captain to force him to divulge your location so he could send Cheng to kill you."

"I figured as much. I hope my son didn't die in pain."

"He was tossed into the sea."

"After he was no doubt tortured to give up my location."

Shao didn't respond. He fiddled with his ring.

Mei Ling asked, "Who else has Zhou killed?"

"Bao Yin, the Minister of Intelligence; and your friend Qua Ping, on the Central Committee."

"No!" Mei Ling said in horror.

Shao wasn't finished. "Zhou also killed his Russian mistress, Androshka."

Shao looked around nervously. Then reached into his pocket, removed a cell phone, which he slipped it into Mei Ling's black bag.

"What's that?" she asked.

"On the phone is a video of Zhou killing Androshka. It shows the behavior of a crazed man."

Mei Ling was astounded. "How did you get it?"

"One of Zhou's servants, who hates him, took it. He forwarded it to Wei Fuzhi on the Central Committee. Wei knew I was coming to Paris. He asked me to meet with you and give you the video. I also have a message from Wei," Shao paused and leaned his face close to Mei Ling's ear. "Wei asked me to tell you that when you believe the moment is right, he wants you to return to China to seize the Presidency from Zhou. The country needs you, and he will line up support in Beijing."

Mei Ling swallowed hard. "You're asking a great deal."

"You'll have broad support. The business community is unhappy with Zhou's erratic behavior. Though I have no proof, I heard that even Zhou's brother, the billionaire industrialist, Zhou Yun, is finding his brother to be an embarrassment."

Shao's words made a deep impression on Mei Ling. Also, the risk he took by meeting with her and carrying the video from Beijing.

"You're a brave man doing this," Mei Ling said.

"I care deeply about my country. Our country. We cannot afford a lengthy rule by another Mao. Now I must get back to my conference."

Mei Ling told Shao to leave first. "I'll wait fifteen minutes before going myself."

As she sat alone on the bench, she decided she had to get the video of Zhou's murder of Androshka into Elizabeth's hands. Craig and Elizabeth would know what to do with it.

Washington

Craig left Jill's house with two copies of the fake CDs she had prepared, following Craig's directive: describe a long-range missile system, close to PGS in content, but containing only public information. Craig could have had someone pick them up. But he wanted to meet with Jill, provide her with a status report on the operation, and check on security at her house.

It seemed solid. Two men in the house around the clock. At least one awake at all times. A third man to drive Tracy to and from school, baseball games, and anywhere else.

Jill had to be feeling cabin fever, but she was in good spirits, Craig thought. She told him, "I work out on the exercise equipment in the house. Also, I tell myself, suppose you were on a submarine. You couldn't leave that."

Back at CIA headquarters, Craig gave Betty Jill's bogus CDs.

"I'll have techies install micro tracking devices on each set."

"Any luck tracing where the million dollars came from that Orlov wired to Jill's account?"

She shook her head. "The trail stops at an Andorra bank that won't divulge a thing. We could ratchet up the pressure."

"Leave it alone. We don't want to scare Orlov into going into a hole."

After Betty left, Craig's cell rang. It was Elizabeth. "I just received a video on my phone that you have to see." Her voice was charged with emotion.

"Where are you?"

"Home in Georgetown. Are you at the office?"

"Yeah. I just got back from Jill's."

"Is she okay?"

"All things considered."

"Don't leave. I'm on my way."

Twenty minutes later, Elizabeth arrived and handed him her phone. He activated the video; then nearly flew through the roof of the CIA headquarters building.

On the screen, he saw President Zhou and Androshka naked in bed. Zhou pulled a gun from the end table. Androshka was running toward the door. Zhou shot her once in the back. She turned toward him and fell to her knees. He shot her two more times. She wasn't moving. Zhou walked over and felt her pulse. He threw a blanket over her head.

"Where did you get this?" Craig asked.

"From Mei Ling. Before forwarding it, she called and told me that she got it from a friend who hates Zhou along with many others in

Chinese leadership positions. According to her friend, a member of the Central Committee received the video from a servant of Zhou's in the Presidential House who also hates Zhou.

"This is a game changer for us," Craig said. "Now we can seize Orlov when he meets you in Rock Creek Park Thursday night. I'll show him the video of Zhou murdering his beloved sister. That should be enough to turn him against Zhou and persuade him to work with us to nail Zhou."

"I figured as much. That's why I raced out here."

"What'd you tell Mei Ling?"

"I thanked her and said we would use it carefully."

"Your relationship with Mei Ling has been invaluable."

A cellphone in Elizabeth's bag rang. Craig watched her pull out Jill's cellphone with a worried look on her face.

Craig heard her say, "Yes. I understand what you're saying . . . No. I don't know if I can do that . . . You have to give me some time to think about it . . . Of course I heard you about the two million . . . I need time. I'll let you know tomorrow."

She put down the phone. "That was Orlov. He wants to move the location for our exchange to the Czech Republic. I'm supposed to fly Thursday evening to Paris. Then connect to Prague, bringing the CDs with me. He'll meet me at Prague Airport. As a sign of good faith, he'll transfer two more million to my bank account as soon as I agree to come."

"Did he tell you why he made the change?"

"Just that it would be easier that way. I still want to go through with the exchange the same as I was planning to do in Washington."

"It'll be much more dangerous."

"I'm prepared to take the risk."

"Hey, wait a minute," Craig said. "I'll bet I know why Orlov made the change."

"What do you think's happening?"

"They've learned Jill's a dangle. We have a leak on our team. Orlov was tipped off. Or Zhou was tipped off and told Orlov to change the location."

"You really think so?"

"There is no other explanation."

Craig thought about the last Task Force meeting. Leeds and Hennessey were so vocal in their opposition. One of them could have been the source of the leak.

Craig called Betty into his office and explained the situation.

"You'd probably like me to tap the phones of Leeds and Hennessey," she said. "Well, it's a nonstarter. Not the FBI Director and Assistant Secretary of State."

"Even I know we can't do that without Treadwell's approval, which we'd never get."

"So what's the backup plan?"

"We start more modestly. Get me bios of Leeds and Hennessey."

Ten minutes later, Betty handed him and Elizabeth the bios. Leeds had a boring resume. Lawyer, federal district judge in Nebraska, then FBI Director. Married with three children. Not a damn thing of interest.

Craig turned to Hennessey. Not married. No children. Princeton undergrad. Harvard MBA. Then ten years of employment with Hansell Gray Investment Banking firm in New York before joining the State Department.

Craig read the last sentence. Hansell Gray . . . Hansell Gray . . . Bells went off in Craig's brain. Loud, clear bells. Hansell Gray was William March's investment bank.

March, the devil incarnate. March, the worst traitor in United States history to receive a free pass . . . a get out of jail card . . . an escape from the electric chair . . . a presidential decision not even to prosecute.

Thinking about Brewster's decision on March made Craig's blood boil.

He closed his eyes and saw March pointing a gun at him in Kirby's father Aspen home. March would have killed him but for Elizabeth.

Craig opened his eyes. "Well isn't that nice," he said.

"William March," Elizabeth said, before Craig had a chance to explain what he was thinking.

Damn, she was smart. She always got it.

"Where does Hennessey live?" Craig asked Betty.

"I have an address on River Road in Potomac, Maryland."

"The land of mansions. He must have made a bundle at Hansell Gray."

"Or it's family money," Elizabeth added.

Craig turned to Betty. "Check with Hennessey's secretary. See if he's in town. Tell her I'm thinking of scheduling a Task Force meeting tomorrow."

Betty placed the call. "He's here," she said.

Craig checked his watch. A little past four. "Rush hour traffic to Potomac is a bitch. I better get started if I want to get there before Hennessey. Meantime, I'd like you to stay in the office this evening, Betty." He turned to Elizabeth. "You should go home. I'll see you there."

"You want to tell us what you're planning to do with Hennessey?" Betty asked.

"You don't want to know."

*   *   *

Hennessey lived in a huge estate that Craig estimated to be in the eight million plus range. With three large, round white columns in front, the house was set back from River Road, at the end of a long driveway that gradually sloped upwards. The grounds were perfectly manicured.

As Phillip, his driver, made the circle in front of the house, Craig noticed the house was dark inside. Craig reached for the door handle and asked Philip to go back to River Road and wait about a quarter of a mile away.

It only took Craig twenty seconds to pick the lock and another twenty to disarm the security system in the dark house.

Craig walked through the house to make certain it was empty. Even into the wine cellar. Hennessey had good taste. Only cases of Margaux, Mouton, and Haut Brion. Must be nice to be rich and drink five hundred dollar bottles of wine every night.

Satisfied no one else was there, Craig sat down in the living room; and he waited.

An hour and a half later, he heard a car drive up, the garage door go up, and a key in a side door.

As soon as Craig saw Hennessey walk into the entrance hall, and turn on the lights, Craig stood up and came forward. "Hello, RJ."

Hennessey jumped back in surprise. "How'd you get in?"

"Your security isn't very good."

"What do you want?"

"Come with me into the living room. I think we should talk."

Hennessey turned on a couple of lamps and sat down on the sofa. Craig was in a wing-back chair facing him.

"What do you want?" Hennessey repeated.

"Tell me the last time you met or spoke with William March."

"We had dinner in Washington last week at the Capital Grille. The same day as the Task Force meeting. Whichever day that was. Why do you want to know?"

"What'd you talk about?" Craig said in a sharp, accusatory tone.

"Why are you asking me?"

"You're in a lot of trouble. Now answer the question."

"I want to call a lawyer."

"Is that how they taught you to respond at Princeton? Or maybe in the Harvard MBA Program. Plenty of those hot shots on Wall Street need lawyers."

Hennessey pulled a cellphone from his pocket.

Before he had a chance to dial, Craig removed a gun from a shoulder holster. "Drop the phone and answer the question."

"Or what?"

"I'll shoot your left knee cap first. Then I'll move onto the right one if I have to. Generally I don't. The pain is too great."

Hennessey was perspiring. The phone fell out of his hand and hit the floor with a thud. "You can't do this."

"But I am. You put Jill Morgan's life at risk. The woman whose safety you were so worried about. You don't deserve to live."

Hennessey's hands were shaking.

"Now answer my question."

"It was a social dinner. Bill and I talked about lots of things."

"And you told him about the Task Force meeting that day. How upset you were that I was putting Jill Morgan out there as a dangle. Didn't you?"

"Yes. Because I thought what you were doing was wrong." Speaking in a self-righteous tone, Hennessey continued, "And your attitude toward us was outrageous. Nobody elected you president. You were treating us like schoolchildren. Not your professional equals who could have helped formulate policy. It made me so sick that I decided to leave the government. I wanted to go back to Hansell Gray. I was treated with more respect there."

"What did March say?"

"That you were a real shit and didn't care about anybody else."

"Are you aware that your friend, March, committed treason against the United States a year and a half ago, when he was Ambassador to China, and wasn't charged because of political considerations?"

The color drained from Hennessey's face. "Is that true? I had no idea."

"Give me all of March's contact info. Telephone numbers and home address."

Hennessey reeled them off from memory while Craig wrote them down.

Then Craig called Betty and explained what he had learned from Hennessey. "Have someone check the records of all of March's phones and email. I'm looking for any communications with anyone in China. Also check flight manifests for the last week. New York or Washington to Beijing or Shanghai. See if William March was a passenger."

Thirty minutes later, Betty called with the information.

"At ten forty-eight on the evening March had dinner with Hennessey, March used his cell phone to call Beijing. The next day he flew from New York to Beijing. He returned the following day."

"Perfect," Craig told Betty. "Set up the safe house on Route 29 near Charlottesville for a visitor this evening. Have two agents come out to Hennessey's house to pick him up and take him to the safe house."

Craig called Philip to come to Hennessey's house. Then he turned to Hennessey. "I'm putting you into protective custody for a few days for your own protection. If March learned what you just told me, he'd kill you. Besides you leaked confidential information to him. It'll be up to the AG to decide whether to charge you."

"You can't just do this summarily. I'm an American citizen. We have laws in this country."

"That's true, but since 9/11 they've gotten a little squishy where matters of national security are involved."

While waiting for Philip, Craig instructed Hennessey to call his office and put a message on his secretary's voice mail, telling her that

Hennessey would be going out of town on State Department business for a few days.

Once Philip arrived, Craig handed him the gun and said, "Watch Hennessey until two of our people come to pick him up."

"Will do, Mr. Page."

"Oh, and give me the keys. I need the car. They'll drop you somewhere convenient when they're taking Hennessey to Charlottesville."

Once Craig got into the car, he checked his watch. Eight o'clock in the evening. He called Ralph Donovan, the president's Chief of Staff. "I have to see President Treadwell."

"Can it wait until morning?"

"Unfortunately not."

Craig heard a sigh, "Hold on. I'll check."

A minute later, Donovan was back. "The president will meet you in the Oval Office at ten o'clock this evening."

"Thanks. Please tell him I'll have Elizabeth Crowder with me. Also, I think it would be good if you could have Attorney General Wilson there or someone high ranking from DOJ. It's time to make this legal."

*　　　*　　　*

Exactly at ten, Craig and Elizabeth filed into the Oval Office. The AG, Treadwell, and Donovan were already there. The AG and Donovan, dressed in suits and ties; Treadwell in slacks and an open collar shirt.

There was a fourth man whom Craig didn't recognize. Dignified and patrician was how Craig would have described him. About sixty, with a full head of gray hair, dressed in a starched white shirt with diamond studded French cuffs and a red silk Hermes tie, loosened at the neck. No jacket.

Treadwell made the introductions. "Craig and Elizabeth, you know Donovan, my Chief of Staff, and the Attorney General."

Craig and Elizabeth nodded. Treadwell pointed to the other man. "This is Edward Bryce. He's a close friend, powerful Washington lawyer, and my informal advisor on certain sensitive issues. We were having dinner upstairs, so I asked Edward to join us."

Craig picked up the ball. "Sorry to disturb all of you, but I believe this is extremely important."

"You have our attention," Treadwell said.

Craig described everything that had happened beginning with Orlov's call to Elizabeth changing the meeting to Europe. He left out the threats he made to Hennessey. At the end, he said, "I want you to arrest William March, charge him with treason, and put him in solitary confinement. No phone calls permitted so he can't tip off President Zhou."

"That bastard, March," Treadwell said.

Wilson, heavy-set, jowly and ruddy-faced, looked as if he'd had several drinks at dinner. And why not, Craig thought. He hadn't expected to be called to the White House this evening.

"You won't like to hear this," the AG said to Craig. "But the evidence you presented to arrest March, much less subject him to the drastic treatment you want, is simply insufficient." The AG held out his hands, palms up, as if he were making an argument to a jury. "What do you have? A dinner discussion and a call and trip to Beijing, where we have no idea whom he met. Talk about circumstantial evidence."

Craig felt as if the air was sputtering out of his balloon.

The AG continued. "I sense that you have a history with March that I'm not aware of, but that won't fill the gap."

The AG looked at the president. "You understand what I'm saying?"

Treadwell replied, "I do. However, the history here is quite relevant. This all happened under your predecessor, Attorney General Wes Simmons, when Brewster was president. Craig had built an iron-clad case of treason against March. Simmons studied the evidence and concluded it was sufficient. But he persuaded Brewster that a public trial would have a devastating effect on our relations with China. So Brewster let March walk. It was all kept secret. I was then Chairman of the Senate Intelligence Committee. Brewster briefed me. I disagreed with his decision and tried to convince him to prosecute, but he wouldn't budge."

The AG perked up. "What kind of case was it? Give me the short version."

Craig responded, "March aided Chinese General Zhou, now their president, in a plot with Iran to cut off the flow of imported oil to the

U.S., wrecking the American economy, and leapfrogging China over the United States in world domination."

"When was this?"

"About a year and a half ago."

The AG replied, "So the statute of limitations hasn't run."

Bryce interjected, "You could arrest March now and charge him with both that prior situation and this one. All of which would justify the solitary confinement Craig wants."

Treadwell was nodding. "I'm on board."

"Where's March live?" the AG asked.

Craig gave him the Park Avenue address he'd gotten from Hennessey. The AG said, "I'll go outside and call the head of the New York FBI office. Have them arrest March immediately. I'll let you know when that happens."

Craig glanced at Elizabeth who was smiling. He mouthed the word, "Yes." She rolled her hand into a fist.

After the AG left, Treadwell said to Craig and Elizabeth, "Now tell me the status of your operation in connection with PGS. Let's decide where we go from here after the leak."

Craig replied, "Since we're now finished with legal issues, I don't know if Mister Bryce . . ."

Treadwell cut him off. "I fully trust Edward with our most confidential information."

Craig didn't like airing this information with a non-governmental employee who might not have security clearance, but that wasn't something he could tell the President of the United States. So he swallowed hard and said, "First, I'd like Elizabeth to show you a video."

She handed Treadwell her phone. As Treadwell watched General Zhou kill Androshka, his face registered shocked disbelief.

"We have to get him out of power," Craig said.

"But how can we do that?" Treadwell asked.

"The Spanish government has an outstanding charge of murder against Zhou in connection with the battle for southern Spain last March."

"Zhou won't just walk into a Spanish courtroom."

"I have a plan for getting him there."

"Before you tell me about that, Craig, how do we know that whoever succeeds Zhou in Beijing will be any better?"

Elizabeth explained about Mei Ling. "She's waiting in the wings. So to speak. In Paris. If we get rid of Zhou, she could fly home and take over the presidency."

"And she'd be better for us?"

"Both for the United States and China."

Craig said, "I believe Russia is involved in this as well as Zhou. But I won't be able to do anything about Kuznov."

The president replied, "I can live with Kuznov. The Russians don't pose a threat to us now. China is a much different matter. Okay, Craig, now tell me about your endgame."

Before Craig had a chance to respond, the AG stuck his head in the door. "March is in custody. Being taken to a federal prison in Lewisburg where he'll be held in solitary. He's protesting furiously all the way."

"That's too damn bad," Treadwell said. "Good work. You can go home now. What I'm discussing with Craig and Elizabeth doesn't raise legal issues."

The AG withdrew and closed the door. Treadwell was looking at Craig, "What's your next move?"

"Elizabeth wants to fly to Prague to meet Orlov. At least, that's what she told me a few hours ago."

She was nodding.

Treadwell looked at her. "You don't have to go."

"I know that, Mr. President, but safeguarding PGS is critical for this country. Making Zhou pay for what he's done is also important. I'll do what I can to accomplish both of those."

"You're a brave young woman," the president said with admiration.

"Not so young after spending the last year and a half running around with Craig."

They all laughed nervously.

The president added, "I know Craig will do everything he can to protect you."

"And then some," Craig added.

"Now tell me your endgame," Treadwell said.

Craig began speaking.

Prague

On Tuesday, Orlov checked into the luxurious Intercontinental Hotel in Prague, along the river. With the money he had received from Zhou, he could live well without spending his own money.

Then he made two calls. The first was to Kuznov, asking the Russian president to arrange to have Vladimir Drozny fly to Prague tomorrow and check into the Intercontinental.

"But you are Vladimir Drozny," Kuznov said.

"No. No. The real Vladimir Drozny."

"You want to tell me what you're planning to do?"

"Not over the phone. And I don't have time to fly to Moscow."

"Okay, I'll do it, but this better not come back to bite me in the ass."

Orlov powered off the phone before saying, "Let's hope not."

Orlov's second call was to Franz Beran, a former Major in the Czech military intelligence when Russia ruled the country. Franz and Orlov had collaborated on a project to gather information and crush dissidents. After the Russians pulled out, Orlov made a trip to Prague to see what it was like. He and Franz had gotten plastered on Slivovitz in the old town. As they staggered out of the tavern, fireworks were exploding over the river. Franz said to Orlov, "If you ever need anything in this country, call me first."

Orlov was now ready to take Franz up on his offer. They agreed to meet in the same tavern at nine that evening.

On the way to his meeting with Franz, walking along the cobblestone streets in the old town, crowded with tourists speaking a multitude of languages, Orlov thought about how precarious his situation had gotten since Zhou had told him the FBI had surveillance on the members of the Epsilon Unit including Jill. They might have focused on her bank account. He probably screwed up there. He should have opened a new account for her in Switzerland instead of transferring to her Washington account the million, then the two million. That was a mistake. Perhaps the FBI didn't move that fast. He was hopeful given the lack of speed with which they moved up on Angie in

Los Angeles. Another red flag might be raised by Jill making this trip to Prague after she had been to Monte Carlo.

Orlov brushed aside these concerns. If all went with Franz as Orlov hoped, it wouldn't matter if the Americans sent CIA agents or anyone else to follow Jill to Prague. All Orlov had to do was get Jill to the Czech Republic. Orlov would not only have the home field advantage, he'd control the entire field. Those CIA agents, or whoever the Americans sent, would be at Orlov's mercy.

Orlov arrived at the tavern first, sat down in a dark corner and ordered a Slivovitz. Waiting for Franz, he went over the operation in his mind one more time.

Originally, Orlov had thought of meeting Jill at the airport, taking her to his hotel, and making the exchange there. But now that he anticipated American CIA agents, Orlov decided to change the plans. He had to separate Jill from those agents before making the exchange.

Orlov had a good plan for doing that, but he needed Franz to supply the remote location and a group of former army officers who, like Franz, preferred the old days and would be thrilled to see action one more time. Orlov was confident that after an evening with Franz and plenty of Slivovitz to lubricate the brain, and to pump up the testosterone, he'd have a willing ally. Success would be assured.

*　　　*　　　*

Wednesday, Craig arrived in Prague and checked into the Four Seasons hotel. Giuseppe was waiting for him.

They sat down to lunch in an isolated corner of the hotel's dining room overlooking the river. How are you enjoying the job," Craig asked.

"Ever day's a challenge, but you left me a good organization."

After they ordered lunch, Craig said, "Elizabeth arrives Friday at noon at Prague airport on AF 964 from Paris. That gives us two days to get ready."

"What's your likely scenario?"

"Orlov said he'd meet her at the airport. My guess is he'll take her somewhere outside of the city to make the exchange."

"We could pick him up at the airport."

"I don't want to do that because I'm hoping Orlov will have high-ranking Chinese and Russian officials at the exchange. Having Elizabeth see them will enhance our case. Also, I want the exchange to take place. We've installed micro electronic tracking devices on the CDs Elizabeth is turning over."

Giuseppe was smiling. "Same old Craig Page. I'm glad you're on my side." Thoughtfully he added, "So that means following Orlov and Elizabeth to the rendezvous point. Not losing them."

"Exactly."

"I assume she'll be wearing a wire or tracking device."

"She refused. I argued with her, but couldn't persuade her."

Giuseppe was shaking his head. "Elizabeth is one strong-willed woman. I admire that about her."

"I do, too . . . *most* of the time."

"Sexist."

Lunch came. Seafood salad for Giuseppe. "I'm trying to watch my weight."

Steak for Craig. And a bottle of Brunello from Antonori. They paused to eat and drink. Then Giuseppe said, "I'm worried. This could be a very difficult assignment for us."

"What resources has the Czech government put at your disposal?"

"That's part of the problem. Not much, I'm afraid. Four soldiers and an unarmed helicopter that I can call upon. For anything else, I'll have to go back to the Defense Minister. To get even that much, I had to twist arms."

"What's their problem?"

"When Dalton was president, he made lots of enemies in Europe."

"Well, he's not president any longer."

"Attitudes are slow to change in the old world."

"Okay. I've got it. I'll have a helicopter on alert at the nearest American base in Germany and some combat Marines ready to climb into that chopper if I need them."

"My guess is you will. I don't have a good feeling about this."

"You worry too much. Didn't we save the Pope?"

"Saving Elizabeth may be more difficult."

Prague and Czech Republic

At ten minutes to noon, Elizabeth bounded off the plane in Prague, full of adrenalin and not exhausted because she'd forced herself to sleep in a comfortable first class seat on the two flights. Somewhere over the Atlantic, she managed to brush aside her anxiety and stop thinking about the tremendous risk she was facing. She had learned from Craig to compartmentalize: focus only on completing the job.

In the terminal, she headed toward passport control, clutching a leather bag that held the CDs and wheeling her carry-on. As she cleared customs and entered the arrival hall, a distinguished looking gray haired man in a suit and tie approached her. He was in his sixties, she guessed.

"Come with me," he said in English with a thick Czech accent.

"Who are you?" Elizabeth asked.

"Franz is my name. Vladimir sent me to meet you. I'll help you with your bag."

He took the wheelie suitcase from her hand.

Elizabeth didn't resist. It contained clothes and cosmetics. She had no intention of parting with the leather bag containing the CDs.

Outside, the air was hot and humid with thick clouds in the sky. It felt as if a fierce rainstorm was approaching. In front of her, at a distance, were a range of high mountains, with patches of snow near the jagged peaks.

She followed Franz to a black Mercedes sedan in the parking lot. He popped the trunk and loaded her bag inside. As he did, she noticed two men, also in suits and ties, seated in front and no one in the back. Franz opened the back door and held it for her, motioning for her to get inside.

"Where are we going?" she asked.

"We're taking you to Vladimir. Isn't that what you want? You agreed to meet him for your exchange."

"Why don't we go into the airport coffee shop and make our exchange there?"

Franz smiled faintly. "We're just messengers. We can't make any changes."

That narrowed her choices. She could get into the car and hope Craig would follow her as he promised. Or she could cut and run, hoping that Franz and his two friends didn't overpower her and force her into the car. Not much of a choice. She was determined to follow Craig's plan so he could obtain the information they needed. She climbed into the back of the car. Franz went around and sat down beside her.

Once the door shut, the driver activated the rear door locks. No turning back now. The front passenger barked orders to the driver. They were moving toward the exit of the parking lot.

The driver of the Mercedes sped along the highway that snaked around Prague, cutting in and out of lanes. After twenty minutes, they were climbing into the mountains. The air conditioning was blasting. Elizabeth was shivering.

"Where are we going?" she asked Franz for the third time.

Her question was again met with stony silence. I just hope to hell Craig has been able to follow, Elizabeth thought.

She was afraid to look through the back window for fear of tipping them off.

An hour later, they were driving through a forest. Rugged oaks and silver beech lined the narrow road. Looking through the front windshield, she didn't see any other cars.

Ahead was a narrow bridge over a deep gully. The Mercedes raced across. They were climbing higher.

Fear was beginning to grip her. You're being foolish, she told herself. Craig won't lose you. He won't let anything happen to you.

*   *   *

Craig was in the front passenger seat of a gray BMW, the first of two cars following the black Mercedes. A Czech soldier was driving; another was in the back seat. Behind them, another gray BMW held two more Czech soldiers.

As they traveled outside of town, Craig worried. Where were they taking her? Had he underestimated Orlov?

Through binoculars, Craig watched the Mercedes speed across a narrow bridge over a deep gully. His car was about a hundred yards from the bridge when a large truck carrying hot asphalt moved off the apron and blocked the narrow road. A man climbed out of the truck and held up a stop sign. The driver of Craig's car slammed on the brakes and pulled up next to the truck.

"Ask him what's happening," Craig said to the driver.

He got out, talked to the man with the stop sign, and returned to the BMW. "He said the bridge isn't safe. They're making repairs. I asked him to move over and let us cross before they make the repairs. He refused."

"Go around him," Craig said.

"I'm not sure I can. He hasn't left us much room."

"Try it anyhow."

The driver shook his head in disbelief. "Okay, you're the boss. He threw the car in reverse to swing around the truck. Then to Craig's horror, he heard a loud explosion and part of the bridge collapsed.

Craig knew exactly what had happened: Orlov had arranged to have the bridge blown to stop anyone from following. Helplessly, he stared at the deep gully in front of them, while metal and concrete fell through the air. No way they could drive down one side and up the other. He asked the driver if there was parallel road that they could circle back and take.

"You would be adding fifty kilometers," the driver said. "We would never catch the Mercedes."

Craig cursed under his breath, removed his cell phone and called Giuseppe to explain what happened.

"I'll get in the Czech helicopter," Giuseppe said. "Try to find the Mercedes and get a fix on their location. It'll be tough in these clouds. I hope to hell the storm holds up. Meantime, you might as well come back to Prague."

Feeling helpless, Craig followed Giuseppe's instructions.

*   *   *

Elizabeth heard a loud explosion behind the Mercedes. She guessed that Orlov's friends had blown the bridge to stop Craig from following. Suddenly, the Mercedes slowed and pulled off the road.

Franz said to Elizabeth, "Give me your tracking device."

"I don't have one."

"You're lying."

"Why would I have a tracking device?"

"Get out of the car."

She dutifully obeyed.

He removed a ten inch black instrument shaped like a cricket bat from his bag. She watched him open the trunk and run it over her suitcase. It never made a sound. Next over the leather bag she was clutching. Nothing. He passed it over her blouse rubbing against her breasts.

"Pick up your skirt," he said.

"Go screw yourself."

He snarled, then ran it over her skirt, front and back. The device was silent.

Franz took out his cell, made a call, and announced, "She's clean."

Elizabeth guessed Franz was calling Orlov.

How in the world would Craig find me?

Elizabeth tried to keep her increasing fear under control. Don't panic. Craig will think of something.

Franz told her to get back into the car.

They were moving again.

After thirty minutes, looming ahead, she saw an old gray stone chateau with four turrets and two towers. Either it was from the Middle Ages or an incredible copy. She felt as if she were dreaming.

Before they reached the chateau, the skies cut loose with a torrential downpour. The Mercedes turned onto a dirt road, leading up to the castle. A tree branch was blocking the center of the road. The driver braked, causing the car to skid into a ditch along the side of the road. He tried a couple of times, unsuccessfully, to blast out, the tires spinning and squealing.

"Halt," Franz said. "We're close enough. "We'll walk the rest of the way."

Dressed in brown pumps with a medium heel, Elizabeth wasn't exactly ready to walk in the mud. But that was the least of her worries.

Franz pulled her by the arm along the muddy road. She was gripping her bag tightly. The two other men from the car had guns aimed at her, fearful that she might try and escape.

By the time she reached the entrance to the chateau, her hair was soaked and water was running into her eyes. All of her clothes were sopping wet. Half a dozen armed men, all elderly, dressed in Red Army uniforms, were standing outside the chateau, seemingly impervious to the rain.

Once she passed them, Franz led her inside, then up an old wooden staircase that creaked. A rat scurried out of their way.

At the top, they entered a large living room with a crackling fire. Armed soldiers in old Red Army uniforms stood guard in each of the four corners of the room.

She spotted Orlov across the room. He came forward to greet her. "Thank you for coming all this way to meet with me. Let's make our exchange and Franz will take you back to Prague. You'll have your twenty million dollars. Then you can go anywhere you want."

Franz and the two who had been in the Mercedes remained in the living room.

Orlov held out his hand. "Give me the CDs."

Reaching into her briefcase, she extracted two boxes of CDs and held them up. "I even made a duplicate."

"PGS is on these?" Orlov asked.

She nodded.

"Give them to me."

"Aren't you forgetting something?"

"What's that?"

"My twenty million dollars."

"First the CDs."

"No! The money. I insist."

Elizabeth knew she was playing a dangerous game. They could shoot her at any time and take the CDs, but she wanted to reinforce her credibility.

"Okay," Orlov said. "We'll do it your way, but if you're trying to trick me, I'll make certain you'll never spend a cent of the money. And I'll kill your daughter as well."

He said it a cruel, sadistic voice.

She handed Orlov a piece of paper with a bank account in Brazil.

"That's different than the account you gave me for the one million and the two million. That was in Maryland."

"With the risks involved, I needed a place where I'm safe from United States extradition."

Orlov nodded.

Once she confirmed the transfer to her account, she handed Orlov the CDs.

"Before I can let you leave," he said. "I must have them examined for authenticity to make sure you're giving me what I paid for."

His words cut through Elizabeth like a knife.

"How do you intend to do that?" She was trying to keep her cool.

Orlov shouted, "Vladimir. Come in here."

A man entered from one of the back rooms. He was about Orlov's height, but twenty pounds heavier. As the man approached Orlov and Elizabeth, Orlov said, "Vladimir, I'm sure you've met Jill Morgan at one of your international conferences."

Vladimir calmly replied, "Of course I've met Jill Morgan. But this woman isn't Jill Morgan. I've been listening and watching from the other room. She looks a lot like Jill Morgan, but there are differences. And she doesn't sound at all like Jill Morgan."

Orlov's head snapped back in surprise. "What the hell?" He looked stunned, his face white as a sheet. "Who are you?" he said to Elizabeth.

*   *   *

Midway back to Prague, Craig told the driver to pull over in a grassy area. The rain was coming down in sheets. The car behind pulled over as well.

Craig called Giuseppe. "Were you able to locate them?"

"I was getting ready to call you. We had to land the chopper because of the weather. But I managed to find out where they've taken Elizabeth. An old deserted chateau. I have precise coordinates."

"Good. I'll call for the Marine helicopter on standby at our German base. Have them pick me up here. Then we're going in."

"You have one problem."

"What's that?"

"I called the Czech Defense Minister to get approval for your chopper in their airspace. He said positively not."

"Fuck him. We're doing it anyhow. What'll he do. Shoot the chopper down?"

"That's what he threatened. And I think he means it. You have only one way around it."

"What's that?"

"Have President Treadwell call the Czech president. The Defense Minister claims he's acting on direct orders from the Czech president."

"I don't fucking believe it."

Craig knew he had no choice. But time was precious. "I'll get on it right away."

As he dialed Washington, he realized minutes were ticking away and Elizabeth was in great danger. The only good news was that the rain appeared to be passing. At least the chopper would be able to fly . . . if he managed to get approval.

*   *   *

All I can do now, Elizabeth thought, is stall for time hoping Craig would be able to get to her. So she said to Orlov, "I work with Jill at Rogers Laughton. She was afraid another trip to Europe might make people suspicious so she sent me. But none of that is important. You have the CDs. That's all you care about. Let Vladimir check them. He'll confirm that."

"Okay. I'll do that," Orlov said. "But you better not be lying."

Vladimir went into the other room, brought back his computer and inserted a CD.

Elizabeth sat down to watch him. If he asked her a technical question, she was dead.

He was working for about thirty minutes. Jill had done a good job preparing the phony CDs. Finally, he stood up from the computer and told Orlov, "They're phonies. Carefully done, but all public information."

Orlov raised his hand and slapped Elizabeth hard on the side of her face. "Lying bitch."

Then he said, "I want you to get Jill Morgan on the phone and have her explain the differences between PGS and what's on the CDs."

"Jill may not be in the office. She may not have access to the PGS CDs."

Orlov was smiling sadistically. "So what? Jill has a photographic memory. She'll be able to tell Vladimir from memory."

"I won't call her," Elizabeth said.

Orlov walked over to the side of the room, picked up a metal case and opened it. What Elizabeth saw inside terrified her: electrodes for torture.

Orlov turned to one of the soldiers. "Tie her to the chair. We'll test her threshold for pain."

I'm being stupid, Elizabeth thought. If I call Jill, she'll be smart enough to know what's happening. She'll never give Vladimir the true PGS, but I'll buy more time for Craig to get here. Elizabeth took out her cell phone. "What if Jill won't give me the information?"

"Tell her that I'm calling Russian friends of mine attached to the Embassy in Washington. They'll go to Jill's house, wait for her daughter to come home, and kill her."

Orlov then removed his cellphone from his pocket. He made a call, speaking Russian, which Elizabeth didn't understand. Except she heard in English, "Jill Morgan . . . Tracy Morgan . . . and Jill's address in Gaithersburg." If Orlov was bluffing about the threat to Jill's daughter, he was doing a good job. Elizabeth remembered Craig had stationed two CIA agents in Jill's house, but she didn't know how many Russians would be coming. It could be a real bloodbath.

Orlov said to Elizabeth, "Stop stalling and make the call to Jill. Put it on speaker."

Hurry, Craig! Hurry, Craig!

Elizabeth called Jill. In a shaky voice, she said, "They've discovered that the CDs are fakes. They're threatening me and your daughter unless you explain over the phone to Vladimir Drozny, a Russian engineer, the differences between what's on the discs you gave me and the true PGS. I have you on the speaker with Vladimir and some other people."

For ten seconds, Jill didn't respond. She must be trying to evaluate what I told her and how to answer, Elizabeth thought. God, I hope she knows how to play it.

*   *   *

Treadwell's secretary told Craig, "Hold for just a minute. He's in a meeting, but I was instructed to interrupt him if you called."

While he waited, Craig looked through the car window. The rain had stopped. He got out of the car. Cell phone plastered to his ear, he anxiously kicked his foot on the muddy ground. Then he heard, "Yes, Craig," in Treadwell's tense voice.

Craig explained the situation to Treadwell. At the end Treadwell said, "That goddamn Jan. When he called to congratulate me on becoming president, he invited me to visit the Czech Republic and told me how anxious he was to strengthen relations with the United States. Now he pulls this shit. I'll call Jan right now with you on the line in case he raises logistical issues."

For a full two minutes, Craig didn't hear a thing. He worried technology had failed him. That he has been disconnected. He considered hanging up and redialing the White House. He decided to wait another thirty seconds. All the while, he was kicking his foot on the ground, digging a hole deeper and deeper.

At last, he heard a voice in a Czech accent saying, "I have the Czech president." Then, "This is Jan, President Treadwell. I understand we have a problem."

Craig listened as Treadwell succinctly summarized the issue for Jan. Concluding, he said, "I can't believe you would withhold approval for us to fly a single helicopter through your airspace. For us, this is a critical issue. And you told me that you wanted to improve relations."

"I'm sorry. But before you called, I didn't know anything about this matter. I had no idea."

Craig wanted to scream: "Bullshit. Your Defense Minister told Giuseppe he was acting on your orders." But Craig kept still.

Treadwell responded. "Well now that you know, can we proceed?"

"You realize, of course, that more than one helicopter flight is involved. There is likely to be a battle at the chateau."

"Hopefully not."

"It's a question of our territorial integrity. We're not a third world banana republic."

"I understand that."

"I'll need time to think about it."

Craig's heart sank.

"We don't have time," Treadwell replied firmly. "Lives are at stake."

There was a pause, then Treadwell added. "Okay, Jan. Tell me what you want in return."

"A reduction in tariffs on Czech steel," Treadwell said without hesitation.

"You'll get it. I'll cut them by fifty percent."

"Permission is granted for your Marines."

"Good. I'll tell Craig Page to move now."

Craig took that as his signal. He hung up the phone and called the Marine base in Germany.

*   *   *

Elizabeth was watching anxiously as Jill and Drozny were speaking on the phone while Drozny worked at his computer, making changes dictated by Jill to the CDs. The discussion was highly technical; and Elizabeth had no idea what Jill was telling Drozny. She just hoped Jill wasn't disclosing the true PGS.

*   *   *

Craig was en route to the chateau in a Blackhawk helicopter with a pilot, Marine Captain Curtis, and the five armed members of his unit.

"ETA, six minutes," the pilot said.

Craig told the Marines, "Remember, I need Orlov and Elizabeth alive."

He had distributed pictures of both of them. "You can kill everybody else."

Through binoculars, Craig surveyed the grounds around the chateau. What he saw amazed him: six elderly soldiers, dressed in Red Army uniforms, were gripping automatic weapons. Orlov must have gathered up some of his buddies from the Soviet era. He couldn't underestimate them. He passed the word to the Marines.

The chopper landed in a clearing about fifty yards from the chateau.

Craig was the first one out. The Czech soldiers were running toward the helicopter. Craig aimed at the one in front. His shot hit the man in the chest. He was down. The others didn't retreat. Instead, they scattered into the trees, firing as they ran at the Marines, who were now on the ground. Captain Curtis and the Marines gave chase while Craig ran up to the entrance to the chateau, prepared to fire if Czech reinforcements came out of the building. None did. He held his position, waiting for the Marines before he entered.

Meantime, Craig heard a constant firing of guns as the firefight raged in the forest. Five minutes later, Captain Curtis came racing up to Craig with his five Marines intact. "All enemy combatants are dead," the Captain told Craig. "We're ready to go in."

Craig raised his gun, preparing to blast off the front door lock. Before doing that, he smashed his foot against the door. It gave way.

Inside, he saw a wooden staircase. He pointed up to Captain Curtis and they were ready to move. Craig and the Marines put on their gas masks.

*   *   *

Inside the living room, Elizabeth stood next to Orlov and close to Drozny, seated at a table, still engaged in his technical discussion with Jill.

Suddenly, Jill heard the shots outside and she knew what was happening: Craig had made it with the Marines he planned to bring. She sized up the situation. In the house were seven armed Czechs with her, Orlov and Vladimir. When Craig and the Marines raced up the stairs, all hell would break loose with bullets flying everywhere. Orlov could easily be killed in the crossfire. She couldn't let that happen. They needed Orlov alive.

In response to firing outside, Franz had directed the Czechs to take positions behind the bulky furniture. Suddenly, she saw a metal canister flying up the stairs. It landed on the floor with a thud, filling the room with tear gas. In the haze and pandemonium, she grabbed Vladimir's computer and smashed it against the side of Orlov's head, knocking him out.

Coughing and gagging, she dragged Orlov into a bedroom and opened a window. She leaned out, gasping for breath. When she could breathe normally, she picked up Orlov and held his head out of the window. He was semiconscious, but breathing and alive. She left him hanging on the windowsill while she opened all the other windows in the bedroom and moved a dresser away from the wall. She dragged Orlov behind it and hid there with him.

For the next five minutes, she heard endless rounds of automatic weapons firing. The noise was deafening. She held her hands over her ears.

Finally, all was silent. Still, she didn't move. Then she heard it from the entrance to the bedroom. The most wonderful sound in the world. Craig's voice. "Elizabeth . . . Elizabeth . . . Elizabeth, are you in here?"

"Yes," she called out. "Behind the bureau."

He pulled it away from the wall. She stood up, threw her arms around him, and kissed him.

"Did they harm you?" he asked.

"No. I'm fine. And I have Orlov."

As if on cue, Orlov stood up and, woozy, staggered out from behind the bureau. Then he collapsed onto the bed.

"I think he'll be alright," Elizabeth said. "I just gave him a tap on the head. What happened in there?"

"All seven Czechs are dead. The other Russian, too."

"He's Vladimir, a Russian aerospace scientist enlisted to help Orlov. The real Vladimir Drozny."

"Two Marines are wounded. Not seriously."

He handed her a gun. "Stay in here and keep your eye on Orlov. Also send that video of Androshka's murder to my phone. I'll be back in a few minutes. I have a little more cleanup. Then we move on."

"One important thing. Orlov threatened to kidnap or kill Jill's daughter. I don't know if he set it in motion with people at the Russian embassy or if he was bluffing, but you better call Washington."

"Thanks." Craig reached for his cell phone. "I'll call the agents at Jill's house. Tell them what you've learned. I'll put them on alert and have them beef up security. Hopefully, they'll get there before the Russians."

*   *   *

Craig walked back into the living room. Two Marines were bandaging their wounded comrades.

Captain Curtis told Craig, "Once we've stopped the flow of blood, I'd like to take my people back to the base in the chopper if that's okay with you Mr. Page?"

"Absolutely," Craig said. "And thanks for a job well done."

Giuseppe walked into the room. At the end of Craig's report, Giuseppe said, "I'll call the Czech authorities and have them pick up the bodies. I have the Czech helicopter on hold outside the chateau with the pilot inside. Can I transport you, Elizabeth, and Orlov somewhere?"

"Yes, but first I want to have a little chat with Orlov."

Craig returned to the bedroom. He told Elizabeth, "I called Washington. Nothing has happened at Jill's house. We've expanded security. She's fine and wanted me to tell you that she never gave Drozny the true equations for PGS."

"I'm so glad she's alright."

Orlov was coming around, but not fast enough for Craig. In the bathroom, he found a bucket and poured cold water over Orlov's head. The Russian was now conscious. Elizabeth had the gun aimed at him.

Craig wasn't sure Orlov recognized him. So he said, "I'm Craig Page. CIA Director."

"Who's she?" Orlov said, pointing to Elizabeth.

"You don't have to know."

"She sure had me fooled. I was convinced she was Jill Morgan."

"Let me show you something."

Craig handed Orlov his phone, set to the video of Androshka's murder.

While Orlov watched the video, Craig studied his face. Horror gave way to pain. He cried out, "That dirty bastard." Then Orlov put his head into his hands and cried. "She never hurt anybody," he said through muffled sobs. "She took care of me when I was wounded in the army . . . I loved her."

Craig took back the phone and converted it to the record mode. He placed it on the bed close to Orlov.

"Do you want Zhou to be punished for your sister's murder?"

"More than anything in the world. I want revenge. Zhou has to pay for what he did. He can't get away with killing Androshka."

"I can help you get that revenge."

"How? I'll do anything for you."

"First, tell me what Zhou had to do with your effort to obtain PGS?"

"Everything," Orlov replied without hesitation. "It was all his idea. I never even heard of PGS. He and his chief military scientist taught me everything I needed to know. They even . . ."

"Who was the scientist?"

"Jiang Hua. He gave me the names and bios of the Epsilon Unit of Rogers Laughton. You think I found Paul Walters and Jill Morgan on my own? Jiang told me about the conference where Jill was speaking. Then Zhou ordered me to move the rendezvous point with Jill outside the United States."

"What about Dalton's assassination?"

"Zhou's idea, too. He was afraid Dalton would impose trade sanctions against China for human rights violations."

"What did President Kuznov have to do with these operations?"

"Kuzov went along. He helped me with logistics on the Dalton operation, including giving me the name of Valerie Clurman, a Secret Service employee whose computer I broke into to obtain the schedule for Dalton's flight to Camp David. Kuznov had known Valerie at Oxford a long time ago. On PGS, Kuznov supplied Vladimir Drozny."

Kuznov's involvement didn't make sense to Craig. "What did Kuznov stand to gain?"

"He hated Dalton and feared American economic coercion. On PGS, Zhou told me that Russia would have access to PGS as well as China. I reported that to Kuznov. Also, Kuznov desperately wants an alliance with China. He wants Zhou to come to Moscow to solidify that alliance. These were just preliminary steps to show Kuznov's good faith."

"Why's he so concerned about an alliance with China?"

"He views it as a critical step in Russia's military and political resurgence. I was just a small cog in all of this. An intermediary brought in by Kuznov because he knew my sister was Zhou's mistress."

Craig now had recorded as much of the story as he needed. Enough to forward to President Treadwell and have Treadwell authorize Craig to proceed with his endgame.

Craig said to Orlov, "Take me to Moscow with you. I want to meet with President Kuznov as a representative of President Treadwell. If you do that, you will get your revenge. I promise you that."

"I don't know," Orlov said, sounding nervous. "I don't know."

Craig could read his mind. "You're worried Kuznov will turn on you. Say you're a fuckup and he had nothing to do with any of this. Is that it?"

After a silence of thirty seconds, Orlov nodded.

Craig added, "You're between a rock and a hard place. If you won't take me to Kuznov, you'll not only lose your revenge against Zhou, but I'll fly you back to the United States to stand trial for the murders of Dalton, Angie, Paul Walters, and a trucking agent in Pittsburgh."

"I didn't push Walters into the Potomac. He jumped."

"Doesn't matter. Nobody will care about that. You'll be headed straight for the electric chair."

Craig handed Orlov his cellphone. "Call Kuznov and tell him to expect us."

Orlov placed the call.

Afterwards, Craig told Giuseppe, "Arrange a plane at Prague airport to take me and Orlov to Russia."

"Will do. I'll get you to the airport in the chopper. Elizabeth, too."

Once they were airborne, Craig's cell rang. It was Betty. "Don't you ever listen to your voice mail. I've been trying to get you."

"Sorry. I've been busy."

"Hang up with me. I want to send you a text that'll knock your socks off."

Craig knew that Betty wasn't prone to hyperbole. This had to be something. As the chopper tossed around in the wind, Craig read the text Betty forwarded. The CIA had finally been able to break the code and prepare a transcript of the encrypted call between Zhou, when he was still in Bali, and his brother in Beijing. In astonishment, Craig read:

Zhou Yun: The anesthesiologist has been paid off. He will mix potassium chloride with the anesthetic. Then he'll appear to be doing everything he can to save President Li. No one will suspect him. The medical examiner is with us as well. He'll conclude it was one of those unfortunate situations that sometimes occur in surgery.

President Zhou: Excellent.

Elizabeth was staring at Craig. He didn't want to say anything with Orlov in listening range. So he told her, "I'm going to send a text message from Betty to your phone. Read it. We'll discuss it at the airport."

As she read, Craig thought: if all goes well with Kuznov in Moscow, careful distribution of this text will ensure that no one will be upset about Zhou's passing from the scene. In Beijing, they'll be happy to have Mei Ling replace Zhou.

When they reached the airport, Craig asked Giuseppe to take Orlov onto the private plane that Giuseppe had arranged.

"Guard him," Craig said. "I have to call Treadwell."

Craig was able to get through to the president immediately. After giving Treadwell a report, Craig obtained the president's approval for the endgame.

Then, Craig took Elizabeth aside. "The phone conversation between Zhou and his brother is a huge asset. We have to find a way to use it." He was thinking out loud. "Suppose you sent it to Mei Ling?"

"Better yet, I'll fly to Paris and show it to her, then help her plan her strategy. She was the runner up to Zhou in the election for president. She could forward it to people in Beijing. And then if you succeed in getting Zhou out of China . . ."

He completed the thought for her. "She could fly to Beijing. And take over the Presidency."

"But she can't leave until you have Zhou in custody."

"Correct. The timing will be tight. It all depends on what happens in Moscow."

"We'll stay in close touch. We can make it work."

Craig nodded in agreement.

"Wait here for a minute," she said.

"Where are you going?"

"To check airplane schedules."

She returned a couple minutes later. "There's a flight to Paris in an hour. I'm on it."

She came over, hugged and kissed him. "Be careful, Craig."

"Don't worry. I'll be okay."

"Remember Bali. You can never underestimate Zhou."

Moscow

Craig and Orlov entered Kuznov's ornate office in the Kremlin. The Russian president looked grim.

"I have to convince him to cooperate with me, Craig thought. Not merely throw Orlov to the wolves.

After coffee was served and they took seats around a marble topped table, Kuznov said, "I received a call from your President Treadwell. He told me that you were speaking for him as his official emissary. But he refused to tell me what this is about."

Craig took a gulp of espresso and tossed a grenade on the table. "I'm aware that you and Chinese President Zhou conspired to assassinate President Dalton and to steal PGS from the United States. Orlov was your joint agent for both of these operations."

Kuznov looked outraged. "You have no business making such serious charges with no factual basis." He said it in a loud, confrontational tone.

Craig calmly replied, "Well, let me describe the evidence I have. From a Chinese source, I have dates of Orlov's meetings with Zhou in Beijing. I have Orlov's fingerprints on the throat of a trucking company clerk in Pittsburgh, Pennsylvania, whom he strangled to obtain the grenade launcher to kill President Dalton. I have Orlov's fingerprints in the house of the Pakistani who fired the grenade; and the shooter's wife ID'd Orlov as visiting her husband right before the attack."

Craig paused for few seconds, letting his words sink in. Then he continued, "I have Orlov's fingerprints on the throat of Angie, a prostitute in Los Angeles who he killed to silence about his efforts to obtain PGS from Paul Walters, a Rogers Laughton engineer. I have witnesses who will testify that Orlov and another Russian, Boris Vereley, used the Oligarch, a yacht owned by Yuri Rosnov, to recruit Jill Morgan to turn over PGS. So I have lots of evidence of Russian involvement."

Kuznov was glaring at Orlov. Guess he wasn't supposed to leave a trail that leads back to Moscow, Craig thought.

Craig continued, "Also, Orlov used people at the Russian Embassy in Washington in an attempt to kill Jill's daughter."

"I never took steps to implement that," Orlov said. "It was just a bluff."

"That doesn't matter," Craig said, believing Orlov and feeling relief. "Without it, we have plenty to try Orlov for several counts of murder. A trial that will make it clear the Russian government's responsible for these crimes."

Kuznov pounded on the table. Coffee cups bounced. "That's an absurd leap. Orlov is a fool and an incompetent. His sister, Zhou's mistress, got him involved in all of this. I appreciate your bringing this information to me. Orlov is a Russian citizen. He will be properly punished here."

Well, there it was, precisely what Craig had feared. He glanced at Orlov. The man was white with terror. Craig had to bring Kuznov around. "It won't work," he told the Russian president.

"What do you mean, 'it won't work'?"

"Unless you cooperate with me, President Treadwell will circulate the evidence I presented to key leaders in the United States. It will leak out to the public. No one will believe you were not personally involved. The United States will initiate strong trade reprisals against Russia. We will persuade the Western Europeans to do the same. We will cripple your economy, and one other thing . . ."

Craig paused to take a breath. He'd have to be careful how he expressed this—to make it a threat, but subtly. "The difficulty in killing one nation's leader," he said slowly, while staring at Kuznov, "is that the leader of the nation which does the killing places himself at risk for retribution, if you know what I mean."

Kuznov looked pale. He understood.

"But if you cooperate with me," Craig said, "President Treadwell is prepared to ignore all the evidence of Russia's involvement. None of it will see the light of day."

"What do you want me to do?"

"Choose between the United States and China."

Craig took out his cell and continued speaking to Kuznov. "As you consider whether you wish to entrust your country's economic viability and your own safety to President Treadwell and the United States, or to President Zhou of China, let me show you two things."

Craig then handed the phone to Kuznov, first to view the video of Androshka's murder. Then the text of Zhou's encrypted conversation with his brother when Zhou was in Bali.

While watching and listening, Kuznov pressed his lips tightly together. Veins were protruding on his neck and forehead. His head was shaking.

"Personally, I wouldn't want to place my balls in Zhou's hands," Craig said.

The phone slipped from Kuznov's hand onto the table. Craig retrieved it and said, "The choice is yours."

"Suppose I pick the United States. Just suppose . . . I'm not saying that I will. What would I have to do?"

I'm making progress, Craig thought.

"It's very simple. You call Zhou and tell him Orlov just returned from Prague. You have CDs for PGS, which several of your aerospace experts have confirmed are accurate. You made a copy of the CDs for Zhou. You're prepared to give it to him. But he must come to Moscow next Tuesday, four days from now, to get it. You'd like not only to give the CDs with PGS to him, but to discuss future joint operations with him."

"What if Zhou won't come?"

"You have to persuade him."

"That won't be easy."

"Play tough with him. What we Americans call hardball. Make him believe that you have PGS and the only way he'll get it is by coming to Moscow. Tell him to fly into a Russian airbase, outside of Moscow. Tell him that you'll meet him there. It will be a secret meeting. You'll give him the CDs for PGS and the two of you will talk."

"What happens if he comes? What do I do then?"

"Nothing at all. You won't be at the airbase. You will have turned over the portion of the base where Zhou's plane lands to my control for several hours, keeping all Russians out of the area except Orlov, who will supposedly be taking Zhou to meet you. I will be there with people I bring. Do you understand or should I spell it out any further?"

"You've said enough."

"Well, how do you choose: the United States or China?"

Kuznov stood up and paced for a couple of minutes, his hand up to his face. Craig and Orlov remained still.

Finally, Kuznov returned to the table. "I will cooperate with you," he said with hesitation in his voice.

Craig was relieved, but he didn't show it. "Good. Then I think you should call Zhou. My suggestion is that you put it on the speaker phone. He may ask for details that Orlov will have to supply. So tell him you only have Orlov with you. I'll be quiet."

Kuznov turned to Orlov. "And you . . . you fool . . . you better not warn Zhou. Or I'll kill you myself."

"You don't have to worry about that. He murdered my sister."

Kuznov placed the call, explaining that he had Orlov with him and following the script Craig had outlined. When Kuznov was finished, Zhou said, "Are you certain that you have the CDs for PGS?"

Craig thought Zhou sounded surprised. "Absolutely," Kuznov replied.

"And you're sure they're authentic?"

"They were verified by several of our top aeronautical engineers."

Kuznov was convincing, Craig thought.

"You didn't think I could do it," Orlov said.

Zhou replied, "Frankly, no. After you began your Czech operation, I learned that Jill Morgan was a dangle working for Craig Page. I had no time to alert you."

"No problem," Orlov said with a swagger in his voice. "I assumed that might be the case and I took steps to overcome it."

"What steps?"

"First, I noticed that Page or one of his people was following Jill, so I separated her from her followers before taking her to the meet. Then I had an engineer at the rendezvous who examined the CDs and concluded they were bogus. So I threatened to kill Jill's daughter. That made her cough up from memory the differences between PGS and the phony CDs. Our engineer revised the bogus CDs and made them accurately depict PGS."

Orlov had said it all calmly. He sounded credible.

"I underestimated you, Orlov," Zhou said.

Smiling, Orlov looked at Kuznov. "People often do that."

Craig hoped Orlov didn't overplay his hand. Craig closed his mouth tight and raised a finger to his lips, hoping Orlov would shut up. The Russian kept still.

Kuznov picked it up. "Then I'll plan to see you next Tuesday in Moscow."

"I'll be there."

"Good. Let me know when your plane is in the air and your ETA."

"I will do that," Zhou said.

Once Kuznov hung up the phone, he said to Craig, "Orlov will help you on logistics for next Tuesday. And I assure you that Orlov will do a good job, won't you?"

"Yes sir."

Kuznov stood, signaling that the meeting was over. "This had better work," he said to Craig.

"Don't worry. It will."

As soon as he left Kuznov's office, Craig called Carlos in Madrid. He told the Spanish Defense Minister, "I may have failed in Bali to bring Zhou to you for trial, but I intend to succeed in Moscow. Now here's what I want you to do."

Beijing and Paris

Zhou was pleased when he put down the phone. Orlov had come through. He couldn't wait to get his hands on those CDs and begin China's implementation of the PGS technology.

As far as going to Moscow to retrieve the CDs, Zhou wasn't surprised Kuznov had insisted on it. The Russian president had wanted this meeting from the first time that Orlov had come to Beijing. Besides, Zhou couldn't blame Kuznov for directing Orlov to bring the CDs to Moscow rather than Beijing. Kuznov had no doubt deduced that if Zhou got his hands on them first, he never would have shared them with Russia.

What troubled Zhou was leaving China right now. He had heard from allies on the Central Committee that there were increased rumblings about Zhou's behavior after the murder of his Intelligence Chief, Mei Ling's son, and a member of the Central Committee. Rumors were circulating that Zhou had done something to Androshka because she hadn't been seen in days. Some were beginning to suggest that perhaps they had made a mistake selecting Zhou rather than Mei Ling to become president.

Zhou was a student of history. He knew that coups often occur when the leader leaves the country. The good news was that Mei Ling was in Paris. But if her supporters informed her that Zhou had left China, she could rush home to initiate a coup.

Zhou brooded for several minutes about this quandary. Finally, he had a solution: keep his trip to Moscow absolutely secret. When he had negotiated the agreement to cut off the flow of imported oil to the United States with the Iranians, he had taken two trips to Paris and kept them both secret. Captain Cheng had made all the arrangements including the plane. And Zhou didn't take anyone other than Cheng and the crew with him.

Unfortunately, he no longer had Captain Cheng to make his arrangements. Cheng's death in the unsuccessful effort to kill Mei Ling in Paris was a tremendous blow to Zhou. Cheng's successor, Captain Tong, wasn't nearly as savvy and Zhou had to spend much more time explaining what to do.

Even with all of that, Zhou was confident that he could arrange the Moscow trip so that only Zhou, Captain Tong, and the airplane crew knew about it.

*   *   *

Elizabeth waited for Craig to call and tell her that Kuznov had scheduled a rendezvous with Zhou next Tuesday before she called Mei Ling to meet with her.

It took Jacques's personal intervention for Elizabeth to gain access to Mei Ling in the safe house. Six armed guards manned the perimeter.

She looks haggard and pale, Elizabeth thought with sympathy. The woman's undergoing an incredible ordeal, and she can't properly grieve for her son.

Mei Ling smiled when she saw Elizabeth, but it seemed forced.

"We should go out into the garden to talk," Mei Ling said. "The skies don't have ears."

Did she suspect the French of spying on her? Was she becoming paranoid?

They carried glasses of ice tea out to the grassy yard in the back of the house and settled into chairs around a wrought iron table with an umbrella to shield them from the midday sun.

"Now that we are together," Elizabeth said, "I want to express to you in person how sorry I am for the loss of your son."

Mei Ling sighed. "Thank you. I appreciate that. Zhou has now killed my husband and my son. He would have killed me as well if it weren't for you and Craig and your friend Jacques."

"I believe that Zhou's killing days may soon be over."

"What do you mean? What have you done," Her voice had some of her old liveliness.

"Do you have your cellphone? I want to send you a text."

Mei Ling pulled it from her skirt pocket. "I'm ready."

As Elizabeth forwarded the text of Zhou's call from Bali with his brother, she said, "It's good you're sitting down."

When she was finished reading the transcript of the call, Mei Ling nodded her head vigorously. "This confirms what I fully believed."

Elizabeth wasn't expecting this response. "Then you're not surprised?"

"No. I was standing in the observation booth above the operating theater during President Li's surgery. I was there with our country's Health Minister, Yin Shao, who is a physician. We were both convinced that Zhou had used the surgery to murder Li, but we didn't have proof. This gives us that proof. It's invaluable. Can I share this with others . . . important supporters?"

"Or course."

Mei Ling turned back to the phone and reread the text message while Elizabeth sipped ice tea.

When Mei Ling was finished, she looked up at Elizabeth. "You told me that Zhou's killing days may soon be over. What will happen to him?"

"I will tell you, but this cannot be mentioned to anyone. Even your closest supporters."

"I understand. You don't have to worry. You and I have never betrayed a confidence . . . or we would both be dead."

Elizabeth had no hesitation in telling Mei Ling, "Craig has arranged for Zhou to fly to Moscow for a meeting next Tuesday with Russian

President Kuznov. If Craig succeeds in Moscow, Zhou will never return to China."

Mei Ling wrinkled up her forehead. "Do you recommend that once Zhou is gone, I return to China and try to take over the Presidency?"

"That's your decision alone to make. The risk is huge. I cannot guarantee that Craig will succeed. If Zhou escapes from Craig's trap and returns to Beijing, your fate would be horrible."

"I understand that. The tape of the phone call between Zhou and his brother will be helpful to me if I decide to try and seize the Presidency."

To Elizabeth, it seemed as if Mei Ling was thinking out loud. Elizabeth kept silent. Mei Ling had to decide for herself. It was Mei Ling's life on the line.

After a pause that seemed interminable to Elizabeth, Mei Ling said, "I'll do it. Tell me when I should leave for Beijing."

"Zhou has promised to tell Kuznov when he is airborne. Craig will let me know. At that time, you should take the next flight from Paris to Beijing."

"Good. I will do that."

"Until then, I would like to stay here with you, if you don't mind."

"I would welcome it."

*   *   *

Tuesday morning at five, Elizabeth's cellphone rang. She hadn't been sleeping. She had been waiting for Craig to call."

"Zhou's in the air," Craig said in a tense voice. "I've reserved a seat for Mei Ling on the six a.m. Air France nonstop from Charles De Gaulle to Beijing."

"She can't make that."

"Jacques has a car waiting outside the safe house. He's arranged to hold the plane until Mei Ling's on board."

In minutes, Mei Ling dressed and grabbed her suitcase.

Thirty minutes later, at the curb in front of the terminal, Mei Ling hugged Elizabeth. "I'll never forget what you and Craig have done for me and for China."

"I just hope you'll be able to take over the presidency."

Moscow

At ten in the morning, three hours before Zhou's arrival at the Russian airbase under a blazing sun during a Moscow heat wave, Craig rode out with Orlov to check on preparations.

Kuznov must have given strict orders to the base commander, Craig decided, because Orlov had freedom to do what he wanted. With Orlov behind the wheel, they drove in an air-conditioned sedan across the landing field to a remote location. "Here's where Zhou's plane will be landing," Orlov said.

Orlov coughed, cleared his throat and continued, "I will meet with Zhou when he comes down the stairs of his plane, no doubt accompanied by the one aide he is bringing. I will then drive them to that hangar." Orlov pointed to a freshly painted white metal structure about a hundred yards away. "I'll explain to Zhou that's where Kuznov is, in an air-conditioned office, the site of the meeting. Completely private. No press. Very limited staff. Does that sound good to you?"

"Yes," Craig said tersely. "Let's look at the hangar."

Orlov drove across the field and into the hangar. Craig saw an unmarked, midsize airbus passenger jet. Once the car stopped, Craig and Orlov got out. Carlos Sanchez immediately came over and threw his arms around Craig. "I'm glad to see you again."

Craig introduced the Spanish Defense Minister to Orlov. "He's in charge of all our arrangements," Craig told Carlos.

"Pleased to have your help," Carlos said.

Craig pointed to the plane, "Who'd you bring with you?" he asked Carlos.

"A dozen armed special ops troops."

"That should be more than enough. Zhou only has the airplane crew and one aide."

"After Bali, I'll never underestimate Zhou."

Carlos's words gave Craig pause. With Zhou, nothing ever went according to plan. There were always surprises.

"Where do you plan on positioning your troops?" Orlov asked.

Carlos pointed to a wooden partition inside the hangar. "There's an office behind that wall. Eight of my troops will be waiting there, out of sight, ready to move when I signal them. Four others will be on the plane."

"I like it," Craig said. "I'll be remaining here with you while Orlov brings Zhou."

"How's Elizabeth?" Carlos asked.

"Doing well."

"Tell her I asked about her, and I hope she covers Zhou's trial in Madrid for her newspaper."

Craig noticed Orlov rolling one hand at his side into a fist. "We're doing this peacefully," Craig said while looking at Orlov. "We're here to make an arrest pursuant to a Spanish court order. We don't want any violence."

"I understand," the Russian replied.

Craig didn't know what was running through Orlov's mind. He realized that the Russian was a bit of a wildcard, but Craig didn't want to change the plan. Didn't know how he could alter it without alerting the savvy Zhou.

Carlos invited Craig and Orlov onto the plane for lunch. The tension was heavy enough to cut with a knife. After paella, barely eaten, Craig and Carlos chatted about the economic situation in Spain to pass the time while Orlov, appearing bored, sat in a comfortable chair and dozed.

An hour later, Craig heard Orlov's cell ringing. He answered. Craig heard, "Yes . . . Yes . . . Yes . . ."

Orlov stood up and said to Craig and Carlos, "The tower reported that Zhou's thirty minutes out."

"We're good to go," Craig said.

"I'm leaving you," Orlov told them. "I have to get in my car to meet our guest."

Despite everything that happened so far, Craig didn't fully trust Orlov. He wasn't sure why. Just a feeling in his gut.

Craig spotted an opening in the side panel of the hangar. He asked Carlos for binoculars and positioned himself at the opening to watch Orlov and Zhou.

The Chinese Air Force jet landed. Perfectly according to plan, Craig watched Zhou bound down the stairs in a dark suit, white shirt, and tie, followed by a young Chinese man in an army uniform. The new Captain Cheng.

Orlov greeted Zhou with a handshake. Then Zhou and his aide climbed into the back of Orlov's car. Craig watched them approaching the hangar.

Orlov continued following the script. He stopped the car at the entrance to the hangar. All three climbed out. Maybe, I was wrong, Craig thought. Maybe, Orlov will stick with the game plan.

"Where is President Kuznov?" Craig heard Zhou say to Orlov.

"In an office in the hangar waiting for you."

Orlov began walking toward the hangar. Zhou was two steps behind him, the aide taking up the rear.

Craig signaled to Carlos and the two of them stepped out from behind the corner of the building to confront Zhou.

Craig watched Zhou pull back in surprise. "What is this?"

According to plan, Carlos responded, "Mister Zhou, I am here as a representative of the Spanish government to arrest you, to take you to Madrid, and have you stand trial as a co-conspirator in the death of Spanish civilians in the March and April attack in Southern Spain."

Carlos lifted his hand and his eight Special Ops troops stepped out from behind the wooden partition and took battle ready positions.

"This is an outrage!" Zhou shouted in a furious voice. His face red, saliva dripping from his mouth, he turned to Craig. "This is all your doing. And you'll pay for it. I am the president of the most powerful nation in the world. The Spanish government will never get away with this. Civilized nations do not behave in this way."

Craig responded, "After all of your crimes, you can't claim to be civilized."

"Please come with me into the plane," Carlos said.

Zhou ignored him and looked at Orlov. "You, Dimitri Orlov. You're a lying piece of dog shit. Not a man. And your sister Androshka was no better. She . . ."

Before Zhou finished the sentence, Orlov yanked a Beretta from his jacket pocket.

"No, Orlov! No!" Craig cried out as he reached for his own gun.

Craig watched Orlov raise his gun and level it at Zhou. At that instant, Craig could have fired at Orlov. Could have shot the gun out of Orlov's hand. But he hesitated. Racing through his mind was Francesca's murder and the litany of Zhou's crimes. The fear that faced with political pressure with Beijing, Spain would in the end buckle and release Zhou, rather than try him.

So Craig held his fire. He watched Orlov blast two rounds into Zhou's chest.

Too late. Zhou's aide removed a pistol from a shoulder holster and blew away much of Orlov's head.

Spanish troops then opened fire on the aide, who went down.

Craig walked over to Zhou, lying in a pool of blood, not moving. Craig checked Zhou for vital signs. He was dead. Craig's long battle with Zhou was over.

Craig checked Zhou's aide. Dead also. Orlov, too.

Perspiration dripping down his face, Carlos looked mortified. "Believe me, it wasn't supposed to end this way. I truly thought he would get into the plane and fly with us to Madrid. There, all hell would break loose politically. I just hoped that Zahara would have the political will to stick with the prosecution. But I guess we'll never know."

Craig didn't share with Carlos his fear, vividly in his mind in the instant he could have stopped Orlov, that once Zhou was in Madrid, China and those nations beholden to the economically powerful Chinese government would have leaned so hard on the Spanish government that Zahara would never have hung tough. He would have caved and released Zhou to go back to China.

But those were all political and diplomatic considerations. Craig realized that they played no role in Orlov's thinking. Zhou had killed Androshka. That was all that mattered to Orlov.

I was no different, Craig concluded. My long battle with Zhou is over. The man responsible for my daughter Francesca's murder is now dead. He finally paid for it. I have avenged her death.

Washington

Craig left the Oval Office after briefing President Treadwell, who thanked Craig for a job well done.

As Craig passed the secretary's desk in the reception area, he saw a copy of the *International Herald*. Craig picked it up.

The lead article in the upper right hand corner was entitled "Leadership Change in China" with the byline of Elizabeth Crowder.

Craig read, "President Zhou of China died yesterday of a sudden heart attack moments after he arrived in Moscow for a secret meeting with Russian President Kuznov. Efforts to revive Zhou were unsuccessful.

"In order to achieve a speedy transition, the Chinese Central Committee met three hours later. They named Mei Ling to be Zhou's successor."

From the White House, Craig drove to the cemetery in Virginia. He stood for ten minutes in silence at Francesca's grave. Then he said, "At last, I've avenged your death."

He would never forget his beautiful, talented daughter. But for Craig, it was time to move on.

About the Author

Allan Topol is the author of eight novels of international intrigue. Two of them, *Spy Dance* and *Enemy of My Enemy*, were national best sellers. His novels have been translated into Japanese, Portuguese, and Hebrew. One was optioned and three are in development for movies.

His new novel, *The Russian Endgame*, is the third in a series of Craig Page novels, following the successful *China Gambit* and *Spanish Revenge*.

In addition to his fiction writing, Allan Topol co-authored a two-volume legal treatise entitled *Superfund Law and Procedure*. He wrote a weekly column for Military.com and has published articles in numerous newspapers and periodicals, including the *New York Times*, *Washington Post*, and *Yale Law Journal*.

He is a graduate of Carnegie Institute of Technology, who majored in chemistry, abandoned science, and obtained a law degree from Yale University. As a partner in a major Washington law firm, he practices international environmental law. An avid wine collector and connoisseur, he has traveled extensively researching dramatic locations for his novels.

For more information, visit www.allantopol.com.